ABOUT THE AUTHOR

Sam Youd – who would go on, as John Christopher, to write *The Death of Grass* and *The Tripods* – was born in Lancashire in April 1922, during an unseasonable snowstorm.

His teenage love affair with science fiction was short-lived, and by his mid-twenties his ambition had turned to literary fiction. His first novel, *The Winter Swan,* came out in 1949; he brought out a total of ten non-genre titles, before turning his attention entirely to genre fiction.

As a writer of genre novels his range was extensive. Alongside John Christopher the dystopian and young adult writer, there was William Godfrey the cricket novelist, Peter Graaf the thriller writer, Hilary Ford whose stories centred on female protagonists, Stanley Winchester who chronicled the carnal tendencies of the medical profession …

But writing literary fiction meant a lot to him, and he turned his back on it reluctantly. The novels written under his own name are eclectic in their themes and outlooks: from a woman's life told in reverse, to crises of faith amongst Jews and Catholics, to anti-heroes and deserters in World War II, to séances in post-war London. The last of the series, a bitter-sweet comedy of errors set in a large decaying country house, was published in 1963. He would continue to write, in a more popular vein, for several more decades.

John Christopher

The Death of Grass

The Caves of Night

The White Voyage

Cloud on Silver

The Possessors

Pendulum

Hilary Ford

Sarnia

A Bride for Bedivere

THE WINTER SWAN

SAM YOUD

THE SYLE PRESS

For Joyce

Published by The SYLE Press 2018

First published in 1949
as *The Winter Swan* by Christopher Youd

Cover photo: *Aphrodite on a Swan,* The British Museum
© Marie-Lan Nguyen / Wikimedia Commons

ISBN: 978-1-911410-06-5

www.thesylepress.com

Contents

Introduction

In the early spring of 1947 Sam Youd heard from the Atlantic Awards committee that he was in the running to obtain a bursary from them. As he wrote to a friend at the time:

> … strangely enough, on the morning the letter arrived (before it arrived) a stray idea struck me and – the letter from the Atlantic people providing the stimulus – I have already done two chapters amounting to 10,000 words … it occurs to me that such a recommendation as an Atlantic Award is about the only thing that might persuade a publisher to accept the unbalanced and graceless novels I am likely to write.

Aged 24, and having already 'fallen out of love with SF', he looked towards a future as a writer of serious fiction. As he was later to explain:

> I knew first novels tended to be autobiographical and was determined to avoid that. So my main character was a woman, from a social milieu I only knew from books, and I complicated matters further by having a story that progressed from grave to girlhood.

Over the course of writing, and as perhaps befitted a tale whose end was known before its beginning, the book took on a series of titles, including – quoting from William Blake – *The Desolate Market*, before finally settling down as the somewhat less desolate *Winter Swan*.

The Atlantic Award was bankrolled by the Rockefeller Foundation. Targeted at 'young British writers whose literary careers had been interrupted by the war', it offered a sum intended to be sufficient to 'free the successful candidate from financial anxiety and allow him to live modestly for a year'. Sam's award was obtained on the strength of the promise of a book; by the time it came through the book was effectively written, and a publisher (the first to read it) had already agreed to take it.

The Winter Swan was published in 1949 under the name 'Christopher Youd'; subsequent serious novels as by 'Samuel Youd'. The author was later to recall a jingle that his father (also Sam) had chanted to him: 'There's Old Sam / And Young Sam / And Young Sam's Son ...', commenting:

> At my christening the parson tried to insist on Samuel as the more proper version, but my father, in any case an atheist and with natural combativeness sharpened by a prior fortification in a nearby pub, would have none of it. It had been Sam for him, and would be Sam for me ... In early teens ... I turned it into Samuel, and later, in a dodgy confirmation into the Church of England, added Christopher.

Sam viewed *Swan* as an experimental work: more so, possibly, than anything else he was to write, and in that sense perhaps typical of the risk-taking that a first-time novelist can afford. His sheer enjoyment in writing shows through. Following the practice of Kipling he prefaced the novel with a piece of his own verse. He was also much under the influence of the lyrical, thoughtful prose of Aldous Huxley; he would remain so over the course of the next few novels, until, writing under other pen-names, he would eventually become drawn into the relative material security offered by genre fiction.

Much later, when quizzed about the main character's appearances from beyond the grave, over the course of the novel, he explained:

Swan wasn't about reincarnation, in which I have never been able to believe ... If anything, it related to an outdated suggestion by Ouspensky (I think) that we are four-dimensional creatures, the fourth being (of course) time – and that at the end of our lives we lumber away into infinity burdened with every moment of our earthly existence. My chief character was interacting with other such entities, as part of a learning process ... The theme of the book – that relationships matter more than anything and spiritual isolation is hell – was sincerely felt. It is only towards the end of my life that I have come to accept this intellectually, as well as emotionally.

February 2018

Death in spring is a paradox,
And mourners, unbelieving, sing
Where a butterfly dances with flickering wing
Among the lifting buds and flowers,
Taking its time from the thistledown clocks.

Death in summer is death too soon;
The mourners stand under flaming skies
With hearts made numb by their aching eyes,
And hurry away from the grave to find
New toys, new wonders, in fruitful June.

Death in autumn is peace at last;
The harvest is taken, the webs are spun,
The fields lie shadowless under the sun,
And, sober and quiet at Festival,
The mourners dream of the blossoming past.

But death in winter kills everything,
Forgotten in frost the swan lies still,
Songless under the jewelled hill.
The mourners have mourned too long for grief,
And only the dead remember spring.

CHAPTER ONE

1949

Cedric Garland

IT HAPPENED SUDDENLY as Mr Garland watched, his eyes intent – for it seemed indelicate somehow to gaze at the open grave – on the curving roof of the church. The snow which made the church look like some cotton-wool cottage in a Christmas window shivered and slipped. Before Mr Garland's eyes it slid forward several feet, and piled in rippled waves in the gutter. In the empty space the grey slates gleamed wetly. But higher up the snow still clung, and higher still there was the frosty blue sky and the golden, indecently ardent sun.

Such moments, Mr Garland felt, were a revelation. Throughout the world there was change, violent and uncompromising. Wars, tidal waves, volcanic eruptions; and the relentless revolution of the seasons. But to see it, to catch the monster with claws outstretched, was hardly to be hoped for. All his life, it seemed, things had been taking place behind his back. Most vividly he remembered in his childhood how the railways had leaped across the country and his own immature horizons, secretly and by stealth. From the time the family left Charnock the outside world had always been ahead of him, always presenting accomplished facts. First there had been London, busy with its vast Victorian flux. On all sides new buildings, new constructions, towered and flowered. And though one might watch day after day the slow toil of the workmen, the swinging into place of iron girders and mountains of masonry, always at the end the thing slipped away, and presented itself suddenly as completion. And then, when he went back to Charnock to stay with Aunt Sara, he found that the monster had been there before him, and left a railway station.

So it had gone on, always quietly, always illicitly. For tap as Mr Garland would the barometer of his soul, it was always set steadily to Fair, and always the weather of the world stormed in on him, shocking him by its insistent Change. Out of the golden haze of the future three wars had rushed on him, like ignoble, devouring waves, and with their recessions sucked away each time more of the fragments shored against his ruins. Time, his unsuspected friend, continually betrayed him.

But now, in this momentary apprehension, he felt an achievement. For once he was on equal terms with the hurrying years. While he had watched, absently but intently, change had taken place. Complacently he listened to the sound of water dripping from the church roof, as the snow melted. And through it he became aware that the Vicar had ceased to speak. His gaze returned from the high, glinting roof of the church to the snow-hillocked churchyard, and to the rough brown gash at his feet. He watched with furtive fascination as the first clods fell, rapping vainly on the polished oblong box. Mrs Hallam would not hear their impertinence. Realising her new aloofness, her inability to touch or be touched, he ventured on an impertinence himself. Rosemary, he thought. Rosemary.

As the few mourners filed away through the brilliant snow, he remembered how he had first made a breach in the careful wall of her reserve. It had not occurred until several weeks after her arrival at Mrs du Cros's. At first, passing her on the stairs as she went to and from her attic room, or watching her at dinner, quietly withdrawn, she had been a gracious, gentle wraith. The anonymity of her widowhood shielded her. For most of the women Mr Garland met, in his leisurely forays from boarding house to boarding house, widowhood was a banner; if not to be flaunted, at least to be held ready for flaunting. But with Mrs Hallam it had been a vague, illusory quality, definable – so far as it could be defined – as a shield. From the start he had been interested in and attracted towards her conscious aloofness.

He had inquired discreetly among the others at 'Twilight View', but none had been able to help. Even Mrs du Cros, floridly eager to chatter about all her paying guests and unaffected, as Mr Garland felt he was himself, by any meticulous regard for truth, had been at a loss. She knew simply that Mrs Hallam had written from a small hotel in London, and had engaged one of her cheapest rooms, paying in advance. Beyond that her knowledge did not extend, and her eager surmises fell back baffled. Infrequently official-looking letters arrived, their envelopes addressed in neat, typewritten characters to Mrs R. Hallam.

It was on a grey afternoon, early in January, that Mr Garland opened the first breach. As he came down the stairs into the hall he saw Mrs Hallam's slender, withdrawn figure cross to the lounge, and immediately afterwards the afternoon's mail cascaded into the letter basket. With his usual willingness to help he sorted the letters for the others, after he had picked out his own. And amongst them he found a pale-green envelope on which, in spidery handwriting, was written the name. Mrs Rosemary Hallam.

He seemed to be following a course of action that was almost automatic as he picked it up and hurried with it into the lounge. There Mrs du Cros was presiding over afternoon tea. The room was a shadowy forest, gloomy with aspidistras and ferns, bright with white linen and silver, rosy behind Mrs du Cros where the fire bloomed. The voices of the guests rattled like the subdued, nocturnal depredations of tree-rats, punctuated by Mrs du Cros's parakeet scream. Looking beyond them Mr Garland saw Mrs Rosemary Hallam, sitting by herself at the little table under the window. She was looking out into the luminous greyness of late afternoon. Her quietness seemed to shine.

Mr Garland walked across the room, and paused beside her.

'Mrs Hallam,' he said, in his portentous, solemn way. 'I believe this letter is for you.'

She looked up at him, as though he were a messenger from some strange, alien world.

'Thank you,' she said. 'Thank you, Mr – '

'Garland,' he replied. 'Cedric Garland. I am honoured to assist you.'

She smiled. 'You are extremely kind, Mr Garland.'

The original acquaintance ripened firmly, though not so swiftly as Mr Garland might have wished, into a quiet form of friendship. The outer barriers of her reserve she let down graciously, almost casually, but with discrimination. Always, Mr Garland felt, she was testing him, and although on the whole she approved it was as a link with the world of Mrs du Cros and the gnawing tree-rats that she accepted him, and never as an equal on her own remote plane.

But despite the barrier that he knew could never come down, Mr Garland felt a surprising warmth in his enjoyment of this new pleasure, blossoming like a rose in the golden desert of his life. He himself had always had the feeling of watching the world and its scurrying populations from a distance, and although in his case it was the world that had refused intimacy to him, while Mrs Hallam so clearly played the active part in the refusal, yet he could feel closer to her than he had been to any person since his youth. Even, in a way, he realised, she came to depend on him for certain things. She had in herself a fragile but invincible strength. Like diamond she could never bend; but like diamond she might shatter and break at a tap of the world's hammer. The pomp of Mr Garland's presence was a cushion for her brittleness. He felt that she knew this and was grateful for it.

They had known each other a few months when spring touched 'Twilight View' in its passing. Mr Garland woke one morning to find that once again a transformation had taken place overnight. Throughout the winter the garden behind the house had been a cold, wet desolation, with lank grass and trees that seemed to drip continually like leaky taps. Now from Mr Garland's second-floor window, the vista of the garden roared in a tumultuous riot of green. A volley of starlings, startled into flight, shook the budding lilacs in exultant ecstasies. From its kennel Mrs du Cros's retriever barked sharply, and the noise whirled out through time as well as space, identified with so many barking dogs on so many halcyon spring mornings. Leaning well out of his bedroom window Mr Garland was able to see the sun, gloriously unchanging. He glanced upwards and saw that Mrs Hallam, too, was leaning out of her window, a white shawl wrapped about her thin shoulders.

He called out impulsively.

'Good morning! We must go for a jaunt on such a lovely day as this.'

She smiled down from her window in the roof.

'That is a very kind suggestion, Mr Garland. It is a lovely day. Where do you suggest we go?'

'Anywhere, anywhere!' Mr Garland was suddenly boyish. 'I will see you at breakfast in a few minutes, dear Mrs Hallam!'

They smiled and nodded and withdrew again into their own cool privacies, refreshed by the bold warmth of the sun. There Mr Garland chose his tie with a certain ebullience, and tied his shoes with care. He met Mrs Hallam outside the dining-room and gravely steered her to the small table they now habitually shared. Over dried egg omelet they made plans for the day. Mr Garland, reassured of the permanence of things by the spring sun, was almost gaily inventive. Mrs Hallam in return parried his more fantastic suggestions with flickering verve. Twice she laughed musically, causing Mrs du Cros to look up titteringly from her chair of state at the head of the big table.

In the end they walked out to the Market Square where, to Mr Garland's great delight, Mrs Hallam consented to a trip in the first omnibus that should come along. This, reflected Mr Garland, was adventure! Only momentarily was he saddened

– a small cloud crossing his permanent sun – by the thought of the wasted years in which for him omnibuses had run greyly and prosaically straight. Now Mrs Hallam was choosing the top deck of the bus, and even leading the way to the very front seat. And sitting uprightly beside him she watched with interest as the town thinned out until at last there were fields around them, and green copses, and the glint of water.

Within an hour the bus reached Wenning and they climbed, a little stiffly, down. They found a would-be Elizabethan café overlooking the river, and ordered coffee and biscuits. While they sipped their coffee they gazed out over the tumbling silver water whose radiance rippled in reflected shadow across the white, low-raftered ceiling. One of the Wenning swans stood, ungainly, on a flat rock around which the water swirled with fantastic venom. While they watched it waddled to the edge of the rock and slipped into the bubbling water, becoming suddenly graceful as it breasted the cauldron into its natural element. Mr Garland, breaking a digestive biscuit between his fingers, yielded to an impulse.

'You remind me greatly of a swan, dear Mrs Hallam,' he said.

'A swan on dry land?' she asked curiously. 'That waddling thing we saw a moment ago?'

'No, indeed!' Mr Garland declared. 'I mean the swan as we see it now, effortlessly graceful, and riding serenely over the troubling waves of the world as though they never existed. All the rest of us are swans on dry land. Perhaps there is an element somewhere in which each poor one of us might be at home and in grace. Yes, even Mrs du Cros! But you carry that element always with you. Where we flounder, you float. You are to be envied as well as admired.'

She smiled at him in acknowledgement. 'A pleasant compliment.'

Briefly he felt a pang, that she could not meet him here. He went on talking, ostensibly to his companion but aware that the gulf was still there, marking her off from the rest and even from himself.

He said, musing: 'One supposes that there are different forms of grace, and that all lie in the eye of the beholder. Does the swan feel an inward bursting of light as its webbed feet cleave the water? Or is it our peculiar taste that says there – at one moment – stands a crude, ungainly bird, but there – at the next – glides a swan? Perhaps to some eyes even Mrs du Cros has a grace of her own; elephantine, maybe, but still a grace. And all these graces are a grace of parts, as each finds and loses again its element perhaps without knowing of the miracle that has come and gone.'

She smiled at him, remotely, tolerantly.

'Can one always live in one's element?' he asked. 'Surely not. The swan must leave the water now and then. And yet you do, dear Mrs Hallam. As though' – he smiled in deprecation – 'your element were a vacuum which always clings about you.'

It was the nearest he could come to criticising her, and he was relieved that she seemed to find no criticism in it. They left the café and set off down the banks of the river. Soon, even at their slow pace, they were outside the town. They rested frequently, and once paused for more than ten minutes watching the activities of a water-rat under the opposite bank. Under the blanket of detachment Mr Garland thought he detected an interest in the new, thrusting life of the country. And once, gazing away from the river towards the unruly spring fields, she quoted softly in her small, cool voice:

'When weeds, in wheels, shoot long and lovely and lush;
Thrush's eggs look little low heavens, and thrush
Through the echoing timber does so rinse and wring
The ear, it strikes like lightnings to hear him sing.'

'Ah, yes,' confirmed Mr Garland, happily:

' … that blue is all in a rush
With richness; the racing lambs too have fair their
fling.'

'Dear Mrs Hallam,' he went on, 'the earth is indeed a wonderful place, especially in this season of the year. I had almost forgotten that it was possible to escape into such unravished perfection; a perfection that has stayed unchanged through the years. Do you feel, as I do, a sense of fullness and completeness, here where time leaves no mark, but annually renews his charge?'

The small head looked out over the stumbling waters and the steady fields beyond. He waited, expectant for the revelation, the vacuum's break, the intimacy. But she said only:

'I was born in the country. Remembering … And I suppose it can be a consolation when one has outlived the things the other world had to offer.'

Across the river a willow shivered in a faint breeze. Mr Garland was conscious that, as a small boy in the setting gold of Victoria's age, he could have come here on just such a day and seen just such a tree, patiently absorbing the sunlight. What consolation could the other world of trains and transition offer to put beside this?

'I am sure you could never need the offerings of the other world, Mrs Hallam,' he said, 'and for my part I cannot say that I ever enjoyed them, though that may be because little was offered me.'

They turned and walked slowly back to Wenning. By the time they had had lunch, an austere meal, heavy clouds were rolling up the valley with a chill breeze that promised rain. So they took the next bus back to 'Twilight View', and Mrs du Cros's screams among the tea-cups.

But after that they made several trips together, finding an increasing pleasure in each other's company. With the onslaught of summer, Mr Garland revealed to Mrs Hallam his one delight in the vast world of men, and on especially sunny days she went with him to watch the course of county cricket matches. She would sit, slender and erect, beside him in the stand while he explained the skill and beauty and subtlety of the game. She had a quick apprehension, but always she remarked on things quietly, as though even here she realised the absurdity of trying to impose herself on the crude pattern of life.

In the autumn their walks in the country brought new delight in the rich, warm kaleidoscope of the trees. The year seemed to have bent its efforts towards perfection. In its youth and maturity and autumn ageing, this year had displayed a charm that to Mr Garland's mind stamped it as a frame to the grace of his companion. Always afterwards this would be the year of grace, inseparable from his memories of Mrs Hallam.

But winter returned, and their walks became less frequent as the brilliant days slipped one by one into the past. Quietly they returned to the quiet world of 'Twilight View', to the wranglings over the soup and baths, the days gnawed away by the tree-rats, the evenings when Mrs du Cros's high laughter shrieked through the jungles of bridge. They played cards themselves occasionally, but more often sat together near the fire reading. At times Mr Garland would look up from his book, and then Mrs Hallam would look up from hers and they would smile. For each of them their companionship was a way of preserving into winter the past summer delights.

Christmas was the season in which Mrs du Cros excelled herself. For weeks before she moved around, like some vast spiritual beaver, building an atmosphere of goodwill. And for once the shambling chaos of 'Twilight View' responded to her shrill ordainments. Bath rosters miraculously took coherent form, and although the soup at dinner was still burnt somehow it became possible to overlook it. As evening advanced on the shortening days, afternoon tea in the lounge assumed the mystic dimness of a cathedral service, for even in her spirit of maturing goodwill, Mrs du Cros was adamantly a fuel-saver. In the shadowy room the guests, under her keen benevolence, voluntarily restricted their helpings of butter and jam, even refused sugar in their tea. All was to be saved for the Christmas festivity. Even when, as happened frequently now, Mrs du Cros was absent during the day, to return in the evening squealing beneath an avalanche of Christmas shopping, her spirit seemed to linger and chide and inspire. Co-operation was the keynote of 'Twilight View', and if Mr Garland and Mrs Hallam still stayed without the charmed circle, at least they fell in with the measures of economy adopted.

So Christmas Day came. It began with Mrs du Cros's own special ceremony, a ceremony that her husband had brought with him on being invalided from the cavalry but which had become Mrs du Cros's own as the years of his increasing illness imperceptibly changed into the years of his death. Promptly at seven she launched her body into the frigid air and, quickly washing and dressing, made her way down to the kitchen where she and the cook exchanged seasonal greetings and warmed their twin bulks by the stove. Then at seven-thirty, aided only by the living-in maid, her procession through her kingdom began. From room to room she went, preceded by the pungency of coffee vapour, leaving behind her the steaming coffee itself, spiced – except only in the case of the most rabid abstentionists – by the little extra something that to Mrs du Cros was the true herald of Christmas.

Warmed and cheered by the bringing of cheer to others, she then went down again to assist in the preparation of the Christmas breakfast. For absence from this meal there could be no excuse but genuine illness. The voice of Mrs du Cros, raised in shrill command, swept through the house, exhorting, imploring, almost tearing the guests from their warm beds. Down they came, pretending unwillingness but greedy for the spread. Grapefruit! Bacon and egg! And butter on their toast. Mrs du Cros sat at the head of the big table, praising, presiding and promising. Wait till dinner. Such a turkey, such liberality of pork! Outside the rain dripped from the tattered lilacs, but inside Mrs du Cros was sacrificing her fuel-saving to more lasting values, and huge fires roared in all the living rooms.

Mr Garland enjoyed a quiet amusement at these signs of

cheerful hysteria. Leaning over their small table, he whispered didactically to Mrs Hallam:

'A legacy from the pagan world, dear Mrs Hallam. Can you not visualise our hostess as a white-robed priestess, flourishing a flaming torch before some primitive altar, proclaiming the turn of the year?'

Almost immediately after breakfast, it seemed, there was lunch, and lunch had barely been cleared away before the first harbinger of dinner appeared, and Mrs du Cros brought round sherry. As she walked, majestically bearing the tray before her, light shivered from her ear-rings and gleamed on the glasses with their amber cargo. She was toasted in the sherry she had brought and her flustered, embarrassed delight rocked round the shining room.

Mrs Hallam, by the window, twirling her glass of sherry, suddenly stopped smiling and drew her breath in sharply. Solicitously Mr Garland bent over her. He knew of her turns, and had helped with them before. Now he raised the sherry to her lips, where its rich shades marked the whiteness of her face. Soon she could smile again, and the warmth of Mrs du Cros's Christmas lapped around them. But a shadow lingered.

After the immensity of dinner there was bridge as usual, for Mrs du Cros had a talent for not taking things too far. The success of her Christmas could now be consolidated by the orthodox. The green baize tables came out, and the cards, and soon the remembered cries – 'One No Trump', 'No Bid', 'Three Diamonds' – rose in the familiar jungle. Away on the fringe of things, Mr Garland was able to talk seriously with little fear of being overheard.

'Dear Mrs Hallam,' he said, 'there is a matter I should like to put to you. It is a delicate one but I have little gift for subtlety, and I can only hope that you will forgive my inexperience. Would you tell me first why you choose to live here at "Twilight View"?'

'There is no real choice,' she said easily. 'As you must have guessed, I have no friends and little money. It is the only way I can live.'

Mr Garland sipped his brandy. Something in his mind shivered against the irrevocable step, on whose brink he hovered. Throughout his life he had watched men and women rushing together, fighting to abandon themselves and each other to the whirlpool of darkness and deceit and anger. As his susceptibilities had turned in shock from contemplation of them, so now they asserted their querulous, protesting doubts. But memory rejected them. This wraith, this pleasant vacuum, would not claw him down into the whirlpool; but rather act as a further barrier against it.

'Forgive my saying it,' he said, 'but I had guessed that. And as far as your first reason is concerned, why that explains my own residence here. In my youth I did not acquire friends easily, and the few there were have all gone, in different ways. But I have a little money.'

He paused in embarrassment. Here, inescapably, one clawed oneself; the whirlpool thundered suddenly nearer. The rush, the abandonment – all these impended. But already it was too late for withdrawal.

'In fact I have enough,' he continued, 'to make a home for the vintage years that still may lie ahead. Small, but' – across his words Mrs du Cros's voice shrieked a savage commentary: 'Three down, doubled and vulnerable!' – 'but … aloof. I was wondering, dear Mrs Hallam, if you could possibly consent to share it. Will you marry me?'

She drooped her head a moment and he thought, with a small shock, that she was going to unbend, cast off her cloak, suddenly be warm and human. In part he longed for, in part dreaded it. To see a butterfly swarm from the tinted chrysalis … And yet, the whirlpool, its tumult rocking now in deep and steady nearness … She looked up, and he knew there was no butterfly; only the chrysalis.

'How very kind of you,' she said. 'But no. It's too late, isn't it?'

Then her face whitened and she caught her breath again, and even the swift application of Mr Garland's brandy did not ease her. He had to abandon her to Mrs du Cros, and sit apart while the women fussed with cushions and smelling salts. When Mrs du Cros had helped her up the stairs, Mr Garland made his way to his own bedroom where he sat for some time thinking of the years, and realising as he had not done so clearly before that they take away as well as give.

Mrs Hallam's illness advanced swiftly. She came downstairs a few times after that, but each time she looked whiter and more frail. Mr Garland sat with her a lot, reading to her Thoreau and Jefferies and Hugh de Selincourt. He was reading to her one dim afternoon when the final attack came and the diamond cracked. For a few minutes after he knew she was dead he stood looking down at the still, white face that had held so many secrets and would never yield them up now. Then he went to call Mrs du Cros.

Now, standing in the snow, he looked at the rough, fresh clay and thought how strange it was that of all the people who must have known and been drawn to her throughout her life, it was left to him to stand by her grave and renew, when they withered, her meagre flowers. She had told him so little of her life but surely, he felt, she must have known fullness as he had never known it. And of the fullness only this was left – an elderly mourner in the snow, the last of her suitors.

Beside the church a tree raised skeletal branches, thinly mounded with snow. There was another tree, he thought, that flowered once; flowered fantastically in colour and scented strength. Those flowers … Punch … horseless carriages proudly flagless … the ordered pageant of the hunt … garments enveloping, rich in line and swathe … balls in the Season … the great years – oh, my Hornby and my Barlow long ago … That was the tree of which we were the leaves, he thought; leaves that are scattered now and lost beneath the relentless winter.

To swim back, he thought, along the river of time, through storm and tempest to that halcyon summer! To rest, a leaf, with the other leaves on that broad tree. All had been anchored to it, even when seemingly alone. Even himself, even Mrs Hallam. Now it was dead and the last leaves underfoot, this strange one resting here among the snow and clay. This very strange one.

Strange, he thought, but – realising it gladly – no mystery, no glacial secret. That empty grace went back unchanged, through storm and fall of leaves, to the rich summer. Watching the dappled grave-stones – the white, the blue, the transcendent gold – he knew that nothing was mysterious in itself. Man made mystery. Others, as he had done, must have been fascinated and puzzled by her, but the fascination and puzzle alike had been rooted in themselves. They were the puzzle; she but the calm screen of its projection.

The snow was melting everywhere. As he paused by the lych-gate, Mr Garland heard it melting in trickle and whisper from gutters and runnels all round him. Change was raging about him, but the sacred moment of apprehension was gone and once more he was on his own and must face the horrors of transformation. He could not expect again to surprise the monster at its feast. Now there was snow. To-morrow he might look from his window and see the brown earth straining with green. But all too insidiously slow to catch and savour.

As he walked back over the slushy pavements to 'Twilight View' he thought without much emotion of the years ahead; the struggles for the bathroom, the burnt soup, the afternoons chattered away and the evenings devoured by cards. And he thought again of the tree, and the summer that now bloomed only in his mind, beyond the curtaining mist. The tree was dead, the leaf beneath the snow. As the house came in sight, and the snow-blossomed lilacs, he remembered that he had never even called her by her name.

He whispered it to himself:

'Rosemary.'

Space. Oddly an effect of blueness. A thought of blueness, a feeling of blueness, unrelated to sight or any of the senses. Hold it. Visualise it. Blue ... blue ... blue fading. Space. Colourless. Lightless. Soundless. Intangible. Space.

A thousand, thousand years. No movement. No vision. No thought.

This is what I wanted, she remembered. There would be peace, a merging, perhaps sleep. She wanted to let her mind drift away into it, into the blankness, away from all thoughts and memories. But memories clustered insistently about her. Lacking the constant flow of sensations from her body, the memories themselves were strangely real and solid. They seemed to drift round her like circling satellites, plucked from an inexhaustible galaxy below. They would not be disregarded. They edged in about her. Like vortices they pulled. She felt herself falling through long agonies of emptiness into the rejected warmth. The senses returned with the numbing pain of activity. Light and sound, roaring through eyes and ears, shocked and dazzled her.

... There was a breadth of green, and figures walking on it in white. Above, beyond it, the sky swelled into an immensity of azure, limitless and unclouded. Sound rose rhythmically and ebbed away – a tide of clapping. A smell of petrol and grass and blistering paint; all the mingled perfume of summer.

But all somehow distorted. Vision particularly. She stared, trying to resolve the hazy outlines at the corners of sight. Staring, she began to feel the sensations of body around her, but they were not quite the familiar, expected sensations. A pain, pulsing gently in the le

a sense of greater physical bulk

again. The vague outlines were

She realised suddenly, triumphan

But she had never worn spectacles.

Then a woman's voice, tantalising

'He is out then, Mr Garland?'

The head turned. Although almost ex

shock. Through the filmy brightness of sp

at her own body.

She remembered now. She remembered th

man walked away from the wicket, his bat ha

less salutation. And the fielder just below the st   ..no took

off his cap and lay down, sprawled on the yellowing turf. A

return to life in the middle of a county cricket match. But

surely a mistake. She listened to the voice from the body she

tenanted.

'Yes indeed, Mrs Hallam. A fine ball. It came in from the

off. Did you see? It beat him all the way.'

There was a rising joy about her that did not seem to be

part of her own apprehension. It deepened as the eyes looked

down at the body of Rosemary Hallam into a confused, ea-

ger exultance. A strange, undisciplined emotion. She realised

what it was only slowly, and then with an instinctive revul-

sion. It was the love for herself of Cedric Garland; and in his

body and his mind she was spying on it.

She fought against it, striving to separate herself from this

knowledge and unwanted intimacy. It was unfair that she

who had all her life refused emotion should now be sub-

merged in another's. Unfair and somehow frightening. But

as she struggled she became more and more intensely aware of the thoughts and feelings of Cedric Garland; sank into them more and more deeply until her real self was nothing but a confused and helpless participating spectator. She was Cedric Garland. She knew a fraction before it happened that his hand was going to his waistcoat pocket to bring out his big, gold hunter. While his eyes read the time she knew his happiness in being there on such a day with Mrs Hallam. She felt his mind forming words before the words were spoken:

'Some refreshment, Mrs Hallam?' he suggested.

She would not submit. It was a mistake, a fantastic mistake. She strove against the entangling web of thought and feeling.

Her other self said: 'Why, yes. That would be nice.'

She resisted, with all her strength of will. The plain of green began to tilt, the white figures blurred, scent and sound twisted and faded. She was winning. The green tilted faster and faster, until sight faded with the other senses. And she was back again, exhausted, in the longed-for peace of non-existence.

She wondered with tired curiosity. There must be an answer to things, a purpose, an end. But what end could there be but peace and sleep and emptiness? The gleaming gates, the haloed angels – although they would have surprised her, they would have been in their way logical. But there were no gates, and no angels, and no quiet oblivion. There was only herself, and her past life hanging about her like the coils of a serpent. She did not want the past.

Without warning, she fell again.

A different body. Shorter, more bulky and – sensed at once – inescapably female. The lounge at 'Twilight View'. Christmas decorations on the walls, the huge, billowing fire, bridge tables, and the brightness of cards on the green baize. She was Mrs du Cros.

Mrs du Cros, leading against a small slam in Hearts, turned at the sound of a fall. She saw Mr Garland looking up, frightened and bewildered, and beside him the slumped figure of Mrs Hallam. Waddling across she directed expertly; administering smelling salts, propping up cushions, chafing hands. She thought: poor Mrs Hallam. Afraid it's something serious. A mercy her rent is paid in advance.

She said: 'There now. I'll help you upstairs. You'll feel better in bed.'

Mrs Hallam was too light to weigh heavily on her as she helped her upstairs to her room. She helped her to undress, and brought her a hot-water bottle.

Mrs Hallam whispered: 'Thank you.'

Mrs du Cros left quietly, switching the light off at the door. On the way downstairs she slipped into her own bedroom. The bottle, the season's gift, stood on her dressing-table and, barely hesitating a moment, she lifted it to her lips and drank. The whisky soaked through her like a hot shower of pricking needles. Poor Mrs Hallam. Had she enough to cover the funeral expenses? But Mr Garland would see to that. Darby and Joan, she thought sentimentally, Darby and Joan. She glanced at the old double bed, and remembered the Major with a vivid clearness that she had not known for years. How he loved Christmas … Darby and Joan. Joan left desolate through the long years and now – how soon? – another Darby also abandoned. She drank from the bottle, feeling her body tingle with renewed sensibility. Even if he doesn't, she thought generously, I'll bury her properly …

There was the struggle again as revulsion concentrated into

strength. The struggle, and the distortion, and at last the liberation. Emptiness and peace, lapped round by an absolute of oblivion. Lapped round, but not absorbed. She was real and separate, and chained in some way to the phantoms of her life.

She fell again, and struggled back, and fell once more into the maelstrom of senses and emotions. She was a spy, a reluctant, bewildered eavesdropper on the lives of others. Mr Garland, Mrs du Cros, a bus conductor, Mr Garland again ... All who had crossed the thread of her life, idly or purposefully, in love or indifference, were hosts now to her visiting spirit. She was astonished by the chaos of emotion in their minds; a whirlpool of feeling somehow indecent, and altogether unfamiliar. Did they really think like that, she wondered, or is this the fantastic exaggeration of a nightmare? She resisted still, but knew her resistance weakened by the constant struggle. The descents were just as swift; the struggling return to nonexistence each time steeper. She tried to will herself into her own body, hoping to rest in that quietness and serenity. But it was denied her. Instead she fell, more and more deeply, into the unknown jungles of the minds of others.

Strength and resistance faded. Free for a moment she hovered in the timeless, dimensionless void, waiting and resigned. There must be some purpose. She relaxed and felt the vortices of memory spreading round her. She would resist no longer. There was a strange conviction that if she waited she would find an answer.

She fell slowly and more gently, and slowly floated up through the distortion into light.

She was Elise Walters.

CHAPTER TWO

1942

Elise

ELISE, OPENING THE FRONT door with her key and walking into the hall, became Elsie. It was the usual transition, and she accepted it without rancour. Now that her life away from home was becoming the more real one she was able to accept home itself more easily. She pulled off her coat and hung it next to her father's patched and rank-smelling working coat. Then she pushed open the door into the kitchen and walked into the flood of raw light and the almost tangible smell of kippers.

Her father was already sitting in his high-backed wooden chair mauling the remains of a kipper in his hands. He looked up as she came in, blinking in the light.

''Ello,' he said. 'You're late, Else. Been workin' late?'

'Yes,' she said. 'Missed my bus, too. My kipper ready, Mum? I haven't much time.'

Her mother trotted out of the scullery like a small terrier. She carried the dish with the kippers and her cheap horn-rimmed spectacles were misted as usual.

''Ello, Else,' she said. 'What's the 'urry?'

Elsie sat down and, reaching for the teapot from the hob, poured herself a cup. The tea hissed as it came out of the spout, but there were still the tea-grouts she hated swimming on the surface when the cup was full. She began picking them off carefully with a spoon.

'Going out to-night,' she replied. 'Mum, you didn't let the water boil properly.'

'Where are you going,' her father asked. 'Pictures?'

'Yes,' she said.

He insisted coyly: 'With a boy?'

'No,' she said shortly, 'with Hilda.'

She wondered why she lied about it to them. There was no real need, as far as hindrance was concerned. Had she told them about Lance they would not have pried far; they were too humble and beaten by life to have more than an idle curiosity over their daughter's activities. She thought with some bitterness that if she had said: 'I am leaving to-night to live with my Boss,' they would only have remonstrated mildly. And yet it was essential to lie about Lance, about everything in the world of Elise. That world and the world of Elsie could not be permitted to touch.

She ate her kipper quickly, gagging a little on the bones. Her father was sitting back in his chair, sucking his teeth and reading the evening newspaper with a bewildered pretence at interest. As her mother came in, slamming the scullery door behind her, and sat down to her own tea, he relinquished the paper, realising the completeness of his audience.

'I'm to go away for four days nex' week,' he said proudly, 'to learn gas. They've chose me and Dan Stevens out of the works' Fire Brigade. We've got to learn gas, an' instruc' the others when we come back.'

'Fancy that!' said her mother. 'You'll 'ave to learn a lot if it's goin' to take you four days. 'Ear that, Else? Your dad's to go away an' learn gas.'

'Yes,' she said. 'He'll have to have some notebooks. I've got a couple upstairs he can have.'

'Notebooks?' her father said. 'Why, that's right. I will want notebooks, to take notes in. Thanks, Else.'

'I'll bring them down when I come,' she said.

Pushing her chair back under the table she went into the scullery. There she soaped her hands under the hot tap, and ran a flannel over her face and neck. As she came through the kitchen again to go upstairs, her mother called to her.

'You 'aven't eaten much, Else. Feelin' aw right?'

'Fine,' she called.

She ran upstairs and shivered in the chill of her bedroom. It was bitterly cold, although the room itself looked warmer than the others in the house. In the others there were no shades on the lights, her parents considering it rank folly to pay for brightness and then darken it. Here the orange shade pretended a warmth where no warmth existed. She hesitated a moment, wondering whether to change out of her jumper and skirt into something cleaner. But after all they were only going to the pictures, and the room seemed icier merely at the thought of taking her outer clothes off. She tidied her hair, made her face up briefly, and changed her stockings and shoes, rubbing her frozen toes for a moment before putting clean stockings on. Then, gathering the notebooks from her drawer, she went downstairs.

Her father said: 'Thanks, Else. I'll 'ave to increase your pocket money.'

He smiled at his own familiar joke.

'That's right, Dad,' she replied. 'Must be off now. Goodnight. I'll probably be back about eleven.'

They heard the front door slam behind her, and settled back into their rut of timidity and content.

Elise met Lance, as usual, in front of the Odeon. She saw him while he was still some distance away, moving diffidently through the crowd surging in front of the cinema, and ran towards him.

She said: 'Hello, Lance. Let's go in before they start queueing.'

He said: 'Wait a moment, Elise.'

He paused.

'Yes?' she prompted.

'I was wondering,' he said, 'whether you would like to come home with me for a change. You could meet Mother.'

Elise inventoried rapidly her hastily made-up face, her office clothes and the ladder she had intended to darn in her stockings.

'That will be lovely, Lance,' she said.

He smiled. 'Good. We can get a bus at the corner.'

In the bus he said suddenly: 'Did you know I have to register next week?'

She said: 'No. So soon? What are you going to do, Lance?'

A muscle in his face twitched nervously, pulling the corner of his mouth down. She saw his thin shoulders shudder slightly.

He said: 'I don't know yet. I suppose I've been letting things slide, hoping for some late revelation that would make it easy and positive for me to decide. And instead I get more dithery than ever!'

'Then you should object. If you're not sure you should object.'

'No,' he replied obstinately. 'If I'm not sure I should go with the rest. I suppose most of them aren't sure either. Millions of them like me; too weak to be sure about things. Why shouldn't we go and do as we're told if we haven't anything constructive to offer?'

She said weakly: 'That's not right, Lance. You know you don't want to kill anyone. Why should you? It's a mess, but it's not your making.'

Lance said: 'I don't know.'

The bus jerked round a corner, and he pressed the inside of her arm.

'This is where we get off.'

They walked a few yards before turning into Grenoble Gardens. The sky was light with the diffused brilliance of a full moon behind the clouds. High up they heard the mutter of an aeroplane. Elise was able to see that Grenoble Gardens was a wide road, flanked by rows of large houses standing well back. They seemed to tower tremendously high after her own home.

Lance, walking beside her, broke the calm silence.

'The decay of grandeur!' he said. 'They still look quite good in the dark, don't they? During the day one sees the flaking paint, the trampled garden plot, the pram on the top floor balcony. But at night they are as grand as they were in the time of their glory, the time of one family to each house, the days of triumph of the merchant princes.'

He pushed a gate and held it open for her. She noticed that there were steps leading up to the door and pillars on either side.

'It's a big house, Lance,' she said.

He keyed the door open, and pushed her inside.

'It has to be,' he said, 'with five different sets of people living in it. We are merely second-floor troglodytes. Come down in the world, like all the rest round here. Or so we pretend. We need some excuse for our inefficiency.'

As they climbed the stairs a shaft of light above them broadened swiftly into a square, framing the figure of a woman.

A voice said: 'Is that you, Lance? And have you brought Elise?'

Lance answered: 'Yes, Mummy. I've brought her.'

Elise walked before Lance into the lighted room. The walls and the ceiling were cream, and the room itself seemed to swim in a creamy light. She noticed how high the ceiling was, and the green carpet, worn but still luxurious, that covered most of the large floor space. There were two or three easy chairs, a polished table, a small dressing table with bevelled mirrors, a massive radiogram, and a single divan bed with a rich scarlet cover falling in folds round it. On the walls were a few framed prints which she took to be reproductions of famous paintings. An electric fire of the reflecting mirror type glowed in front of the armchairs. Everything was clean and seemed to have a faint polish.

A voice behind her said: 'You should introduce us, you know, Lance.'

Lance said: 'Don't be silly. Mother – Elise. Elise – Mother. There you are.'

Elise turned round to see a thin woman of between fifty and sixty. Her grey hair was almost white in places and blue veins stood clearly on the back of the hand she held out. But there were few wrinkles in the thin, white face, and Elise realised that only a few years ago she could have been called beautiful. In the level grey eyes there was a quiet, assured power. Her cultured voice said:

'How do you do, Elise.'

Elise said: 'Pleased to meet you, Mrs Hallam.'

The room swam round and she felt her throat suddenly tighten. Of all times and places, for Elsie to appear now! The horror of it fogged and sickened her. She wanted to scream: 'I do know what to say properly; really I do. I'm Elise. I'm not ignorant and common.' But through her horror and confusion she heard the quiet voice continuing, as though nothing had happened.

'I've asked a lot of questions about you, but Lance is so vague about things. I hope you don't mind. Mother's curiosity, you know. It's very nice to find you so charming. Will you have some coffee?'

Elise said, weakly: 'Thank you.'

Lance guided her to a chair in front of the fire.

'I'll have some too, Mummy, if it's strong enough,' he said.

Mrs Hallam, who had left the room, came back carrying a tall metal coffee-pot.

She said: 'It's been percolating for hours.'

She smiled at Elise. 'This is a horribly battered old jug – we've had it for years. You take sugar, of course. Lance, bring Elise some biscuits.'

They sat drinking coffee. There was a clock ticking rhythmically in the room. Elise looked up and saw it on the mantelpiece; a grotesque, elaborate affair painted with blue, quartered moons and displaying brass gears.

'Horrible, isn't it?' Lance said. 'Oh, listen!'

Above the ticking they heard the night wailing outside. Sound rose and fell like a sea washing in over the city. Right on its heels, as it shuddered into silence, they heard the padded shunting of guns in the distance. They rumbled for a few minutes before quietness flooded back over them.

'Nothing yet, anyway,' Lance said. There was relief in his voice. 'Perhaps we'll have a quiet night.'

Mrs Hallam said: 'I suppose Lance has told you he has to register the Saturday after next?'

Lance stirred restlessly . 'Yes, she knows. She thinks I should register as a C.O.'

Mrs Hallam said quickly: 'Oh, surely not! Surely, Elise, you would not try to influence Lance towards such a course of action. It would be disastrous for him. All the uncertainty and isolation and guilt. He couldn't avoid cracking up.'

Elise said: 'I only think Lance ought to do as his ideals tell him.'

Mrs Hallam said: 'And what do they tell him?'

Elise said: 'I don't know. But they couldn't approve of killing.'

She felt that it was a weak answer. Mrs Hallam didn't reply directly. She poured more coffee into their cups. As she was pouring, she said:

'I met a young man after the last war who had been in prison for his pacifist views. Believe me, Lance, any discomforts you have to endure in the Army will be less severe than prison life would be. And although I know you do not count it, the danger of being killed is just as great, here as a civilian in London, as it would be if you were in uniform.'

Lance got up and walked round the room restlessly.

'No, I don't count it,' he said. 'But at least I don't have to do any harm to others sitting here, even if I am just as likely to be killed. The whole thing's so damned ridiculous. Can't you see, the whole point is what you *do*, not what's done to you. That doesn't matter. Putting me in uniform and making me obey silly orders wouldn't do me any harm. But if under those orders

I had to go forward and murder someone ...'

He shook his head. 'Oh, I don't know!'

Mrs Hallam said: 'They tell me that for every man in the fighting part there are over twenty who merely supply things. I'm sure they would realise that you are too sensitive for sitting in trenches.'

Lance looked at her sharply. She caught his arm, smiling.

'But sit down, darling. You must do as you think best, of course. I should hate to think of you doing anything against your will.'

Lance smiled. 'That's all right, Mummy. I'll work it out before the time comes.'

Elise drank her coffee in silence. She felt there was a way in which she could help Lance, but she lacked the courage to attempt it. She felt the impossibility of breaking through the fabric of security that lay around him here. The quiet, unstrained intimacy between him and his mother was so strong, and her own tenuous attachment to him so weak. He would not be able to avoid resenting her if she tried to force things in any way, when his whole environment was so calm and unforced. She, after all, was Elsie as well as Elise. Elsie was persistent, however fiercely Elise tried to repress her. She had won through once already this evening; she might do so again.

When, later in the evening, Lance was taking her back to the bus-stop, she tried to say something but didn't have the right words.

She said: 'Lance, don't let anything ... force you ...'

He laughed, almost resentfully. 'Don't worry. I'll think things out on my own. It's about time I learned how.'

The All Clear bellowed like a herd of sick cattle as they reached the bus-stop. A bus was coming round the corner towards them.

'Shall I come back with you?' Lance offered.

She thought of taking him back to watch the comedy of Elise turning into Elsie, to smell the never absent reek of gas, to listen to her father monotonously telling dull tales.

'No thanks,' she said. 'I'll be all right.'

She swung on to the bus. ''Bye, Lance. See you to-morrow.'

There was the usual little ceremony at the office when Lance left. Two other clerks had also received their papers, and one of the girls was leaving to join the A.T.S. Mr Bengear himself paid for the afternoon tea and cakes, and presided over their serving in the typists' room. His small, fat paws stretched out as though to bless, and tiny drops ran down from his hair to settle in the grooved scar that ran across his forehead.

He said: 'Well, young men, you've got to go. You must exchange your clothes for uniform, your sheets for Army blankets, your five and a half days a week at the office for seven days a week, twenty-four hours a day, in the Army. I don't know how you are feeling about it now, but I can assure you that within a month you will be looking back on your life here as a snatch of earthly paradise.'

The typists giggled. Mr Bengear quelled them with a pudgy wave.

'Despite my fat,' he went on, 'I have a vicious nature. In 1916 in the trenches, and even more in the arid desolation of Base Depot when I had at last managed to wangle a job there, I thought of this happy future. I thought of how I should wave good-bye to the next generation as they went forth into slavery. Such thoughts. Such happy fulfilment!'

His round, merry face clouded.

'Though, after all,' he said, 'perhaps you will like the Forces. Perhaps I am unusual in that respect. Certainly, although I met few who liked the life while I and they were in it, all I meet now speak of the old days with a certain, sentimental regret.'

Mr Bengear lifted his cup and drank the steaming tea.

'Anyway,' he finished, 'we shall miss you. I shall miss you even while I gloat. And I beg you not to take the gloating too much to heart. Set your minds instead on the next war when you will be waving good-bye to the youngsters yourself, and old Bengear will, very probably, have passed beyond.'

Letters came from Lance only rarely. He had been posted to an artillery training regiment and, after a first wild outburst of disgust and hatred for his new life, his mind seemed to tighten up, and his letters skated on thin satire over the abyss that, Elise guessed, hung always beneath him.

He gave her no warning when he came on leave. It was Saturday afternoon and she was ironing in the kitchen when the door-bell rang. She ran out to open the door, her face flushed, and saw Lance. He stood before her in shapeless uniform.

He said: 'Hello, Elise. Can I come in?'

She thought for a moment of throwing herself on his mercy; of saying: 'Please, no. I'm ashamed of it – of my home, of my family, of myself for being ashamed and for being part of it. Please let me stay outside with you and be Elise.' It might barely have been possible with the old Lance, hatless and in flannels. But she had no means of contact with this uniformed stranger. She held the door open.

'Of course, Lance. Do come in.'

She saw him wrinkle his nose as his senses caught the smell of stuffiness and leaking gas. Then her mother who had been peeling potatoes in the kitchen came out curiously.

'Who is it, Else?' she asked.

'One of the boys from the office, Mum,' Elsie replied. 'He's on leave, so he dropped in.'

She realised, with a strange feeling of relief, that the clash she had avoided for so long had arrived, and that in the battle Elsie must always win. Elise was all right for the office or afternoons at the tennis club, but Elsie was the real thing. She turned to Lance, defiantly:

'Mum will make you a cup of tea.'

He said: 'Thanks. I am rather dry.'

While they were having tea she saw that his eyes were examining the small, badly wallpapered room. His gaze flickered over the tradesman's cheaply-printed calendar, the old family photographs enlarged from snaps and hideous in oval walnut frames, the religious prints, the cheap set of Dickens given away by a newspaper. Out of her embarrassment, Elsie said:

'Are you getting to like it any better, Lance?'

He seemed a little nervous. He looked down at the shortbread biscuits on the Woolworth plate.

'Oh, I suppose it's all right,' he replied. 'One gets used to it. Schemes are the best part – when we get away from the barracks a bit. Sleeping and living rough don't seem to matter beside the sense of freedom they give. So perhaps it will be all right when we get out of training depot.'

Elsie's mother said: 'It must be terrible. I 'eard one woman sayin' in the grocer's 'ow 'er boy 'ad to go across raging rivers on a greasy, slippery pole, while they fired bullets at 'im all round. What a thing to 'ave to come to.'

Lance said: 'They haven't got to that stage with us yet!'

He looked up at the mantelpiece, where the battered tin alarmclock said five o'clock. He turned to Elsie.

'Would you like to come to the flicks or something?'

She said: 'Hang on. I'll slip upstairs and put something on. Would you mind putting the iron away, Mum?'

As they opened the front gate she saw her father's figure slouching down the street towards them. She pulled Lance in the opposite direction. Once again the old struggle in her mind, and this was the outside world, Elise's territory. She glanced back. Her father was standing by the gate, peering after them. She looked ahead, gripping Lance's arm.

The film bored both of them. They had seen the tail-end of the supporting film at the beginning, and when it started again, Lance asked:

'Want to see it through?'

Elise said: 'No.'

It was still light when they came out. The sky was deep, soft violet, except where one thin cloud was surprisingly green. Riveting the blue were the silver studs of barrage balloons, like man-made stars. They saw one rising to join them from somewhere behind the cinema. It twisted slowly as it went up, a huge, wallowing aerial slug. Soon, by the metamorphosis of height, the slug would become another star, twinkling in the distant sunlight.

Lance said: 'Feel like going for a drink?'

She said: 'Have you started drinking, then, Lance?'

He laughed. 'Please don't embarrass me by being tactful about my coming of age. Just come and drown with me in the oblivion of the vine.'

In the saloon bar of a nearby pub he got sherry for Elise and beer for himself. He carried the glasses over to the table in the corner where she was sitting. He drank a draught from his own, and put it down.

'You know, Elise,' he said, 'I felt rather embarrassed back at your home. I couldn't help feeling that with all the – solidity – of your background you must despise a middle-class throw-out like myself.'

Elise flushed. 'That's rather a cheap sort of insult,' she said.

Lance looked at her blankly. 'Insult? No, I'm really serious, Elise. There was a solidness there, and I envy it. Oh, I know it's cramped and must be rather a trial for you at times, but there is something real there which those of us sliding down the ladder in Grenoble Gardens lack.'

Elise sipped her sherry. 'I hate it,' she said slowly. 'I hate every rose on the wallpaper, every crack and crease in the old oil-cloth on the kitchen table. You can't imagine how I hate it.'

Lance said: 'God! How awful for you. And yet you seemed – contented enough there.'

She said: 'Oh, I fit into it, all right! After all, it's my proper environment, that station into which it pleased God to call me. But being ashamed of one's parents, being ashamed to bring friends home – you can't imagine how bad it is.'

Lance said: 'That's just snobbishness. There's nothing wrong with your parents, and if there were why should it affect you?'

She flared on him suddenly. 'It's all very well for you to talk like that with the background you have. You have everything. You can conform to all the little conventions unconsciously, as though you had forgotten they existed in themselves. You don't have to watch your aitches all the time. You don't even have to bother about the clothes you wear – you are so sure of your own superiority that it doesn't matter.'

Lance said: 'Hang on, I'll get some more drinks.'

She watched him walk over to the bar, easily confident and assured of himself even in the swaddling uniform. He came back, and raised his glass.

'Here's to us,' he said. 'Who's like us? Damn few, and they might as well be dead.'

He drank solemnly and Elise sipped her sherry.

Lance said reflectively: 'It's funny how knowledge of our own weaknesses only makes us more ready to assume strength in others. For instance, you seem to think me a strong, assured character; while I am convinced that beside you I'm just a two-dimensional projection, as far as will and security goes.'

He laughed.

'For instance,' he went on, 'I had plans for to-night. To be brutally frank, I intended to ply you with liquor and then se-duce you. But as soon as we got here I realised that I didn't have the nerve to go through with it. There's such emphasis on sex in the Army, and for days I've heard the others talking about the conquests they would make as soon as they got home for a few hours. And all of them probably as weak and dishonest about it as I am. What a cowardly lot of boasters we all are!'

Impulsively, warmed by the sherries, Elise said: 'Oh, Lance, I love you!'

He looked at her closely. 'Do you really mean that? One thinks of oneself as so completely unlovable.'

He paused and laughed weakly.

'It's ridiculous! I outline my petty lascivious imaginings, and you tell me you love me. The whole thing's fantastic.'

She said: 'You're so honest. And – better than I am.'

Lance drained his glass.

'There you go,' he said, 'idealising. Most of the time I'm petty and irritable, and a hell of a coward.'

He stood up. 'Shall we go?'

She said: 'Lance, we can do all sorts of things together next week. Like dancing and – whatever you want.'

He laughed. 'Next week? Next week you can think of me sleeping on the marshes and by day idling about imitation gun-posts, snatching a pint at a pub when the instructor isn't looking. Didn't I tell you this was just a short week-end? I have to go back to-morrow, and on Monday we go out on a super-scheme. Five days of it. Still, it will be a change from blanco-ing.'

Elise said: 'No. I thought you were on proper leave. You should have told me. What about your mother? Won't she be hurt at your going off with me, when you have so little time?'

They were outside the pub now. A light wind had sprung up. The early stars looked as though they were brushed by it into a high polish. One or two of the nearer barrage balloons could still be made out, but they were no longer shining. Lance took Elise by the arm.

'She may be hurt,' he said, 'but it's her own worry. After all, she wanted me to be a fine soldier like her first husband. She must expect soldiery to be crude and licentious.'

Elise said: 'Please, Lance. Don't try to be callous.'

'Anyway, she'll have me to-morrow.' He sounded guilty. 'Shall I come home with you?'

Elise said: 'No. Please don't. Go back home now.'

The light was still bright enough for her to see him clearly. For once she felt the stronger and more capable of the two. His face was very young.

She said: 'You will write more often, won't you, Lance?'

A bus was lumbering towards them, a scarlet, devouring monster in the dim canyon of the night street. As the monster paused to snatch him up, Lance said:

'I'll write the very first day. And I should get some real leave soon.'

Elise began to walk home, realising he had not kissed her.

The bell clanged on her typewriter as she heard her name being called. She looked up. Mr Bengear was standing in the door of his office.

He called: 'Miss Walters! Wanted on the phone.'

He pointed to the receiver as Elise entered, and returned silently to his study of a document.

She said: 'Miss Walters here.'

The line was bad, and she could not grasp the name. The voice sounded rather familiar.

She said: 'I'm sorry. The phone is very bad. Who is it, please?'

The voice said: 'Rosemary Hallam. Lance's mother. Could you come round straight away?'

Elise said: 'I finish work in an hour. Will it do then?'

Mrs Hallam said: 'No. Please come round now. It's so difficult to explain things over the telephone. But it is urgent. Can't you get away?'

'Wait a minute,' Elise said.

She said: 'Mr Bengear – could I leave now? It seems to be urgent.'

The pudgy hand waved blindly in the air.

He breathed: 'Of course.'

Elise said: 'I'm coming,' and rang off.

Mrs Hallam let her in at the front door. Elise was surprised to see that she was wearing a half-length fur coat and gloves.

'What's the matter?' she asked. 'Is Lance all right?'

Mrs Hallam handed her a telegram.

'It came half an hour ago,' she said. 'I've rung for a taxi for us. It should be here any moment.'

The telegram read: REGRET INFORM YOU YOUR SON LANCE HALLAM GRAVELY INJURED ON MANOEUVRES CRITICALLY ILL SWANDOWN HOSPITAL.

Elise said: 'No. It can't be. He only went back last night.'

Mrs Hallam said: 'I wish I could think so. That it's someone else; that there's been a mistake. But there never is with bad news.'

Elise said: 'He didn't want to go. You practically forced him to go. I'm sorry for Lance and myself, but not for you.'

She was aware of the unfairness of her attack, but her anger could not now be checked. She looked round the room, her hate swelling against the careless, expensive symbols of the gulf that had always divided her from Lance. She pressed the toe of her shoe into the luxurious green carpet.

Mrs Hallam said: 'Please. We're both upset. Let's not say harsh things.'

Elise said: 'No. Let's not say harsh things. Let's not cause ourselves any pain. It doesn't matter that Lance is lying in hospital; perhaps dying.'

She looked at Mrs Hallam, at the remote, white face still untouched by her anger. She thought: why should she escape everything? All the bitterness and pain, the black fury of anger. Why should she be free?

Mrs Hallam said: 'Please, Elise. It doesn't do any good.'

But doesn't it, she wondered, doesn't it? She looked again at the cold calm of Lance's mother, and felt her anger strangely dissolving into pity. Pity not for herself, nor for a wounded – perhaps maimed – Lance, but for this old, frozen woman before her.

She said: 'I'm sorry.'

Small stones glistened on Mrs Hallam's wristlet watch as she raised her arm to look at it. Elise saw that it said four-thirty.

Mrs Hallam said: 'There's a train at five-fifteen. The taxi should be here.'

They heard the bell ring in the front door.

'The taxi,' Mrs Hallam said. 'Will you come, Elise?'

When they opened the door a messenger stood there, holding a telegram. A taxi was coming slowly down the road, the driver peering at numbers.

The messenger said: 'Telegram for Hallam.'

Elise said: 'It was a mistake! It was somebody else, not Lance. Oh, open it quickly!'

As Mrs Hallam opened it, they looked at it together.

It read: REGRET INFORM YOU YOUR SON DIED IN HOSPITAL THIS AFTERNOON MATRON SWANDOWN.

CHAPTER THREE

1938

Lance

THE LIBRARY AT CARVEL's looked out over the terrace, and so
over the huddled town of Bullcaster beyond. Lance Hallam,
sitting facing the leaded glass windows, admired the serenity of
the view. The cathedral looked all its six hundred years in the
morning sunlight. At its side even the industrious granite of the
council offices relaxed in the quiet of early summer. To the left,
the white parade square of the prison dazzled thirstily. Beyond,
the city was indistinct, already half hidden in haze.

At nearer hand the school sports field extended on either side.
The dew was gone from the roped-off 1st XI cricket pitch, and
the big roller lay up against the terrace. During break, a press-
gang of small boys and minor delinquents would man it for
a final assault on the wicket, fighting and scrambling for the
privilege of sitting on top and, in the case of the unsuccessful
ones, working off their resentment by digging their heels into
the turf. Beyond the cricket pitch were the high boards guarding the swimming bath and, further still, the pines marking the
school's boundaries. As they swayed in the slightest breeze, the
yellow of their pollen drifted down over the grass and made the
water golden in the swimming bath. They drew out and deepened the colour of the scene, their darker green offsetting the
more brilliant grass and the smoky brown city.

Lance's eyes came back to the book lying on the green baize
cloth in front of him. The Odyssey, Books XIII to XXIV.

'And now the pious Odysseus ...'

He looked at his watch. Twenty-to-eleven. In another five minutes, break. And after break another free period before Greek. He could mug up his prep then. At the worst he had a rhyming translation to fall back on, though it was a chancey business reading cribs to Grange. But school life was taking risks. Lately, in the Sixth, it had also drifted into a policy of delay. There was so much to find out about oneself, and so many outside distractions. Obligations, in the way of prep and set books, mounted into successive climacterics, each more nerve-wracking than the last and each leaving a greater residue of work to be done by July. At times Lance still felt that an orgy of work might bring Higher Schools within his grasp, but as the weeks dwindled so did his chances of achieving that miracle of labour. Mainly now he was occupied with getting past everyday obligations.

The Library, decreed as a place of private study for industrious Sixth Formers, was as conducive to the laziness of the rest. Lance felt at ease here, surrounded by the mellow leather bindings. Even the silently reproachful gold letters on the Roll of Honour were somehow endowed with the calm for which he longed. To him, at seventeen, they still meant very little, and nothing at all in the compass of his own existence.

There were only a few others in the Library; most of the Sixth had a full timetable on Saturday mornings. On other days the large, quiet room filled up fast enough; sometimes it even overflowed into the Hall when a master claimed the table near the door for some minor set. But the table at which Lance always sat was reserved for a certain group, and notorious. It was placed in an alcove by the main window, out of sight of the table to which masters sometimes came. Here the fast set passed its porno-pensive time, despised and disliked by the harder working Sixth Formers, and known by them as the Leisure Club. Lance blamed the Leisure Club for his own idleness but now, solitary and unmolested, he still made no attempt to work.

A jackdaw walked jauntily across the fresh strip of green. From the Hall a bell rang sharply and Lance got up, closing his Odyssey.

He spent break walking with Mackensen along the far boundary of the school field. This was as far as they could go from the restricting school atmosphere. They spoke briefly about various things, but always slid back to Carvel's, their one real contact. Finally, with relief, they fastened on the afternoon cricket match, an event connected with school but remote from the routine of work.

Mackensen was a solid third man in for the 1st XI. His batting was unspectacular but very even. Lance, an eccentric and occasional member of the 2nd XI, admired but did not envy his stolidness. At times he tried to get behind the façade that was Mackensen. He probed for a human being like himself, interested in all the aspects of life. But gradually he realised that the surface Mackensen was a logical and undeceptive projection of the real Mackensen. There were no under-water abnormalities in his iceberg. Lance reviewed his own lazy, undisciplined mind, and was irrationally pleased with himself.

After break Mackensen went off to Main English. Lance walked unhurriedly to the Library and sat down. He opened his Odyssey as Bennett came in, closely followed by Heath and Welling. They came over to the table by the window; the large, unruly figure of Bennett followed by the other two.

'Here's old Hallam,' said Bennett. 'Slacking as usual. Hallam? Christ, do you ever work?'

'Busy bloody Bennett,' Lance said affably. 'Do you mean to say you've actually done two periods of work this morning? You didn't even cut English?'

Welling laughed. 'Gas-bag nearly had a fit when he saw us. He was too shaken at first even to try sarcasm. Later he said something about the prodigals returning. Billy turned to me and said how lucky Gas-bag was to have two fatted calves, and the old fool blushed like hell.'

'Poor old Gas-bag,' said Heath. 'He's so scared.'

Bennett was sitting in his usual place with his back to the window. Welling and Heath ranged themselves on either side of him, and rocked backwards in their chairs until the backs rested against the stone window ledge.

Their conversation drifted away to the fascinating subject of the girls attending the school on the other side of the town. Lance, listening to them, half believed and half ridiculed the grubby tales of their imagined conquests. Bennett's tales he enjoyed because Bennett had a breadth of imagination, even in salaciousness, which was stimulating. The others, trying to emulate him, were only boring.

Bennett reached the climax of an adventure at the public swimming pool and they all laughed.

'You can shut up now, Billy,' Lance said. 'I have some Greek Set Book to do for Walrus by next period.'

'Why not cut it?' said Heath.

'Don't try to be helpful, Blasted,' Lance said. 'You're better in your normal idiocy. Even Walrus would notice a fifty per cent drop in his Classics set.'

Bennett grinned. 'I like to think of you isolated with Goodrich and that refugee from the Zoo. Punishment for your sins, Hallam. Why the hell take Classics, anyway?'

Lance shrugged. 'One has to take something.'

'I always take Epsoms,' Welling said.

They laughed. Goodrich, at the next table, looked up mutely. Lance noticed that he was reading a translation of *Antigone*, one of the recommended books. He had done his prep at home, of course. Encountering this contrast to his own shiftlessness, he suddenly felt violently angry.

'Goodrich doesn't like us talking,' he said loudly. 'Goodrich thinks we ought to be working for Higher Schools like good little boys. Don't you, Goodrich?'

'I don't mind what you do,' Goodrich said, mildly. 'But I would be glad if you could do it with a little more consideration for others.'

Lance recognised the justice of Goodrich's remark but it was impossible to climb down or even remain silent while the other three were watching. He looked at Goodrich's pale, square face, and then at his cheap, careful clothes and lank body.

He said: 'Before you instruct us in manners, my opulent Goodrich, I suggest that you learn the elements of dress. You can button up a sports coat like a pair of combs. when you're at home, but in civilised society the top and bottom buttons are left undone.'

Goodrich flushed and turned silently to *Antigone*. Heath laughed, and then broke off. The other two gazed blankly at the row of *Punch* volumes on the opposite wall.

'Got the cards, Billy?' Lance asked, uneasily. He wanted to forget the whole episode. Bennett, too, seemed glad of the diversion.

'No,' he said. 'Woof confiscated them in German. We shall have to stick to dice. Anyway, cards are too difficult to hide in a hurry.'

He brought out his set of three tiny dice, contained in a hollow cork, and threw them absently. They rolled across the green baize. Then he retrieved them hurriedly as the door swung open. Carp came in.

Carp was stocky and sandy-haired. He was stand-off half and captain of the 1st XV and a good middle-weight boxer. These qualities magnified his legal authority as prefect into near-omnipotence. He was working for the Indian police, and regarded school as a training ground for his discipline. His affection for authority was not satisfied by a sergeant-major's rank in the O.T.C.

He came over to the table by the window, and sat down beside Lance.

'I hope we shall not disturb each other, gentlemen,' he said, pleasantly.

They glared at him. His habit of addressing non-prefects as 'gentlemen' had all the conscious superiority of the Head, from whom he had derived it.

'You couldn't disturb us, Jacky,' Bennett told him. 'We love you too much.'

Carp made no protest against the diminutive use of his christian name. Instead he turned to Lance, who was busily copying the translation of Homer into his rough book.

'Dear me, Hallam,' he orated, 'not – surely not – cribbing?' He took the translation up between finger and thumb and put it on top of his own books. 'All for your own good, Hallam.'

Lance's smile was sickly. 'Could you let me have it just for now, Carp. I have Walrus next period, and he's in a difficult mood this morning.'

Carp patted the book decisively.

He said: 'I'm sure Mr Grange would prefer to have you stupid and honest. Your work may then be a poor thing, but at least it will be your own.'

Lance got up. He said to Bennett:

'I'm off to the Hall. The atmosphere here gets a little strong. Drains, I fancy.'

He slammed the swinging door of the Library viciously. The Hall looked even more bare than usual. He sat down at the table on the rostrum and opened Homer. Forty lines to translate in thirty minutes. He might manage fifteen. After that forty-five minutes of Walrus, and the reproachful Goodrich. He walked across to the sports board, to make sure that Bennett had bagged a tennis court for the afternoon.

With one hand holding the saddle, Lance propelled his bicycle forward so that the front wheel jammed securely between the wall and the lawn-mower. Then he walked out, slamming the garage door behind him. Sometimes the emptiness of the garage looked strange even now, although Gordon had been dead for three years. He walked across a corner of the lawn, swinging his racket, and entered the drawing-room by the french windows.

He called: 'Mummy!'

His mother came through the door leading from the kitchen, carrying a blue fruit dish. She was wearing a brown, flowered pinafore over her grey costume.

She said: 'Hello, Lance. Did you have a nice game?'

Lance threw himself down listlessly on the settee. He pressed his head down between the cushions, so that the cool leather rubbed against his face. At the same time the cushions, pressing up against his thighs, yielded a lazy, sensual satisfaction. He kicked his legs up in the air behind him.

He said: 'It was all right. I had Bill Bennett for a partner. We won the first set easily but then we got fed up and mucked about. So they beat us eventually.'

Mrs Hallam said: 'I think that a most unpleasant word, Lance.'

Lance asked: 'What? Oh, "mucked"? What's wrong with it? Sorry, anyway.'

'Ready for your tea?' she asked.

Lance said: 'Oh, rather!'

He followed her into the dining-room.

Half an hour later, his mother said: 'If you really *want* another chocolate biscuit, of course, darling. But you've eaten over half a pound already.'

Laughing, Lance helped himself.

'Really, Mummy,' he said, 'anyone would think we couldn't afford them. Grudging me my healthy appetite!'

Mrs Hallam smiled. 'Don't be ridiculous. They're only one-and-six a pound. It's just your tendency towards hoggishness I deplore. You know very well what I mean. You are just forcing that last biscuit into an overcrowded stomach because it makes a nice taste in your mouth.'

'You may be right,' Lance acknowledged. 'I'll stint myself and not have another after this. Mummy, when can I have a car?'

'Never, while I have the power to prevent you,' she said. 'You know that.'

Lance lay back, replete. 'That's silly, you know, Mummy. It's rather unfair, too. Gordon had a car as soon as he was seventeen.'

'Let's not talk about it, dear,' his mother said.

Lance said: 'Because of Gordon? But that's not an argument, Mummy. Gordon was mad on the road. He wasn't fit to be trusted with a go-cart.'

Mrs Hallam said: 'Lance, that's too much! Are you forgetting yourself?'

'Sorry, dear,' he said, 'but we have to be reasonable. After all, it's three years now since it happened. And we have to admit that it was Gordon's fault; he really was crazy on speed. You know I'm a careful chap. I shouldn't approach blind corners at sixty.'

Mrs Hallam stood up. There was a barely perceptible tightening of her face. She said sharply:

'Lance, I won't have any more of it. You will be silent on my instructions, if you haven't yet developed a sense of propriety.'

Lance felt his own weakness, spreading like a giant cancer across his body. Fear; blind, instinctive fear. Fear of harsh words, of exposure, of disgrace. So small a thing to dry up his mouth, and weaken the muscles behind his knees. He tried to fight it. He told himself: it's only Mummy. She will do no more than jaw you. You are quite safe. But nothing could halt the onrush now until it died slowly by itself. He stared sullenly in front of him, and felt his heart thumping.

Mrs Hallam said: 'And there's something else, Lance.'

He hated her even more than he feared her. Guiltily he thought of all the things she might have found out. But it wasn't, he told himself, any error of his that mattered, in comparison with Mummy's deceit. To have sat through tea, smiling, joking – quite ordinary – and at the same time have been storing something up against him. She had done it before but each fresh betrayal had the power to stun him. The ordinary world had its hidden gulfs and abysses. They were real enough and fraught with terror. But when the smiling grace of his mother turned hard and forbidding, it seemed as though one giant abyss opened beneath all the others, sweeping him into the extremities of fear. By now he knew the intonation in her voice that preceded the horror. But that could not prevent the abyss from opening.

Mrs Hallam went on: 'I met Mr Grange at the Skinners' this afternoon. I asked him how you were getting on. Lance, he said you are almost certain to fail Higher Schools.'

'He's a rotten master,' Lance said, sullenly. 'He never *teaches*. Just sits and grunts all the time.'

'He was quite frank,' Mrs Hallam said. 'He told me you were lazy; that you had a good brain if you would only use it. But it wasn't that that shocked me.'

She paused, looking at him closely.

'Lance,' she said, 'I've asked you several times why you have no preparation to do these days; you have always told me that the Sixth have special time allotted during the day for that kind of work. Now Mr Grange tells me that those private study periods are meant to be used for the study of recommended books, and for revision. It does shock me to find that you have been lying to me.'

Lance was falling; falling into those unknown, uncharted depths. The horror of being caught in deception – of being defenceless against attack – bore down on him heavily. Desperately he fought upwards, beating the wings of twin hatred against Grange and his mother. They were despicable spies. And how hypocritical of her to minimise the laziness and pin her attack on the deceit. Hypocritical and unfair. It was the laziness that had made him follow the Leisure Club in doing prep in private study periods. The deceit rose out of it; inevitably, justifiably, in reply to his mother's questions. How could she have expected him to be open about it; to say: 'Oh, yes, Mummy, I'm supposed to do prep in the evenings still but I prefer going to the pictures with Bennett?' Lance hovered on pinions of hate above the hell of defeat.

Mrs Hallam said: 'Haven't you anything to say?'

Lance lay back in his chair. Through the bay windows the sun flung a dying bolt of flame into the great mirror on the wall. Rivers of sunlight on the wallpaper rippled into life as a breeze shook the edge of a curtain. From the direction of the garden next door, the cries of the children were golden also.

His mother began collecting dishes.

She said: 'I think you had better go to your room and begin the week-end's preparation. I mean it, Lance.'

At last he said: 'I haven't got anything with me. I left it all in my locker at school.'

She said: 'Get on your bike and bring them then.'

Lance got up silently, and went out towards the garage.

Higher Schools, as usual, was taken in the Library. Dust sheets hung from the tops of all the bookshelves, in case the lettering on the spine of a book might give assistance to some boy sitting opposite. A master sat by the radiogram, reading magazines. The only noise was the scratch of pens, with occasionally the rustle of paper or a strangled cough.

Lance's first paper – a Classics paper – disillusioned him of any hope that he might scrape past the examiners. Looking over his work just before bell his emotions were a mixture of fear, relief and amusement. His translation of Greek Unseen was notable only for its gaps, where the best of guesswork had been unable to produce a sensible possibility. The gaps were even and regular in his neat handwriting. As the papers were handed in he saw the top sheet of Goodrich's work. Slovenly, loose writing; a blot halfway down the page. But undoubtedly a translation.

Grange was invigilating. Lance saw him look casually at his work and at Goodrich's. He put them into their envelope with no trace of surprise. Lance hated him fiercely. He imagined him to be gloating; enjoying his revenge for the long months of inattention. Later he was to understand that to have one pupil of a class of two fail wretchedly did not help Grange's reputation as a teacher of Classics. And he was to understand something of the apathy which made Grange accept it without rancour or surprise.

Lance left the Library at 11.30. He had no other examination before the afternoon, and an hour to waste before there would be any point in going home to lunch. He took a Latin grammar, to placate any magisterial interference, and walked up the field away from school. In the back of his mind he had an idea that he might do some late swotting. Still further back he knew he would do nothing of the sort.

The ground yielded to his feet without being muddy. It was like walking on a sloping expanse of green rubber. The sky was rubber, too; grey, opaque and infinite. He came on two worms, still, at this late hour, clasped in sexual unity. He pressed his right foot gently and firmly into the ground beside them. They unclasped, leaped apart, snapping like elastic back into their holes.

As he had anticipated, he found others on the far side of the sports pavilion. There were half-a-dozen Sixth Formers who had preferred the dank morning air to the close supervision inevitable in the Hall. Cartwright, Morris, Mackensen, Bennett, Heath and – surprisingly – Goodrich, sitting with the others and openly ignoring the Latin Set Book in front of him.

Lance walked over to Bennett.

'Hello, Billy,' he said. 'Where's Welling?'

'Taking Main French, poor bastard,' said Bennett. 'He's got ants in his pants about it too. Been working like Goodrich for the last week.'

'I haven't been working for the last week,' Goodrich said, unexpectedly.

There was a local whine in his voice that irritated Lance.

'That's right,' he said, 'you're so bloody good you don't need to swot. You love Homer like a brother.'

'Last minute swotting doesn't do any good,' Goodrich said, mildly. 'But if you want to know, I do like Homer.'

Mackensen and Heath looked at him with respect; Bennett with a dubious contempt. Cartwright, slightly built, with small eyes and a blue stubble of beard, got up and leaned against a strut of the pavilion.

He quoted:

> 'Seven cities vie for Homer dead
> Through which the living Homer begged his bread.'

Fat lot of good it does Homer to have you like his stuff now.'

'Seven towns contend, surely,' said Goodrich.

'That doesn't matter,' said Cartwright. 'It's the sense that counts, not the words. What that shows is that art is bunk. Economics is the only thing that matters. Homer didn't give a damn about what cities would contend for his birth hundreds of years after he died. He would have swopped the lot for a comfortable life.'

'That jingle deceives you,' said Goodrich. 'There is nothing to show that Homer was poor. In fact it is very unlikely that he was. Certainly whoever wrote the books down could not have been poor. It's not the sort of thing a eunuch slave would do, and apart from slaves only the rich were educated.'

'Swine!' said Cartwright, passionately. 'Slavery and capitalism, provincialism and patronage. And some fools call it the Golden Age.'

He glared at Goodrich.

'Don't include me with them,' said Goodrich. 'I am the last to favour such a system – for obvious reasons. But it *was* a Golden Age of art.'

Goodrich's frank implication of his poverty infuriated Lance. Faced with such a situation himself he knew he would have hedged and boasted. Now he said, pointedly:

'To hell with Greece, and for Christ's sake don't mention economics. My mother only told me this morning that she might let me have a car if I got Higher. If she had had the sense to say that six months ago …'

'A new car?' Bennett asked.

'Good Lord, no,' said Lance. 'But I know of a nice little wreck going for about thirty quid. Well, it's too late now.'

'Think it might still be available when the results come through?' asked Bennett.

'Yes, why?' Lance said.

Bennett considered the matter carefully. At last he said slowly: 'Because I might be able to buy it.'

They were all incredulous, but Lance chiefly.

'In the first place you haven't got the money,' he said. 'In the second you display a mean spirit in wanting to get your hands on a property rightly mine, before I even lose it.'

'Don't be a b.f.,' Hallam,' Bennett said. 'If I get it we can all use it. As for the money – my old man has promised me twenty-five quid if I get through.'

Lance laughed. 'If that's your only ground for hoping, I can't see you buying the car.'

'Don't be too sure,' Mackensen said. 'I called at Billy's one night and found him up to the eyes in German. I didn't say anything at the time, but since he has let the cat out of the bag …'

'Have you really been swotting?' Lance asked.

A small abyss was opening again. The knowledge of his own laziness was bearable only when others were implicated with him. From this gulf of self-disgust only companionship could save him. To fail Higher along with Bennett, Welling and the rest would be bad enough; to fail it alone would be unbearable.

'I think I've done enough to get by,' Bennett said. The statement itself, quite apart from the complacent tone of his voice, was unusual. Those in the Sixth who did not decry their ability in false modesty generally went to the opposite extreme of conceit.

Goodrich said: 'I'm glad you are not the kind of fool who thinks it big to do no work.'

Lance was stung. The insinuation was only applicable to himself and Heath, and he knew Goodrich would not have wasted it on Heath. It was wrong, too; that was the injustice of it. He did not slack because he thought it was the thing. He had tried hard enough. It was just that he was incapable of concentrated and sustained effort. But he could not counter Goodrich without revealing that part of himself that must be hidden. The pathetic yearning for guts, for stamina; that was the last thing to disclose to Carvel's.

He said: 'Who did you mean by that, Goodrich?'

Goodrich said: 'You can wear the cap if it suits you.'

Lance said: 'You stinking bastard! Get up if you have the nerve.'

He stood over Goodrich as he got up. When he was on his feet, he punched wildly at him. But Goodrich parried, and drove a straight left hard against Lance's jaw. It rocked him back against the pavilion. When he recovered he could see Goodrich only through a haze. His jaw was hurting badly, and from the smarting in his eyes he knew he was on the verge of irretrievable tears. Having started a fight he knew he should continue it, but he had not anticipated that Goodrich would be strong and capable. He wanted to drive his unwilling body forward, to smash at Goodrich and bear him down by sheer force of attack. But his own fear and the welling tears stopped him. He hesitated, and turned away. The others were watching him. He had to do something.

He said to Goodrich: 'I'll see you in the gym to-night.'

Goodrich grinned contemptuously.

'You aren't worth fighting, Hallam. You're all wind. I don't suppose you will ever learn manners. And it isn't up to us to instil decency into you.'

Lance said nothing, and walked back in the direction of school. He was relieved to be free of the obligation to continue the fight, but Goodrich's off-hand contempt bit deeply. He wondered what it must be like to be Goodrich. To know you could handle anything your mental instructors put up to you; to be capable of slow, slogging effort as well as intuitive brilliance; to know your body strong and your mind clear. Yes, but also to be poor; to live surrounded by cheapness; to wear patched, shabby clothes.

From his brief orgy of self-abasement and reviling, Lance passed automatically to fantasy. In fantasy he ran the whole scene over again, but this time making all the points where he had previously failed. This time he floored Goodrich contemptuously with the first blow and, more contemptuously still, helped him to his feet. Goodrich lying on the ground before him, Goodrich flushed and apologising. Perhaps even Goodrich next term, amazed to read the Classics results:

1. Hallam.
2. Goodrich.

Almost automatically Lance took his bicycle from the shed and started off down the Drive. Already the ground had healed beneath him.

On the first morning back at home Lance woke up with a sense of relief. His own spring mattress was very comfortable after the hardness of the spare bed at Aunt Sara's. And it was a pleasant change from the early farmyard din to hear the drowsy sounds of suburban Bullcaster. The milk van delivering down the street; bicycle bells ringing; an occasional car humming past. He could hear the noises of his mother and Nelly moving about downstairs. The smell of bacon was beginning to flood upwards. Lance got out of bed and began dressing.

The front door was open as he came downstairs and he could see Nelly beyond, scrubbing the doorstep. He called out to her, and she looked up with appraising, frightened eyes. His mother looked out from the kitchen, smiling.

'Hello. Sun drive you out of bed? Living on a farm seems to have given you an ability to get up if nothing else.'

Lance said: 'Bacon, not sun. It smelled lovely upstairs.'

He picked up the *Telegraph* and wandered into the dining-room. The table was already laid, so he propped the paper against the toast-rack. He had just finished his cereal when his mother came in, carrying a tray. She put down two plates of egg and bacon, and sat opposite him.

Carefully rinding his bacon, Lance said:

'Nelly gets more scared-looking every day. When I said good morning to her I thought she was going to burst into tears.'

'I expect it's her father,' Mrs Hallam replied. 'I believe he drinks heavily and beats them all.'

Contemplating the abject weakness of Nelly, Lance felt strong. He felt the security of the distance lying between him and the Nellies of the world. For him, comfort, strength, a holiday on a farm as a preliminary to the real holiday at Torquay. For Nelly, squalidness and brutality so great that scrubbing steps in his home must seem a bliss in comparison. How horrible, how grotesque to think that an accident of birth might have made one a Nelly! Such engrained humility and compliance. His mind wandered furtively. Perhaps when Mummy went out shopping he might try something on with her. She wouldn't resist. He tried to control his growing excitement.

There was a knock from the front door, and Nelly's voice calling weakly:

'Post, Mum.'

Lance said: 'I'll get it.'

He went through to the hall quickly, but his excitement died away at the sight of the postcard, addressed in his own writing, on the hall table. He thought of hiding it, but there was no other mail to cover it up. He looked down the list anxiously. Passes in two subsidiary subjects: Fail in all the rest. The abyss was opening again as he took the card into the dining-room.

He said casually: 'It's Higher results, Mummy. I'm afraid I've failed.'

His mother held out her hand for the card. She read the results carefully. Lance, watching her, saw her face tighten.

She said: 'It could hardly have been worse. It's very disappointing. Can you account for it at all?'

Lance said: 'I'm only good at things I'm interested in. I can't concentrate very well on others.'

Mrs Hallam laughed suddenly; a hard, brittle laugh that tore across his nerves.

She said: 'And you aren't interested in much. Another way of putting it is that you are lazy and shiftless, and inclined to be vicious. I suppose I must be partly to blame. It isn't easy to rear a child without a father.'

She looked again at the results card.

'So very strange! Your father with all his energy . And you – lazy and stale.'

Lance said: 'Mummy – please. Don't.'

His mother looked at him reflectively. 'No,' she said, 'you don't like being hurt, do you? You want everything to be pleasant and easy. There's not much of value in you.'

Lance stood up. 'I'm going out,' he said. 'If you want me to leave I can leave. I'll get a job somewhere.'

She said: 'I'm afraid you will have to. But don't talk nonsense about leaving home. If you are at all honest with yourself you must know that it would only involve the humiliation of having to return to me when you found you could not live on the wages you earned.'

She turned the results card over in her hands.

'University is out of the question now, of course. And I see very little point in having you stay at Carvel's another year in the faint hope of your developing enough energy to work for Higher Schools before next July. I worked out once that the money I have left would be enough to see you comfortably through college. But now I suppose I must start planning.'

Lance said: 'Planning what? It will save you money if I get a job.'

His mother said: 'I am being selfish. You are only fitted to be a junior clerk, and even with normal promotion that means seven or eight years before you will be able to support yourself. By then you will probably have married, and I don't fancy a subsidiary position in your household. I must hoard my money against that time. I shall go in to Darwin's this morning to see about selling this place. We can get rooms somewhere.'

Lance said: 'I'm sorry.'

His mother looked at him with tolerant contempt.

'Yes,' she said, 'I suppose you are. I suppose you always will be sorry about the things in which you fail, and always too lazy to succeed. Anyway, I suggest that this morning you write to the Head and ask him if he can help you to find a job.'

She put the breakfast dishes on a tray and took them out to the kitchen. Lance went through into the drawing-room. He found notepaper and a pen. He was half-way through the letter when his mother looked in. She was pulling on her gloves.

'I'm going out now,' she said. 'I'll probably be a couple of hours.'

He heard the door close behind her. Then he heard the light, scurrying steps of Nelly as she went through to the kitchen, and shortly afterwards the noise of washing-up. He felt the excitement rising again. Going into the kitchen, he came up behind Nelly and put his arms round her fiercely.

She had a litheness that surprised him. She twisted herself free and stood in the doorway. Steam rose from her wet arms, and tears were beginning to roll down the thin, white cheeks.

She said incoherently: 'Oh, you monster! I'll tell your mum. Don't you dare touch me.'

He said: 'Sorry, Nelly, it was only a joke. Don't tell Mummy. I'll give you half-a-crown.'

Nelly's abjectness was transformed into power.

'Keep your money,' she said. 'I know me rights. I'll see what your mum 'as to say. And my dad, too. 'E'll 'ave somethin' to say. You monster! I'm respec'able.'

Desperately, persuasively, he offered: 'Look, Nelly – here's five bob. It's all I've got. You're not hurt. Go on, take it.'

Surprisingly the tears turned into derisive, searing laughter.

'Scared of your mum, aren't you?' she said. 'I 'eard 'er this morning telling you off for bein' no good at school. An' you tryin' to lord it about. You are a poor thing.'

Lance said humbly: 'You won't tell her?'

Nelly was triumphant. 'I may do, and I may not. You get out of the kitchen for a start. Go on – scoot.'

He went out, back into the drawing-room, and finished writing the letter. There was nothing in his world but fear and disappointment. Somehow, he was sure, Mummy was to blame. There was nothing he could blame in himself; he tried hard, but weakness and inability drove him on like storms behind a ship.

He realised suddenly: no Torquay this year. But the abyss was so wide that it could hardly open further.

CHAPTER FOUR

1935

Gordon

HE WAS REMEMBERING HIS PROMISE to Rosie all the way through the tortuous streets, and even feeling a certain detached pleasure in treating the car gently, coaxing it through the traffic. But here the tramlines finished in a final net of confusion and beyond the road stretched wide and straight, under a low, wide bridge and away off into the distance. It ran into the west like a swift river, dotted only infrequently with the floating specks of other cars. Over the whole scene spread a thunder cloud, so thick and deep and heavy that it seemed to crush the countryside beneath it. His foot moved automatically to the accelerator – smoothly, blandly, like a well-remembered dream – and he felt the car surge forward into its rightful element. Soon it was shrieking triumphantly through the wind and his eyes, steady and exultant, were watching the little finger crawling round.

50 … 55 … 60 …

A field away a secondary road ran across, but the hedges were low and he could see that it was empty. Then he was beyond it and breasting a rise that gave on to a tremendous dip – down, down and then up, up, over another rise, with the forest pressing close to the road so that the afternoon was even darker in the close embrace of the trees. Open fields, a farm, a village. He braked carefully, triumphing in the completeness of the response. A child waved gravely from the grass beside the road.

He smiled to himself, soaring out into the open, watching the little finger patiently crawling back.

He told himself cheerfully: it's all right. You can control it. There won't be any more trouble. You can go as fast as you like and as slow as you like. Everything's going to be fine. There won't be any more trouble. Everything's going to be fine.

Light flashed on the windscreen – silver and gold and a rainbow-tinted whiteness – and he looked up at the sky. A spear was striking down from the edge of the retreating storm-cloud, tunnelling through the heavy air as though it were solid gold. He looked up through the gold into blindness, and looked down quickly again to the road. For a moment there was only a dancing, multi-coloured haze ahead, but his hands held steadily until his eyes could see through the dazzling colours to the less dazzling whiteness beyond. He thought of them caressingly; his own fine, steady hands.

There was shadow again for a moment, and then the full flood of sunlight as the blue lake above lapped over the diminishing black. By the time the road twisted into the valley and he could see Bullcaster lying under the hill five miles away, there was no trace left of the storm. He let the car roar in a final burst of speed, revelling in the mastery of his tumultuous passage. As the outlying houses of the town loomed up, he let the finger sag back. Soon he was turning decorously into York Street, halting at the traffic-lights. He felt like singing in the exultant knowledge of his own power. The car crawled obediently through the scrambling traffic until he turned into Greycotes Road. Lance was kicking a tennis ball against the garage door, but stopped as he saw the car approaching. He ran towards it, waving.

'Hello, Gordon,' he called. 'Don't get out. I'll open the gate.'

Gordon lay back grinning while his brother pulled the gates open. He saw Rosie come to the front door, and waved to her. She was wearing a light, flowered frock, with a shawl round her shoulders, and her dark hair was slightly ruffled by the spring breeze. He thought how ridiculous it was that she should be over fifty and his mother. Watching her erect slimness he felt heavy and old himself.

He drove into the garage, and came out with Lance hanging on his arm. Rosie came round the side to join them. Gordon kissed her heartily.

She said: 'Darling. You did drive carefully?'

'Like a snail,' he assured her. 'I thought once or twice I would land a summons for loitering.'

He led the way into the house.

He said: 'I'm ravenous, Rosie. I say – visitors coming?'

Rose said: 'Yes, dear. Eve Graham and her mother.'

'Must I stay to tea?' Lance asked. 'Please, Mummy.'

'You must learn not to be frightened of things,' she said. 'Deformities are always rather unpleasant because we are unused to them. But it is ridiculous to run away from what seems unpleasant.'

'Let him go out, Rosie,' Gordon said. 'No point in keeping him in against his will. She can be a bit disconcerting, especially over a meal.'

Lance shivered, remembering the deformity; the crooked arm ending in that claw hand, the short twisted leg and foot. Gordon talked about it so casually, as though it were not he who had been driving the car that day but some other person. Lance tried to shut his mind against the picture of that drive. The car leaping along the road. Two people laughing and talking. And then Gordon waking up, miraculously unhurt, to find the girl beside him cradled in twisted metal, spouting blood, and screaming … But Gordon never seemed to worry about it, even to avoiding the subject. He would sit with the girl and her mother at tea as though they were just ordinary visitors.

Lance said: 'Need I stay, Mummy?'

She replied: 'Have your tea in the kitchen if you feel you really cannot stick it. You disappoint me a lot, Lance. Go on, then. They will be here any moment.'

'I hope so,' Gordon said. 'Lord, but I'm hungry.'

The front door bell chimed. Gordon heard the new maid trotting from the kitchen to open the door. He went out himself into the hall. As the door opened he saw Eve in the wheel-chair, with her mother hunched behind it. He came forward quickly.

'Here,' he said, 'let me lend a hand.'

He lifted the chair easily over the step. Once in the hall he helped Eve out of it, and carried her into the dining-room. Her sound arm clung to him. She smiled up at him winningly. Her face had escaped with only one small scar, running away from the right-hand corner of her mouth. Gordon noticed that it was much less pronounced than it had been when he had seen her last.

Her mother wheezed in behind them. She went over to Mrs Hallam and shook hands.

'You must be proud of your big, strong son,' she breathed asthmatically. 'And he's so charming. A great pity more young men aren't like him to-day.'

'Now, now,' Gordon said, boyishly, 'not too many compliments or you'll turn my head. How's little Eve keeping?'

The oval face smiled up from the twisted body. Her mother looked across cheerfully.

'Why, our Eve's as fine as ever. She's been sleeping a lot better at night lately. It's since she found a way to occupy her time during the day. She's making raffia mats. Show Mrs Hallam and Gordon your new one, Evie.'

Eve said: 'It's in my work-bag on the chair.'

'Not another word,' Gordon said, jovially. 'To hear is to obey.'

He left the room and was back in a moment with the bag.

'Can I look inside,' he said, 'or are there mysteries there?'

The face smiled coyly. 'Perhaps there are,' Eve said. 'There might be love letters.'

She fished with her good hand in the recesses of the bag. The claw lay limply on her lap. She brought up a rolled, square mat of multi-coloured, woven raffia. Gordon took it and unfolded it.

'Golly,' he said, admiringly, 'isn't it cute? I wish I could do things like this. Will you teach me some day, Eve?'

She laughed. 'No. For you might do them better than I do. But this one is for you, to put in your room.'

Gordon carried it across to Rosie.

'Look, Rosie, look at my mat! Isn't it a beauty? Eve, I can't thank you enough. It's one of the nicest birthday presents I've had.'

Smiles trembled across the face, like convulsive ripples wagging a dog's tail. Eve said:

'Oh, but that isn't your birthday present – that's just a little thing. Wait a minute.'

This time the claw reached down into the bag, but after a moment's futile scrambling she had to use her other arm. She held out to Gordon a small box. He took it and opened it. A set of studs and cuff-links lay in a white satin bed, gleaming with mother-of-pearl and gold.

He said, awed: 'I say, Eve, you shouldn't spend money on me like this. Really ...'

Eve said: 'Don't forget I'm rich, Gordon. All that insurance. I've more money than I know what to do with. Do you like them?'

'They're lovely,' he said. 'Though I shall hardly dare to wear them with my old shirts. Look at these, Rosie. Isn't it kind of Eve?'

Mrs Hallam took the little box and clicked it open. She looked down at the smooth, finished perfection of the fittings, and up at the twisted body, surmounted by that wistfully eager face. The blue eyes were intent on Gordon's long, lean figure.

'Yes, they are lovely,' Mrs Hallam said. 'You are spoiling Gordon with such lovely presents, Eve.'

She walked over to the hearth and pulled the bell-cord. 'I hope you are both ready for tea. Gordon has told me twice already that he is ravenous, so I hardly dare to keep him waiting longer.'

'I'm always ready to eat a horse after an afternoon's driving,' Gordon said, cheerfully.

'I would love to go for a drive with you again,' Eve said, wistfully.

'Oh, you must!' Gordon said. He paused. 'Can she, Mrs Graham?'

Mrs Graham struggled with her breath for a moment before finding words.

'I'm sure a drive would do her good; if you can find time to take her for a run.'

'What about both of you coming with me for a spin on your way home this evening,' he suggested.

Mrs Graham's smile ran out from her mouth and eyes through the fat wrinkles of her face.

'That's very kind of you, Gordon,' she wheezed. 'But sitting in a car takes my breath away terribly. It all rushes away from me in the wind. A motor-car ride might be the death of me. You take Eve; she hasn't been having much excitement lately. I think she misses trotting off to dances and things.'

The maid was bringing the tea in. Gordon lifted Eve up again and carried her to another chair at the table. He felt her lightness clinging to him. She spoke, vehemently, against his chest:

'Of course I don't. I think dancing is stupid, anyway. I can't imagine what I ever saw in it.'

Gordon put her down carefully. Mrs Hallam, watching her across the table, saw the blue eyes gazing after the thick legs of the maid as she came in with another tray. Mrs Graham, panting heavily, said:

'Well, I'm glad of it. There's a blessing in misfortune if it enables us to find the true comforts early in life. When I think of the wasted years before I found the comfort of religion … Now Eve sits with me and listens to all the services and uplifting talks on the wireless, and I wheel her to church both morning and afternoon on a Sunday. That's the true joy for all of us. And Eve has it so young.'

Mary clicked in and out again on thick legs. They began tea. Gordon ate eagerly and quickly. Eve picked at her food. He remonstrated with her, waving a piece of bread.

'You're not eating properly, Eve. I've known canaries with bigger appetites.'

The blue eyes smiled up guiltily. 'I'm sorry. But I really have very little appetite, even for such a lovely tea. I don't do anything to get hungry.'

'Such a change,' said Mrs Graham, for the first time lamenting. 'She used to bolt her food. I would rather have her bolting it than pecking at it.'

There was a knock at the door, and then Lance came in. He stood for a moment, white-faced, seeming to stare right through the room. Then he came forward.

'Good afternoon, Mrs Graham. Good afternoon, Eve.'

He looked directly at his mother.

'Billy can't come out to-night,' he said. 'May I stay in here while you finish tea?'

'Of course, darling,' Mrs Hallam said. She turned to Mrs Graham. 'Lance had his tea early because there was some expedition planned for this evening.'

Mrs Graham wagged a finger at him, and gasped with the vigour of her exertions.

'Ah,' she said, 'these schoolboy expeditions! Which was it to be, Lancelot, rescuing maidens from dragons, or digging up buried treasure?'

Looking at Mrs Graham, Lance felt reprieved from the need to watch the twisted body at the other side of the table; to be natural and smile to it, and treat it as though everyone had a claw hand and a leg twisted underneath.

'We were only going to play cricket, Mrs Graham,' he said. 'But Billy has an impot to do for talking in prayers this morning.'

'The wages of sin,' Gordon announced. 'I say, though, it's a bit early for cricket, isn't it? Could you sling over another piece of cake, Rosie?'

Lance, concentrating on Mrs Graham and Gordon and the cake-stand being lifted in his mother's fingers, heard Eve's soft, cheerful voice breaking in relentlessly, testing to its limit the courage that had brought him back from the kitchen.

'Let me have a look at you, Lance,' she said. 'It's ages since I saw you last.'

He turned quickly, in the same way that at night when his bedroom window creaked he would run across the room and gaze out, searching the night sky for the bat-man hovering in the shadows. The only other time he had seen Eve since the accident he had made his eyes concentrate on her face, to avoid seeing the crooked body. But her deformities, seen vaguely from the edge of his vision, had been as terrifying as the thought of the bat-man hanging just below the window-sill. Now he gazed fully at her.

'How you've grown,' she said. 'Tell me, Lance – *is* it too early for cricket?'

The claw held a saucer, while her right hand lifted the tea-cup to the small, red mouth.

Lance said: 'I suppose it is, but we're keener on cricket.'

'Yes,' Eve said, 'it's a good game. Do you play for your House, Lance?'

The bat-man had disappeared before the intensity of his gaze. He said eagerly:

'I did last season for the Juniors. I'm a Senior this year. I might get picked, though. Our Seniors aren't much good.'

Eve said: 'I played for my school. I used to bowl. Under-hand, of course. They didn't let us bowl over-arm because we were girls.'

Lance felt himself whitening as the horror drifted back. He felt quite helpless. Desperately he tried to wrench his mind from its contemplation. He looked across the room. Mrs Graham had paused in her eating to indulge in another paroxysm of choked breathing. Gordon was munching a cake. Mummy sat quietly, watching and yet seeming not to watch. The horror was not touching them. There was no help for him. This was more real than the bat-man, and would not disappear when he looked at it. He could only run away.

He said: 'Mummy, there's some homework I should do. May I go?'

Mrs Graham had recovered again, and was eating heavily.

'Go on,' she said. 'That's right. Do your homework. That's the way to get on.'

Mrs Hallam nodded agreement, and Lance turned to go.

He said, breathlessly: 'Good-night, Mrs Graham. Good-night, Eve.'

The clear voice followed him out of the room: 'Good-night, Lance.'

Gordon, watching his step-brother go, thought of him with curiosity. Funny little devil. First of all scared to come to tea; then marching in with that trumped-up story about his pal not being able to come out; and now dashing out again like a young rabbit. He himself felt warm and happy after the meal and ready – he thought to himself – for a hundred mile spin on a super motor-road. He watched his own hands tapping on the edge of the table, strong and leanly muscular.

He said impatiently: 'How about this run? Ready, Eve?'

Rosie said: 'Don't be ridiculous, Gordon. They haven't even finished tea. Really, I'm beginning to think you are obsessed with that car.'

'Oh, I'd love to go,' Eve said. 'I'm quite ready.'

Gordon stood up. 'What about you, Mrs Graham. Can't I persuade you to come?'

She wheezed her refusal. 'No. I'll walk it when my tea is down properly. But you could put Eve's chair in the back.'

Gordon said: 'I'll take it round with me now. Then I'll bring the bus round to the front for you, Eve. Won't be a sec.'

They heard him wheeling the chair down the hall and through the kitchen. There were noises of the car engine revving, and the car appeared at the front as Gordon guided it carefully on to the road. He left the engine running, and came back to the house. He looked magnificent in driving gauntlets and his leather jacket.

'Ready, Eve?' he asked.

She smiled and nodded. He picked her up easily, and stood holding her for a moment.

''Bye all,' he said. 'We won't be long. You sit here and have a talk with Rosie for an hour, and we'll probably get back before you do.'

He looked down at Eve. 'Got a key in case we do, Eve?'

She said: 'Oh, it's in my bag. Would you give me my bag, Gordon?'

Mrs Hallam said: 'Drive slowly, Gordon.'

He looked at her reproachfully, but made no reply. He carried Eve out of the room, and a moment later they saw him crossing the lawn with her, and lifting her into the front seat of the car.

'Gosh,' Eve said, 'it's a lovely car – much nicer than – than the old one.'

In the driving seat Gordon paused to look round with pride.

'Yes,' he confirmed. 'It's a beauty. Cost a bit more, but it's worth it. I can get up to seventy easily.' He looked guilty. 'Of course, only on an absolutely clear road.'

Eve said dreamily: 'We were doing nearly seventy when it happened.'

He said: 'The speedometer was crooked. It was only just over forty, really. It seems more on some roads.'

Eve laughed, and the scar was suddenly vivid on her cheek.

'I shan't tell anyone, Gordon. I thought at first … But it seemed so silly and dishonest. Like a girl complaining of rape only when she finds she's pregnant. It wouldn't have done any good. Things just happen; lucky and unlucky. I suppose I was unlucky.'

Her voice became suddenly bitter.

'Though I count my blessings. Raffia work, and religious services on the B.B.C.'

He said: 'You're wonderful to be able to stand it and be so cheerful.'

York Street lay on either side of them, slowly fermenting with the gathering crowds of early evening. They moved to strange purposes in patternless eddies; the late back from the office mingling with the early off to the pictures. Outside the Regal cinema at the corner of the Square, a queue was already forming.

'You must come to the pictures with me some night,' Gordon said.

Eve looked up at him, smiling. Sitting on his left in the car she looked almost normal, the claw hidden and the twisted leg drawn up behind the sound one.

'And you would take me there and carry me upstairs to the best seats?' she said. 'No, thanks, Gordon. I'm not hardened enough for that yet. I suppose I will be some day, though it's difficult to imagine it.'

Looking down, Gordon saw the blue eyes staring ahead into the shadowy streets.

'We met Gwen Norton while Mummy was wheeling me to your house this afternoon,' she went on. 'Funny how old feelings persist! Ever since I've known her I've felt sorry for Gwen. When we first came to Bullcaster we lived next door to each other. We worked in the same office. Her face was always covered with spots, and she was always running after boys and never catching any. It was rather pathetic.'

A long, sleek car glided past them with headlights gleaming, although it was still quite light.

Eve continued: 'I still felt superior to her when she stopped by us this afternoon. I didn't think of her as having two legs and two arms. I just thought of her as poor little Gwen Norton who was always mad with me because I monopolised all her potential boy-friends at local hops.'

She laughed clearly, a small bell ringing from a ruined church.

'She had been talking to us for five minutes before I realised that she was patronising me, forgiving me for all my trivial successes in the past, pitying me for the years I've still got to live.'

The road they were taking ran round the side of the hill towards Weybrook. There was little traffic on it now. The light seemed to be fading rapidly from the sky ahead. The little finger began to crawl round unwatched as Gordon thought of Eve's last words: 'the years I've still got to live.'

He said at last: 'I'm sorry.'

The small, flawless bell rang clearly.

'Sorry? Oh, Gordon, you don't know what it means! It isn't something you can be sorry for, like treading on a cat's tail. When you find something – horrible – like me, the only possible kindness is to ignore it. Praise my accomplished raffia-work, and my zealous preparations for a life everlasting (when the blind shall see and the lame be made whole!) – but don't be sorry for me. You have some imagination, Gordon. Think how you would be yourself. Think of never driving again – of being alive and knowing you would never drive again. And ask yourself if sorrow and pity can do anything but hurt.'

The little finger had crept to 50. Gordon saw it, and began to ease it back. But the excitement was mounting in his brain, and his hands and feet moved of their own volition. The road tilted round the hill away from Bullcaster and he saw the full moon floating in the air, still wan in the lingering twilight. The little finger pressed on 50. He felt power surging in him, communicated from the throbbing engine; power to outrun the winds, power to kill and maim.

Beside him Eve moved, leaning forward to look at the moon.

'I love full moons,' she said. 'They're so – complete.'

A pheasant whirred low over the road, just in front of the car. The finger dropped back, to 40, to 30.

Eve said: 'Don't slow down.'

Gordon said: 'If that bird had waited another second our

windscreen might have hit him. I might have run the car off the road. But it is silly to slow down now it's over.'

Eve began singing softly:

> 'The night is young, and you're so beautiful.
> Here, among the shadows, beautiful lady,
> Open your heart.'

She put her hand on his sleeve and smiled at him.

'Am I beautiful among the shadows, Gordon? Do tell me I am. The shadows are quite thick now.'

He said: 'You'll always be beautiful, Eve. Don't let a thing ever change you.'

'I won't change,' she said, 'I promise. They tell me at the hospital that if I do the proper exercises I'll be able to limp round the house in a few months. My left leg will only be six inches shorter than the other. But I'll sacrifice that. I won't change.'

'You're wonderful, Eve,' Gordon said. 'I think you're wonderful. Eve, will you marry me?'

The bell's small carillon shook slightly, as though the church were conscious of its tragedy.

'I wanted you to say that,' Eve said. 'Somehow I seemed entitled to it. And I day-dreamed from the time we met Gwen Norton until we reached your house. There was going to be the biggest wedding reception Bullcaster has seen. Gwen was to sit at our table and writhe while I made my last and greatest score off her. It was all so easy. But when I saw you again I knew how silly it was.'

Gordon said: 'It's not silly. We'll have it just as you say. It's going to be wonderful.'

Eve said: 'Gordon, will you do something for me?'

He said: 'Anything.'

She said: 'Will you get out just above Shepherd's Dip, and let me drive on over the top? You could come down after me and wedge yourself in the wreckage.'

He said: 'Eve! You mustn't talk like that.'

She said: 'I know. It wouldn't be fair on you. Getting you a reputation as a dangerous driver.' She laughed shakily. 'And smashing up your new car.'

'It's not that,' he said.

Eve shivered beside him. 'Oh, if only it were! I could leave you money to buy a new car … Oh, I'm being silly. Gordon, you will come and see me at times when I'm old, won't you? It will be worse then, much worse. To look back on forty or fifty years of raffia-work and broadcast services, and being wheeled about.'

'I want to look after you always,' Gordon said. 'Won't you let me, Eve. Wouldn't it help a bit?'

She said: 'Turn round, please, Gordon. I want to go back.'

He slowed down, and reversed the car in a farm lane. The moon slipped behind them, out of sight and reach. In front of them, over Bullcaster, a fresh barrier of cloud was moving up, discernible in the waning dusk and the waxing moonlight. The lights of the car probed weakly ahead. They sat in silence until Gordon halted the car outside Eve's house.

She stirred and sat up. She said:

'Sometimes I lie quite still for a long time and know that I am – just as I was before. It's a more ecstatic feeling than I ever knew existed – knowing that when I move at last I will be able to jump up and walk about. Stand on my hands if I want to. Perhaps it's just because it can't happen that it feels so wonderful.'

Gordon carried her to the door, and opened it with her key. The house was still empty. He switched lights on, and carried her into the drawing-room. In the artificial light the deformities of her body stood out clearly.

She looked up from the chair in which he had placed her.

'You're awfully kind, Gordon,' she said. 'And I'm sorry for burdening you so with the weight of my self-pity. It's a relief to talk about it, and perhaps in a way I do resent you being unhurt, and feel I am entitled to have you as an audience. But it is unfair of me. I know that. Will you go now, please? I really would like to be by myself. Leave my raffia in reach. Good-night, Gordon.'

He bent over to kiss her. 'Good-night, Eve.'

Rosie was sitting by herself when he got home. The pink, shaded light of a table lamp fell across her face and across the book she was reading. Everything was as it should be; calm, peaceful and well-ordered. There was no raw pain or sick despair. She looked up and smiled as he came in.

'Did you have a nice drive, darling?' she asked. 'I don't suppose Mrs Graham could have got back before you did. She only left ten minutes ago.'

Gordon said: 'Lance in?'

'He's gone to the cinema. I felt quite ashamed of him this evening, though luckily I think the Grahams didn't notice. Lance is too wrapped up in himself.'

Gordon said softly: 'At least he won't get many nasty shocks.'

Rosie looked at him enquiringly.

'It's morbid and unpleasant to concentrate on oneself too much,' she said.

Gordon sat down heavily on the divan, pulling off one of his gloves.

'Oh, I don't know,' he said. 'I was just thinking … Lance, mulling over himself all the time, knows pretty much what to expect. But taking oneself for granted, one never really knows what's going on underneath.'

His mother leaned over and patted his arm.

'You have nothing to worry about,' she said. 'Little depressions aren't worth worrying over. Think how lucky you are. It might have been you who were crushed in that accident and poor Eve who got off unhurt.'

Gordon looked at the level, untroubled eyes; searching for something he could not define. He said slowly:

'I almost wish it had been.'

Rosie said: 'Of course, we all sympathise with her, but you mustn't take it too much to heart. These things happen. We can't help them.'

Gordon said: 'I asked Eve to marry me this evening.'

'Gordon!' Rosie exclaimed. 'That was silly of you. It's going to hurt the poor girl when she – when she realises how impossible it is. You and Eve were never more than friends.'

Gordon laughed. 'Don't worry, Rosie. She turned me down.'

His mother said with relief: 'She's a sensible girl. It makes me feel sorrier than ever for her. Certainly no one else will ask her.'

Gordon said: 'Does "being sorry" do any good?'

'What else can we do?' Rosie asked.

She placed a book-mark carefully and laid her book back on the shelf.

'I'll make this an early night, I think,' she said. 'Are you staying up for a while, Gordon?'

Almost to himself he said: 'There must be something. There must always be something.'

'Good-night, darling,' Rosie said. 'Are you staying up?'

He looked at her and realised that he had been expecting her to help him. But there was no help in anyone else.

He said: 'For a while, Rosie. I think I'll take the bus for another little run. It's such clear moonlight.'

She shook her head. 'You are too obsessed with that car, Gordon. Don't be too long.'

He kissed her good-night, and watched her climb the stairs. Then he went to bring the car out again. He scraped a bumper against the gate, and his mind automatically reminded him to see to it to-morrow. Bullcaster was quiet and almost deserted as he drove between the avenues of street lights. The moon was over the brow of the hill now, but the cloud-bank was advancing inexorably towards it. He drew up outside the Grahams' house, and went up to the front door.

Mrs Graham opened it. She wheezed happily at the sight of him.

'Is Eve still up?' he asked.

She motioned him in. 'Lord, yes. It's barely nine o'clock. We stay up late and get up late. There are some good programmes on the wireless late on.'

Eve was plaiting blue and red raffia, in the chair where he had left her.

She said: 'Why, Gordon! Did you leave something?'

'There's such a fine moon,' he said. 'It's fine driving through the moonlight. I thought you might like to come for another spin before bed.'

Something inside his mind was insistent that she would refuse; that he would soon be saying good-night again, and driving back home. But she didn't refuse.

'I'd love to,' she said. 'Mummy, will you get me my white shawl? Gordon is taking me for another little ride.'

Mrs Graham panted incredulously. 'Another? At this time of night! Oh, dear. You young people.'

She came and draped the shawl round Eve's shoulders. Gordon lifted her up easily, and carried her to the door. He stood for a moment on the threshold.

'Why!' exclaimed Mrs Graham. 'You look like a bride in that white.'

'I feel a bit like one,' Eve said. ''Bye, Mummy. We shan't be long.'

Gordon thought he had never known the car to run so smoothly. It seemed that no effort of his was needed to achieve a perfection in response; it ran with absolute sweetness, almost – he thought – like a well-trained horse. Bullcaster sagged away behind them, and as the little finger began to leap forward he let the excitement take his brain, unchallenged, welcomed. There was only the noise of the engine, and Eve humming softly: 'Stay as sweet as you are', and a strange, inaudible *sense* of sound that seemed to embrace all, like the voluptuous moonlight. The excitement swelled. He was a god, restored to his dominion, sweeping forward on eagle wings of speed. The transient was the eternal, and now the whole world was transient. He laughed inside with joy for the climbing finger.

Eve said once: 'You are going to do it?' but to neither of them did there seem any need of answer. When she spoke again the first ragged edge of cloud was drifting over the moon.

'Slow down, Gordon,' she said. 'You will have to get out just before the corner.'

He looked down at her, laughing, but made no reply.

She said: 'Gordon! You mustn't. You've got everything to live for. Oh, Gordon, I didn't mean that.'

He said: 'I wouldn't like you to be lonely, Eve.'

His voice was thick, as though with intoxication. The moon tore free of the ensnaring clouds, and she saw the exultation in his face.

She said: 'Gordon, you're so good to me. I feel just like a bride.'

The moon was caught again, and hidden away completely. The headlights of the car, stretching ahead, rebounded from the flimsy, white-painted fence that guarded Shepherd's Dip. The little finger tottered on the brink of 70. Gordon looked down, laughing, at his consort. Above the eager roaring of the night he heard her singing softly:

'Don't let a thing ever change you.'

CHAPTER FIVE

1930

Lance

L ANCE WOKE VERY EARLY. He could hear Gordon's heavy breathing on the other side of the room, but he did not look at him. He lay very straight in bed, his gaze limited to the ceiling and the largest of all the cracks, running from the corner above his head away out of sight across the white, inverted plain. He had grown used to that crack. It was hard to visualise to-morrow when the crack would still be there but he would be back in Bullcaster in his own small bed and room.

Feet padded along the corridor outside. He guessed – he knew – that it was the man with the shoes. He pictured him, festooned with shoes, putting each pair carefully down at the proper door. Overwhelmingly he wanted to rush outside and confirm his knowledge. But what if it should prove to be not the man with the shoes after all? Or worse, if it were – and the man with the shoes stared at him standing there in his pyjamas, and asked him what he was doing? Lance shivered with embarrassment at the thought and snuggled down into the security of his bed. He drifted in and out of the borders of sleep.

Later, through the haze of sleep, he became aware of a molten pool of sunlight lying on his counterpane, stretching from below the bulge of his hip almost to his face. It poured down from the window opposite, and the air above it was liquid gold and shimmering with tiny movements. Lance put out his hand and let it lie in the pool. He felt warmth lapping round it.

There were noises outside of other people moving about. The day had begun. The preliminaries were over – the man with the shoes, the drifting in and out of sleep, the sense of being alone. Now the whole machine had started up again. Lance climbed out of bed and ran over towards his brother. He shook him carefully, and called:

'Gordon!'

Gordon stirred and mumbled something. Lance looked at him silently, feeling himself awake and rich in sensations. The pool of gold lay where he had left it, across his bed. Above it the motes of dust jigged frantically, twisting and spiralling, rising and falling in a fine, sunsplashed frenzy. He ran back quickly and thrust his hands in it, so that the warmth burned caressingly along his skin.

From outside rose the clatter of a milk-cart, as though tangible, metallic sunbeams were resounding from tin roofs. Voices rose with it, cheerful and rich. Lance ran to the window and pushed it open. The street below was almost empty; there was only the milk-cart, throwing off sound like an anvil, and the noisy puppets in orbits about it. A man came to the door of the small hotel opposite, paused, and then, like a stray comet, walked quickly along the road and round the corner leading to the station. In the road the milk-cart was a majestic sun, gleaming in all its brass-work, attended by subservient planets.

Lance stretched himself high, his palms pushing hard against the window ledge. In front of him there were only roof-tops, rising in limitless ranges. He brought a chair over, and climbed on to it. Then, standing on tiptoe, he could see, beyond and between the roofs, the limitless glitter of the sea. He gazed at it, leaning forward lightly against the window pane.

With decision he climbed down. Leaving the chair where it was he hurried over to his bed and began to dress. For a while he wrestled with a tie. Gordon usually helped him, but Gordon still lay immobile in the strange, unreachable world of sleep. He stowed the tie away in a pocket and went out into the corridor, closing the door quietly behind him. He tapped at the next door, and whispered:

'Mummy! Can I come in?'

There was no reply. On either side of him the corridor stretched away, remote and high and rather frightening. A door opened abruptly, and a man carrying a towel walked briskly towards and past him. He looked at Lance curiously as he went by, to disappear through another door further along.

Lance whispered 'Mummy!' again very quickly, and without waiting for a reply walked hurriedly away towards the stairs.

He passed no one on his way out of the hotel. The sunlight was not so warm outside as he had expected; a wisp of cloud dimmed the vehemence of the sun. The milk-cart had moved almost to the end of the street, and rested in the shadow of the corner frontage. It needed painting, and the milkman carrying bottles away from it had a sad, wrinkled face. Lance began to run in the opposite direction, towards the invisible sea.

He knew the way quite well, but without the reassuring surge of crowds about him he felt unsure and doubtful. Some streets seemed wider and some narrower than he had remembered them. All the shops were shuttered, and he saw the Parade for the first time unencumbered by postcard-racks and rows of buckets and spades and coloured flags and trinkets. At the end where five roads straggled away like a nest of dead snakes he paused for a moment, trying to translate this unfamiliar calm into terms of the peopled confusion that he knew. Then, away to his left, he seemed to hear the penetrating, almost inaudible surge of water. He ran down the left-hand snake and at the first corner saw it, irresistible and unresisting. The sea.

As he walked across the promenade the sun came out again in vigour and the sand was glimmering gold between him and the sun-stippled blue of the water. But he saw a heavier bank of cloud lying under the sun. He ran down the steps and over the sand, glad to feel the sand yielding beneath his feet, sifting over his ankles into his shoes. The unpeopled beach was not so strange as the unpeopled town; it seemed right here that he should be alone, trudging across this golden softness. As though it were the Sahara and he a gallant soldier of the Legion. In the haze there were Arabs and camels, miraged oases and beleaguered forts, until he reached the water's edge and they dissolved into the lazy, lapping certainty of the sea.

Sitting down a few feet from the water, Lance pulled off his shoes and socks. Barefooted he advanced to where the sand turned firmly damp and brown, a few inches in front of the moving water. He pressed his toes in, feeling the damp sand squirt up, as though alive, between his toes. Slowly, savouring each inch of the transition to cool wetness, he allowed his feet to be drawn in, until the water clung above his ankles and each liquid attack splashed against his shins.

He paddled about in the shallows, walking out until the water rose above his knees and lifted him a little as it moved past him towards the town. It was much clearer than he had ever seen it. Against the brown sand moved the darker, darting shadows of the small flat fish he and Gordon had fished for unsuccessfully the previous day. He lunged towards them with one foot and the uprush of water nearly carried him off his balance. Suddenly frightened, he waded quickly in to shore, and picked up his shoes and socks. He returned to the edge of the water carrying them, and paddled off along the verge, away from the town, towards the quiet cliffs and the rocks beneath them.

As he reached the first rock-encircled pool he wondered if he would find the little girl there, until he remembered that she had gone home the previous morning. They had hunted crabs together every day without bothering to ask each other's names or anything beyond the immediately practical questions of the hunt. Standing now by the pool which had always been the starting point of their forays, Lance felt the small, clear voice calling, distinct in memory:

'Oh, look! A red one. A whopper. I say, he's lost a claw!'

He sat down on a round, damp rock, suddenly feeling very

sad. He would not hear the small, clear voice again, and after to-day he himself would be gone, and the silent, reproachful pools, rich with crabs and seaweed, would lie unwatched. He felt the damp seeping through from the rock to his skin. Purposefully he stood up and waded out into the middle of the pool. Through his feet he felt the thin slime coating the rocks, and his toes brushed through thick clusters of weed. Before he had always walked warily and slowly, frightened of his quarry as it lurked behind rock and under weed with claws ready to tear. But now, knowing it to be the last time, he hunted boldly; reaching down fearlessly with his hands to pry away loose stones, and even kicking through the weed with his feet to disturb the hoped-for prey. He searched the pool carefully for some time, but found nothing.

From this point the pools and hollows, with their accompanying rocky eminences, stretched almost continuously away to the curve of the headland. Lance paddled and clambered through and over them, never relaxing the intensity of his search. But there were few crabs, and those he found were too scattered and mean-looking to make the real game worth playing. In the real game it had been fun to gather them all together in the smallest and clearest pool, where they could be prodded and compared and even incited into battle. He did collect a few medium-sized crabs in one pool but they were somnolent and unsatisfying. He could find no stick to prod them with and even when one did advance, claws erect, towards his attacking finger, there was little fun in it. It had been, he realised, a game for two. In his solitariness, crabs seemed unimportant.

He abandoned the crabs and scrambled on towards the cave. This had always been the furthest point of their excursions since here, even at low tide, the water swept in, deep and troubled and quite unbridgeable, to disappear under the cliff in the cave's recesses. A few yards further on the rocks rose again, against the wash of the sea. In their hollows and crevices lurked what gigantic monster-crabs, brilliantly clawed and coloured? But as remote and unattainable now as the rocks on which he stood would be to-morrow.

A ledge of rock, over a foot wide, lay between the water and the arching wall of the cave. Lance moved along it carefully, feeling his way into the cool darkness ahead. A little way in, he knew, the ledge broadened into a shelf. They had sat here and talked in whispers; whispers that ran up the glistening heights of rock and creaked back at them from the echoing dimness beyond. Now he called loudly, bawling meaningless phrases into the watching shadows, but the echoes came back in dull, empty tones. He tried to remember the stories they had made up; of ships sunk under the water, and buried treasure at the back of the cave, and a skeleton guarding a cask of rum. But there was no reality to them now. He stood up and began edging his way back towards the light.

During the few minutes he had been inside the cave, clouds had moved up over the sun. The sea-wind, racing in from the bay, was sharp and the sea itself was suddenly grey and old. The rock pools looked dull and somehow threatening. Lance remembered with a shock of fear that back at the hotel Mummy would be looking for him. Clutching his shoes and socks he scrambled back towards the beach.

He stopped only at the pool where the quest had started. As he peered into it a great red crab scuttled across the bottom. It was the largest crab Lance had ever seen; he wondered how it could possibly have escaped his earlier searching. He dropped a stone from above it but it sank down through the water and landed harmlessly behind. The crab disappeared into the seaweed.

A thick mass of pimpled seaweed floated on the surface of the pool, half-severed from the rock to which it had been attached. Lance kneeled over and tugged it free. Then, sitting down, he pulled stockings and shoes over his wet feet. Clutching the dripping weed he ran off, across the grey, unfriendly sand, towards the town.

Gordon

Gordon leaned, smiling, across the breakfast table and spoke to his mother:

'Don't worry. He'll be back any moment. He's a little devil for scooting off on his own, but he's not reckless.'

Mrs Hallam said: 'It's so thoughtless of him – disappearing like this.'

'Kids don't think,' Gordon said. 'I must have been just as big a worry to you a few years ago.'

'But you weren't,' she denied. 'If you had been I should have been more prepared for Lance's queer ways. You were a misleadingly easy child to handle, Gordon.'

'More tea?'

Gordon poured carefully, weakening his mother's tea with hot water.

'You shouldn't worry,' he went on. 'With kids – especially queer kids like Lance – the best thing to do is leave them to their own devices. Fussing over them only makes them nervous and destroys their confidence. You will have to be careful with Lance; he's very sensitive to scolding.'

Mrs Hallam laughed. 'You're a great relief, Gordon. There you go, talking like a wise old parent of the right way to rear children. You must remember that in my eyes you are still only a boy yourself.'

Gordon smiled at her. 'And in my eyes you are the eternal, the incomparable belle of the ball, Rosie,' he replied. 'I *do* get older, even if it's hard for you to realise it. You only seem to grow younger. Come on, let's slip down to the club for a set of tennis.'

She shook her head doubtfully. 'No. I don't think …'

Gordon said: 'Hang on – is that him coming through the hall now? Lance!'

Lance sidled uneasily into the breakfast room. His shirt hung untidily open at the neck, and shirt, knickerbockers and stockings were thickly caked with dried salt and sand. From one hand the tangled mass of seaweed still hung limply.

He said: 'I'm sorry, Mummy. I just went along the beach. I didn't think I'd been so long.'

Mrs Hallam sighed. 'Really, Lance, I don't know where to begin. Your clothes are in a dreadful state and you know all your other things were packed last night. It will mean unpacking again to find you something presentable. And couldn't you have told us before going off so early in the morning?'

Lance looked at them; Mummy gently accusing behind the teapot and Gordon lounging in his chair, both of them so remote from and superior to the world of crab pools and caves. He shuffled, and clutched his seaweed.

He muttered: 'I didn't want to wake anyone.'

'Really, Lance. You should think before you do these things. You should realise that it is bound to be far more worrying to find you gone. Anyway, sit down and have some breakfast. No, run upstairs and wash first; changing will have to wait until I've found some other clothes for you. And do get rid of that terrible, smelly seaweed.'

Gordon watched his brother go.

'Bravo, Rosie,' he applauded. 'Quite well done. Though even a mild ticking-off seems to frighten the poor lad. He's scared of you, Rosie.'

'Don't be ridiculous, Gordon,' she said. 'What is there to be frightened of? He cannot be so very frightened, anyway. He never takes any notice of the things I tell him.'

'Probably can't help himself,' Gordon said. 'I should never have dreamed of sneaking out in the early morning when I was his age but I can imagine it's the sort of impulse that needs some restraining. Anyway, he's safely back. Let's trip away for a couple of keen sets.'

Rosie smiled at him; sparkling Rosie, so incredibly close to fifty.

'All right,' she said. 'Let's slip up and change. It won't take me long to root something out for Lance.'

He took her arm as they walked towards the stairs.

'It's been a very pleasant holiday,' he said, 'but it will be nice to be home again.'

They had played tennis quite a lot during their fortnight's stay, and as they walked into the club house several people nodded and smiled. Gordon, guiding his mother to a deck-chair on the verandah, felt mature and rather pleasantly pompous. The sky was filling up with black and white clouds, but it was still very warm. They lay back, chatting and watching white figures darting in front of them against a background of red asphalt and high, arching trees.

On a court away to the left a set had broken up, and the foursome was drifting back towards the pavilion. One of the figures detached itself and ran across to them. She was a small, slim girl, with curly black hair set off by her white costume.

Gordon said: 'Why, it's Eve.'

'Eve?' Mrs Hallam asked.

'You know. The girl we met at the dance last night.'

He leaned forward, calling to the girl as she ran towards them.

'Hello, Eve! I didn't know you played here.'

She stood before them, breathless, her small breasts rising and falling quickly under her blouse, the short, curly hair falling round her face.

'I haven't before,' she said. 'Hello, Mrs Hallam. It's awfully nice to see you again. I say, isn't it a wonderful morning? Have you had a game yet?'

'Not yet,' Mrs Hallam said. 'We're summoning our energies for it.'

'May I sit with you?' Eve asked.

Gordon leaped up, contritely. 'Oh, do sit here,' he said. 'I'll drag another chair out.'

He came back with one and set it up. Eve had flung herself back into the chair he had left. The bar came below her knees and her small feet dangled clear of the ground. She made even Rosie look moderately large. He himself felt immense beside her.

'Heigh-ho,' he said, 'summer is over.'

Eve said, indignantly: 'Oh, Gordon! Don't be silly. It's only a few clouds. There'll be lots more summer.'

'We go back this afternoon,' Gordon explained. 'And then, back to work and an end to holiday. How much longer have you got?'

Eve wriggled in the deck-chair.

'I don't want to think of it!' she said. 'Eleven – no, ten days.'

'It will soon go,' Gordon prophesied. 'Almost any minute now it will be time for you to pack and leave. I feel quite sorry for you. We packed yesterday.'

'Oh, you pig!' Eve cried. 'You're a dog in the manger – trying to spoil my holiday because you have to go back.'

'Stop tormenting her, Gordon,' Mrs Hallam said.

Gordon grinned. 'I'm interested to see how far into the menagerie her vocabulary extends. Pig. Dog. What next, Eve?'

'Camel!' she said, promptly. 'What about a game, Camel?'

'Altogether too active, these children,' he declared. 'Have you no reverence for my age?'

She got up swiftly and grasped his hands.

'Come on, Camel,' she said. 'You are going to play. Will you play, too, Mrs Hallam? I'll rake up a fourth quite easily.'

Mrs Hallam said: 'I think I would rather watch you.'

'Oh, come on, Rosie,' Gordon said. 'I'll collect a partner for the infant here, and we'll give them a thrashing.'

Rosie shook her head. 'No. Much too exhausting. You go and play. I prefer to watch.'

They came back, hot and breathless, an hour later, and bore her with them to the pavilion. Gordon brought three tall glasses of iced lime juice and soda to their table. Eve buried her nose in hers like an eager puppy. When she had drunk half-way down she relaxed, gasping.

'Mmm!' she said. 'Nice.' She looked up. 'It must be rather pleasant for you, Mrs Hallam, having this giant as a slave. He's quite handy for bringing cool drinks and things.'

Mrs Hallam smiled. 'Oh, yes, he comes in useful in all sorts of ways.'

'I suppose you must drag him away to-day?' Eve asked. 'Just as I'm getting used to him.'

'It needn't be for ever,' Gordon said. 'Where do you live? My bus has a good range from Bullcaster.'

Eve drummed her small fist on the table.

'Golly,' she said, 'what a coincidence Daddy's applying for a job there. If he gets it he will be surveying your boundaries or mapping your drains or something. And we'll go there to live. Can I borrow your giant now and then if we come there to live, Mrs Hallam?'

'I think so,' Mrs Hallam said. 'Provided you look after him.'

'Oh, I will,' Eve promised. 'Has he got a car, too? That's awfully handy.'

'I've got it here,' Gordon broke in. 'We came down in it. It's a beauty. We have time for a spin before lunch, haven't we, Rosie?'

'He's only had it a few months,' Mrs Hallam said, 'so it's still quite a new toy to him. Do you feel like a jolting-up before lunch?'

'I'd love to,' Eve said. 'If we can go as we are and not bother about changing.'

'I think we can,' Mrs Hallam said. 'It's our last day. I let Lance go back to the beach after he had muddied his clothes before breakfast. Let's just walk round to the garage and get the car out.'

'Don't bother,' Gordon said. 'I'll get it and bring it round here for you.'

He bowed to Eve. 'Don't go. I'll be back.'

'Clever giant!' she said. 'We'll be here.'

Ten minutes later Mrs Hallam listened attentively to an approaching roar.

'There he is,' she said. 'Let's go out and meet him.'

They reached the front of the club as Gordon opened the car door. Mrs Hallam insisted that Eve should sit in the front with Gordon while she sat behind.

Gordon drove slowly at first through the crowded streets; down the station road to the promenade and then to the east. On their right the sea rolled in across the cloud-flecked sands, sinking further below them as the road climbed up over rising ground. Gordon stopped the car on the cliffs, and they walked a few yards to stand by the railings that marked the edge. Far below them the waves hammered in over the rocks, breaking into brief efflorescences of spray. But further out the water was a level, unbroken grey-blue, stretching away until it merged with low clouds on the horizon. Some large bird was drifting down to the sea in wide, unhurried spirals.

Eve leaned impulsively forward over the railings.

'Oh, look!' she exclaimed. 'Isn't it lovely – like icing!'

Gordon felt strange. His head was dizzy from gazing down the depths below them and he had an unusual feeling of despair. There was nothing to which he could relate it. Even the end of the holiday was welcome in a way; it would be pleasant to be home again. But this feeling of despair, embracing the white fence and the long drop below it, was real enough to upset him.

He stepped back, almost involuntarily.

'Let's get on,' he said, brusquely. 'We shan't have time for a decent drive before lunch.'

Lance

Gordon brought the car round to the front of the hotel just after three. Lance had been leaning out of the window in his mother's room and announced its arrival. The clouds that had gathered during the morning were now thickly ranked across the sky, and trailing ragged, grey rain-banners behind them. He was glad that the fine weather had broken. It would have been terrible to go home in sunshine.

They accompanied the porter downstairs with the last instalment of luggage. Outside they found Gordon busily erecting the car's hood. Eve was standing by, watching and encouraging him with advice. It came over at last with a click, and Lance quickly climbed in to the seat next to the driver's. With the hood closed the car was wonderfully snug and impregnable. It felt like the times when he was allowed to stay up in the evening, drowsing on a settee, with the old, thick overcoat weighing on his legs and the voices of people spreading away in high, echoing, meaningless ripples. He crouched down in the seat, deliciously aware of being completely enclosed in a box that would soon be moving.

He could hear the noises of bags being stowed away or tied behind, and Eve or Gordon chaffing, and the cool, remote voice of his mother occasionally directing. A door opened, and Gordon was helping Mummy in to the back and then, with a shock, he roused himself to find Gordon clambering in beside him. Eve tapped against the window, and Gordon leaned over him to turn the little handle that opened it. She looked in at them, laughing.

'I believe Lance was asleep!' she said. 'What have you got in your bucket, Lance? Crabs?'

Lance looked down at the painted bucket between his legs. He felt somehow ashamed.

He said: 'It's just seaweed.'

'Seaweed!' she echoed, laughing. 'Are you going to grow it at Bullcaster?'

Mummy said, from behind: 'He's incorrigible. I've tried to persuade him to throw it away but he stubbornly refuses.'

'I always used to insist on taking sea-shells home with me when I went to the seaside,' Eve said. 'I used them for money when we were playing shop. Do you play shop, Lance?'

Mrs Hallam said: 'He seems to prefer playing solitary games. It's quite a relief for me. Gordon used to have all the children in the neighbourhood round playing with him; the house was in a continual uproar.'

Lance wondered vaguely how one managed to get lots of children round to play games. His own tentative advances to other children never seemed to achieve anything. There had been only the unknown girl on the beach, as a wonderful exception. He wondered if perhaps he would meet her again in Bullcaster, and they would play shop as they had played the crab games. He drifted off into reveries. They could use the seaweed as cabbage.

Gordon looked at his watch.

'We should be off,' he said. 'We're late already.'

Eve said: 'I won't keep you. Bye-bye. Think of me sunning myself on the beach when you are back at work to-morrow.'

Gordon grinned. 'It will be over sooner than you imagine. Anyway, send us a card – you know the address. And we'll hope to see you soon.'

The car began to move. Lance leaned out of the window and waved obediently. Soon they were round the corner and he was able to sit back again and pull the window up. They were taking the inland road so there would be no chance of seeing the water again. Lance put his hand down and squeezed the seaweed. It felt excitingly damp and soggy.

Once the town was left behind they found the roads fairly free from traffic. Gordon was able to build speed up, unobtrusively. The road leaped eagerly under the wheels of the car; hedges sped by, almost as fast, on either side. For a few miles they ran through the edge of a rain-belt, and the windscreen wiper was busy pushing away the lances of rain that hammered towards him. After that the roads dried out again, and there was even a brief trace of sunshine.

The sun had gone in when they came up with the column. They could not tell how far it stretched, because the road here twisted through an untidy village. For this reason they could not pass it, but had to trail behind at a slow walking-pace.

Mrs Hallam said: 'What is it, Gordon?'

The men were walking, with a ragged attempt at precision, four abreast. In the back row one turned round to look at the car slowing up behind them but the others marched silently on, their heads for the most part bent forward, intent only on the painfully-traversed road. For the most part they wore thin jackets that were wet from the last shower of rain. Less than half-a-dozen in that part of the column that was visible seemed to have raincoats.

Gordon said: 'Hunger marchers, I think.'

In the ensuing silence, Lance's mind revolved about this strange new term. He tried to remember the day when he had been sent to bed early, without tea or supper, and had cried himself into hungry oblivion rather than go downstairs and make the necessary amends. But the sensation would not return. He could only remember waking again to find the night fallen, and looking from a window at the large, improbable moon, and being pleased with his own determined refusal to bow to circumstance. But how could grown men be hungry? What strange circumstance could withhold food from them, without even sending them to bed?

He touched Gordon's sleeve.

'Are they *really* hungry?' he asked.

Gordon said: 'No. They call them that. They are just looking for work.'

It was a strange idea, and it haunted Lance. He had not thought much of the days when school would be over and he would be grown up like Gordon, and these men walking through the damp summer afternoon. He had always found it impossible to visualise himself in any state different to his present one. But this was a terrifying idea. Would he, too, have to walk with these bent, silent men, hunting elusive work along lonely roads?

He said: 'You aren't going to do it, are you, Gordon?'

Gordon said: 'What? Hunger march? No fear!'

'Do you think I will when I grow up?' he asked.

Gordon laughed. 'I shouldn't worry about it. These are the men from the factories that have been closed down. You won't be working in a factory.'

Lance remained silent, trying to resolve the puzzle. He supposed it was something to do with the boys who went to the elementary school and were rough and noisy and sneering. The road was clear of the village now and Gordon was able to increase speed and pass the trudging lines of men. Lance gazed curiously as the car slid past them. Few bothered to look up. They all seemed very tired and he was not reassured by Gordon's claim that they were not hungry. One of them on the outside was wolfing a crust of bread.

They went through a large town and followed tramlines that ran alongside the road out into the country. It was funny to see a tram lurching towards them and green fields and trees beyond it. As they slowed up for a bend, a huge wooden signboard rose in front of them advertising HOVIS and adding, in smaller letters underneath: WAYSIDE CAFÉ – 200 YARDS.

'Tea, Rosie?' Gordon called.

Mrs Hallam said: 'I think so. If there's a pull-in.'

It was a double cottage, Elizabethanised with white plaster crossed by black beams. A rough, cobbled drive wound round to a small yard at the back of the cottages, where there were already two small cars and a number of bicycles parked. Two cabins had been converted, with bright, striped paint, into tea-rooms, and one of them flaunted a stiff bronze banner with the slogan CTC. As Gordon switched off the engine, a small, fat, cheerful woman bounced out of one of the cottage doors, and hurried towards them.

'Come right in,' she said. 'There's a table free in the Blue Room – that's the one that's painted blue. Make yesselfs at home an' I'll be along to see to you the next minute. The lavatory's outside, just behind the lilacs, and there's a wash-room next door to it.'

She had an Irish brogue; dulled by years in England but still unmistakable. But the small boy who came running up the garden path towards her had the local Southern whine. He seemed to be about Lance's age and was dressed in a small, rough suit of overalls. He had thick, yellow, curly hair.

He called to her: 'Mam, Dad's pouring all my tadpoles out o' the tub. Stop 'im, Mam. 'E's pouring all my tadpoles away.'

She wheeled on him furiously.

'Be out of my way!' she shouted. 'You an' your tadpoles when there's customers. Your Dad knows best what he's doin'. You should be helpin' him in the garden instead of messin' about with tadpoles. Go an' play in the wash-house or somewhere.'

She turned back, smiling, to the car.

'Indeed, children can be a trial when you're busy,' she informed them. 'But do be goin' along to the Blue Room, an' I'll bring you a pot o' tea to start with straight away.'

The Blue Room was light and airy and seemed so much more pleasant than the other tea-room they had passed that Gordon suggested it was kept for the motorists, who could be charged a few pennies more for the Special Home-Made Teas than could indigent cyclists. The tea, at any rate, was pleasant and quite cheap. But Lance was not hungry, and sought permission to go outside while the other two were still eating.

His mother said: 'All right, Lance. But don't go too far.'

There was a wood behind the tea-rooms and he found a gap leading in to it. The trees grew close together and were mainly easily climbed sycamores and chestnuts. He climbed one and swayed perilously among the thin green branches at the top, looking out over the sea of green around him, as it tossed into lighter and darker shades with the afternoon breeze. On the other side the sea broke against the red bricks and blue slates of the backs of the cottages. He climbed down carefully.

The yellow-haired boy was waiting at the foot of the tree. He glared at Lance, pugnaciously.

'That's our tree,' he said. 'You ain't got no right to climb it.'

'I'm sorry,' Lance said. 'I didn't mean any harm.'

The boy laughed. '"Didn't mean any 'arm"!' he mimicked. 'Lar-de-da!' He stepped closer to Lance. 'I can climb every tree in this wood,' he challenged.

Lance looked round rebelliously.

'Let's see you climb that one,' he said, pointing to a slim, smooth birch trunk.

The boy ignored the proposal. He raised a grubby fist, threateningly.

'I'll bet I can fight you,' he said.

Lance said nothing. He wondered why other boys always wanted to fight, as though there were some pleasure to be gained in hurting or being hurt.

The yellow-haired boy suddenly jumped high and caught at a branch of chestnut, pulling a few leaves down in his hand.

He said: 'That's your car in the yard, ain't it?'

'It's my brother's,' Lance replied.

'Can I 'ave a look at it?' the boy asked.

Lance said: 'Of course.'

They went back through the wood and the gap in the fence into the yard. Lance realised suddenly how superior he was to a young, overalled ruffian whose brother, if he had one, would never have a car. He watched the boy tolerantly as he admired the car.

'Can I 'ave a look inside?' the boy asked.

Lance opened the door for him and allowed him to touch the dashboard. He knew he was the unquestioned leader now. The boy looked down at the bucket on the floor.

'Seaweed!' he said.

'Yes,' Lance told him, 'we've just come away from the seaside.'

'I went for a day last year,' the boy said, mustering his pride. 'An' I went in the Fun Fair an' dug the sand on the beach an' rode on a donkey. An' I brought some rock back.'

Lance said, crushingly: 'We've been for a fortnight. We stayed at a hotel.'

The boy said nothing. His mother, hurrying past them with a loaded tray, called out to him:

'Mind ye be careful, ye young limb!'

Then Lance heard Gordon's voice calling. He closed the car door.

'I've got to be getting back,' he said. 'Good-bye.'

He ran back to Mummy and Gordon, who were getting ready to leave. As they all came out of the Blue Room he saw the car door was open, and the boy was bending inside. Gordon shouted loudly at him and he looked round, frightened, before running off down the garden path, clutching something in his arms. Gordon ran ahead to the car.

'Can't see anything missing,' he said.

'The seaweed!' Lance said. 'He's taken the seaweed.'

The small, fat woman came out, raging.

'Has the young child of Evil taken something of yours?' she asked, anxiously. 'I'll have the hide from him if he has.'

Mrs Hallam said: 'It's all right. Only a bunch of seaweed that would have been thrown away.'

'I'll have the hide off him anyway,' the woman said, 'for poking his nose into people's property. Andrew!'

She hurled herself away down the garden path in pursuit of her son. Mrs Hallam got in the car.

'Let's go before she comes back, Gordon,' she said. 'So – nerve-racking.'

Lance climbed in beside Gordon. He realised it would be fruitless to ask anybody to help him recover the seaweed. Even if they were to admit its value they would probably declare it was better to leave it with the boy, who had had no fortnight at the sea. There was nothing to do but hug his loss dumbly. Now there was no link to bind him to the crab pools, and the little girl, and the mysterious cave. No link but memory, and already that was fading.

My sons, she thought, my failures …

She gathered her self-inviolability round her like a cloak, but it was tattered by the storms and seasons of others. It was as though she were more diffuse, less strong and less sufficient. A torment, she wondered briefly? A hell specially designed for the strong who could be assailed in no other way? Fantastic. But so was all of it.

One knew secrets, but the knowledge did not help. How could she have saved either of them? Their doom was written on them like a birthmark. Lance … From weakness to weakness, down and down, a deepening spiral of defeat. Always more fear and more agony … she had not thought a person could live with so much fear. Her mind shuddered, recalling it. And Gordon, throwing away years of life in an evening's folly …

Her sons, yes, but not her failures. They failed in themselves, where all must inevitably succeed or fail.

Why then must she, too, suffer the agony and the defeat? She protested the unfairness of it, but there was nothing to which she could protest. The nothingness did not change. It was all round her, merging with the tattered edges of herself but never encroaching. If only it would … If only it would sweep in like a final, devouring wave, and spill its peace on her. But it waited on the frayed boundaries of her thoughts, patient and obstinate.

She felt the vortices of memory pulling her back. What part have I in their failures? she thought angrily. The pull strengthened, the distortion crystallised about her.

Roger, she thought with surprise. I'd completely forgotten Roger.

CHAPTER SIX

1926

Roger

R OGER SAID, 'But, Norman, I *said* we'd go down.'
Slow and imperturbable, Norman Danvers weighed the matter.

'Still,' he pointed out at last, 'you didn't know how quickly things were going to come off. We could send a wire, explaining.'

Roger said: 'Damn it, let's not take it too seriously. Nothing will happen before Monday. We can travel back Sunday night. Let's have a rest before the battle joins.'

Norman said: 'They might need us for meetings. It's a tricky time just now.'

Roger laughed. 'We're not indispensable. They won't need us till Monday.'

He wondered if Norman suspected how anxious he was to convince him. Probably he did – he was an astute old devil, he thought affectionately. But he had to see Rosemary again. How long was it? Eight years. And he realised now that for those eight years he had had a question mark in his life. How could he forego the possibility of solving it?

Norman looked at him shrewdly.

'In a way I'm sorry I gave you that telephone number,' he said. 'She's a bit of a bitch, you know. And you were at an impressionable age when you knew her.'

'Who?' Roger asked, casually. 'Oh – you mean Rosemary Hallam. I wasn't impressionable – I was all-conquering. Those were the days when my tailor used to measure me for three-legged trousers. And she was getting on even then, anyway.'

Norman walked across from the divan to where Roger sat in an armchair. He slapped him on the knee, affectionately.

'All-conquering, all right,' he said. 'Apart from the time I booted you through a sheet of glass. Remember?'

Roger looked up, laughing.

'The bad old days! Don't you feel a sort of tingling excitement when you think of them? The war just over, and all the bottles and bedrooms open? It was at Jessica's you kicked me through the glass. You were even drunker than I was that night.'

'Not too drunk to keep such a shocking little tick as you were in his place,' Norman said, grimly. 'You were a horrible little pimple in those days.'

'I couldn't have been as bad as you officers and gentlemen were. You insufferable war-winners. The drunken toasts and the haggard silences and all the talk about what happened up Death Alley ten minutes before zero hour ...'

Norman grinned. He walked across to the window of their basement bed-sitting room, and looked up through the bars.

'Threatening more rain in the outside world,' he reported. 'Are you quite sure you wouldn't rather go down yourself? More chance to get the lady alone.' He leered grotesquely.

'God!' Roger exclaimed, disgustedly. 'The inside of your skull must echo. One idea in it and it's positively overflowing. The woman's married now and has another kid. Even if I hadn't changed, she must have.'

'She didn't seem to have changed much,' Norman murmured reflectively. 'I don't think she's the sort that does change. Leaves that to her husband.'

They laughed together.

'The political merry-go-round,' Roger commented. 'You knew him quite well at one time, didn't you?'

Norman grinned. 'Yes. He was spouting revolutionary communism when I first met him.' He looked at his watch. 'Well,

I suppose we should pack a thing or two if we are going down there.'

'It'll be interesting to see him,' Roger said. 'He's a talkative chap, isn't he?'

Norman shut his eyes. 'Very,' he agreed.

As he packed, Roger wondered about things. It was so strange to be renewing links with that early immature self. He could have been, he realised, a very different young man of twenty-five to the one he was; several different ones for that matter. One of them, he thought with a pang, might have married Rosemary. His common sense laughed at him. When she had been just twice his age! It was stupid to fool himself into a romantic attitude towards this middle-aged, married woman. Even then he had never dreamed of marrying her. The initiative, he remembered suddenly, had always been with her.

And on her initiative she had picked up this Hallam fellow instead. He folded pyjamas neatly into his small attaché case. She must have changed; how old would she be now – nearly forty-five? An unromantic age. And he had the friendship of Norman, and a purpose in life with which he could create. How strange that one could never imagine other people having useful and pleasant purposes in life!

She must have changed ... But her voice on the phone had been so well – so very well-remembered! She had said: 'Roger!' with just the same cool, amused surprise that she had shown to the remote and shadowy Roger in the last year of the war.

She had said: 'I rather expected you would ring up. Norman Danvers said you and he were rooming together.'

He had replied – stammering, the stumbling Roger of twenty-five against the assured seventeen –

'Yes. That is ... He said he'd met you. He gave me your phone number ...'

That quiet, not-quite-taunting laugh. She said:

'I guessed as much when you rang up. But won't you come down and see us? Are you free this week-end?'

'Well,' he replied, uncertainly, 'Norman and I … There are always things that may crop up.'

'Come down both of you,' she said. 'There's a train at 11.37 from Victoria that gets you here in time for lunch on Saturday. Stephen will meet you with the car.'

The same calm assumption of authority. Remembering, he sighed. Norman was plunging like a bewildered ox in their joint chest of drawers. Roger called out:

'Throw over a pair of socks from my left-hand drawer.'

Norman turned round, baffled.

'I can't find anything,' he said. 'Not a damn thing. I can't find my clean pyjamas.'

Roger walked over to the wardrobe and opened the door.

'You put them in here when the laundry came back,' he said.

Norman grinned. 'Did I?'

In the end Roger took over the packing for both of them. Norman watched him and smoked a cigarette, lying back on his bed.

'You're a shocking anal type, Roger,' he commented lazily. 'All this neatness and passion for order.'

'Nothing so complicated,' Roger replied. 'My formative adolescent years were grossly influenced by the sergeant in charge of my O.T.C. platoon. As an Army officer you didn't have to be tidy.'

Norman lifted his tremendous body from the bed and walked over to the window, to stand idly looking up towards the street. He flicked the ash from his cigarette on the carpet.

'Roger,' he said, 'don't you think you've been leading rather too celibate a life the past few months?'

Roger looked up briefly. 'No more than you have. Why?'

Norman laughed deeply.

'I'm a dried-up gourd,' he declared, 'settling into old age. You should still be young and vigorous.' He looked critically at Roger's delicate, almost pretty face. 'You have the figure for it still.'

Roger closed the second case, pressing his knee down on it as he snapped the catch.

'Why this sudden interest in my sex life?' he asked. 'Have you decided to find me a wife?'

Norman, his great bulk suddenly lithe, fanned at a fly with a rolled-up *Daily Herald*. It buzzed frantically, up and over the window, out into the raw morning air. Norman turned towards Roger.

'I just wouldn't like you to get into a mess.'

Roger went over and lifted their raincoats from the wardrobe. With some irritation he said:

'Don't worry. I'm all right. I'm not seventeen now.'

Norman looked at him reproachfully.

Roger smiled. 'But thanks for worrying, anyway.'

There was a car waiting outside the station at Bullcaster, a square black Standard. A small, pale, nervous-looking man in plus fours was standing with one foot raised on the running-board, watching the crowd drifting out. Norman gripped Roger's arm.

'That's Hallam,' he said. 'Remember him?'

Roger shook his head. 'I only met him once.'

They went across. Stephen Hallam smiled in recognition of Norman's bulk. He looked much better, Roger thought, when he smiled. It relaxed his face and with the relaxation brought sincerity. And his was the kind of face which sincerity improved. Which should mean, Roger reflected, that he was essentially worth-while, but probably didn't.

Stephen said: 'Norman! You haven't changed at all.'

Norman rumbled with amusement.

'You've certainly taken on the badge of the bourgeois,' he said. 'Plus fours ...'

Stephen looked down with deprecating pride.

'Oh, these ... As a matter of fact I've come straight over from the club.' He extended a small, scrupulously-groomed hand to

Roger. 'You're Roger Staines, of course. We did meet once, I think.'

They climbed inside. Stephen went round to the front and flung himself on the starting handle. The engine caught at once, and he came back and got in. As the car moved off he said, over his shoulder:

'As you probably know, Norman, I'm not so scornful of badges of the bourgeois as I once was. I don't think they've done such a bad job when everything's considered.'

'That's a very pleasant optimism,' Norman said, drily, 'when one considers the state of the nation at the moment.'

'Still waiting for the dictatorship of the proletariat?' Stephen asked, humorously.

Norman winked at Roger.

'Yes,' he admitted. 'That same dictatorship we worked out together during my leaves from France.'

A policeman's hand forced the car to a stop, and Stephen seized the opportunity to glance back. He looked serious, and insincere.

'But one develops,' he said. 'One has to.'

Roger lay back, wondering. With the implication, though, he thought, that development is really a private preserve of one Stephen Hallam. Doesn't he consider the possibility of people developing along lines divergent to his own; or even developing more deeply along the same line, as Norman has done? Obviously not. He must have a strangely lop-sided view of the world. Though perhaps so outrageously twisted a view of things was at least as justified as the more subtly malformed personal approaches we must all utilise.

The car stopped outside a medium-sized detached villa.

Stephen said: 'Here we are. I shan't bother to garage the car now; I may need it after lunch.'

He led the way, opening the heavy gate labelled 'Santa Chiara', along the meticulous red gravel drive, past the lawn of quarter-inch grass, up to the front door flanked by hanging pots of fern and topped by a sun-blind in orange and black stripes. As he let them in, a maid's head peered into the hall, and retired swiftly again into the further recesses of the house.

Rosemary Hallam was waiting in the lounge that looked out over the shaven lawn. She rose from an armchair, putting down a Boots' library book on the small table beside it, and came over to greet them. With an unexpected feeling of relief Roger thought: 'But she's old!'

Only her voice was unchanged. She said:

'Roger, how nice to see you again.'

Norman grinned. 'And me, too, I hope.'

Rosemary smiled, and Roger saw the wrinkles running away from her mouth and eyes.

'Of course,' she said, 'but I met you last week. Outside Fortnum and Mason's, wasn't it? I haven't seen Roger for – how long will it be now?'

'Eight years,' Roger said, gravely. 'Seven-and-a-half, anyway.'

Stephen went over to a rawly modern roll-top cabinet near the window.

'Lunch is nearly ready,' he said. 'Sherry or cocktail?'

Roger said: 'Sherry, please.'

'Ah, a man of taste!'

What an appalling business were these clichés and attitudes of so-called civilisation, Roger thought. He wished now he had asked for a cocktail.

Stephen nodded significantly: 'Norman? Whisky?'

Norman smiled broadly. 'Nothing, thank you, Stephen. I don't drink at all now.'

Rosemary gurgled in her own private amusement.

'Don't drink, Norman? I'll have a Martini, Stephen.'

She glanced at Roger as though identifying herself conspiratorially with him against her husband's smugness. It was difficult to resist. Roger smiled.

Stephen brought the drinks over.

'An aperitif for you and me, Roger,' he said, 'and rot-gut for my wife. What made you give up drinking, Norman? Ethical objections?'

'I developed out of it,' Norman said with courteous irony. 'I used to drink because I felt I needed it. Now I don't need it so I don't drink. One has to develop, you know.'

Stephen smiled understandingly.

'Clearly it's better not to *need* to drink,' he said, gently, 'but why cut out the occasional sociability of a glass of good wine? That's on a par with stopping smoking because excessive smoking can damage the respiratory system. The only man who would do that, I feel, would be the man who knew he couldn't smoke without doing it to excess.'

Shrewd, Roger thought. Not a fool, at any rate. Certainly not a fool.

Norman said openly: 'You're probably right, Stephen. I haven't drunk for five years. Maybe because I had enough before then to last me a lifetime, and maybe because I don't like to trust myself with it at all now. I wouldn't like to say.'

Stephen nodded his head in wise, rather gloating agreement. Roger drank his sherry quickly. He wondered if Stephen ever guessed how such small lapses into brutishness must ruin his laboriously achieved effects? Though in a way they were a reflection of the poor devil's inadequacy. A man accustomed to making his points without emphasis would not need them. Stephen must be very unsure of himself all the time.

A small, fat, staring maid whispered: 'Lunch, Ma'am,' and Rosemary led them through into the dining-room. Over soup, she turned her attention to Roger.

'What have you been doing all these years?' she asked him.

He said: 'Oh – brushing about on the verges of politics. A little editing, a little writing, licking stamps, addressing envelopes. You know.'

'And making some very fine speeches, too,' Norman put in. 'We'll have him in Parliament soon.'

'Labour?' she asked.

'Approximately,' he replied.

'I don't think you can win,' Stephen said, pugnaciously. 'The country is fundamentally against you. This strike business … You're not going to be so foolish as to try it, are you? It will put you back a generation at least.'

'Or it may advance us several generations,' Norman pointed out. 'Though it's not Labour's choice really. It will be a defensive strike. The working class just can't let their standard of living drop again.'

'Will be?' Rosemary echoed. 'Is it settled?'

'Quite settled,' Roger affirmed. 'The first wave come out Sunday midnight. By the middle of next week it should be properly in swing.'

Stephen said, in a strained voice: 'I suppose the T.U.C. realise it's a direct incitement to civil war?'

Rosemary said deflatingly: 'Well, it's a long time since we had one. New potatoes, Roger?'

He said: 'Thanks. I don't suppose the strike will affect Bullcaster as badly as some places. London, for instance.'

Stephen seemed to have recovered his complacence.

'The whole thing is farcical,' he said. 'I give it less than a week. The people I'm in touch with have been ready for it for some time. Several of us are going up to London to lend a hand. There will be millions of volunteers. The strike can't succeed.'

Norman looked across at him, a smile broadening on his face.

'You wish you could be sure of that, don't you?' he asked.

They played bridge after dinner. Roger had a good grasp of the game and found a real delight in playing. Norman as a partner was limited but predictable. They amassed points slowly but surely. Stephen began the evening with fine, intuitive brilliance, but began to waver and make mistakes as the score mounted against them. Rosemary played coldly and competently, undisturbed by the state of the game or by her husband's increasing nervousness.

Soon after ten they broke up, with Roger and Norman nearly three thousand points in the lead. Rosemary, who had been dummy on the last hand, came in with cocoa and biscuits.

'How did it go, Stephen?' she asked.

He took a biscuit. 'Two down,' he said, peevishly. 'Another misfit. Really, Rosie, you should have shown me those diamonds.'

Rosemary sank down in an armchair, her skirt pulling back over her knees. Those sheerly sheathed legs at least looked younger than ever, Roger thought. She caught his eye and leisurely smoothed her skirt down.

'I didn't have the strength to show diamonds,' she explained. 'You would almost certainly have gone on to game, and been more than two down in the long run.'

True, Roger thought, but not calculated to soothe. Stephen's brow furrowed in annoyance but relaxed as he looked over towards Norman. He smiled boyishly and became again for an instant as likeable as a cheerful, unworried boy should be.

'It seems very funny, Norman,' he said, 'to see you knocking back cocoa.'

Rosemary yawned. 'Me for bed, I think. You know your rooms, don't you? I hope you don't mind sleeping in the lounge, Norman. We're a little cramped for space with young Lance in the house. Good-night then.'

She stood for a moment in the doorway, looking back at them with a faint, amused smile on her lips. And Roger felt a sudden ecstatic lift in watching her slender, drooping body. Stephen got up and walked across to the side-board for the whisky decanter.

He said: 'A night-cap, Roger?'

Roger shook his head. 'Not after cocoa, thanks.'

Stephen poured himself a drink, and held the glass up between his eye and the electric light. He turned nervously to Norman.

'Honestly, Norman,' he said, 'do you think this strike can be a good thing?'

Norman was amused. 'Since I support it, I must either think so or else be a blackguardly cynic. Shall we re-frame the question that way?'

Stephen laughed, but his face didn't relax.

'That was a silly way to put things,' he agreed. He drank off his glass and poured out again. 'Though it's difficult to tell – about self-interests, I mean. I've thought sometimes ... Some people might think I've sold out on my beliefs.'

He looked round at the new expensive furniture.

'I know the system supports me in my dingy glory,' he said. 'I know I consume more than I produce. But I don't think there is any alternative system which could fix that up without putting others just as worthless in my place. Your Socialism, for instance. I suppose you will get it eventually; if not now, later. And it sounds wonderful as you sit planning out what the future is going to be like. But don't forget the future is in the hands of men as human and fallible as those in the Government to-day. There will be graft and nepotism and good jobs for old pals, irrespective of their usefulness. You may get more efficiency into State-run industries, but I doubt it. Will a government answerable to its electors be any keener on long-term planning than a board of directors answerable to shareholders? And to get it you will run the risk of losing all individual freedom and enterprise. It's a long shot.'

Norman said, surprisingly: 'Sometimes, in some ways, I agree with you, Stephen. But I don't think now it's a question of holding on to the old or accepting the new. The new will come no matter how hard some of us fight against it. It's a question of moulding it the best way we can.'

Roger said: 'There need not be graft and nepotism. You can legislate against it. The men running State industries will be public servants, not profit seekers.'

Stephen said softly: 'Yes, but who legislates for the legislators?'

Norman said, glancing apologetically at Roger:

'After thirty-five you have to be a fanatical humanist to pre-serve much faith in human nature. That's the amount of truth there is in that tag about the man who isn't a socialist at twenty having no heart, and the man who is still a socialist at thirty having no head. But even without believing in human nature you can plan things. I'm for doing away with that individual freedom and enterprise Stephen talked about. I'm for tying mankind down, with good, stiff moral chains backed by ade-quate, unobtrusive force. There's less damage done that way.'

Roger smiled uneasily. 'I'm at a disadvantage. I still believe the human race isn't irremediably hopeless.' He looked point-edly at Norman. 'Another thing about being over thirty-five would seem to be that you get depressed easily. This time next week we may have won. We may really have the dictatorship of the producing class.'

'The producing class?' Stephen queried. 'Not the workers? A nice distinction! I'll try to think of it when they move an Under-Commissar in here and take me out and shoot me.'

Norman stretched his great bulk luxuriously.

'Don't worry, Stephen,' he grinned. 'We're a peaceable lot. You'll probably get away with ten years hard in the mines. Any-way, I can see you drinking sherry and playing golf for many years to come. Now ...' He stretched again. 'Bed, I think.'

'Good-night,' Stephen said. 'I'm staying down for a while to do a few things.'

Norman went on to the bed that had been made up for him in the lounge. He parted from Roger in the hall.

He said: 'It's difficult to trust anyone when you can't safely trust yourself. Good-night, Roger.'

Roger climbed the stairs slowly. As he reached the landing he saw that a door on the left was half open, so that he could see part of a cream wall and the end of a dressing-table littered with small feminine debris. Lust glowed in him as he thought: Rosemary will be sitting up in bed reading, in a flimsy, silk nightgown … He checked his mind, hating it. Damn it, he'd just said good-night to her husband. He walked resolutely past the door towards his own bedroom.

But he stopped at once, although her call was only faint. He heard: 'Roger?'

He walked back and stood by the door. He heard himself whispering: 'Yes?'

She said: 'Come in.'

He pushed the door open and walked in. She lay back against pillows, not in a nightgown but in carefully cut silk pyjamas. Her dark hair was braided back behind the clear oval of her face. A book rested on the hollow of her lap; one smooth, small hand marking the place. Verse, he noticed. With the lamp-light shaded on her face, she looked no more than thirty.

He said awkwardly: 'You wanted me?'

She smiled at him enigmatically.

'Just curiosity,' she said. 'I remember you saying once you only read poetry at school. Have you read any since?'

He said hoarsely: 'A bit. I don't have much time …'

She patted the bed beside her. 'Come and sit down. I'll read you some.'

Roger advanced reluctantly. 'But Stephen …'

She smiled; that seraphic purity, faintly accented with malice.

'Don't worry about Stephen.' She looked at her small, gold wrist-watch. 'He works from eleven to one on his new book analysing the defects of socialism. He thinks more clearly then.'

Roger sat down carefully beside her. She looked at him critically.

'I do believe you've slipped back, Roger,' she said. 'And you were a most promisingly gallant boy. The sort that can be relied on for tasteful, harmless decoration. The pale cast of thought does make you look sickly.'

Roger said: 'Why do you read poetry, Rosemary? It's never seemed right for you.'

She stared at him. 'Red herrings. And clumsy ones. I believe you are trying to understand me.'

He insisted. 'But seriously …'

She fingered the book. 'Dead men make no demands.' She added with her curious, flat malice: 'Though live men should.'

She took his wrist and drew his face towards her own.

'Don't be ungallant, Roger,' she whispered. 'Don't tell me I look old.'

He let the last thread of detachment go, and drowned voluptuously in the senses.

Retiring, later, to his own bedroom, he could feel only a confused pain of loathing and disgust. Less than half an hour ago he had been championing, he remembered, the innate goodness of man. Including the goodness of sneaking in to your host's wife's bedroom at night. He remembered Norman's words: ' … when you can't trust yourself.' Good, thick chains, he thought despairingly, and force, even to the point of torture.

Stephen

In the morning there had been steady rain, but on Sunday afternoon the sun came out and after lunch they had the deck-chairs out in the garden. Norman and Roger sat on either side of Rosemary but Stephen had fixed his chair a little way from them, under the early white rambler roses that were just beginning to bud. At the bottom of the garden, Lance played quietly in his sand-pit. Occasionally he looked round at the group of adults. Stephen wondered vaguely whether he was resenting their continued presence, or welcoming it.

He would have liked the boy to be more boisterous. He was quiet and well-mannered, which was perhaps better than being unruly, but there was an aloofness about him incongruous in a four-year-old child. He might have suspected a derivation from Rosemary, except that it was not her kind of aloofness. It was the aloofness of timidity, not of rejection. Though surely there was nothing to make him timid.

From the depth of his deck-chair, Norman Danvers said lazily:

'You would never guess there was a child in this house. I don't think I've known one so quiet.'

Rosemary said: 'Lance is very self-sufficient.'

Roger said: 'Long live self-sufficiency. To hell with you, mate, I'm all right.' His voice was curiously bitter.

'Yes, it can be carried to excess,' Norman said.

Rosemary said briefly: 'I don't agree.'

Stephen roused himself and sat forward.

'It's not altogether natural in a child,' he said, 'and anyway I'm not convinced that it's so much self-sufficiency as self-withdrawal.'

'And do you consider that worse?' Roger pursued harshly. 'It seems better to me. If there were more self-withdrawal and less self-sufficiency ...'

He hesitated, lost for words, and Rosemary finished for him:

'We'd have liberalism and socialism and pacifism and internationalism and old More's Utopia and all,' she said calmly.

Roger retreated into brooding silence. Stephen looked across at Rosemary affectionately. Like ice, he thought, like diamond-hard ice. He had long since ceased looking for gratification of affection in her, but she continually delighted his sense of property more deeply. Her well-groomed, languid repose; the delicate, liquid lines of her body under the cool, linen frock; the obscure mystery of her face, shaded by the floppy, straw hat. She was so wonderfully decorative; he had not imagined a woman could be so decorative at forty-three.

Ours, he thought, is a successful marriage. Mutual respect, mutual restraint, mutual trust without intrusion on privacy. He thought, with momentary embarrassment, of the callow dreams of his bachelor days. That longing for lavish, all-surrendering love. How naive. Possible for some, perhaps. For the dull, coarse, unimaginative ones, insensitive enough to stand the close buffetings of separate personalities so closely linked together. But even there he doubted if such calm, settled satisfaction as he and Rosie had could be attained. When the sensitive are bound together they must wound and be wounded. Far better to revolve, discreetly distant, about a common axis.

He saw Roger writhe angrily, shifting his position in the chair. He had been strange all day to-day; nervously depressed. Worrying, perhaps, about the Forces of Revolution – as well he might. Danvers had been right last night in claiming it as defensive. Of course it was, and very well manoeuvred by the Government too. The wedge was already deep between the workers and their shaky, treacherous leaders. One hard blow now and there would be a division that might last half a century. The strike could only win if the leaders stood by their rank and file. Baldwin knew that. The fact that he was letting the strike take place meant that he knew those leaders would crack.

A doubtful manoeuvre, he admitted, and one that must bring suffering – not to the leaders but to the poor devils who obeyed their injunctions. And yet, necessary. The alternative, despite Roger's optimism and Norman's promised chains, was too grim. Power for the masses eventually, perhaps. But first they must learn how to use it.

Roger got up suddenly, startling him and disturbing his chain of thought. He began to walk down the garden path towards the sand-pit where Lance played silently. Stephen thought he detected a kind of baffled anger in his walk. He had been curt and sharp to-day, but especially to Rosemary. It might not be the strike that was making him depressed. It might be … He remembered suddenly that when he first met Rosemary, Roger had been with her. Perhaps the poor young fool had fallen in love with her!

A delightful thought. It would amuse Rosemary if she knew. It excited Stephen himself. To think of a young man envying him his wife was to have that sense of property most delicately gratified. He got up and walked after Roger, more deeply, more voluptuously aware of the home and child and wife that were so clearly his.

He overtook Roger as he paused near the sand-pit. Lance was engrossed with his tottering, dusty fortifications and still unaware of them. Stephen bent towards him.

'What are they, Lance?' he asked, cheerfully. 'Forts and castles?'

Lance looked up quickly and looked away again. He whispered something quietly, his fingers digging nervously into the sand.

'Speak up, old man,' Stephen urged.

'Hills,' Lance said. 'Just hills.'

He looked up, shyly smiling. Stephen smiled back, acutely, happily conscious of Roger's morose figure beside him. In a few years, he thought happily, he will be growing into all the wonderful adventures and explorations of youth. I shan't lose him; I'm determined to hold him with the sympathy I always wanted. I'll grow with him. Gordon was all right, but he hadn't been able to reach Gordon before school began taking him for three-quarters of the year. And Gordon wasn't his own. How delicious was ownership.

A symbiosis, he thought. An emotional symbiosis of generations.

Stephen was thinking of Lance several days later as he drove his bus out towards its terminus. The initial excitement of the unfamiliar had already palled, and now he was looking forward only to the end. It seemed an age since he had left 'Santa Chiara'. Surely it could not last long now. But improbably, frighteningly, it went on lasting. What if they managed to stick it out after all? A stop loomed up, and he braked obediently.

Two thumps above him. Young Harris must be collecting money on the top deck. He looked back. There was a jammed mass inside but the footboard was clear. He drove off again more cheerfully. At least driving was better than conducting.

It must be agony to collect money and hand out tickets in that swarming mob.

He glanced briefly at his watch. Just turned five. The afternoon was fading but it would be another three hours before he would be relieved. At least, though, there was the terminus, and the prospect of a cup of coffee and a sandwich before the long drive back into the centre of town began. He watched for the already customary landmarks. The Regent cinema on the left. Then the crossroads, with the church on the corner, and a glimpse of tram-lines where trams were no longer running. Almost there. He looked back again. The bus was nearly empty now. Most of them had got off at the cinema stop.

At last, the terminus. He swung the heavy vehicle round the island and parked it by the kerb. Harris came round leisurely to meet him as he got down from the driver's seat. There were beads of sweat in the wrinkles on his forehead under the shock of fair hair.

'Sticky trip, sir,' he said.

Stephen looked up at him, envying him for a moment his long, sturdy body and active youth.

'Like to be back at school?' he asked.

Harris hesitated. 'Well … I don't know. I just hope it doesn't go on too long. We take Higher in July. This is a nice break. It's interesting. But I hope it doesn't go on too long.'

Stephen led the way into the Cosy Café. He noticed at once that it was unusually full. The round, yellow-painted tables were crowded with men who were quite obviously strikers. For a moment he felt an impulse of almost intolerable fear, as he had done on a day almost twenty years before when his schoolboy enemies had banded together against him, and he had walked out of the classroom door into their silent, watchful midst. He looked round warily at these new silent faces. One or two of them were reading the four-page British Gazette. They seemed tame enough, and there had been no sign of trouble before. He walked up to the counter and put down a florin.

'Two teas and sandwiches, please,' he said.

A small, swarthy man got up from a nearby table and limped over to stand beside them. Ignoring them, he said softly to the fat, uneasy man across the counter:

'You goin' to serve 'em, Joe?'

Joe laughed and his face looked more uneasy than ever. 'I'm non-political, 'Arry,' he said. 'I serve anybody, ev'rybody. I don't want no trouble. I don't give no trouble. I don't want coppers rahnd 'ere askin' questions. I mind me own business.'

The swarthy man looked round casually, but with a proprietary air, at the others round the tables. He leaned over the counter again. His voice was still soft and almost expressionless.

'I been in 'ere practically every day since the war. That's right, ain't it, Joe? We've all been in 'ere.' He straightened up and turned away. 'Well, bye-bye, Joe. Comin', mates?'

The uneasy laugh returned, like a comic face painted on an empty balloon.

Joe said: 'Don't go. You know I'm wiv yer.'

He looked deferentially at Stephen, hitching his shoulders into a grotesque shrug.

'Don't seem to 'ave no more tea an' sandwiches left, sir. You might try further along the road.'

Had the strikers seemed aggressive, Stephen would have left without argument. But their restrained, co-operative blackmail fed his cold fury. He said icily:

'Those sandwiches in that case are for sale. I'll have some of those.'

The swarthy man limped up to the counter again, looking this time directly at Stephen. He was about Stephen's own height but strongly muscled in body and face. Still looking at Stephen, he said:

'Those sandwiches aren't for sale, are they, Joe? They're reserved, ain't they? Reserved, like the tables in the Ritz. Per'aps the Ritz 'ave a branch dahn the road. They might try there, mightn't they, Joe?'

Harris laughed awkwardly.

'Be a sport,' he said. 'I know we're on the other side, but it's not sporting to cut us off from a cup of tea. It's thirsty work conducting.'

The swarthy man looked at him implacably.

'I 'ate you kids,' he said. 'I 'ate you kids worse than the men. A man's responsible, but you young bastards come dahn from school to blackleg for a lark. Sport! Bloody fine sport you'd find it if you were 'avin' your wages cut an' 'ad a wife an' kids to keep.'

'You won't keep them with your mouth,' Stephen said.

The man turned towards him as fast as a dancing boxer, his hands half-raised. Stephen could not prevent himself from flinching. The man said:

'By Christ, if you've ever used anythin' but your mouth to earn your wages I'm a Dutchman. You keep it shut 'ere. Or I'll shut it for you. Understand?'

Stephen picked up his coin from the counter. He said to Harris:

'Come on. Let's go.'

They walked out together past the silent men. The sky was heavy with untidy clouds, and darkening early. The street here was practically deserted. Two or three people were aboard the bus.

Harris suggested: 'I suppose we might as well push off?'

Stephen said: 'Yes. Another hour before we get a cup of tea now. Blast those fools.'

Harris wrinkled his forehead even more deeply than usual.

'Can't really blame them, I suppose,' he said. 'It's more serious for them than it is for us.'

Stephen began, hotly: 'I don't agree …' and then stopped. The strikers were coming out of the café, talking among themselves, orderly and purposeful. They went past Stephen and

Harris, and the swarthy leader climbed on to the back of the bus.

'All change,' he called. 'This one ain't goin'.'

The few passengers came out, grumblingly obedient. Stephen went round to where the men stood in a bunch.

'What's the idea?' he asked. 'The police will clear you if you try picketing.'

The swarthy striker answered him.

'We're not picketing,' he said. 'Keep yourself an' the kid out of the way. We're turnin' 'er over.'

He waved his arm to the others. 'All right, boys. All together. Give it a swing. Not a MINUTE on the day, not a PENNY off the pay.'

Stephen could feel only a sick, nauseating anger. These were the masses, the masters by weight of numbers. It had been almost happening for a long time and now it was happening. Their offhand refusal to bother with Harris and himself made it worse. His anger and disgust and despair twisted and grew, scalding his mind out of logic and apprehension, out of everything except the certainty that they must not win, whatever the cost. They were not men, he saw now, only misshapen sub-men. They were the despised and the rejected, and they must not win. He shrieked sudden, meaningless vilifications at them. Through air that was stifling like cotton wool he heard them chanting:

'Not a MINUTE on the day, not a PENNY off the pay.'

The huge wheels began to lift away from the ground. He ran round to the other side of the bus and pitted his puniness against them, pushing, straining, to keep it level on its wheels.

He heard Harris's voice calling in horror and confused shouts from the sub-men on the other side. He looked up, smiling, to see the red wall leaning over him like a petrified flame. A shrill whistle tore the cotton wool to echoing shreds. They must lose. They must lose.

Then the flame dipped towards him.

CHAPTER SEVEN

1921

Stephen

D URING BREAKFAST HE THOUGHT a lot about the Irish question, rolling in his mind those balanced, sonorous phrases, framed in rhetoric, for which his writing was – even though only in a narrow circle – famous. By the time he had reached toast and marmalade he had achieved a fine fervour. He drank his coffee slowly, sitting well back in his solitary chair and murmuring his snatches to himself as he savoured their authentic ring. He had to admit that he was gaining a certain reputation, and gaining it – he could proudly affirm – without compromising in any way with his beliefs. How many writers, after securing a regular and envied niche in *Populus,* would have gone out into the journalistic wilderness as readily as he had done? *Liberal Comment* had, it was true, recognised his value immediately. The valuable was hard to suppress.

As always he left a quarter of toast uneaten, lying on his plate thickly spread with butter and marmalade, almost like a libation. He walked through to his study, noting with satisfaction that his watch and the old brass-geared clock, painted with blue moons, agreed in declaring that it was just nine o'clock. The silver and brass replied to the morning sunshine unusually brightly; but then, of course, it was Friday, and Mrs Ganner would have spent the previous evening polishing them. He passed a slender, complacent finger along the dustless mantel, and turned to sit down at his desk.

Everything was in perfect order. He picked up his favourite pen and, pulling the pad of faintly lavender-tinted paper towards him, began to cover it with his small, neat, rounded, regular writing. He wrote quickly, without losing the initial neatness. And as he wrote he felt the words carrying him away; out of the realms of argument and compromise into those brilliant rainbow worlds where his intellect and logic scintillated like remorseless Excalibur in the costly, jewelled sheath.

The Irish, he explained with gentle ruthlessness, had had a case to present; a case that all lovers of liberty and democracy must have heeded, a case that might have won for them the applause of the civilised world. There they were, an ancient, freedom-loving race that had been for centuries oppressed by their more powerful and capable Anglo-Saxon neighbours. They had had martyrs, but they had borne their martyrdom like a laurel wreath. Theirs was the glory of a refusal to descend to the methods of the enemy; they, indeed, were the true noble savages, bowed under national serfdom but still with a light in their eyes and a song on their lips. They had endured, and they must surely have won as their oppressors felt the sting of their consciences, and humbly unloosed the chains.

But now, dragged down the slope of disaster by a Gadarene few, see how they threw away their victory!

How could even those corrupt and degraded men who now held the Irish spirit in the palms of their perverting hands hope to win England over by force? Could they not realise, did they not remember, that three years had not passed since the greatest tyrant of the world had stormed at that same England, and fallen back, defeated? The conscience of England was always ready to attend to the wrongs of weaker nations. Cynical Tories might for a while prejudice her name by opportunism, but the warm mass of England outlasted and eventually overpowered them. The only argument that England would never listen to was the argument of force. Nor did it help the Irish when they calumnised so ridiculously our troops, stationed in

Ireland merely to protect the minorities from the excesses of the mob. Could anyone, remembering the part these men had played against the brutal masses of the Kaiser, believe the stupid fabrications of atrocities alleged against them?

The telephone on his desk rang sharply, an irritating summons from the inferior world where clear issues blurred and became confused. Still with the feeling of speaking for England he picked up the receiver and spoke gruffly:

'Hallam here.'

He recognised Kenton's calm, precise voice.

'Oh, is that you, Stephen? Just the usual reminder since there's nothing from you in the mail that we'd like your piece by this afternoon.'

He said irritably: 'Damn it, Arthur, you know I never send it by post. You know I always bring it round after lunch. Why all this nonsense of phoning? I've never let you down, have I?'

Kenton laughed, his small, careful laugh.

'Just our absurd routine, Stephen. And, of course, it's so nice to hear your voice again. But I'm sorry if I interrupted you. Were you working on it?'

'Just starting,' Stephen said shortly.

'Starting!' Kenton repeated. His cooing laugh returned. 'Such facility and certainty,' he exclaimed. 'What are you doing this week, by the way?'

'The Irish question.'

'Ireland *again*,' Kenton said. 'Oh, dear. These Irish. I say, Stephen?'

'Yes.'

'I hope you're not being too – violent.'

'In what way?' Stephen asked.

Kenton said: 'We – ell. The last two you did were a little on the thank-God-I'm-a-Briton line, weren't they? We've had a few nasty letters. We are supposed to be a liberal paper.'

'I thought liberalism was opposed to the use of force in politics?' Stephen asked, heavily.

Kenton said: 'Of course! But you might drop a hint that there is something to be said on both sides. I know it's very difficult …'

'Are you inferring that my attitude is biassed?'

'No,' Kenton said. 'I'm taking that for granted. All our attitudes are biassed. I'm just expressing a delicate hope that your attitude is biassed in the same direction as the attitude of *Liberal Comment.* Somehow you seem to be slipping away from us.'

Stephen said: 'I remember you saying something about a free hand, when I came over from *Populus.* You know how I work. I have to have a free hand. I've never written to order. I couldn't write a word if I didn't know I were completely free.'

'God forbid that we should prejudice your freedom!'

Kenton's voice was amused in its rather spineless, tittering way.

'Anyway, bring it along this afternoon. And now I'll hang up and let you get back to those admirable arguments of yours.'

Stephen turned to his article again, but the grasp he had achieved over his subject seemed to have slipped away. He read through the part he had written, anticipating in his mind the comments Kenton might make. He could hear the weak, whispering voice raised interrogatively. 'But what about such? And he's omitted to consider so-and-so.' Such ridiculous, bloodless carping. The *New Reader,* even though Tory, could show Kenton a few things in vigour.

He was relieved when the phone rang again. He said eagerly: 'Yes? Stephen Hallam speaking.'

Her voice had its usual, tingling coolness.

'Hello, Stephen. Are you doing anything important?'

'Rosemary!' he said. 'I am, rather. Relatively important, anyway. If I don't get it finished by lunch old Kenton will be dashing round rather frantically for a page of material.'

She said: 'Kenton?'

'You know – the editor of *Comment.* You haven't forgotten I do a little journalism?'

Rosemary laughed. 'Don't be silly. Look, Stephen, I'd like to see you soon. Will you be free this afternoon?'

Stephen said: 'I have to drop my copy in at Kenton's office. After that I'm free. What have you in mind?'

She said: 'We could go on the river, if it keeps fine. Shall I meet you for lunch?'

Stephen said doubtfully: 'I can't see quite when I'll finish this. I will by lunch-time, of course, but I can't give an exact time.'

Rosemary was decisive. 'You can pick me up. I'll stay in till you come round. 'Bye now, Stephen.'

He paused for a moment to examine her photograph, before going on with his work. It was an enlargement of the snap he had taken at the Griffins' the previous summer. She was wearing a fantastically wide-brimmed hat and a flimsy, flower-splashed summer frock – the sort of ensemble that you expected to go with a rather generous fleshiness and much coy simpering. That delicate, clear face, those barely-laughing eyes, were a constant happy surprise.

He directed his attention back to the Irish problem. Soon the rounded, regular writing was rolling forward again across the expanses of pale lavender. At ten-thirty Mrs Ganner brought in coffee and three cheese straws on a small willow pattern plate. At a quarter to twelve Stephen ran his eyes again over the last, crushing paragraph; read it aloud to savour its true impact, and pushed the whole into a long, stiff envelope.

He was pleased with the speed he had achieved. Generally he was much later in finishing. It was forceful, too; one of the most forceful he had done. It should make Kenton sit up. He realised, remembering how the words had flowed, that the second half was a good deal more provocative than the first. He chuckled to himself. It served Kenton right for exasperating him.

In reply to his ring, Rosemary came down with coat and handbag, and in a moment he was helping her into the waiting taxi.

'Where do you suggest?' he asked.

She said: 'Oh … *Chez Raoul*? Or *Alberto's*.'

He directed the driver and pulled the door shut.

Rosemary looked up at him obliquely.

'Had a busy morning?'

He said complacently: 'I finished it early – as you see.'

Rosemary said: 'I can't see why you bother with it at all. Such a nuisance, being tied down. Why do you bother?'

'It brings me in a pittance,' he said.

He felt obscurely that it was important not to discuss it too fully with Rosemary. She was more direct than sympathetic. There was something shocking about that incurious directness, so closely paralleled by Kenton's anaemic prying. Life, he felt, should be lived on a high but personal plane. A great man did not expose or explain his motives. But at the same time he was conscious that there was a discrepancy. His own function as a critic was, after all, a method of exposing motives.

'But you don't need the money, do you?' Rosemary went on.

He sighed. Beyond the windows of the taxi he could see the streams of traffic converging and diverging in their interlinking channels about Hyde Park Corner. A policeman's white hand beckoned, and they moved on into Piccadilly. The trees of Green Park slipped past; green, irregular, unquestioned and unquestioning. He pointed to their shade.

'See the happy clerks and clerkesses, gambolling in their lunch hour. Does it ever occur to you, Rosemary, that we too might easily have been like them?'

'Not at our present ages, surely,' she said.

She lost interest in the question of his motives for being a journalist as casually as the interest had been casual. Although it was what he had wanted, he felt hurt. He drew away from her in the cab.

He found a table he liked at *Raoul's*; in the corner, by the window. Rosemary excused herself, and he sat with his back to the wall waiting for her return, drinking a fine, crisp sherry.

There were very few people dining and, he thought at first, none that he knew. Then he saw that someone was lumbering to his feet behind the potted palm on the other side, and recognised Walter Mulready.

Mulready came over, swaying ponderously like a tight-rope-walking elephant. He threw forward a large white hand, like a tentacle, as Stephen began to rise.

'Don't disturb yourself, Mr Hallam,' he protested. 'I just hoped I might sit down with you a moment until the lady comes back.'

Stephen said: 'Will you have a drink?'

Mulready's great hand dismissed the suggestion as trivial. He sat down carefully in the chair opposite Stephen and gazed at him from wide, deep-set eyes.

'Do you read my little paper, Mr Hallam?' he asked, abruptly.

Stephen sipped the sherry, feeling its reassuring tingle in his throat. This was the real fabric of life – the small, enigmatic questions in the not-quite-obscure restaurants, the heavy innuendoes, the cautious slanders.

'I have done, at times,' he replied slowly.

'Read it, read it!' Mulready urged. 'It won't do you any harm. You aren't afraid of being convinced, are you?'

Stephen looked up at him.

'I've never been afraid of that,' he said.

Mulready splayed his large hand across the tablecloth.

'Do you know anything of palmistry, Mr Hallam?' he went on. 'If you do you will know – and in case you don't I will tell you – that the lines of this hand reveal a man who could never betray a confidence or a contract.'

The hand rose, like a traffic policeman's.

'Wait!' Mulready commanded. 'I am not boasting. I have little of which to boast. I am one of the young hopes that could not succeed. It is all there, in my hand.'

He extended both hands, palms uppermost, across the table.

'There,' he said. 'The tendency in my left; the achievement – the lack of it – in my right. Observe the line of talent in my left hand. See how it breaks and scatters. It was deep in my right in the past, but it's gone now.'

The wide eyes flickered, grotesquely self-pitying.

'I don't begin to understand it, Mr Hallam,' he said. 'It was there in my left hand all along. I was bound to fail. None of my efforts could prevent it. There are few things more terrible than to fail in the struggle with words when one has once had the mastery of them.'

Stephen looked at him; embarrassed, but complacent in his own power.

'You're too modest, Mr Mulready,' he said. 'Even those of us who don't share your politics admire the vigour of your statements. I wish Kenton could be persuaded of the need for such vigour. I'm beginning to consider it myself as one of the major necessities in political writing. We need forcefulness in times like the present.'

Mulready lowered his huge head, and looked up at Stephen in heavy speculation.

'How right!' he said. 'I admire strength myself, even in opponents. I feel that we have a lot in common. This Irish business, for instance. Strength is what is needed. Strength even to the point of ruthlessness.'

Stephen said: 'It's a gift with us. Strength – even ruthlessness – against coercion. Determination. Endurance. And then victorious mercy. If the Irish would only remember South Africa.'

'Exactly,' Mulready agreed. 'Steadfastness – that's what we most need. What the world needs rather; what we have.'

He pushed his palms forward again.

'Loyalty. Steadfastness. Observe how it is promised in the left hand; achieved in the right. I'm not boasting, Mr Hallam. How could I boast, a ruined genius? But loyalty is there all right. I have a gift for sensing quality in a man. I pick men of quality for my friends and for my helpers on the *Reader*. And when I've picked them, I stick by them, Mr Hallam.'

Stephen thought of Kenton's cautious, cynical approval. To lack warmth was to lack a fundamental attribute of humanity. And yet there were so many like Kenton; so many chilly theorists condemning where they could not follow, chopping logic on the block of living man. The real men, the warm men, should ally themselves against them. He looked across at Mulready with sudden confidence. But beyond him he saw Rosemary approaching. He gestured awkwardly and Mulready, after looking round, lumbered to his feet.

Stephen said: 'Rosemary. This is Walter Mulready, the editor of the *New Reader*. And this, Mr Mulready, is Mrs Drake, an old friend of mine.'

Rosemary put her own right hand forward to take Mulready's large, pale record of destiny, looked at it for a moment, and withdrew herself again. Drawing a chair out for her, Mulready said:

'I will be going now, Mrs Drake. I just came across to compliment Mr Hallam on the last few articles of his. We could do with him on our side. But it has been a doubly fortunate visit, since I have been introduced to you.'

Rosemary smiled non-committally. Mulready looked at her uneasily and turned, smiling largely, to Stephen:

'Drop in on us at High Holborn some time,' he suggested. 'Come and see if the atmosphere suits you. It's warm – that's one thing about it!'

They saw his vastness retreat until it was lost behind the shadowy sweep of the palms. Stephen turned to Rosemary, laughing.

'Clumsy,' he said, 'but brilliant in his way. I used to hate him a few years ago. Now I can see his point of view rather better.'

Rosemary's cool voice said: 'We all change.'

How strange, he thought, that she should say that, who never seems to change. The rest of us move, advancing and retreating, swinging perhaps in some vast and futile circle, while she stays rigid in a kind of crystalline eternity. Once again he wondered what she really thought behind that casual, unaffected curtain.

Aloud, he said warmly: 'For the better, I hope.'

She looked at him curiously, and the curtain rippled into the contours of a smile. But still, he protested passionately to himself, a curtain. There was no getting behind it – its very unconsciousness was its greatest proof of permanence.

Appropriately, a waiter arrived. Stephen ordered deftly, obtaining from Rosemary confirmatory nods. *Potage à la Bonne Femme. Poulet à la Romaine. Chartreuse d'Oranges à la Royale.* And a dry Lacrimae Christi of Orvieto, 1913.

Savouring the sensual delight of the soup, rich on his tongue, crumbling the *croûton* of fried bread in his fingers, Stephen felt the benediction of food. How hopeless to postulate an austere, discarnate God that could stand against this warmth, this altogether tangible glory! Such dismissal of the senses could be valid only where the senses manifested themselves in crudity. The roast beef and cabbage brigade, the bread-and-cheese-and-ale boys – ascetism had a case against them, as all refined instruments had against blunt and coarsened ones. But match two sensitivities together – the mystic's mental ecstasy on a mountain against a fine dry wine of Orvieto – and who could measure the balance? One lived, inescapably, in the senses; to deny them was a presumption against whatever existed beyond.

The chicken rested on its bed of macaroni, garnished with olives and chervil. He said to Rosemary:

'What was it you particularly wanted to tell me? I'd almost forgotten.'

She looked at him across the table, the curtain rippling again into a smile.

'I'm pregnant,' she said.

He heard her words without incredulity or even much surprise. But he felt elation, like a wave, lifting him and carrying him forward. Here it seemed was his triumph over that cool inviolability of hers that he now knew he hated. It had fascinated as well as repelled him, but the fascination had lain in his hopes – however vague and unformed – of conquering it. In the past, each new advance had promised a breach in that indefinable barrier; only for him to find that the barrier had moved back and still guarded, as impregnably as ever, the secrets lying beyond. Often he had wakened early in the satin-panelled bed at her flat and gazed at her bewilderedly in the soft grey light that was beginning to seep through the drifts of lace against the window. In sleep she did not put aside her armour, but lay half-smiling and remoter than ever. He remembered how he had wanted to touch her, and yet had been afraid lest he should stir the deep, undemanding cold of sleep into the interrogative coolness of her waking self.

But here at last his imposition was achieved. Like Dryden's Jove, he thought. 'He stamped an image of himself, a sovereign of the world.' His stamp was on her, transcending her barrier of reserve. She must yield now. There was nothing to which she could retreat.

He said, smiling: 'I suppose we'd better start making arrangements about getting married then.'

Rosemary said: 'Yes, that is one possibility.'

The words, spoken evenly and reflectively, told him that he had failed. Even in this she would accept no subordination; would make no move towards the dropping of reserves and the fusion of individualities that were, he was convinced, the inevitable prelude to the warm splendour of love. All should be shared in an ecstatic, dual participation. He thought of the way things should be. Rosemary, smiling and deft, presiding over a cheerful house and a small girl-child. Rosemary sitting at his knees while he read his articles to her, and she smiled up into the lamp-light, and made grave suggestions, and wriggled against his leg. Rosemary humming a lullaby …

Rosemary said: 'I love orange chartreuse. So pleasantly gaudy.'

Stephen said, rather awkwardly: 'What other possibilities had occurred to you?'

She looked at him with surprise. 'Well, there are two rather obvious ones, aren't there? I could have the child illegitimately, or I could have an abortion.'

He said weakly: 'I hadn't thought ... Surely they are both sort of last resort possibilities?'

Rosemary spooned up red and green appreciatively.

'Neither of them seems quite so drastic as marriage,' she said. 'An abortion's soon over, and I imagine an unwanted child can be farmed out easily enough.'

'Is the prospect of marrying me so very terrible then?'

She smiled. 'You're quite nice in your way, Stephen, but I don't think, really, that you're the marrying kind. Imagine exchanging that nice little bachelor flat of yours for a suburban house. Because I shan't be able to keep my flat on. It was all right with Gordon away at school most of the year, but if I am to keep this new one I shall have to retire into the suburbs, where I can have a garden to park it.'

Stephen said sulkily: 'I don't know where you get the idea that I'm one of the modern troglodytes, unable to leave my centrally-heated cave. Quite apart from anything else I would like to have a garden myself. I remember what fun it was when I was a kid. I used to go and help old Jevvons in the garden whenever I was able to break away from my governess. I think it was the only time I was really happy as a kid. I used to grub about at his heels all afternoon, watching him pruning and planting and transplanting. There's always so much peace in a garden. Autumn, with the dead leaves blowing about and the smell of frost in the air. And that blessed certainty that nothing is going to change, because it will all happen again next year.'

His sulkiness had changed, as he talked, into a dreamy happiness. He knew the same infallibility that he knew when writing his weekly articles; an infallibility that must not be interrupted or questioned.

The waiter poured Turkish coffee from a small silver jug.

Rosemary said: 'It might not be the same thing with the peaceful air punctuated by an infant's howling.'

'I've always wanted a child, too,' Stephen said, softly.

He saw the curtain of Rosemary's face contract interrogatively, and thought despairingly of the communion of lovers. Perhaps with women it was impossible; and all the talk and writings of it no more than the artificial imaginings of poets and novelists. But a child would be different. To get a child before the barrier came down; to surround it with love and warmth so that love and warmth reflected back, stressed and enhanced by the other's thoughts – that must surely succeed.

Rosemary said: 'I take it then that you want to marry me?'

Stephen said, aggrievedly: 'You're so cold-blooded, Rosemary.'

Rosemary looked at him. 'Cold-blooded?'

She seemed genuinely surprised but not very interested. She went on:

'I think I would have been inclined to have an abortion. I didn't imagine you would want anything else. I only told you about it so that we could fix a fair division of expenses. As you know, I haven't got too much money left, and Gordon's school fees are a big drain. But if you're keen on marriage … I don't see any reason why we shouldn't.'

Stephen felt the grasp of things escaping from him. This was not the warm, breathing love he had anticipated. It was more in the nature of a business arrangement. He remembered Mulready. Strength. Steadfastness. Pushing his coffee cup away from him, he said, incisively:

'It must be on my terms.'

Rosemary looked at him with cool amusement.

'Perhaps we'd better see,' she suggested, 'whether your terms are likely to be compatible with mine. What conditions were you thinking of laying down?'

He tried to stiffen himself into a feeling that he was conquering her aloofness, but his intellect saw more clearly than did his conceit. He went on cautiously:

'You'll have to give up some of this independence of yours, Rosemary. I mean – living with another person involves give-and-take. No one can live for him or herself alone. We must all yield …'

He realised, as his voice trailed into silence, that the imperiousness had turned into weak persuasion. Rosemary was still watching him and smiling. She said gently:

'I have been married before, you know.'

He said quickly: 'Let's go.'

They walked out into the street. Rosemary was on Stephen's arm but in a way, he felt, that yielded nothing. They walked down to Piccadilly in silence. As Stephen waved for a taxi, Rosemary said:

'There isn't really a lot of point in arguing about our respective demands for marriage. I'm inclined to feel that demands are exaggerated things anyway. After all, we've been doing quite well together in the past in an undemanding way. Marriage need not throw us into the sort of gross intimacy that has demands.'

Taxis were slipping by, ignoring them. Gross intimacy! He realised, with a sense of shame, that it was just that he had been looking forward to enjoying. Obviously in Rosemary's eyes all intimacy was gross. Except the grossest of intimacies – physical intimacy – in which she seemed to take a strange, perverse delight. From the intimacies of mind and spirit she drew back, aloof and rejecting. Rejection was the foundation of her standards.

But why accept her standards? Were they any more valid for him than – say – that commissionaire's opposite would be? In himself he knew his desires and dreams were stronger and more powerful than Rosemary's negations. But in a clash the negations would always win. The rejector of life must always triumph over the acceptor. In the short run, anyway. In the long run, who knew? Dreams were so improbably durable.

He helped her into a taxi. For once, not saying anything, he felt he was achieving something.

Rosemary said: 'Well, what's it to be, Stephen?'

'Peace,' he said, quickly. 'I want peace. Rosie, can't you ever accept anything without asking questions? Why must you have everything tabulated and planned in advance? Oh, damn … Rosie, will you marry me?'

Half-turned towards him, she raised her eyebrows.

'But do you really want to, Stevie?' she asked. 'It is rather important, and you're impulsive enough to say things while you mean the opposite. And I'm not making any rash promises. This business of give-and-take and yielding … It's all right to talk about it. But who gives and who takes and who yields?'

Piccadilly emerged into the Circus, spinning with traffic, the sunlit hub of a sweltering empire. And poised above the clockwise currents of traffic, the little god of love, perpetually transfixed in the beat of the city about him. How pleasant, thought Stephen, if he should suddenly stir from his stasis and shoot an arrow to split the world!

Meanwhile a brewer's dray barred the taxi's progress. One of its two horses suddenly reared and backed, and the driver got down to hold its head and curse the reeking, clattering engines about him. The currents checked. On an impulse Stephen leaned out of the cab and bought a bunch of violets. He handed them to Rosemary.

'A small betrothal token,' he said. 'I'll get you a proper one later.'

She smiled, and he thought for a moment she might accept the gesture and with it accept the implications of that rare and brilliant world in which gesture, the prime mover, transcended the pettiness of argument and commonsense. Then her brow furrowed.

She said: 'I can't help feeling that you are avoiding things, Stephen. There are difficulties, and they must be faced. You seem to like letting things drift.'

'Not drift,' he said, ' – crystallise. There's always the germ of the future in the present. Things come out right if you let them.'

Rosemary said: 'I wouldn't be too sure of that.'

Stephen shrugged. 'They always have done for me. Everything develops. So many people try to resist development. They get twisted in resistance. It's best to go along with things.'

'Like a weather-cock?' Rosemary suggested.

'I believe in being true to myself,' he said. 'And then not being false to any man. Or woman.'

That was true, he thought warmly to himself. That is my belief. I am with the warm against the cold, with the steadfast against the temporising. My strength and warmth can cloak her too.

'We talk too much,' he said. 'I'm all for acting. How soon can we get married?'

'In three days with a special licence,' she said. 'Tuesday, if you like.'

She was very surprising. Now, when he was prepared to argue, to override and convince, her sudden acquiescence left him floundering again. Would he ever learn to trace the hard, bright illogic of her mind? Anyway, there was the child, the lovely daughter, which she must yield to him. He had no fear of losing the child to her. A child, like a flower, responds to the sun, and closes against the bewildering coolness of the moon.

He said: 'We'll make it Tuesday then. I'll see about the licence this afternoon. We could slip across the Channel for a few days afterwards, though I wouldn't like to be long away.'

'I'd rather not bother,' she said, drily. 'It wouldn't seem entirely suitable. I think it's more important to find a house, and we may not be able to get the right one so very easily. This is your place, isn't it?'

The taxi had turned up from the Strand, and was drawing in against the kerb.

Stephen said: 'Would you like to come in, or will you wait?'

'I'll wait,' she said. 'Try not to be too long. You're forgetting your despatch case. Here it is.'

He found it difficult to leave her. All the gestures he could think of seemed silly as he reviewed them against Rosemary's probable reactions. At last, feeling foolish, he tipped his hat, and hurried up the stairs to the office on the first floor.

It had not occurred to him before how entirely *bloodless* the atmosphere here was. The girl behind the glass plate labelled ENQUIRIES had presumably been just as anaemic and sallow on previous visits but now he contrasted her pale angularity with Mulready's fleshy immensity. While he waited for the girl to look up, letting his gaze roam about the cramped and dingy room, averting his eyes distastefully from the cracked bust of Cobden on the wall, Kenton's door opened and Kenton himself appeared. He came forward, tittering gently.

'Hello, Stephen. I saw you arrive from my window. Punctual as usual.' The titter broadened, almost into a laugh. 'Come right in, won't you? Excuse the mess. I was rather late back from lunch to-day, and they've been piling things on me. You know how sticky Fridays are.'

Irritably, despite himself, Stephen said: 'I can't think why you have Friday as press-day.'

'Because we come out on Tuesday,' Kenton said, weakly jovial. 'And there's the week-end in between, you know.'

'But why Tuesday?' Stephen asked, petulantly. 'Everything else comes out at the week-end.'

'Ah, yes, but the *Comment* isn't like everything else!'

The titter soared to a treble crescendo. Stephen walked over to a chair and sat down. Kenton went on, offering him a cigarette:

'Tradition, you know. We've come out on Tuesday for over a hundred years. I suppose the idea of week-end reading wasn't so important in those days. Ah, well, let's have a look at the latest.'

He reached out a hand and accepted the manuscript Stephen took from his brief-case. With a last amused snigger, he withdrew his attention from Stephen and began reading.

Stephen sat back, smoking Kenton's cigarette. A hundred years of Tuesdays … Weak sunlight filtered in through the high, narrow windows, palely marking the gold titling on the rows of bound volumes on the wall. During that century of Tuesdays there had been more vigorous sunshine, for the rich olive green of the later volumes gave way by degrees to the faded grey of the early ones. When the *Comment* first started, George III had been on the throne, the poor mad king who was flogged for his madness. Now none could lay hands on an imbecile orphan without encountering the wrath of society. A century of progress? No doubt Kenton would claim some credit for the *Comment* in the change!

Kenton read through the papers quickly, folding each back in turn. Now, closing the folder, he leaned across to Stephen.

'Would you mind very much,' he said, 'if we don't use this?'

Stephen looked at him in amazement.

'Of course I'd mind,' he said. 'You don't think I spent a morning on the bloody thing just for fun, do you?'

Kenton said tolerantly: 'But I suggested to you …'

'I don't need suggestions,' Stephen replied. 'You told me when I came that I could write my own way. Damn it, I can't write any other way. I've never been able to write to dictation.'

'But *course* not,' Kenton agreed. 'You could just – keep off certain subjects for a while. Don't force yourself. After all you have tended to run Ireland into the ground lately, haven't you?'

'Perhaps you could suggest a more important subject?' Stephen asked.

Kenton smiled thinly. 'Well, there's the Trade Union question. All these strikes. And Germany. And America. But I don't need to tell you. Why not take a rest for a few weeks?'

Stephen looked round at the bound volumes fading into grey.

'I think I'd better take a permanent holiday,' he said slowly. 'I'm a hundred years out of place here.'

Kenton smiled incredulously.

'Well, take a few weeks anyway. I don't think you will be able to keep off writing.'

Stephen looked at him, suddenly hating the narrow smugness of his face.

'No, I don't suppose I will,' he said. 'But Mulready's interested.'

Kenton got up and came round in front of his desk, still smiling.

'Mulready!' he echoed. 'Well, well. From *Populus* to the *Reader* via *Comment*. Congratulations, Stephen. You certainly move.'

Stephen stood up. 'I hope the next century's as uneventful as the first for you.'

Kenton gurgled as he showed him out.

'Your wit is more lasting than your principles, Stephen,' he said. 'Don't forsake us altogether. Who knows – you might be the Prince to waken our Sleeping Beauty. You might convert us!'

Cobden leered more grotesquely. The sallow girl gazed apathetically at her switchboard. Stephen ran down the dusty stairs to the street. Rosemary opened the cab door. He climbed in beside her brittle, unwelcoming smile.

CHAPTER EIGHT

1918

Roger

THE HEADLINE declared most boldly: LLOYD GEORGE SPEECH. Below that, in smaller type, he could make out: A POPULAR DEMONSTRATION OF REJOICING. And, straining his eyes, he could see the adjoining column: THE TROOPS COME HOME.

He sang them over in his head. A POPULAR DEMONSTRATION OF REJOICING. A POP-POP-POP-ULAR DEM-DEM-DEM. POP-POP-POP-DEM-DEM-DEM-*onstration* of re*joic*ing. The train slowed down to a stop, and he got out on to South Kensington station.

He passed a paper-seller on the way out, and decided against buying one. It was all over now; the excitement, the shouting, the hysterical attempts to realise that it really had come to an end at last. Now there were only speeches and resolutions and accounts of victorious troops returning. All so very dull. POP-POP-POP-ular DEM-DEM-DEM. He wound his own joy round him like a cloak of radiance. What a glorious mood to get tight on! He lifted the bottle out of his coat pocket and brandished it cautiously. Under a flaring street light he watched the small fragments of brilliance spill away from the metal foil. He lifted the bottle and caressed it, warm from his pocket, against his cheek.

It was going to be a marvellous evening. Such friendly, such exciting, such interesting people. Such a wealth of bottles. And – his mind shying away from the thought with the nervous joy of a stallion – his own, indisputable mistress.

As he walked along Fulham Road the moon slipped free of the heavy clouds that had been hiding it and sparkled frostily over the Brompton Hospital. Its illumination flooded the quiet, dingy street, making the street lights and the late-closing shops fade into cheap, yellow flowers. He turned down towards King's Road, walking briskly through the chilling night air.

Turning the corner into Helvin Street he saw at once that the house was shining with light. The front door was open, flinging out a raw glare, savagely underlined by the nervous rhythm of ragtime music. As he got near enough to see beyond this livid turmoil of illumination, he observed that the Christmas tree Jessica had told him about was already installed in the bay-window. But its tiny lights failed against the starker radiation behind them. The throbbing rush of sound became more closely identifiable. The babble of voices that mingled with the ragtime now gained the ascendancy. Except for the blare of the trumpets and the sickening thuds of the drums, the music was lost.

He rapped on the door with his bottle, but although the party had already flooded out into the hall no one observed the gesture. As he pushed his way through to the door of the lounge, he heard Norman Danvers' gigantic voice baying out the words:

> 'C'mon an' hear, c'mon an' hear
> It's the best ban' in the lan'!'

He paused for a while in the doorway, and saw Jessica unsteadily pouring a drink. She looked up and ran towards him, kissing him drunkenly.

'Roger!' she said. 'You look *shy*. Give auntie a big kiss.'

He smelled the stale liquor in her breath as he kissed her.

'I'm not shy,' he insisted, indignantly. 'Where's Rosemary?'

Jessica leered at him.

'Now, now,' she said. 'Time an' a place. You've only just got here. I'm surprised, at your age.'

Despising her blowziness, he was still flattered by the innuendo as to his precocious boldness. If he had to be regarded as a youth it was better to be treated as a virile one, capable of offering opposition to the uniformed, beribboned mob like Norman Danvers. He crossed to the sideboard, with Jessica hanging on his arm. She poured him a glass of gin, spilling quite a lot. It ran down her dress, but she didn't bother to wipe it off.

Roger said: 'Hasn't she got here then?'

Jessica said: 'She's out in the garden with a great big officer. No, I'm joking, Roger. I just can't help telling lies when I'm drunk. When I get blotto it's even worse, because then I insist on telling the truth. You can't imagine the friendships gin has wrecked for me, Roger. Don't leave me, Roger. Rosemary hasn't got here yet. She really hasn't. I wouldn't fool you, Roger, honest I wouldn't. Aw, now you won't believe me because I told you I tell lies. But that was honest of me – to tell you that. It was, wasn't it, Roger?'

He said: 'You're too far ahead of me, Jessie. Put this bottle away somewhere, so I can have my hands free for drinking.'

She looked at him and giggled. 'Handy little hands you've got, duckie. Is that all they're good for – drinking?'

Roger said: 'Perhaps you'll find out.'

Jessica was leaning back against the sideboard, muzzily tilting her glass with one hand so that the drink almost spilled. She looked up at him and laughed, showing her teeth. Her yellow hair fell untidily across the slack lines of her face. He felt very young for a moment, and rather scared. Behind her yawned the horn of the gramophone, and now it sprayed forth clotting melody like relentless oil.

Jessica let her gaze wander into the distance over his shoulder. She began to sing the words, harshly, absently:

'If you were the only girl in the world,
And I were the only boy '

Roger felt the haunting, cloying melody pulsating the air

about him. The din seemed to slacken. One or two couples abandoned drinking temporarily to dance, with doubtful grace, on the already crowded floor space. Norman Danvers stood by the gramophone and drunkenly bellowed out the words of the song. Several other Army officers joined in with him. They had all abandoned their tunics, and Danvers had torn off his tie as well. Roger felt a spasm of hate for their smug glory.

Jessica filled his glass again and he drank, aware of the excitement of the drink pricking under his skin. Jessica watched him for a moment, and then leaned over.

'You're a nice boy, Roger,' she whispered.

Her fingers tapped along the outside of his thigh and suddenly, as though a tap had been turned on, he began to feel excited. He turned inwards to face her. The room fell away down a very long steep slope and there was only the two of them, buoyantly riding a sea of alcohol with their lust like a coloured bubble between them.

The cool, remembered voice was like a dart that pricked the bubble.

Rosemary said: 'Hello, Roger. Been here long?'

His boldness and lust melted away as he looked at her. She stood beside Jessica, dressed in a dark blue costume, smiling faintly. Her brown hair ran back immaculately into the fashionable bob.

She lit a cigarette, and offered the case to Roger and Jessica. Jessica was watching her in drunken rage. She refused a cigarette awkwardly.

'Coming to collect Baby?' she asked, thickly. 'Aren't you a little ashamed of yourself, Rosie, at your age? You sleek bitch, can't you go and get yourself a man?'

Roger felt there was something he should say, but he was frightened. He knew Jessica was eager for a scene, and he realised he could not come well out of it. He looked appealingly towards Rosemary.

She glanced at him quizzically and smiled.

'I thought Baby might be burning his fingers,' she said to Jessica.

Jessica's face crumpled, the slack lines puckering into wrinkles.

'Oh, hell!' she said. 'Hell, I hate you, Rosie. How do you get away with it? How do you manage not to be ashamed of yourself? You're as filthy as I am. You've no right to look clean.'

Roger edged back and away from the two women. Jessica scared him, and the calm contempt on Rosemary's face was not reassuring. Rosemary saw his movement and smiled.

'Would you prefer to be left with Jessica, Roger?' she asked.

He looked. Jessica staggered to a chair and fell forward, her head resting in the spilled beer on the table. She raised her head slightly for a moment and moaned. Before she dropped it again he saw that her cheek and hair were stained with the dirty liquid. He tugged Rosemary's sleeve.

'Let's get away,' he whispered. 'To your flat.'

'Don't be frightened,' Rosemary said. 'You don't look a bit handsome when you are frightened. But go if you like. I'm staying. I've only just got here.'

Roger said: 'It wasn't anything really. Jessica was just – hinting things. I wasn't doing anything myself. I can't stand her at any price.' He gestured towards Jessica, sobbing into the beer. 'She's a hag when she drinks.'

'Yes,' Rosemary said, 'but you're not really very fussy, are you, Roger?'

He said: 'Let's not fight about it, Rosemary. It's too crowded to dance. Let's go out in the garden.'

Rosemary examined him curiously.

'I do get mixed up with some funny things,' she said.

He was stung into a feeble attempt to fight back.

'Just because Jessica's made you ratty by saying you were as filthy as she is, there's no reason why you should pick on me,' he said.

The gramophone was moaning: 'You great big beautiful doll'. For a moment she looked her age. Feeling his advantage, Roger went on brutally:

'After all, Rosemary, you are thirty-five. You ought to have more self-control.'

Her face tightened and then relaxed. She smiled.

'You know, Roger,' she said, 'I keep forgetting I'm old enough to be your mother.'

Roger smiled back complacently.

'Let's go out into the garden,' he whispered. 'Let's go and see the moon.'

He took her arm and led her, unresisting, through the tangle of drunkards. With the first fine flush of intoxication on him he could feel that his whole body was more responsive to his thoughts, and his thoughts themselves clearer and more positive and assured. Norman Danvers lurched across the floor before them but instead of making way for him Roger abruptly stood still and Danvers cannoned into and off him, falling in a sprawl across a couple on a divan. He looked up, resentful but bewildered. Roger steered Rosemary out through the open French windows and into the garden.

The music, starting up again in the room behind them, had a faintly wistful note even as the trumpets brayed, through its dissipation into the cold night air. Beside him Rosemary shivered. He put a confident arm about her shoulders.

'Cold?' he asked.

She shook her head in the moonlight.

'Just realising the war is really over,' she said.

Roger said: 'Oh, the *war* ...'

He bent down to kiss her but she turned her head suddenly upwards, forcing him to withdraw. He followed her eyes. There was only the moon, racing like a virgin through the clutching ranks of clouds.

He said: 'Nice moon.'

'Fond yellow hornlight wound to the west,' Rosemary said.

Startled, Roger asked: 'What's that?'

She looked at him briefly. 'Poetry. Do you ever read poetry?'

He said defensively: 'I did at school.'

Rosemary laughed. 'School! It must seem terribly close to you. I had forgotten how close it must seem. Do you know, I can't remember a bit of what school was like? I can remember remembering, but there aren't any real memories.'

Roger said: 'I've forgotten a lot of it already.'

Not strictly true, he told himself, in slightly drunk self-confession. If only old Hippo could see him now! Hippo to come along, peering from his grotesque squatness. 'Have you prepared your Virgil, Staines?' And himself replying: 'Go away, you old fool. Can't you see I'm busy with women and drink?' Women and drink, he thought happily.

He said: 'Half a tick. I'll slip in and get a bottle of something. Don't go away, will you?'

'Nowhere to go to,' she replied, gravely.

He patted her on the shoulder and walked back into the whirlpool.

Stephen

Stephen Hallam hovered indecisively by the door. Norman had mentioned a small party, but the din swelling out through a blatantly open door was more suggestive of an orgy. He pictured, with acute, timid imagination, what it would be like to go in. The hard, curious, drunken faces examining him; and rejecting him as all too obviously not of their brand. He felt a spasm of hate for them. With a world in ruins they could find nothing better to do than gratify their appetites for drink and sex. Miners worked in black pits of despair to bring them fuel; farm labourers toiled sixteen hours a day to bring them food. And they drank and danced to this ridiculous ragtime music and fingered each other on divans. He leaned against one of the pillars that flanked the door, shivering with contemptuous hate and the raw chill of the evening.

A bass voice boomed out the words of a popular song, and he recognised it as Norman Danvers's. His hate relaxed a little. Norman would be drunk, of course, with the rest of them. That was a fault in him; he mixed so easily. Those who fashioned the future must be aloof; not capable of being dragged down into the mob by a few drinks or a friendly atmosphere. And Norman was quite uncritical. He made friends with any kind of scum.

As so often happened, his train of thought suddenly turned against him. He thought: am I pretending to despise Norman because I really envy him? It was not an easy question to answer. His mind went on, insidiously treacherous. And do I pretend to hate the rest of them in there because I envy *them*? He laughed. The idea of envying the dwellers in the maelstrom was ridiculous. But hate, surely, was a weakness? All demanding, involving emotions were weak. Only the dispassionate was strong.

But the delving miners, he thought, the scrabbling farm labourers! Without hate for the people who put them and kept them to their delving and scrabbling, how could you force your will through the tortuous, misleading arguments of liberalism? Perhaps a temporary absolution from dispassion? He smiled to himself again.

He started back behind the pillar as a figure lurched towards him down the hall. It was a woman. She staggered past, not seeing him, and made her way over to the far corner of the small patch of garden. She crouched down against the wall. He realised with horror that she was urinating.

He tried to press himself further back against the pillar, and his foot dislodged a stone.

The woman called: 'Peeping Tom! Can't a woman do her jobs in peace?'

He said, incoherently: 'I'm awfully sorry … really awfully … Norman Danvers … I was waiting … Danvers asked me to come round … my name's Hallam.'

The woman got to her feet and came across to him giggling.

'My name's Jessica,' she said. 'Nothing like a proper introduction. I don't always come out here, but there's someone being sick in the lav., and I didn't want to go up to the bathroom. Did you say Norman asked you round? He's *drunk*. Anyway, I live here. Come right in.'

He followed her through the hall into the lounge. The noise and the smell of spirits battered him. A young, plump brunette was lying on her back on the floor, wriggling her body along the carpet in time to the music. Her skirt was rucked up across her rather flabby thighs and a pigtail had fallen free across the small hills of her bust. Her face was flushed into red, maidenly innocence by her exertions. The pigtail, incongruous enough in itself, ended in a pink, girlish ribbon.

There was a shout from behind them and an officer came in waving a small funnel that dripped paraffin. He was a squat, serious-faced man, with a thick ginger moustache.

'This'll do it!' he yelled. 'If she won't get up to drink she can have it lying down. Come and lend a hand, you fellers.'

He picked up a bottle of gin and with two other officers advanced on the drunken brunette. While the others attempted to stay the rhythmic jerkings of her limbs he poured gin through the funnel into her open mouth. It ran down her chin and over her neck into the carpet.

Stephen had stopped by the door, watching. Now Jessica called him over to the other side of the room, and he carefully walked round the girl and the three officers to where she stood by the sideboard. She handed him a glass.

He said: 'I'm not sure … What is it?'

Jessica pushed it into his hand.

'Drink it. Mummy won't know.'

He took the glass, flushing. It was full of gin. He drank quickly and felt its sickly warmth on his tongue.

Jessica said: 'Like it?'

He said apologetically: 'I'm not fond of gin. I don't drink spirits much.'

Jessica leaned towards him confidentially. He retreated a little to avoid the gin that was spilling from her glass. She raised a shaky finger in his face.

'How are you for sex?' she whispered.

He blushed again, hating himself and the woman for his embarrassment. Laughing awkwardly, he said:

'Oh, about normal, I think.'

Jessica shook her head.

'Gosh, that's bad. *Normal.* That's terrible. You must have another drink. Have some Scotch if you don't like gin. Here, help yourself.'

She handed him a half-full bottle of Johnny Walker, and he held it cautiously in one hand.

'What do you do?' Jessica asked, curiously.

'Do?' he echoed. 'I – oh, I'm interested in politics. I do – political journalism.'

She squealed with shaky laughter.

'Oh, how wonderful! How wonder-under-ful! And I suppose, the Election and all that? There's a woman putting up here called – you know what – *Miss Phipps*! Miss Phipps, the Suffragette! Isn't it wonderful? I nearly went to vote for her, but I forgot what day the Election was. Tell me, did she get in?'

'The votes aren't counted until after Christmas,' he said.

Jessica did not seem to pay any attention to his reply. She stared glassily about the room for a moment and drank some more gin. The officers had abandoned the plump brunette, and she lay unmoving, her head on one side and her mouth open. Jessica pressed over against Stephen again.

'How normal are you feeling just now?' she whispered.

Stephen looked at her in bewilderment.

'I'm all for being normal now and then,' Jessica said. 'Let's go upstairs and be normal. Let's leave all these drunkards and have fun.'

He felt her fingers tapping his leg above his knee, reinforcing the suggestion of her words. He looked away from her helplessly. He thought: God, she must be mad! His most urgent need was to get away from her.

In a strained voice, he said: 'I've got to see Norman Danvers first. It's rather important.'

She looked at him petulantly. 'Important! He's drunk. Let it wait till morning.' Her voice declined into a whine. 'Don't I appeal to you at all?'

His weakness moved again into hate; hate for all these drunken, sex-mad, stupid fools, contented in their stupidity. And Norman, the swine, getting him to come round and then not being here. He smiled weakly at the woman beside him. One of her hot, sticky hands gripped his wrist.

The door behind Jessica opened and a woman came in, with Norman Danvers lumbering guiltily after her. He saw Stephen at once and came over, smiling.

'Well, Steve,' he said, heartily. 'So you got here. Have a drink of something.'

He looked at the bottle of whisky Stephen still held in his hand and laughed.

'Have a glass, anyway,' he said. 'Or are they all too small for you?'

Jessica said: 'Oh, for Christ's sake go away, Danvers, and carry on playing with that whore of yours. You're too drunk to talk sense. Run away.'

Danvers looked at her affectionately.

'Sometimes I get too drunk to sleep with women,' he said, 'but I never get too drunk to talk sense. And you shouldn't get upset with me for interrupting you. Steve isn't your type anyway. Go and get young Roger – there's a fine, young stallion for you.'

Jessica said: 'You dirty swine! That's all you think about.'

Danvers patted her on the shoulder.

'Good old Jess!' he said, approvingly. 'Get it off your chest. And now how about going down and seeing to a few more sandwiches, while Steve tells me all about the world that's fit for heroes to live in? You don't know how hungry a man of my size gets.' He leaned towards her, and whispered loudly: 'I'll come down to the kitchen soon and give you a big surprise.'

Jessica looked at him sullenly for a moment, and then laughed. She drank her glass off, and dropped it on the carpet.

'I've always got room for a few heroes,' she said. 'Don't forget that big surprise.'

Stephen looked after her incredulously.

'Is she absolutely sex-mad?' he asked.

Danvers shrugged his massive shoulders.

'Slightly,' he said. 'She's a good girl. Hell of a drinker.'

Stephen said querulously: 'I can't see what you see in this gang of wastrels, Norman. They're no good for anything. It's such a pointless life altogether. I didn't think you would go in for this sort of thing when there are important things to be done.'

Danvers regarded him carefully. 'You must not fall into the error of judging other people's needs by your own, Stephen,' he said.

Stephen said: 'Needs! Drink – and women like that.'

'Careful with me, Stephen,' Danvers said. 'I'm drunk enough now for my natural viciousness to come to the top.'

Stephen said tolerantly: 'I don't think it's vicious. It just seems weak, when …'

Danvers was gazing at him.

He said patiently: 'I didn't mean that. I meant that I might get vicious towards you. So vicious as to remind you that some of us have been doing the fighting that was a rather essential prelude to the creation of this heroic world you're so keen on building.'

'Yes, that is vicious,' Stephen said.

Danvers bowed drunkenly. 'Regrettably so. You haven't been in the trenches, Stephen my lad, and therefore you aren't really qualified to pass judgment on the foolish antics of poor bastards like myself who have. If you had done a couple of weeks at Passchendaele you would have something to get drunk and forget, too. Not that anyone blames you. Don't think that. We're all for the gentlemen of England now abed. And I'm-the-culture-they're-fighting-for.'

He took the whisky out of Stephen's hand and poured out two glasses.

'Here's to the future, anyway,' he said. 'Here's to the glorious proletariat. How do you think the Election's gone?'

Stephen said: 'It wasn't my fault I wasn't out there. I tried hard enough.'

Danvers drank and put the empty glass down.

'Don't mind us,' he said. 'Especially don't mind me. I just talk and talk. What about this Election?'

'How should I know?' Stephen asked, sulkily. 'I suppose we've lost. Everybody thinks Lloyd George is a little tin god for winning the war.'

'Good old Loud George,' Danvers said. 'You don't find them any tinnier. Ah, well, give 'em a few years …'

Stephen said: 'Have you got those papers you said you would let me have?'

'They're in my tunic,' Danvers replied. He looked round the room and grinned. 'I seem to have left it upstairs. I'll go and get it.'

All three doors to the room were open. Behind one of them the moon-clouded night impended. A willowy young man came through as Stephen watched, and crossed Danvers's path. Danvers lurchingly gave way, but the other contemptuously disregarded the invitation to find a path round and brushed heavily against him as he went towards the sideboard. Caught off balance, Danvers fell almost on top of the unconscious brunette.

Stephen said quietly: 'You shouldn't have done that.'

The young man looked at him. His face rose from the long, thin grace of his body like a small, blowzy flower; red-lipped, fat-cheeked, with a strangely aquiline nose between large brown eyes. The sort of face, Stephen reflected, that men think weak and ugly and women find so charming. One ought really to be sorry for them; almost inevitably condemned to some form of gigolo-ing. Power in sexual attraction, as in all else, must ultimately corrupt. In its way a body of that kind was a more damning indictment of whatever god were postulated than was the twisted deformity of the cripple. There was at least a chance that the cripple might be thrown back on the cultivation of his mind. But how could this one escape his destiny?

He watched the blowzy flower open. Roger said:

'He's too drunk to see where he's going.'

Behind him Danvers swayed ponderously to his feet. As Roger, carrying a bottle, made for the garden again, he barred his path. They looked at each other for a moment. Danvers said:

'You're a very careless lad, Roger. That's the second time to-night. You're a very pushing little pansy indeed. I think you'd better apologise, don't you?'

Roger said: 'Don't be an idiot, Norman. I can't help it if you're drunk.'

He spoke half-heartedly. Stephen guessed, seeing the almost imperceptible quiver running from his mouth, that he was beginning to get afraid. Norman's steady, only slightly slurred speech was so much less intoxicated than his rolling gait.

Norman said calmly: 'Leaving aside the insinuation of insanity and your inability to prevent my getting drunk, I am more than ever convinced that I shall have to turn you up and spank you if you don't provide a nice apology. You wouldn't like to be spanked in front of the ladies, would you?'

Roger flushed.

'Forget it, Norman,' he said, awkwardly.

Suddenly, with surprising litheness, he ducked under one of Danvers's arms. Danvers turned with him. Roger had almost reached the open door when Danvers kicked him. He lurched ungracefully forward and there was a crash of splintering glass.

Danvers turned away towards the stairs. Stephen went over and slipped a hand under his arm.

'Let's just make sure you haven't killed him, Norman,' he said.

Norman laughed. 'Impossible! He's straight out of Rupert Brooke – the worm that never dies. All right, let's go and see.'

They went out into the garden, where a figure was already bending over Roger, helping him to his feet. He had apparently fallen against a sheet of glass, propped beside a box. The figure – a woman – said:

'What happened?'

'Hope I've not damaged him for you, Rose Mary,' Danvers said. 'I was just teaching him how to walk. He keeps bumping into things.'

Rosemary said: 'That's a funny way to teach him, Norman.'

The cool, amused voice fascinated Stephen. He moved forward to see her more clearly. Roger got to his feet and examined himself in the light spilling out from the room. Blood was running from one hand. Danvers came forward, too, to look at it. Roger looked dumbly at the blood covering his wrist. Danvers said:

'A blighty one. And without leaving Chelsea, Roger. Better go along to the bathroom and wash it.'

The boy said: 'You won't go, will you, Rosemary?'

The cool, low-pitched voice replied: 'I won't promise anything. You've been rather a tiresome infant to-night anyway. Run along now and bathe your honourable wounds.'

Roger walked away, less gracefully than usual. Danvers said:

'Come on in, Rose Mary, and I'll introduce you to Stephen here, and we'll have a drink to celebrate the victory of the proletariat.'

She came with them back into the room.

'Why – and when?' she asked. 'And I think you've had enough.'

Stephen looked at her eagerly as the full light fell on her. Her face matched her voice; the same fascinating, aloof charm, a tang of the senses like a glass of good sherry.

Danvers said: 'Had enough? I can never have enough. I must keep the divine fire burning within me, and without liquor it goes out.'

'Fires are such tiresome things, aren't they?' Rosemary said. 'I don't think they are ever worth the trouble. So uncontrollable and – messy.'

Danvers poured himself a drink and swallowed it.

'We are all attracted to our own particular hell, Rose Mary,' he said. 'A nice, conventional hot one for me, with hundred feet flames licking round me, fed from barrels of wasted whisky. And for you a lovely, small, frozen one – the worst of Dante's – where you freeze slowly over a million, billion years.'

He poured out more whisky.

'By God, this bottle won't go to feed those flames, though! I've got a more immediate use for it.'

Stephen said: 'You said something about introducing us.'

He saw the woman glance at him curiously, and felt embarrassed but proud of having taken up Danvers's casual suggestion.

Danvers said: 'Good God, yes. Rose Mary, this is Stephen Hallam, who is going to be Commissar for Journalism after we raise the barricades in Whitehall. Stephen, this is Rose Mary Drake, Mrs Rose Mary Drake. There's no Mr Drake now, so she's fair game.'

Stephen took a small, soft hand and, greatly daring, squeezed it. Rosemary looked at him, raising her eyebrows.

'Norman always splits my name because he knows it irritates me. A lot of his other remarks are directed to the same end.'

'You do me wrong, Rose Mary,' Danvers said happily, 'you do me wrong. I would as soon irritate an iceberg. It's true that in my youth I used to do that, ad lib and willy-nilly. But when I started breaking up the polar ice cap the meteorological people came after me. And look at me now – President of the Royal Society for Protecting and Propagating Icebergs.'

Stephen said: 'You were going to fetch me those papers.'

'Straight away,' Danvers said. 'I won't even wait for a drink. You watch the iceberg while I'm away. Watch her carefully. She may look cold but …' He whistled. '*Muy caliente,* as they say in Madrid.'

'Well, that's got rid of him,' Stephen said. 'I must apologise. He's not generally so rude.'

'He's not generally so drunk,' Rosemary said, decisively. 'But you don't need to apologise for him. I've known him for some years.'

'Do you like – this sort of thing?' Stephen asked. He gestured inwards towards the room. The young brunette was still unconscious and one of the officers had gone to sleep with his head resting against her stomach. An empty bottle trailed limply from his left hand.

Rosemary followed the wave of his hand.

'I find it amusing,' she said. 'In small doses.'

Up to this point Stephen had been working out his stratagem carefully and coolly. But now he felt the tightness in his throat, his heart bumping, throbbing. He coughed and said, in a swift gabble:

'I thought – if you were fed up here – we might go for a walk – or something. It's a fine night. Not if you don't feel like it, of course. I just thought …'

She was smiling at him, half derisively.

'What about the papers Norman is fetching for you?'

More confident now, he waved his hand dismissing them.

'They're not really important. He can bring them round to me in the morning. Let's get out of here, shall we?'

Rosemary picked up a glass and slowly lifted it and drank. She turned to look at him directly. The gramophone, which had been silent for some time, began to blare again deafeningly. Across the roaring air she nodded her head slightly two or three times. Stephen watched her warily for a moment, unsure of himself. She turned away from the sideboard and picked up her handbag. Stephen followed her to the door.

Outside they turned automatically in the direction of King's Road. The din softened behind them as they walked and the raw light from the house faded into moonlight. The street lamps flickered faintly, unnecessary in the wide, shining brilliance of the night.

Rosemary said drily: 'I wonder how long the Army intends to go on celebrating its victorious feat of arms.'

'The Army?' Stephen asked.

Rosemary glanced at him. 'The representatives back there at Jessica's.'

Stephen said: 'Oh.' He paused. 'They've had a very rough time out there,' he said, judiciously. 'We oughtn't to condemn them too easily. Especially those like me who weren't out there.'

He looked at her.

'Pacifist?' Rosemary asked.

'Good Lord, no!' he said, swiftly. 'Just medical. Heart or something. So they claimed. I tried the Navy as well as the Army, but they saw through me. So …'

He lifted small, delicate hands into the moonlight.

'King's Road,' Rosemary announced. She shivered. 'It's colder than I had expected. I should have brought a coat. Could we get indoors somewhere?'

The throbbing again, the mutinous bumping, the desperate awareness of the functions of the body being controlled by a frightened, inadequate mind. He said, from a dry throat:

'My flat's just round the corner. If you'd like … to get warm – for a few minutes …'

'It's probably nearer than mine,' Rosemary said, practically. 'Mine's almost in Knightsbridge.'

The dryness, the tightness, persisted.

'Useful, though,' he said. 'Being almost in Knightsbridge, I mean.'

'It's not bad,' she agreed. 'I've not been there long. I packed Gordon off to a prep school when he was six. It's just big enough for me – and for him in the holidays.'

Surprised, he asked: 'You have a son?'

She laughed. 'Don't tell me I don't look old enough!'

Stephen said confusedly: 'No, it's not that. At least … It's difficult to think of you as a mother.'

She glanced at him obliquely. 'How do you think of me?'

As he replied he felt a queer, depressing certainty that she was quite uninterested in his answer. He said awkwardly:

'Oh, cool. And aloof.' He paused, finishing with a note of stubbornness. 'And exciting.'

Beside them the regular iron saplings of area railings misted away into the moonlight. Stephen stopped, feeling for his key.

'Here we are,' he said.

His flat was on the first floor. He showed her round it with the deprecating pride of the London cave-dweller.

'Very nice,' Rosemary confirmed. 'A bit bachelor-ish but pleasant.'

'Help yourself to books,' Stephen said. 'I'll slip in and warm some cocoa up. You do drink cocoa?'

'Immoderately,' she said.

When he came in with the cups she was sitting in one of his two armchairs, silk-stockinged feet drawn up beneath her, looking like an immature girl. She put a book down and smiled at him.

'The cocoa looks lovely,' she said.

His scheme, he told himself ruefully, could not work. She wasn't an 'easy' woman; Danvers's innuendo must have been merely drunken mischief. He laughed to himself, pitying his own absurd aspirations. To seduce on first meeting this cool, virginal goddess, the mother of a schoolboy. At least he could see the ridiculousness of it now. He shivered. How she would have flayed him if he had made that planned advance! And how rightly. And yet … The thought of those cool defences excited and paralysed him equally. He finished his cocoa regretfully.

'You're very quiet,' Rosemary said. 'I wonder what you're thinking.'

How shocked she would be if she knew. He smiled gently at her.

'More cocoa?'

She shook her head.

He said: 'I was thinking I had better be making a start towards seeing you home. I think it will be best to telephone for a taxi. It's so cold out.'

She didn't say anything at first, only gazed into the blue glow of the gas-fire.

At last she said: 'Would you pass me my handbag?'

Stephen handed it across to her. And now, he supposed, they must get ready to go. Perhaps, at least, in the taxi …

She opened the handbag, and took something out.

'I thought I had it,' she said.

Stephen looked at her curiously. 'Had what?'

She waved it at him, and settled back contentedly into the depths of the armchair.

'I always like to use my own toothbrush,' she explained.

Rosemary

Norman Danvers always hated me, she thought. Even before, when Michael was alive, he hated me. How strange. How could I hurt Michael? He was dead, all our ties and rituals broken by the bullet that killed him, beyond the Mediterranean. The others – Roger, Stephen – were unimportant. The days of keeping blind, sentimental faith with the dead were over. Life had to go on. There was hunger, and one ate. Thirst, and one drank.

At least, she thought, I never lost dignity. Not like Jessica. But Jessica, too, was caught up in that ridiculous tangle of emotion. They were all too violent. Hating passionately, loving passionately, twisted and torn by forces out of their control. How stupid it all was. Jessica in Venice, as though she were the only woman who had ever married a man. And Jessica in Chelsea, with her undignified, sentimental lust …

What could she learn from these? All of them broken and ruined by their own appetites and guilts. But for her appetite had been natural, and she had never forced guilt on herself. What reason was there to be guilty?

She considered guilt, with a curious fascination.

Guilt like Stephen's, undermining the pretentious defences, hollowing the façade. Guilt in not having been a soldier, guilt in sleeping with a woman, guilt in being financially independent, guilt – at last – in being alive. Was that the model for her, the lesson to learn? Was she to abandon her inviolability for that?

There was no answer from the surrounding emptiness. She gathered herself, unyielding, into deeper concentration. She would not submit to the absurdity.

They were the weak; she was the strong, in the strength of her own secure, enclosed remoteness. What could she learn from weakness?

There was Michael. In a way, carefully not understanding too obtrusively, he would have understood. They had been good years. Would they call that love? It was profitless to argue. They had been good years.

She was sliding again into the gulf of years, into the warm distortion of humanity. But this time less resentfully. Almost with eagerness, she became Michael.

CHAPTER NINE

1915

Michael

ALL THE WAY TO VICTORIA it was great fun. One of the others had brought along a bottle of rum, and although Michael only had a little of it he felt it like a lean flame licking over the straightness of his body. They sang for a time, and it was like being one throat of a many-throated animal; singing, all singing, all except the standoffish little man in the corner, self-consciously aware of his second pip. Michael thought of O.T.C. field days; it was the same kind of khaki holiday – the singing and the feeling young and free. There had been no rum then, but they had stopped at a little pub on the white road over the downs, and all the N.C.Os. had bottles of beer in the inner parlour. He leaned his head back against the dusty red plush that lined the compartment and roared like the rest with happiness.

Outside Bromley the train stopped for a while, and on either side there were orchards; green and silent and fruitful under the sun. He leaned out to look at them; to see the way the long, narrow avenues of grass ran away to the distance between the trees, colourful with early butterflies and dustily buzzing with small insects. Further down the train, where the men's carriages were, compartment doors opened and small figures ran out, leaping over the signal wires by the permanent way, climbing over the orchard fence, and returning with tunic pockets stuffed with green apples. Their buttons and cap badges burned like tiny suns. The train began moving slowly and they scrambled back to it, scattering apples as they ran towards the doors held open for them. One soldier's puttee had come loose as he climbed back over the fence and he ran alongside the train for a while with the khaki strip fluttering behind him. Then he was hoisted inside with the others.

From there the train ran into London without a further halt. As the town began to crowd in beside the line their excitement increased. Michael looked at Second-Lieutenant Jennings who was perched on the seat opposite him, an animated barrel. His red cheeks glowed roundly. Giggling a little, he leaned forward and tapped Michael on the knee.

'Seven full days!' he said, 'and eight full nights. Make the best of them. I'm staying at that new hotel – the Regent Palace. All the best for the boys on leave. How about you?'

Michael smiled. 'My wife and I are staying in London for two or three days; then we're going down to Hampshire for the rest. Our little boy's down there.'

Jennings laughed squeakily.

'Of course,' he said. 'You old men are all tied down to the domestic life. Me for bottles of bubbly and all the fun of the fair. They say skirts are getting shorter.' He laughed again. 'There's only one drawback.'

'What's that?'

'Going back the day the Derby's run,' Jennings said. 'I got five to one on Pommern a few weeks back. God, I'd like to get to Newmarket!'

'You could over-stay,' Michael pointed out.

'Ha-ha,' Jennings said. 'Don't want to miss that boat for the sunny south.'

'For where?'

Jennings looked secretive for a moment, but his cheeks were flushed with rum and excitement. He leaned over confidentially.

'Don't breathe a word of it. I was in Regimental Office by myself one day. Did a bit of rooting around. We're going out with a new Army to chase the Turks out of the Dardanelles.'

'Gallipoli?' Michael asked.

Jennings laughed affirmatively. 'Where you earn your V.C. before breakfast.'

The others were singing again and Jennings joined in. Michael leaned back, watching the hot slate and brick of sweltering London slip past and thinking of the Mediterranean. To see it again so soon; the dry, blue sky, the warm dust, the little waves gleaming like a million brass mirrors as their insides tilted to the sun. They might glimpse Italy, or Sicily at least, as they went by. They might even land in Italy for grouping, now that the Italians were fighting with us. Pity he couldn't take Rosemary and Gordon with him. Perhaps next year, with the war safely over ...

The long coolness of the platform moved past them, slower and slower, until it finally stopped. Michael left his bags with a porter and walked very quickly towards the barrier.

Rosemary stood away from the crowd, waiting for him. He went up to her and, lifting the veil away from her face, kissed her. Holding her he marvelled again at her lightness and slenderness.

He set her down and she adjusted her hat.

'In public, Michael,' she said. 'How indecorous the Army has made you.'

He clutched her firmly round the waist as his porter came up with the bags.

'Times have changed,' he said. 'Look, I can see both your ankles quite plainly.'

He turned to the porter.

'Find us a taxi, will you?'

She said: 'You didn't tell me how long your leave is to be.'

'I go back a week to-morrow,' he said. 'Hang on while I get a *Times*. The papers hadn't arrived when we left this morning.'

He rejoined her, struggling to open it. She said:

'Eight days. I've made reservations at the Piccadilly for three as you wired.'

He said absently, glancing through the paper:

'Three? Oh, yes. Fine. I thought we could go down to Tall-wood for the rest. How's the youngster?'

'Thriving,' she said. 'Your mother is perhaps a little too keen on hardening him to be a future officer. But the air's good for him. He loves the stables, especially.'

Michael said: 'Don't mind Mother, if you can help it. She means well. How is everything with the stables? How's Chafer? And how's this new fellow doing?'

'All right, I think,' she said. 'Of course, he's not like Hawkes.'

'I can't think why Hawkes volunteered,' Michael said. 'He must be getting on for forty. And he knew how indispensable he was.'

'You're over thirty-five yourself, darling,' Rosemary pointed out. 'And you volunteered.'

His mind appraised fumblingly, genuinely bewildered. He said, at last:

'Well, it was different, wasn't it? I was expected to.'

He concentrated again on *The Times*. Churchill seemed to have been making a hard speech over the week-end. Hard but optimistic. He wondered how much one could rely on the optimism of these politicians. Victory certain in the Dardanelles. If Jennings were to be trusted that probably meant the new Army, and he would go out with it. It would be wonderful to get the war moving again after this deadlock in France. The Government must be banking on knocking the Turks out in the autumn; and obviously the Germans couldn't hold out long after that. Perhaps this time next year it would be all over.

Rosemary, beside him, said: 'Couldn't you read *The Times* later?'

He folded the paper with a laugh.

'What a brute I am! And I haven't even told you I love you yet.'

She smiled. The porter came up standing on the running board of a taxi, and they got in.

'The Piccadilly,' Michael ordered.

The taxi moved off with a grinding roar, startling a horse between the shafts of a nearby hansom. It reared, its front hooves striking the air. Rosemary watched it fearlessly and he felt his pride in her courage. He drew her body towards him, unresisting, unobtruding. The heat, stretching in from the petrol-reeking street, was dull and heavy; unlike the clear, lazy hotness of the country. He thought of the river below Tallwood, with a pang of pleasure in the realisation that he would be seeing it in a few days. How absurd it was to stay in town at all. It was Rosemary, isolated down at Tallwood, who needed the change. He resolved to be especially attentive and careful. Take her to the opera. They were doing *Lakmé* again and she had liked it when they saw it before. When – two, three years ago? And a play if there were any worth seeing. If only the heat would break, though, until they went down to Hampshire.

Rosemary stirred towards him.

'You've forgotten all about me again, Michael,' she accused.

Tuesday was hotter still, as though life were being throttled from the town by a burning, gauntleted hand. They went shopping in the afternoon and, finding the West End almost deserted in its stifling heat, were pleased with their own courage in braving it.

Coming out of the Army and Navy Stores, where Michael had been making up his equipment, the sun was a red-hot flail. They stood under a sunshade in front of a tobacconist's, watching the heat-waves lapping round their pool of shade.

He said: 'I'm half inclined to slip back and change into something cool. This uniform's stifling.'

Rosemary looked up. 'Come under my parasol, then. Shall we go back, anyway? I don't think there's anything else.'

After months of Army life, the feeling of someone caring about him, looking after him, was delicious. Irrelevantly, he thought: poor little Jennings and his gay time in the Regent

Palace! Was it fair that one should be so fortunate as to have a wife like Rosemary, a son like Gordon, a home like Tallwood, a horse like Chafer – all of it real and waiting, a more substantial background than the shadowy, unreal foreground of service life could outbalance? Those others – some of the men in his Company – what did they have beside this? Could one expect them to fight for the meagre existences they must go back to complete?

He mopped his forehead with a handkerchief.

'Not *quite* finished shopping,' he said. 'I saw something on the way up. Just along here I believe.' He put a hand under her elbow and led her from shade into prickling heat, and back into shade again. 'Ah, here we are!'

It was a small jeweller's shop, coldly gleaming with silver and stones, swimming in coolness like a mountain pool. In the centre, resting in its satin box, there was a delicately worked silver brooch, set with diamonds. Michael pointed to it.

'Like it?'

Her face moved slightly in surprise and pleasure. It was exquisite to provoke spontaneity in her, by suddenness plunging through her delicate barrier against stimulation. He squeezed her arm happily.

She said: 'Lovely! But we can't possibly afford it.'

'We can afford anything,' Michael stated grandiloquently. He raised his arms, embracing the hot air. 'Anything. You would prefer, perhaps, a Schloss am Rhein?'

She smiled faintly. 'We can't though. You know we can't. Let's go back and get you into a suit of cool flannels.'

He looked down at her for a moment; happy, secure, wondering, anxious. He said:

'There's something I haven't told you yet. This leave. You know we weren't quite due for one. It's … We're going abroad almost at once.'

Rosemary put her hand against the window of the shop, the small palm pressed against the glass.

She asked: 'France?'

He grinned, reassuringly. 'No fear. The colonel's much too cunning a bird to land us out there.'

She said: 'Then where? Gallipoli …?'

Michael caught her hand between his own.

'Darling, it might be a hundred different places. Italy, as like as not. I'll probably spend my time drinking marsala, or lying on the sands at Lido. But you see why you must have the brooch. I may not be able to get you anything for your birthday, or even for Christmas.'

As they came out of the shop, Michael took the box from his pocket and opened it, holding it in the direct sunlight. The stones accepted the hot, lancing beams; accepted and distilled them into cool greens and blues and transient, liquid silvers. He turned it over in his fingers.

'A safety fastener. That's useful.' He held it out to Rosemary. 'Put it on now. I'd like you to wear it always.'

She said: 'We could hide it away – until you come back. You know I always feel rather silly with jewellery.' She smiled. 'I know I'm handy to hang things on. A portable Christmas tree. But now …'

He fastened it firmly on her dress, catching the scent of her perfume as he bent towards her.

'I'll try not to be gone long,' he said, 'but while I'm away you must carry on as though nothing had happened. Don't accept the war and the separation as real. The only thing real is the after-the-war; all our past and our future.'

He stepped to the edge of the pavement, feeling the stone hot beneath his feet.

'Hi, taxi!' he called. 'Taxi!'

Thick, woolly clouds had rolled up over the sky, but Wednesday seemed as hot as ever. The afternoon sagged across their shoulders like a heavy, stifling burden. Although he had changed out of uniform, Michael felt little relief. Walking through Hyde

Park was like walking along the bottom of a vast warm ocean of air; a viscosity impeding their progress as though liquid. There was a glassy, stagnant air about the Serpentine where the boats that were out drifted aimlessly in one direction or another, with few bothering to direct them. They sauntered down towards the Row.

Michael looked along its dusty emptiness, avenued by trees.

'It's going to be wonderful to get a horse under me again,' he said. 'I've missed it a lot. At times I've wished I'd taken Chafer with me and joined the Yeomanry. Though they would probably have managed to separate us anyway.'

Rosemary said: 'We could get horses out here tomorrow morning if you like.'

Michael shook his head. 'Not the same thing. I'd rather wait now. This place is for fashion, not for riding.'

They walked up towards the Achilles Statue, and were startled by the sudden burning beauty of rhododendron blossoms. They were everywhere, all colours and all shades, lividly brilliant under the monochromatic sky. And in between them, torchlike azaleas and lavender-blue lupins. Familiar, Michael thought. It reminded him ... Rosemary nudged his arm.

'Do you remember – the Villa Gambetti?'

'Of course! But they weren't rhododendrons. They were ...'

'Roses,' she completed. 'But there were azaleas and lupins. And orange blossoms.'

'And Vino Nobile di Montepulciano,' Michael added.

She smiled. 'Oh, that wine. Nobility was the last quality you could grant it. Do you think we'll ever get back there?'

'Next year,' he promised. 'I give you my most solemn undertaking. I'll arrange it personally.'

She said restlessly: 'It's hot. Michael, let's go back to Tallwood straight away. Let's go to-night. There's a train about six.'

He said gratefully: 'Are you sure? Wouldn't you prefer to stay till to-morrow? We have tickets for the opera to-night.'

'Give them away, then. Someone will want to go.'

It began to rain as they hurried down towards Hyde Park Gate; great liquid coins splashed down into the dust of the Row. Rosemary put up her parasol to protect her clothes, but by the time Michael had called a cab the rain had stopped again, leaving as the only sign of its presence the coins transmuted into large wet stars on road and pavement. The languid burden of the afternoon sagged hazily back.

In the evening, as the train travelled down towards Tallwood, the vast grey curtain of the sky began to tear and split, falling into threads and ropes and wisps of whitening cloud. Looking out of the window at one point Michael saw, far-away and unreal, a landscape brushed with sunshine; impossibly golden against the still sombre foreground. Everything in it was tinily distinct; fields, hills, a wooded slope, and farmhouses with motionless pillars of smoke above their chimney stacks. It was all suspended as though on canvas, but at the same time more real and more illusory.

The whole evening was golden by the time they reached Winchester, and small particles of gilded dust leaped in the narrow rivers of light between carriages and platform roof. Two station trucks were piled high with baskets of strawberries, and the fragrance of them stirred in the air like a cloud.

Rosemary said: 'Oh. The infant.'

Michael looked at her questioningly.

'We forgot to get any chocolate for him. Get some from the machine, will you. Chocolate cream. Have you any pennies?'

He rattled his pocket and nodded.

'Give me my ticket,' Rosemary said. 'I'll go and find Rogers and get him to take the luggage out. I do hope they got our wire in time.'

Michael watched her go, gliding smoothly away towards the barrier. He smiled to himself. ' … hope *they* got our wire … ' It was funny that Rosemary always had difficulty in knowing how to refer to his mother, even after all this time. She would go to extreme lengths to avoid saying 'Mummy'. That orphaned youth … Others, he knew, thought her haughty and remote. Norman, especially, was never really comfortable with her. His reflections swerved away. Norman! It would be fine to see him again; to walk down Far Acre with him and talk over all the things that were so much more important than this exciting but ridiculous war.

As he left the station a young lad in gaiters, grotesquely bow-legged, went through in the opposite direction. He turned for a moment to look after him. Rosemary's voice called him, and he turned again to see her sitting up in the big trap. Snowball was between the shafts, looking as woe-begone and dignified as ever. As he came up, Rosemary said:

'That was Rogers who passed you. He was getting the bags.'

'He should sit well,' Michael said. Rosemary giggled.

Michael gave her five bars of chocolate cream, retaining one. He went round to the front with it and stroked Snowball's nose. The long, melancholy head jerked up, rubbing against his arm in recognition. He broke the chocolate into small pieces, and fed Snowball with them from his open palm. On the last piece the yellow teeth nipped his flesh, and he cuffed the horse amiably. The long muzzle peered round after him as he went back to rejoin Rosemary.

Rogers fixed the luggage on and soon they were away. He was capable with the reins and managed to stir Snowball into an unusual energy. They clipped along the lanes at a good pace. Michael sat back, watching the known fields, the familiar hedges, and smelling the keen, damp scent of the countryside. It was all so familiar and yet so startlingly vivid. And then, round the last corner, there was the wall suddenly beside them and the gates looming ahead. Snowball's hooves clopped and the trap wheels crunched gently along the gravel of the drive. The close-pressing evergreen bushes opened out like a fan, and there was the lawn and the statued terrace and behind them, gleaming oddly red in the late sunshine, Tallwood itself.

Spennerby came through to the terrace as the trap drew up.

He had probably been watching the drive since Rogers left to meet the train. For the first time Michael wondered what justification there could be for a man's life being devoted to the menial service of others. Spennerby was happy enough, but could any happiness outweigh the debasement of those futile hours wasted in watching for traps to arrive; the years of darting to anticipate vague wishes and discontents? There was something ugly and insidious as well as old about the thin, stooped figure straining to lift the luggage into the house.

He said harshly: 'Drop those, Joseph. I'll take them in.'

Rosemary was beside him as he carried them into the hall. He could see Spennerby hovering uneasily in the background like a hurt puppy, unconscious of its wrongdoing and anxious to please.

Rosemary said: 'What's up? You've hurt his feelings.'

He put the bags down by the stairs.

'Will you look after them from here, Joseph?' he asked. 'There are a couple more outside. But take it easily. There's plenty of time. Don't rush yourself.'

Spennerby said devotedly: 'We thought you weren't coming till to-morrow, sir. The mistress was so pleased. She showed us the telegram.'

Damn it, Michael thought, I'm an ordinary subaltern, one of thousands. Spennerby treats me like a Turkish prince. And yet I suppose he always has done; what makes it seem so unnatural now? Perhaps the Army. The stairs creaked and he looked up quickly. His mother was coming down. He went to the bottom of the stairs to meet her.

'Mummy!' he called. 'You look splendid.'

She seemed, in fact, more vigorous than ever, despite her seventy years. Even her voice was clear and direct. She came down and held out her hands.

'How fit you look, Michael,' she said. 'I haven't seen you looking so healthy since you left the University. Are you staying with us long?'

'Only till next Tuesday, I'm afraid,' he said. 'Then we're going overseas.'

'How splendid,' she said. 'I had a letter from Cynthia to-day. John has got a D.S.O.'

Michael laughed. 'Don't expect any such vulgarity from me.'

'Don't be flippant, Michael,' his mother said. 'Things are much too earnest for flippancy. Heroism is the only answer to-day. And John is a hero.'

'So was Alfred,' he said, 'but they gassed him all the same. Mummy, I hope you don't write this sort of rot to Cynthia and Jane. These men are their husbands, not some puppets written up by a newspaper reporter.'

Rosemary said: 'Gordon? Is he all right?'

'Perfect!' Michael's mother replied. 'I've just left him sleeping. Go up and look at him, my dear.'

She led Michael towards the drawing-room.

'You must be tired, my dear. I didn't expect you so early. Dinner will be at eight as usual.'

She lived, Michael thought, in a life of multiple attitudes. A life in which heroes were always heroic and mothers so maternal that they must dash up to see their sleeping child as soon as they arrived home. But a life, another part of his mind insisted, that has been tested and has succeeded, that bears rich fruit in graciousness and achievement. The confusion, he suspected, lay in the times. Before the war he had accepted the life he lived without challenge. It was real and workable, and there was no incentive to question. After the war it might be real and workable again; things might slip into place like parts of a jig-saw puzzle, and the confusion solve itself in a richer and more stable life than ever. That richness and stability, at least, must surely come from the war. This sudden, frightening whirlpool must inevitably give way to broad, calm waters, more securely calm by reason of the universal knowledge of suffering and misery.

For now, one must live in the whirlpool, questioning as little as possible, waiting till the waters calmed about one. Mother, clinging to the past, was in her way as right as anyone could be. Tallwood was still here, an outward and visible sign of the old grace. And, yes – Chafer's in his stable, all's right with the world! Now, he thought, to complete the pattern. Mother to the sleeping child; man to the horse. How fantastic. And yet, how real a pleasure.

He said: 'Half an hour, Mummy? Do you mind if I slip round to the stables?'

She smiled approvingly. 'I'll come with you. Wait till I get my stick. No – you can be running into the kitchen for some sugar. I know you'll take it anyway.'

Rogers met them as they approached the stables, and saluted respectfully.

'I'm glad you've found time to come down, sir,' he said. 'There are one or two things I'd like to ask you about.'

'Chafer?' Michael asked eagerly.

'Him? Oh, no. The horse is all right. It's about the motor-car. You will be using it while you are down here, won't you, sir?'

'The … ? No. I shan't bother. But Chafer – Hawkes wrote just before he left that there was a sore fetlock that wasn't healing properly. How is it?'

'It was nothing much,' Rogers said. 'He's all right. I gave him more greens in his feed. Now the motor-car, sir … It's been laid up for so long. I go over it every week but an instrument like that needs using.'

'Not by me,' Michael's mother said firmly. 'Railway trains are bad enough. These – monstrosities!'

She hammered the ground with her stick.

Michael said: 'Doesn't my wife use it?'

Roger's head shook like a pear on the stalk of his body.

'She says horses don't break down, sir. But no more will a motor-car if it's properly looked after and driven. They need a bit of looking after, but so do an 'orse. You've got to 'ave an interest.'

Michael stared. 'Are you – God forbid! – comparing that mess of metal with a living, breathing horse?'

The pear quivered but stayed firm.

'It's the future, sir,' he said, obstinately.

Michael said: 'Oh, the future!'

He heard Chafer's whinny of greeting and went on into his stable. The graceful, chestnut head shook once or twice and then came down to nudge the curve of his shoulder and neck. He felt an exquisite tremor shivering through his body, making his shoulder hunch convulsively.

'This gammy leg now,' he said to Rogers.

Rogers opened the door of the stall and slipped in under the bar. He patted the horse briefly and lifted up its right front leg. He showed Michael the pastern.

'You can see, sir,' he said. 'We had it shaved. Healing beautifully now.'

'Is he all right for a trot?'

'Right as rain,' Rogers affirmed. 'But I wouldn't jump him yet.'

Michael leaned over towards the nuzzling head. Under the soft dark nose he unclasped his fist and revealed the lumps of sugar. While the horse crunched them, he examined him. In good condition and good grooming. It was a pity to lose Hawkes, but this new man was obviously no fool.

He whispered: 'Up early to-morrow, Chafer, and a canter up to the wood.'

He patted the horse again and turned away. Rogers bobbed grotesquely beside him.

'Would you like to have a look at the motor-car now?' he asked.

Michael shook his head. 'No time now, I'm afraid.'

Rogers said: 'It should be used more. It's a great waste having it idle in here.'

Michael laughed. 'I'll tell Mrs Drake you guarantee no breakdown,' he said. 'After that it's up to you.'

On Saturday morning, as Michael left the stables to go up for breakfast, he called out to Rogers:

'By the way, would you have the motor at the front at half-past ten? I'm going down to Knight's Cross for the match.'

Rogers looked grateful.

'It'll be there,' he said. 'I'll give it another going-over before then.'

'Yes,' Michael said, 'do. The ladies will be going down to watch after lunch, and I'll try to persuade them to use it too. We can't ignore the future, can we, Rogers?'

'We can't, sir,' Rogers said, quietly. 'The horse ... It's a fine animal but times are changing. I notice they're not so fond of cavalry charging over in France these days.'

'Well, at least they haven't got to the point of charging in motor-cars!' Michael said.

'No, sir,' Rogers agreed. 'Not yet.'

Michael found his mother eating toast and marmalade. He bent down and kissed her forehead.

'Rosemary?' he asked.

'She finished breakfast ten minutes ago,' his mother said. 'I believe she's gone down to the garden to cut flowers.'

'Ah,' Michael said. 'Kidneys. Are you and Rosemary coming down to the village this afternoon? I promised Rogers I would persuade you to use the motor if you were.'

She poured coffee from the gleaming jug. From outside the call of a blackbird sifted through the air, seeming to ring against the polished silver on table and sideboard.

She said: 'Never, Michael. The idea's absurd. It's not the unsafety of these contraptions I object to so much as their ludicrous appearance, and all the Rogers in the world can't alter that. If we come down we'll use the trap.'

Michael laughed. 'It's not much of a joy for ever, is it? Rogers seems to think that before long the troops will be charging the German lines in them.'

'Fantastic!' his mother said. 'They can't get from here to Winchester without breaking down.'

Michael went looking for Rosemary after breakfast. He found her at the bottom of the rose-garden, her dark hair loose to her shoulders and her arms full of roses. She protested when he kissed her.

'Careful! Don't crush them.'

He laughed. 'Roses are made for crushing. I feel fine. I had a grand run. Through the clover field Chafer was raising dew like a spray round his hooves.'

She said: 'I wish I'd come with you. Darling, it's a fine day for your cricket match. I'm sure you'll get hundreds of runs.'

He grinned. 'I might, with my Rose Mary to cheer me on.'

Her lips moved in smiling annoyance.

'Teasing again. You're the only one who ever splits my name like that. I shall call you Micky if you do it again.'

They walked slowly up to the house. At the top of the steps leading from the rose-garden to the croquet lawn, they paused and looked back. There was a light wind amongst the roses, stirring them into swaying, kaleidoscopic motion; at nearer hand it shredded the petals from a blown white rose. Michael watched it idly, his arm loosely held about Rosemary's waist. A fresh breeze, he thought, and from the east. If it doesn't get up any more I should be able to flight them nicely into the wicket from the church end. I suppose old Riley will be playing for Overton. I'd like to get his wicket again before I go out. The old devil's punished me in the past.

Rosemary's cool voice broke the silence.

'Things are always over so quickly.'

'What? Oh, my leave. Yes.'

Michael pulled her head round into the hollow of his arm.

He said casually: 'I'd like you to marry again, you know, if anything were to happen.'

She said: 'Is it – likely to?'

Michael felt the onslaught on his senses – the vastness of sky, freshness of summer breeze, exquisite touch of a wife. He grinned.

'Most unlikely! I wast not meant for death. Forget about it.'

The still morning air shook suddenly under a hammer of noise. Rogers, revving up the engine of the motor-car.

Rosemary moved delicately against him and, smelling her perfume and the scent of the roses in her arms, he thought: this is something you must try to hold against the barren days, along with the dew scattering from a horse's hooves and the feel of a cricket bat, firmly held. These – all these things – that are part of life as it has been as long as you can remember, the gracious days, the golden evening before the night.

He said, half-aloud: 'I like things that don't change. Old houses and institutions and orchards and farms.'

The tumult in the air died for a moment before restarting with larger vigour. The smell of petrol began to overpower the roses. They turned and walked back towards the house.

The match was due to start at eleven. Michael reached the green twenty minutes earlier, and saw the motor-car chug away again up the hill. He leaned against the pavilion rail, watching for the others. To-day he was going to miss none of it.

It was just on eleven when he saw a familiar figure advancing with ponderous deliberation across the green, and ran down eagerly to meet him. It was Norman Danvers.

Michael said: 'Why, Norman! I rode over on Wednesday and they told me you were likely to be in town for the next week. I thought I should miss you.'

Norman said: 'I only got back this morning. I ran into the Reverend Skape at the station and he told me you were a man short. I hope I can borrow your spare bat; I split mine the last time I played and I haven't had time to get it fixed yet.'

'How's the farming going?' Michael asked.

Norman flushed. 'That's what I've been up to town about. I'm going into the Engineers. Old Arnold has promised to look after things while the war's on.'

The Overton team were arriving. Michael, recognising some faces, looked hopefully for Riley.

He said: 'That's quite a shock, Norman. I can't say I approve. You're a damned sight more useful running that farm than you are likely to be messing about with earth-works, or whatever Engineers do.'

Norman said apologetically: 'All the rest of you had gone, Michael. And I'm no older than you are. It gets on your nerves after a while; all the waiting about while other men go and do things. Married men, with children. I've got no ties now Joan's dead.' His voice dropped slightly. 'I haven't the same enthusiasm for the farm now.'

Michael said: 'Just selfishness on my part, Norman. I like to think of everything staying stationary while I'm away; a sort of idealised village and house and country waiting in a trance for the day of my return. I forget other people have lives too.'

'They told me you were going out,' Norman said. 'Happy about it?'

Michael looked at him. 'Reasonably. About the same as you and being in the Engineers, I suppose. As long as someone is doing it we don't want to miss anything.'

'Yes, I suppose that's it,' Norman agreed. 'How does Rosemary feel about it?'

'She's worried, of course,' Michael said. 'Slip across and cheer her up a bit, if you can find the time before you go.'

Norman said: 'I'll try. But you know how I am with her. She's altogether too remote and angelic for me; we don't really get on when you're not there.'

Absently, Michael said: 'Yes, I know some people find her a little – withdrawn.'

He had noticed Riley coming up the path between the churchyard and the green.

Norman said awkwardly: 'I hope you come through all right, Mike. Look after yourself. I want to be able to look forward to seeing you riding up Far Acre for an evening's yarning.'

Michael laughed. 'We had some good times, didn't we? Do you still think there's going to be a wonderful future, as in those novels of H. G. Wells?'

Norman rocked back on his large frame, screwing the heel of his cricket-boot into the grass.

'I think there's got to be,' he said. 'Either that or this sort of hell going on year after year, pausing only long enough to renew its filthy strength.'

'But can't we go back,' Michael said, 'to last year; to the ordinary, quiet, peaceful world? And then gradually improve things from there?'

Norman countered his question. 'Do you think we can get back?'

Michael grinned. 'I don't know. But I'm going to try. I've got a stake in it – it's worth getting back to. I bet we'll find all your forebodings fail to come off. In almost no time we'll be settling back into our routines, wondering if there ever really was a war.'

'I hope you're right,' Norman said. 'If you are wrong … I don't think I could carry on farming with the world in ruins about me.'

Michael said: 'You'll be gathering the harvest next year. I'll lend a hand in my intervals from clearing the more outstanding debts on Tallwood. We'll talk it all over again.'

From the pavilion the Vicar called to them throatily.

'Ah, there you are! We're in first. I've put you third wicket down, Norman, and Michael sixth. All right?'

They sat watching, not talking much, until Norman went in. Left alone, Michael looked at his watch. A quarter to one. Fifteen minutes before lunch; it was unlikely that he would be needed in that time. He settled down again to watch. In the second over he received, Norman swept twice to the leg boundary and the Overton field spread out, whispering. The breeze was still strong and from the east. The ball was flighting well; Michael saw one ball come in under Norman's bat, wide of the off stump but dangerous. At the other end the Vicar batted impassively. The score at lunch was 51 for three.

Soon after three Knight's Cross were all out with a total of 107, to which Michael had contributed nine. He made Rosemary and his mother comfortable in chairs and went out with the rest of the field. He and Norman were together in the slips, alert in the sun and wind, while the Overton score crept up. He felt the leisurely minutes soaking into his mind; an inalienable reality of perfection. The white-flannelled figures moved in patterns, like figures at a dance. A defiance of time – a remembrance of the past, a promise of the future.

The Overton batsman glanced a ball and he dived low, catching it barely a foot from the ground.

The one perfect sound to match the scene … The clapping swelled up like a wave round the green island, falling and rising again as the departing batsman reached the pavilion.

Norman said: 'Lovely, Mike. I thought we were never getting rid of that pair.'

And the Vicar came up, smiling.

'Very nice. I think you might as well take the next over from the church end. We may get amongst them now. And it's your old friend Riley in next, isn't it?'

It was Riley coming out from the pavilion towards them, purposeful, slow, smiling. He put his hand to his cap as he got near Michael.

'Afternoon, Mr Drake. Not bowling yet?'

From the last ball of the over, Riley took a single. He faced

Michael twenty-two yards away, his cap pulled down over the brown wrinkles of his face. Michael weighed the ball in his hand, tightening his finger-grip on the seam. He ran up and delivered; medium-fast on the off stump. Riley blocked carefully. The second was in the same place, but this time Riley cut it hard just out of Norman Danvers's reach for four. The third Michael pitched short and Riley moved across to it, hitting it past cover point for two. The fourth, placed on the leg stump, he drove for another boundary.

Michael took the ball impassively as the Vicar threw it in to him. As he began to run up his fingers tightened and twisted. His arm came over and he knew it was going to pitch exactly on the spot he wanted.

It pitched on the off, a foot from the crease. Riley moved forward with a straight bat. Then there was the click Michael expected, and the wicket-keeper caught one of the bails as the wicket splintered asunder. Still smiling, Riley raised his bat in salute.

'You win, Mr Drake,' he said.

Michael said: 'Thanks! I've been waiting a long time.'

The wave swept exquisitely over the island, as he filled all his senses against the future.

Two days after they left Gibraltar, land appeared on the port side. Michael went on deck with the others, to watch the mist open out into brown hills, flecked with small, incredibly white villages. During boat drill at ten o'clock he looked over the heads of his detachment, beyond the purple and bronze waves, to the sun-brilliant land. When he was able to dismiss them he went to the rail again and strained his eyes towards Sicily. It was fading into the distance when lunch was called.

After lunch the land was a shadowy, brown mist again, slipping by hour after hour, fading to nothing and gradually reappearing. Not until evening did the hills build up again as the troopships moved in towards Taranto. Michael thought excitedly: perhaps a diversion to the Italian front or, at least, a stay here. A week, even a few days …

At seven o'clock he could pick out Taranto quite clearly. With glasses he could see the town beyond the harbour. He watched it hungrily until, just after eight, he was quite sure the troopships were going straight on. For the last time Italy faded into the mist. He stayed at the rail until it was impossible to distinguish it from the other clouds that were rising in long grey bars over the horizon.

At first his mind was petulant. Not even an overnight stay in Taranto harbour where, at least, there would be the boats piled up with fruit – peaches and grapes and melons – as the Italians peddled them. Unfair. But he saw Jennings's red-mooned face checking the guard on the lower deck and thinking automatically: 'Poor devil!' remembered his own leave, the quiet consolidation of love and affection already achieved and known. There was all that solid attainment behind him, whatever happened.

Besides, he thought happily, I spreadeagled Riley in my first over.

As he went below the clouds were high over the vanished land.

Chapter Ten

1910

Adrian

H E HEARD VOICES CALLING for him and crouched down over the table, his arms falling across his books. For a while he sat motionless, active only in his hate for the importunate voices. He heard Cynthia's shrillness, and Michael cheerfully yelling for him through the house.

Cynthia called: 'Tried the Library?'

Lightly, cunningly, he dropped behind the heavy oak table. He heard the door open and, after a moment, swing back. Michael called back:

'Not there. I think I'll try the stables.'

Some sort of ceremony, he remembered. A betrothal? Something to do with the young woman they called Rosemary. And Michael. Michael? He rubbed his forehead, trying to remember. A sound distracted him, and he turned eagerly to look out of the window. It was a stable boy, filling a bucket with water from the pump. He was whistling, a high, piercing sound above the bubbling clatter of water against metal. There was a fine, raw mist, almost hiding the dairy, and promising heat. Michael's figure came round the corner, talking earnestly to Hawkes, and he slunk back to the table.

He ran his fingers over the beloved leather. Opening Horace, he felt his mind swim strongly in the delightful known and charted waters. The bright, sinewy vigour of the Latin was like a twisted rope of diamonds.

The words sang:

'Laeta quod pubes hedera virenti
gaudet pulla magis atque myrto
aridas frondis hianis sodali
    dedicet Hebro.'

Fixing on his spectacles, he peered at his notebook for the translation:

'In the green ivy youth will find its joy
    And in the myrtle's gleaming, dark alloy;
Like wind it blows the withered yellow leaves
    To that far land where frozen Hebrus grieves.'

Good, he thought excitedly. Oh, very good! The noblest Roman ... Ah, those days, those days!

In the high gloom, above the sombre ranks of Gibbon and Cassell's History of England, something moved, and his attention darted to it. He clambered up on to the table, kicking the notebook away with a slippered foot as he strove to follow the fleck, the movement, the gleam of darkness in the dark. Leaning over, his hands touched the top of the bookshelves and he clawed his way upwards. Crockford fell with a crash and he peered guiltily back. Then his head rose above the dusty lintel. It cowered away, six inches from his face. A mouse!

In a moment of startled fear he drew back, and the weight of his body made the row of shelves totter and strain away from the wall. He clung, shivering, while the sweat of fear started out under his arms and along his legs. The mouse was still there when he looked again, seemingly paralysed into beady-eyed immobility. He clung with his left hand while his right fished for a heavy, not unwieldy volume. Then, as fast as he could, he moved, his right arm swinging up and over like a flail. The mouse darted sideways and he struck again. Like a mad, spinning doll it leaped along the top of the bookshelves, and suddenly sprang over his shoulder to the table below. He tottered again, the sweat needling his limbs. By the time he had eased himself to the floor, the mouse had disappeared.

He began hunting for it, looking under the recesses below the books. After a few seconds he squatted back on his heels, resting. Beside him the Crockford lay where it had fallen, spine upwards and pages bent underneath. He picked it up and, settling himself with his back to the table leg, began to glance through it. Carson, Carstairs, Cartwright, Carway … Edward Carway, Bishop. Teddie Carway!

Memories surged back round him, clear-edged and vivid against the dim, unreal present of dust-crowned books and crude young voices calling through the mist. The other voices that rose round him now were young also, but clear with the winnowing of half a century. Clear, too, the acrid scent of smoke, drifting across Big Side from the Doctor's garden where the autumn leaves were burning in piles, and the mud half-frozen under his boots, and the smacking wet thudding of the ball. A punt about, he thought with sudden delight; and after, we'll have fried herrings in the den! Herrings fried in butter over the big fire, and beer saved from supper. For a moment he could feel the heat of the flames on his face as he held the frying-pan precariously over them, jostled by half-a-dozen others, baking potatoes, toasting, frying. And Carway coming out from their study, bawling for another length of candle so that he could finish his Virgil.

Carway, Bishop Carway!

There was something else about the name as well, though; something vague and recent. Had he met him again, and forgotten already? Or someone, perhaps, who knew him. Or his name in *The Times* … Teddie Carway. The term he brought back Jenning's Humanitarian Mouse-Trap and they caught mice alive and tried to tame them. A bishop …

Mice, he thought, a dim, synoptic familiarity stirring his memory. Mice … Mouse-trap … Carway … It was gone. He couldn't remember why he was sitting on the floor. The Crockford, perhaps. Getting up he replaced it, and looked for something to do.

Hesitantly he picked up the Horace. As he did he heard Michael's voice calling, cheerfully, loudly:

'Father! Are you there?'

He cowered miserably behind the table again, resenting, hating the interruptors of his quietness. He heard feet moving, and Cynthia's voice again, and Michael replying:

'We'll have to give him up for now. Come on. I'm hungry!'

They had left him. He tried to feel glad, but knew he could not. He was alone and forgotten, here among the dust and silence. The silvery jangle of a horse's bridle from the stables seemed terribly remote. He called weakly:

'I'm here. In the Library, Michael.'

No one answered. He thought petulantly: they don't care what happens to me. They want only their own diversions. These days, these shabby, run-down days ... No love, no warmth, no affection. I'll find where Teddie Carway is and spend a few days with him. We'll talk it all over. Hare-and-hounds through slippery, wet afternoons ... the rush to get in for call-over ... those savoury, fried herrings ... Carway calling for a candle. He laughed feebly. Teddie will think that funny!

He picked up his notebook and, holding it in one hand, went out of the Library towards the dining-room. He could hear the din of voices and he went towards it, half-eager, half-resentful.

They did not see him at first as he stood, deliberately pitiful and forlorn, just outside the door. There were so many of them. Cynthia and Jane, and Cynthia's fiancé, John, and Jane's husband, Alfred, and Michael's friends, the Danvers, and that girl, Rosemary ... Rosemary, he thought, the mist clearing a moment from his memory – a ceremony. She and Michael ... He looked across at her without curiosity. She was sitting quietly beside Mary.

Alfred saw him and called out in his shrill, drawling voice:

'Ah, there you are, sir. We were wondering ...'

He saw Mary's lips tighten disapprovingly, and went across to placate her. There was an empty chair beside her, and he slipped into it gratefully. Jacob came round behind him with a bottle, and poured it into a glass at his elbow. He recognised the bubbles rising through its transparency.

'Champagne!' he said delightedly.

Mary caught his arm as he reached out. She whispered fiercely in his ear:

'Propose a toast. For Michael and Rosemary.'

He looked up at her, puzzled and disturbed. So difficult to understand. He shook his head, doubtfully.

'Adrian!' she said. Her voice was low but distinct. 'It's the wedding breakfast. Michael and Rosemary. Propose a toast.'

He nodded eagerly, glad to have something he could do. He got to his feet, smiling to himself as they all turned to look at him.

'Ladies and gentlemen … This is so happy an occasion. You all know … I am sure you join with me in wishing every happiness …'

They all looked very funny, watching him from their seats. Like the mouse watching him before he flailed at it. He began to laugh weakly.

'I should tell you,' he went on, 'how I nearly caught a mouse. This morning, or … No, I'm not sure when. It stood looking at me, waiting …'

Mary was pulling his sleeve. He jerked it away from her.

'Every happiness,' he finished quickly. 'So I propose a toast to their future happiness.'

He drank the champagne and sat down. The others were talking and laughing. Ignoring them, he twisted the champagne glass in his fingers, trying to balance it at awkward angles, spinning it round between his hands. Mary reached quietly, and took it away from him. He looked across. Michael was smiling at him watchfully. He leaned over.

'Michael,' he said, 'do you remember what diocese Bishop Carway has now? I'd like to see him again. We were at school together.'

Mary began to speak, but Michael interrupted her.

'All right, Mummy. Let me. Edward Carway, Father? Don't you remember – we showed you in *The Times* a few weeks ago. He died of pneumonia.'

Adrian nodded slowly. 'Thank you, Michael. I forgot.'

Just for a while he sat with the dignity of a king above the tumbled ruins of his mind. A dreadful thing, he thought, and dreadful for Mary and the children. Forgetting Carway was dead like that. They must be ashamed of me. He felt tears gathering beneath his eyes, and hastily dabbed his nose with a handkerchief.

Putting the handkerchief back in his pocket, he stopped to look at it. He started tying knots in it, carefully and tightly.

Michael

Round the bend the Grand Canal narrowed towards the Rialto Bridge. As they drew near it the water was turning to gold until they saw, framed in the narrow arch of the bridge, the whole reach up to the Palazzo Foscari like glass sprayed with the late flame of the setting sun. They were afloat on a gilded sea, lined with palaces whose windows were vivid with crimson. It was all there in front of them, beyond the dark, lifted prow, beyond the leaning silhouette of the gondolier – an incredible river of unconsuming fire. But as the gondola moved swiftly forward the gold as swiftly retreated, becoming black, lifeless oil, rippled with green, dying away into the grim, lapping channels between the mooring-posts. The fire was always just ahead, always a promise.

From a side canal another gondola lunged out close to their own, and then slipped away behind them.

Michael said: 'Happy?'

Rosemary nodded. The gondolier began to croon a song, softly, softly, as his craft leaped on towards the retreating radiance. From somewhere a faint breeze shivered suddenly, scudding the oily darkness behind and around them into transient ripples.

She said idly: 'Do you think we could ever be happier?'

'Much happier,' Michael said with conviction. 'All this … It's charming, but not permanent. And happiness rests on permanence; the rest is only excitement at the best.'

Rosemary asked: 'Permanence?'

Michael smiled. 'Contentment of the soul, if you like. The deep peace that comes from living in a certain way – following a pattern, knowing the future through knowing the past. There will be Tallwood for us some day; I can't think of a better place for finding real happiness.'

'It's your home,' she pointed out. 'Easy enough for you to be happy there.'

Michael looked startled.

'It never occurred to me,' he said. 'Don't you like Tallwood? I hadn't thought of that.'

She smiled. 'Of course. But I'm still a stranger. Yes. I like it.'

Michael looked at her curiously. Through the quiet air the long rays of the sun stretched to gild her, but calmly, without harshness, so that she did not need to raise her parasol. The light glowed on her pale face and against the dark hair under her bonnet. She seemed to be drifting in a dream of light in which he, although sitting substantially beside her, had no part. The tense figure of the gondolier, now fallen silent again, was nearer to her, less remote than he was. He wondered … The remoteness, the dream, was real enough – but why? If he turned now to speak to her she would answer him. If he ordered the gondolier to pull in to the side, he would obey. What was there about them both that rejected him, silently, decisively?

They nosed towards another craft, and the gondolier called out in a low, liquid voice that carried across the placid water:

'A-oe! Sia stali …'

Rosemary stirred, moving against him on the narrow seat.

She said: 'Your friends – the Danvers, all of them … They don't really like me. They put up with me because of you. But that's all a part of why I would hate to be by myself at Tallwood.'

Michael said: 'You won't be by yourself there. I shall be with you when you go. It's really a matter of getting used to the place; its slowness and stubbornness. You will love it eventually.'

She said: 'I hope I will.'

He asked, grinning: 'Do you love me?'

Her fingers joined across his wrist, pressing lightly.

She said: 'How silly. Of course I do.'

He said: 'Then Tallwood will capture you. I'm a complete result of it.'

His eye caught the flash of liquid silver among the sheet gold ahead and he watched it until it drifted dully past them into the dark, a battered tin can. The doubt which had clouded him swept suddenly away. Rosemary … The gondolier … They did not reject him. How could they? The rejection had come from himself. He alone could accept or reject in a world that spun at his whim. The gondolier, hired for an hour, and Rosemary Sedgwick, newly become Rosemary Drake – each in their way puppets dancing to his pattern. He luxuriated for a while in thoughts of fantastic cruelty. The puppets must jump at his whip. When he spoke, they answered; when he commanded, they obeyed; when he contemptuously rejected them they drifted on in a dream of light, silent, gratifying his senses, lifeless until he called them back to life again.

She turned his hand over in her own.

'Of course I do,' she repeated.

He felt guilty and contrite, regretting his thoughts, wanting to call them back. He turned to Rosemary, intent with affection and interest, pointing things out to her across the wide swell of the Grand Canal. She responded to him, smiling, and he thought with relief: she doesn't know – how could she? And yet the guilt would not lift; it stayed there, immune to the new flow of affection between them. He thought greyly: I fix the pattern, even for myself. I order, I reject, I condemn, I apportion my own guilt. But who absolves? God? His mind gabbled quickly; he prayed among the lapping, liquid calm. But there was no response, no absolution. Perhaps that too could come only from himself. He thought clearly: I absolve myself. But he felt no different.

Rosemary said: 'I believe you will be glad to be back in Hampshire.'

He smiled at her, relieved that she should imagine his thoughts so far from where they were. He said:

'I shan't be sorry. We shall be going back into the summer, and things are at their best then. Winter's all right for hunting – misty, damp mornings and those afternoons when you can see everything miles away as clearly as though it were in the next field and the frost just nips your ears – but I'm a summer man. Cricket and fishing and hay-making.'

She said: 'Can you imagine what it would be like to be Venetian – this gondolier, say? To see everything against a background of these canals; everything liquid, fluid. They never freeze, do they?'

Michael laughed. 'No, they never freeze! And I couldn't possibly imagine what it would be like to be a gondolier, except that it would be pretty disgusting. Living on spaghetti and garlic and cheap vino nero. And I'm told the place smells like a sewer in the summer. Not surprising the way they throw their garbage over the garden wall into their wonderful, liquid roads.'

They saw the gondolier lean over to the right, poling vigorously. The gondola turned inwards towards gay, striped poles and wide steps leading to a high, pointed door.

Rosemary said: 'Are we there already?'

The gondolier leaned back, pointing.

'Palazz' d'Argento. Va bene?'

'Va bene,' Michael confirmed. He pulled out his watch.

'We're ten minutes early. Do you think the Craithes will mind?'

Jessica came running down the wide staircase to meet them as the Italian butler took Michael's hat and gloves. She grasped Rosemary's hands eagerly.

'The honeymooners!' she said. 'How sweet you both look. A radiance …'

Michael looked at her with surprise.

'You have the advantage over Bill and me there. We have a fresh honeymoon every year, but the first is' – her voice dropped wistfully – '… oh, I don't know! Different, somehow. We're very wise, but we're not wise thrushes. The song isn't the same the second time. Oh, Rosie, you haven't introduced me!'

Rosemary said: 'I haven't had a chance yet. But I've told you both about each other, so let's take it for granted. Jessica – Michael.'

Jessica said, frankly appraising: 'He looks charming.'

She turned to call up the stairs.

'Bill! Come down, you idler – Rosie and Michael are here.'

Michael, startled by her vivaciousness, looked at her closely. She was wearing a bright blue gown, and her yellow hair fell in girlish ringlets down her back. She returned his gaze bright-eyed; not coyly nor impudently but as though conventions of looks and glances and politenesses were quite unknown to her. He could imagine her embodying all the graces. Except, his mind added, tact, the most important of all. He summed her up – charming, impulsive, uncontrollable through ignorance of control – and thought with relief of Rosemary's decorative calm.

Rosemary said: 'Aren't we terribly early? Is no one else here yet?'

Jessica screwed her face up in attractive petulance.

'Oh, them! The others won't be here for half an hour or so. They always come late and all try to arrive at the same time. When we go out to dinner I always arrive on time, and the poor idiots don't know what to do with me. So silly. But anyway it means we can have a chat over sherry. Bill! What on earth are you up to?'

A voice cried: 'Coming, my own, my sweet.'

Half-way up, the wide stairway turned back on itself, dividing to left and right. They heard feet clattering down the left-hand stair and he appeared suddenly, running down towards them. Michael noticed a clear, rosy complexion, a small, hopeful moustache and that he was rather below average height, before he reached them, breathing heavily and bowing to Rosemary and Jessica.

Jessica said: 'Don't be silly, darling! You know Rosie, don't you? This is her new husband.' She giggled. 'I mean – oh lor' …'

They looked at each other, laughing helplessly.

Bill said: 'She's quite hopeless. You are Michael, aren't you?'

He had a pleasant, light voice and, when they shook hands, a small brisk grip. He looked, Michael thought, almost a mirror image of Jessica in lightness and sparkle. Almost; but where in her there was gay, strong elation, in him the strength was assumed, the gaiety deliberate. Her laughter was unconcerned, as though to her it really was the only valid thing about her. The laughter in him peered out, obstinately.

'Sherry!' Jessica said, gluttonously. 'Oh, Bill, darling, let's have tons and tons of sherry before the Paolinis and the rest arrive.' One hand reached for Bill and the other for Rosemary. 'Let's sneak off to the Library.'

The Library overlooked a side canal. Michael walked over and gazed down from the wide bulge of the window. The alley of water lapped against the wall on either side, flinging small sucking waves against brick and stone. Jessica came over and stood beside him.

'Isn't it exciting?' she confided. 'I love Venice. My bedroom's directly above this. I get up early in the morning sometimes and drop things – peach-stones and things – on whatever's floating by … I'm a wonderful shot.'

Michael looked at her in amazement.

She went on: 'I'm a much better shot than Bill. Aren't I, Bill?'

Bill looked embarrassed.

'Childish games,' he said.

Jessica gasped with horror. 'Oh! And you taught me!'

She pummelled him and he retreated across the room into an alcove. Watching unobtrusively, Michael saw her glance quickly across towards himself and Rosemary and then stretch up to kiss her husband. He felt shocked as though, prying on children, he had suddenly realised how childish they were.

To Rosemary he whispered incredulously:

'How long have they been married?'

He looked at her demureness with relief. To live demonstratively as those two did ... how strange. He thought of them with some unformulated envy, but more with disgust. Like children ... But adult, knowing children.

Rosemary said softly: 'Two years. No, three.'

They came back towards the window arm in arm. Michael shook his head slowly. Was there more to it than childishness? He could not believe so. It was conceivable that some might find it amusing, but surely there was something sinister and unhealthy about it?

As Jessica had foretold, the other guests arrived twenty minutes late, as though by a pre-arranged plan, and they went in to dinner. Michael found himself sitting between Signora Paolini and Mrs van Bein, garrulous respectively in broken English and hard, fast American, and was relieved when they left after the dessert. He sipped his brandy, and looked curiously at Bill Craithes. He had watched Jessica go with a blend – Michael thought – of relief and regret, and now he drank brandy quickly and greedily, and talked rather more loudly.

There were three other men. Van Bein, an American oil-man on holiday; Paolini, a vaguely landed Italian; and a strange, shabby individual with cropped grey hair and a heavy gold crucifix on his chest, who was called Harding and was presumably

English. During dinner he had sat, silently, withdrawn, refusing meat and rich dishes. He sat as silently now, but less conspicuously uninterested in his surroundings. Michael wondered how the Craitheses managed to acquire such dubious acquaintances. Van Bein seemed to be an ordinary, pleasant specimen of the crude American type; modest and arrogant in turn, deferential to a hint of age or family. Paolini was a crank, obsessed with some idea that the future belonged to electricity and motor-cars and all the other gadgets of industrialisation. The silent Harding, dressed in a worn, Napoleonic cloak, was clearly impossible.

Paolini said excitedly: 'Italy is only now rising from the chains of bondage to the church! Luzzatti is gathering strength for the final blow against all the priests who have sucked our country's blood for hundreds of years. Imagine – until a few weeks ago they even travelled cheaply on state railways …'

Van Bein, with the crushing, platitudinous comfort of the American, said:

'Hundreds of years … You know, I don't think anything that has gone on that long can be wholly bad. No, I don't believe it. All these marvellous cathedrals of yours. That St Mark certainly is something. That gold inlay … Always makes me think I'm right inside the golden egg the goose laid.' He laughed briefly. 'Yes, indeed. Right inside the golden egg.'

Paolini replied with fawning indignation: 'It is very fine for you Americans. You live in a great country with a great future; a country with millions of motor-cars and electric tramways and good sanitation. You can come here for a holiday and think how quaint a country Italy is, and how nice that there is somewhere where the romance of the old world is preserved. But what of the people who have to live here? No, we must build a new Italy, regardless of what we destroy.'

Bill Craithes said: 'First your countrymen should learn how to treat animals, Giuseppe. Over in Mestre last week I saw one brute half-killing a horse.'

'Exactly!' Paolini exclaimed. 'Exactly! They are a brutal, half-civilised lot. They ill-treat horses. But give them motor-cars instead, which they cannot ill-treat. All the horses should be sent to England, where the English can make love to them.'

Foreigners, Michael reflected, betrayed their coarseness most significantly in their attempts at humour. At the other side of the table Harding still gazed silently out into the wide dusk beyond the great windows. By his side Paolini burst into another denunciation of the Italian priesthood, who held the Italian nation back from its rightful heritage of scientific gadgetry. Bill Craithes gestured deprecatingly, and Paolini faltered in his denunciations. He turned towards Harding apologetically.

'I hope I am not deeply offending you,' he said. 'I had forgotten how seriously the English take such things.'

Harding smiled, a grim and somehow impressive smile. Speaking almost for the first time, he said:

'All Catholics are deceitful and treacherous and avaricious, but Catholic priests are the baneful, malignant fruit of that tortuous, evil tree.'

Van Bein said clumsily: 'Oh, come now. And aren't you ... ? That is ...'

Harding said: 'Yes, I am a Catholic. It is difficult to explain.'

They waited expectantly, but Harding gave no sign of making the explanation. He relapsed into staring meditation.

Bill Craithes said: 'Mr Harding is an author ...'

Harding still gazed over their heads into the relaxed and languid dusk. Michael thought: ah, an author! Why were authors always so shadily unpleasant? Unhealthy, and dressed with that shabby flamboyance. The life, perhaps ... a drab tampering with and parading of words. How wretched.

Recovering himself, Paolini broke the silence.

'Priests are like carrion crows, like vultures. They kill the countries in which they live to practise their necrophagous rites. If they could they would bring back the reign of the Borgias ...'

Harding said: 'Why not?'

Van Bein looked up, smugly uneasy. Even their age and no-bility could not justify the Borgias. He said:

'Why, they were murderers, Mr Harding. Poisoners every one of them. And more than that, they were downright immoral. I read that they even committed' – he looked round uncertainly – '… incest!'

Harding glanced at him indifferently, his blue eyes impersonal under the close-cropped head.

'Since Creation,' he said, 'there has been only one man wholly good, and none wholly bad. Who are we to condemn the Borgias, who had the courage to commit where others only wish and do not act? They lived.'

His eyes examined the other faces; Paolini's hysterical sallowness, van Bein's wrinkled simplicity, Bill Craithes's smooth roundness, Michael's stolidness.

'Do you?' he finished.

Melodramatic, Michael thought. Melodramatic and foolish. A man like that daring to imply that he knew the secret of living; of really living. A man who had never headed the field on a morning when the rain swept like gusts of cloud across meadows and fences and the hounds splashed through mud by the feet of the horses. Who had never batted stubbornly all afternoon against a good spin bowler on a pitch drying in the sun and a steady breeze. Who had never fished in the dawn on the Itchen; or danced all night at a hunt ball. Pathetic fool.

Bill Craithes knocked out his cigar and looked round.

'Are we ready to join the ladies?'

Michael watched Bill and Jessica when they met. She was almost visibly restraining herself from rushing up to embrace him; and he looked back at her with a kind of scared admiration. The difference between them, Michael reflected, was that Bill, in prep and public school, had had hammered into him the elementary principles of self-control and detachment. Some of them remained, serving as a brake against the emotional looseness in which Jessica wallowed. What would either do without the other? Bill would probably recover. A year of hopeless grief but still the vestiges of discipline to control and so, perhaps, another partner in wallowing. But Jessica – there it really would be hopeless. A convent, perhaps, if she were a Catholic. Or – more likely – this messy spiritualism business; sitting in the dark hearing imaginary Indian chiefs tell tall stories. The whole thing, he decided again, was unhealthy and unpleasant.

Jessica said excitedly: 'Oh, Bill, did you know there's a festa to-night? They will be out on the bay and the Giudecca. Franca told us. Do let's go! We haven't been on the canals during a festa since the first time we came here.'

Paolini said: 'A little festa. It only starts in the evening, this one. But the barges will be out. It should be quaint.'

He grinned maliciously at the van Beins.

Jessica said: 'Oh, darling Bill, get Toni to have the gondolas brought round.'

While Bill was away giving instructions the others crowded towards the windows opening on the Grand Canal. It was dark, and the moon had not yet risen; the gondolas drifting past were remote shadows, black against the black waters. They flickered into brief definition in the rippling lights from windows across the canal, fading away again up towards San Marco. Then a barge went by, many-oared, decked with bright lanterns and articulate with the throaty singing of Venetians. It was crowded with men and women and children.

Bill came back shaking his head.

'Here's a go,' he said. 'Alberto's sick. They're afraid of cholera. Toni packed him away to hospital without saying anything about it. That only leaves one gondolier, and I don't suppose we'll get another one to-night with a festa on.'

Jessica said: 'Poor Alberto. Oh, dear, how dreadful.'

Harding had been gazing out of the window, straining his eyes into the darkness along the canal. He turned towards Jessica.

'I should be delighted to offer my services. I am quite experienced as a *gondoliere.*'

Michael stared at him. Of course, he should know that a guest could not be permitted to do that. He might as well offer to clean the company's boots. So queer. A writer, and some queer kind of renegade Catholic, reviling his own church. My God, how unpleasant to be like that!

Jessica rushed in. 'Oh, Mr Harding … How kind of you. If you're sure you won't mind. We would so love to see the festa.'

Michael gave it up. They were all, presumably, unhinged. He looked at Rosemary for reassurance. She sat, impeccable, smiling, unruffled by the strange eddies about her.

The Paolinis and the van Beins went in the first gondola. Jessica, Bill, Rosemary and Michael were in the second, with the stooping, tattered figure of Harding at the oar. The two boats pushed away from the Palazzo d'Argento and glided out into mid-stream. All around them there was darkness; whispering, liquid, creaking night in which the dim shapes of other gondolas passed and passed. The sky above them was a battleground, fought over by clouds and stars. The stars were gaining; their freckles of light springing out thickly in the wake of the scattering clouds. And between the battleground and the liquid night, between heaven and earth, were the branching chandeliers in the great windows of the *palazzi,* spilling light like a benediction on the middle air.

In a scared voice Jessica said: 'Looking up at these palaces I sometimes think it's all a dream that we live in one ourselves. I think I'm a – a fruit-urchin, or the girl who brings fish round. And I sit and dream how wonderful it must be to really live in them. Isn't it silly?'

'Goose!' Bill said, laughing.

Michael felt another thrill of repulsion. How grotesque all this business of 'if' and 'might-have-been' always was. Women were so fond of it; seeming to find some virtue in an ability to twist the good solidity of the real world into mad, fantastic patterns. Jane, for instance, with her mania for the contorted, badly-drawn sketches of that fellow Blake. And his even more nonsensical, so-called poetry. Why? What was wrong with this world? For men of ordinary strength and will it offered all that one could wish. Perhaps that was the explanation. Women lacked that strength; and poets and artists were often weaker than women.

From the Rio san Stefano a barge nosed out into the canal, its prow almost touching the side of their gondola as it turned with them towards San Marco. It was hung with green branches and flowers like a floating garden, and the small gay lanterns bobbed everywhere. A high, clear tenor was singing *Core Ingrate,* the song rising and falling like a wave along the dark waters of the Grand Canal. Slowly the barge pulled away from them towards San Marco. Ahead they could see the lights clustering on the bay but round them there were shadows and the lapping of water.

Adrian

Cynthia watched him patiently while he finished breakfast. She didn't say anything when he crumbled the bread between his fingers; not even when, to exasperate her, he twisted it into formless blobs and left it on the table. He looked up quickly, trying to catch a sight of impatience in her eyes, but she merely smiled at him. He pushed his coffee away and stood up.

'Going to the Library, Daddy?' she asked.

That had been his intention but he was determined to refute her – refute all of their attempts to run his life and treat him like a child.

He said: 'No. I'm going down to the garden. Lewis hasn't planted those roses I wanted. I've got to see him about it.'

Cynthia said: 'You won't forget, will you?'

'Forget?' he echoed. 'Forget what?'

He watched maliciously as the mask of patience momentarily slipped and her mouth curved up in annoyance. Did he have her? Was she angry, defenceless? She controlled herself almost at once, looking at him too sweetly, too understandingly.

'Daddy, darling,' she said. 'Michael and Rosemary are coming back this morning. Don't be away too long, will you?'

He sat down again uneasily.

'This coffee's cold,' he complained.

Cynthia reached across to pour him fresh coffee and he noticed the heavy sag of her breasts. He resented her bitterly, thinking: she's acting as though she were my mother. They have all grown up and started acting parts. Even Jane a little, at times. And Michael and Cynthia aren't real at all. When they were children they were real. Mary has spoiled them. I wanted them to be children, natural.

Cynthia said: 'Please don't forget, Daddy.'

He thought, in a panic – forget what? For he had forgotten. His contempt and rage against them fell back into torturing self-pity. He had forgotten. They had the mastery of him; how could he defy them when he could not remember? Jane … The thought slipped across his clutching mind. Was it Jane? Surely it was something about Jane … He had been thinking of her only a few moments before. But what – what?

Cynthia was talking again.

'… probably not later than eleven. Hawkes is meeting the train.'

He snatched the scrap gratefully. Hawkes is meeting the train. Someone must be coming. Jane. Yes, yes, Jane is coming to stay! He could show them. He had not forgotten. Jane is coming to stay. Casually, hugging his knowledge, he said:

'Is Alfred coming too?'

She looked at him with surprise, and he knew at once that he was wrong; that he was delivered irretrievably into their hands. In confusion he picked up his cup to drink, but somehow it was hot and his hand jerked with the shock, spilling coffee down his shirt front. Cynthia came round towards him with a cloth. She wiped some of the coffee away.

'Go upstairs and change, Daddy,' she said gently, but behind her gentleness was the triumph of all of them who tried to humiliate him.

He said: 'It is! It is Jane coming!'

He pushed her hand away from him.

She said: 'No, Daddy, it's not Jane. It's Michael and Rosemary. They are coming back from their honeymoon. Their town house won't be ready for a few days and they are coming down here. You will stay in this morning, won't you?'

He felt the tears welling round his eyes as he pitied himself, too feeble to resist their subtle destructions. He remembered now. Michael and Rosemary. Not Jane, the only one who did not try to rule him. He got up and walked away unsteadily towards the door.

Cynthia called after him: 'Go up and change, Daddy. And don't forget Michael is coming. Don't forget.'

A plan lodged in his mind as he closed the door behind him. He fastened on it, narrowing it in focus, ignoring everything else as he rejoiced over it. He listened, but there was no sound from the breakfast room. He sneaked out carefully, making for the stables. He called, querulously:

'Hawkes! Hawkes!'

Hawkes came quickly out of the stables, polishing a stirrup as he walked. He said respectfully:

'Good morning, sir.'

Adrian said in a low voice: 'Get the carriage out at once, will you? I want you to drive me to the station. I'm going up to London.'

Hawkes looked at him for a moment before saying:

'Very good, sir. Won't be a moment.'

While he was waiting for Hawkes to bring the trap round he looked down guiltily at his shirt front. The coffee stain had spread badly. He rubbed it furtively with one hand. When he got to the club he could send someone out to buy him a new one. The thought pleased him. He would show them he could look after himself. He listened with triumphant confidence to the sound of hooves on the cobbles as Hawkes fitted Snowball between the shafts.

He was in a fever of impatience while Hawkes was bringing it round, afraid that at any moment Cynthia or Mary might appear and try to prevent his leaving. He would defy them. He was not a child. But he was glad when the trap appeared, and Hawkes gave him a hand to climb up. The whip cracked, and they were bowling along the drive, round past the front of the house, towards the shelter of the evergreens. He looked back quickly. Cynthia was standing at the open window of the morning room, but she made no attempt to call after him. She merely watched. He felt a chill of fear. But he was safe now.

Out in the lane he drifted into reverie, listening to the clop of hooves and the crunch of the wooden wheels. The fields were wet and green from the night's rain, but the clouds overhead were breaking fast and the air was muggy and warm. Such a morning ... He remembered. When ...?

The ploughing-match! Of course. In the Long Field. They had laughed at him for wanting to enter, but old Penniston had given him lessons every day for two months, and when the morning came he had not disgraced himself. Third, in an entry of over thirty. He could remember his own excitement, and the feel of the plough under his hands, biting into the wet clay, and the storm of birds rising and settling as the ploughs moved, smoothly and raggedly, across the field. On his second run that drunken fool, Layton, had called: 'You're crooked!' and he had looked back, and the plough had jerked against a stone and out of true. But for that he might have been first.

He said: 'Yes, I would have won but for that. I had the best furrow of them all till then, didn't I?'

Hawkes said placatingly: 'Yes, sir, that you did.'

It was all so clear, so clear! The steam rising from the horses' flanks, the mud-crust thickening under his boots, young Layton's drunken encouragements and jeers, and the birds wheeling in clouds across the living sky. This present sky, these fields, were badly drawn scrawls beside them.

He said sadly: 'Things aren't what they were, Hawkes.'

Hawkes said with sympathy: 'No, sir. They're not …'

Beside the road a wall sprang up. Adrian looked at it with confusion. Surely …

He said timidly: 'We're back at Tallwood, aren't we, Hawkes?'

'That's right, sir,' Hawkes said.

He said: 'But … But …'

There was something wrong, but he could no longer remember what it was. Perhaps if he asked Hawkes where he had been, he would tell him. But he couldn't do that. He couldn't ask the servants things like that. He must have been somewhere; he would remember soon. Ploughing … ? One of the farmers, perhaps. But why? He shook his head, trying to clear the dry mists that filled it.

It was not until he saw Cynthia waiting on the terrace that he remembered and felt again the full sorrow of his weakness. Cynthia stood by while Hawkes helped him down.

She whispered: 'Thank you, Hawkes. Take the trap round until it's time to fetch Mr Michael.'

Even the servants were against him; bribed, seduced, cozened into betraying him. All, all were against him. Why? He looked at Cynthia in bewilderment. Why did they hate and thwart him so? His own children, his wife, his servants.

He said softly: 'I cry unto thee, and thou dost not hear me: I stand up and thou regardest me not. Thou art become cruel to me; with thy strong hand thou opposest thyself against me.'

He did not protest as Cynthia put her arm round his shoulders and led him into the house.

Rosemary

The gigantic ruin of his father's imbecility striding over the order and pattern of Michael's life. A joke, she wondered angrily? But how pointless if it were. For the order and pattern had been with Michael; even then she had rejected it, and the years that followed, with their wasteful lunacy, had only pointed her rejection. No, it had been all Michael's, and his death had fulfilled it. For him the world had moved in some unguessed, unquestioned plan, cogs silently meshing and unmeshing to the rhythms of an infinite engineer, destinies known and places appointed. There had been moments of doubt, spaces when the inaudible machinery was listened for in vain, but the basis of his life had been faith. She thought regretfully: all was always well with him.

But his father – the ruin, the mindless wraith, more nearly dead on each visit to Tallwood until at last – 1911, 1912? – death accepted what life had long abandoned. What of him? Where was the pattern in that slow destruction? She remembered – yes, 1912 – the afternoon he had died, when Michael had carried him in from his seat under the ilexes, the white, drawn face anonymous like all the other dead. She remembered thinking: does that, then, go to Paradise, that slipping, furtive mind?

It had all been so easy. Paradise or Nothing; the surprising benediction or the calm oblivion. She had ordered her life with reason. No love, breeding hate. No fervour, breeding disgust. No pity, breeding cruelty. Just Calm, preparing for Calm, preparing for Nothing.

And now Nothing would not obey her. It besieged her like

an army, reminding her always that she existed; separate, inviolable, alone. She challenged it, but it did not move. She laid down her defences, but it would not invade.

The stir where nothing stirred, the tremor of movement in the immovable. Falling, falling again, through starless gulfs. From the order and security of oblivion into the chaos of the senses.

Adrian.

CHAPTER ELEVEN

1905

Adrian

CLOUDS RACED UP THICKLY in the afternoon and by three o'clock the sky was a swift flow of black and grey, racing ahead of a stiff wind from the south-west. Showers dashed in sharp, raging bursts against the windows of the study, and after each attack the broken drainpipe above poured a torrent of water just clear of the sill. At half-past three there was a diffident knock, and Joseph came in carrying the lamp that usually hung above Adrian's desk. Adrian looked at his watch.

'So early, Joseph?' he asked.

Joseph motioned with his shoulders towards the savage sky.

'It's that dark, sir. In some of the rooms you can 'ardly see your 'and. Mrs Drake had the light in 'er room an hour gone.'

Adrian sighed.

'Hang it, then,' he said, 'but don't light it. I'll light it myself when I need it.' He paused. 'Is Mrs Drake feeling – restless?'

'A little, sir,' Joseph said, discreetly. 'Miss Cynthia is reading to her from a novel. She did ring for her salts.'

He hooked the lamp quickly and went out. Adrian put down his book. Since Joseph's intervention it certainly seemed much darker, but he did not want to light the lamp yet. It was pleasant to watch the gloom gather outside in monotonous pattern of wind and cloud; undistracted himself by any light but the quiet flickering of the fire. A gust of rain rattled the window-pane with brief and hopeless siege. Charming! A pity, though, that this dark, boisterous weather always depressed Mary so. Her headaches ... But perhaps Cynthia's reading to her would cheer her up. Although the smelling-salts were an ominous sign.

He wondered where Michael could be. He had gone out directly after lunch and it was unlikely that he would have come back into the house without calling in at the study for a word or two. Probably he was moping round the stables. It would be nice if the weather cleared up for the meet to-morrow; Michael was able to get down so rarely now. It would be fine to have a good day. Cheer him out of the doldrums that working in the City must bring on. For a moment he felt slightly ashamed. It was hard on the boy to be forced into that kind of work. Perhaps if he had scraped more, planned more actively ... But no. There just wasn't the money in the estate now, and those foreign railway shares were almost an Act of God. Anyway, there it was. It was too late to do anything now. Things might yet improve; even the foreign railway shares.

He started to a faint thud, and a jerk of flame in the corner of his vision. Looking down he saw that the fire had collapsed on itself, and his hand moved automatically towards the bell-rope. He paused, clutching it. It was almost teatime, and hardly worth having the fire made up again. He let his hand fall away, relaxed.

The wind had disarranged the ivy; a strand fell like a withered serpent across the top of the window. He watched it as it jerked convulsively, the breeze continually catching it and letting it go. A dance of wet leaves whirled up in a gust of gale, quickly alive and as suddenly dead again. Exquisite, he reflected, to watch wetness and wind fighting, embracing, beyond stout windows. What a direct, simple joy in being in shelter and yet vividly aware of the storm of nature beyond. These clever scientific men and their aeroplanes ... Perhaps they would yet learn to build transparent, floating bubbles in which each man might ride the storm, secure and defiant. The future was very marvellous. But even now there was security, and the impotent, raging wind outside.

He pulled the lamp down and lit it. The soft yellow glow spread out into the corners of the room where the shadows entrenched themselves. By contrast, the landscape outside was lost at once to darkness. He could not see it but the knowledge of it being still there, primitive and untamed, made the thick glow of the lamplight more warmly embracing.

There was a knock, and Cynthia looked in.

'Tea, Daddy,' she said.

He smiled at her. 'Coming, child. Your mother ... How is her head?'

'Almost well,' Cynthia replied. 'I have been reading to her from Ouida. She has asked for muffins.'

'Muffins!' Adrian exclaimed, happily. 'I'll be there in a moment.'

He met Michael in the hall.

'Ready for tea?' he asked. He added shyly: 'I've been wondering where you were this afternoon.'

Michael waved his hands.

'I'm filthy,' he said. 'I've been with Hawkes, giving the nags a good run-over. I think Spaniard will be all right to-morrow. That swelling seems to have gone down.'

He lifted his hands again.

'Lord, I stink of horse! Father, you really will have to have a bathroom installed here.'

Adrian said mildly: 'We've managed without for three hundred years. Surely you can have a bath in your room if you want one. Shall I tell Annie to fill a bath for you?'

'No, not now. I'll make do with a lick. I'm hungry.'

He began to run upstairs, but paused half-way and looked down to where Adrian still stood in the hall.

'But you do need a bathroom now. Everyone has them.' He shrugged quickly. 'Oh, well! See you at tea.'

Mary was sitting in the big chair by the fire, the trolley beside her and Cynthia on a cushion at her feet. Adrian went across and placed a dutiful hand against her forehead.

'How is it, my love?' he asked.

'This weather,' Mary said bitterly. 'I hate the wind.'

Adrian listened. The drawing-room windows faced west and the wind rushed against them, gathering strength across the open space of the lawn to explode in creaking of wood and glass.

'It can't get at you here,' he observed.

Mary shifted impatiently.

'It's the noise,' she complained. 'And the thought of it. So nerve-racking.' She shivered. 'I wish Jane would arrive.'

Adrian bit into a muffin with delight.

'Of course! Jane's coming. Have you sent for her?'

'The trap went an hour ago,' Cynthia put in. 'The train must be late. Or perhaps she hasn't bothered to come after all.' She added bitterly: 'Jane doesn't need to obey the rules, does she?'

Mary said obtusely: 'Oh, she'll be here eventually. She's bringing friends, isn't she?'

Adrian watched Cynthia sympathetically. He said slowly:

'If you envy Jane her life in London … She *is* studying art, you know. If there is anything you would prefer to do, I will arrange it for you. Without being one of these ridiculous suffragists I see no harm in a woman studying the right kind of art or craft.'

Cynthia said quickly: 'I don't envy her a bit. I'm perfectly happy here with you and Mummy.'

Mary selected a chocolate wafer.

'Of course she is all right. Jane would have been better advised to stay here, too. She can never hope to meet the right kind of young man outside the season.'

'She's bringing one down with her,' Cynthia observed maliciously.

'We shall see what he's like,' Mary said. 'I believe he is one of the Gloucestershire Storn-Millers, though I can't imagine what he is doing at this art school. And there's a girl, too, isn't there?'

'We shall have a full house,' Adrian remarked.

Michael came in and bent to kiss his mother on the forehead. His hand wavered over the trolley.

'Muffins!' he said. 'But only two left.'

He went to the door and called: 'Annie!'

'Darling, please,' Mary said, reprovingly. 'Ring, don't shout.' She smiled in pretty apology. 'This wind – my head.'

Michael said: 'Dreadfully sorry, Mummy. Annie! Bring some more muffins, will you?'

He walked over to the window, holding his cup. The glass creaked painfully in another onslaught of furious air. He peered out into the dusk.

'What a tearer!' he observed. 'I'd quite forgotten what a good half-gale is like. London's a bad place. The air can't get at you.'

Reflecting on his guilt, Adrian winced. He said:

'I wish you could stay down here altogether.' He grinned painfully. 'I suppose someone has to retrieve the family fortunes, and I've never been trained for anything but managing the estate.'

'How is everything, by the by?' Michael inquired.

Standing with the fire behind him, Adrian leaned back cautiously until he felt the chimney-piece supporting his shoulders. The warmth from the fire was a cushion behind his legs.

'I'm selling Peaston's,' he said.

He waited anxiously for Michael's comment on the news. Michael was so directly concerned in all this that he felt as though he were springing a surprise on him; as though he ought to have consulted him before taking the step. And yet he knew that if he had written to him for advice Michael would have replied, jocularly or with surprise at being asked: You know best. In a way he now wanted him to protest, to complain that his birthright was being too lightly disposed of. But it was Mary who spoke.

She said: 'Peaston's? You didn't tell me, Adrian. It's rather close to the bone, isn't it?'

'I hope it's the last that will have to go in our time,' Adrian replied.

Mary said: 'Our time! But what about the children?'

From the window Michael said cheerfully: 'Don't you worry about the children. The land just doesn't pay any longer. It's a recreation now. The house itself and the home farm are all that are worth keeping.'

'We're nearly down to that now,' Adrian remarked ruefully. 'I suppose there's a lot in what you say. I want to believe that anyway.'

He propelled himself away from the chimney-piece and walked over, away from the warmth and subdued crackling of the flames to where Michael stood in the draught by the window, listening to the sounding lash of the wind. He said softly:

'Are you quite sure, Michael, that you don't resent my selling these farms? I've tried … Every time I hunt for alternatives, plan economies. But there aren't any alternatives and the economies seem so ridiculous and fiddling. I wouldn't like you to think I do it without considering …'

Michael laughed and placed a hand on his shoulder, and looking up at his tall son, Adrian knew at the same time contentment and an increased feeling of inadequacy. He owed the boy so much and was so excessively rewarded for the little he had given him.

Michael said: 'As long as you don't sell Spaniard on me! No, really, Father, the days when people like us could live on the land that came to us are over. It's quite a minor change really. The land is still there. It's just that now it's our duty, instead of our profit. Duty; and, of course, pleasure. In a few years I hope to be earning enough to support Tallwood comfortably.'

He turned away towards the window. Above the wind they heard the noise of the carriage; first the clipped drumming of the hooves, and then the wheels crunching nearer over gravel.

Michael said: 'Here they are at last.'

Cynthia said: 'Where? Where?' and rushed to the window

to peer out. As quickly, she turned round and darted out of the room to meet them in the hall. Michael looked after her.

'Do you suppose she gets lonely down here?' he asked.

'I think so,' Adrian said, gravely. 'But at the same time she seems to want to stay. I've offered …'

'She always did seem outside things when we played as kids,' Michael said. 'She just tagged along somehow between Jane's pretending games and my battles or hunting, not seeming to want anything herself very much.'

Mary moved her head slowly from side to side.

'This wind!' she said. 'So tormenting. Cynthia is quite happy here, Michael. I hope you won't try to persuade her of anything different. She gets plenty of companionship, too. There's the Hunt Ball next week.'

They heard a bustle of voices from the hall, and Cynthia's, rising unnaturally loud above the rest:

'Annie! Bring lots more muffins and cakes into the drawing-room. And some fresh tea.'

Mary said: 'Oh, dear!'

Adrian and Michael looked anxiously towards her. She smiled bravely. She got to her feet as Cynthia led the newcomers in. The air swarmed with introductions and recognitions; the whole quiet pattern of firelight and impotent, howling wind seemed to flare up into excitement and gradually resettle. Adrian stood apart, watching the others.

Jane had changed. There was a briskness about her and a strange, almost arrogant confidence. Where Cynthia laughed too loudly, with a quick, embarrassed vigour, Jane was amused, unruffled, her laughter darting like arrows of merriment. Beside her the young man who had been introduced as Alfred Storn-Miller watched her with high-pitched adoration. He had silky brown hair, and large brown anxious eyes. He balanced his teacup sensitively, almost with an air.

The girl, Rosemary Sedgwick, seemed lost and withdrawn in the orgy of welcoming. Adrian looked at her dark slimness sympathetically; beside Jane and Cynthia she was thin, though, he supposed, prettily so. For his part – he looked at Mary with a flash of reassurance – he preferred solidity. A brief memory tantalised him and he shuddered. Those thin, bony legs ... He walked over towards her.

'I hope you are going to stay with us for some time,' he said. 'You are studying with Jane?'

She looked at him as though suddenly aware of the room, the people, and Adrian himself.

'Yes,' she said. 'We are at the Slade together. Jane asked us to come down with her. It's very good of you to have us.'

Adrian said: 'You hunt, I suppose? There's a meet to-morrow. I think Michael has hired nags for everyone. The country is quite good here.'

'I have hunted,' she said. 'In the Shires. My guardian ...'

'Your guardian ...?' Adrian prompted.

'Yes. Alfred's father is my guardian. My parents are dead. They were drowned when I was a girl.'

'I'm sorry,' Adrian said.

He was sorry, pitying this thin girl, this orphan. He saw himself for a moment as part of a benediction which his own children possessed but this one did not; the comforting, unquestioned awareness of family. Sensing this, his pity deepened.

'And you are going to be an artist?' he suggested.

She looked at him with surprise.

'Oh, no. Just playing around. Something to do, you know. It's Alfred's brother, John, who's the gifted one.' She paused. 'I knew Jane before, you know. We were at Grail House together. And she stayed with me once at my guardian's place in London.'

Adrian was surprised. 'At Grail House? I'm surprised Jane hasn't brought you down before.'

Rosemary smiled secretly.

'We drifted,' she explained. 'School friends do. We were quite surprised when we met again.'

Adrian said, conventionally: 'I hope we shall see a lot of you in future.'

She smiled. Cynthia came over with tea for her, and Adrian turned away to listen to the wind.

On his way downstairs to breakfast Adrian looked out of the window, over the stable roofs to the east. The wind was still tearing up the carpet of dead leaves but it was impossible to tell its precise direction. He went on down and found Michael already there.

'Wind's still high,' he commented.

Michael nodded and put down his coffee. 'From the north-west, too. Bad for scent. How have they been finding so far?'

'The small bitches have been doing well,' Adrian said. 'Considering how long the drought lasted. In the last week or so as the going got soft they've had one or two really blazing runs. Their first find on Monday they took us a good four miles, right across Blagdon, and didn't check three times altogether. We'll have them to-day. The others have been behaving quite well, but they don't seem to work together the same way.'

'What was it – on Monday?' Michael asked.

'A young dog,' Adrian said. 'Not much cunning but plenty of strength. Didn't even attempt to go to ground. We ran him down on the edge of that little copse by Carford crossroads.'

Michael nodded approvingly. There was a descending clamour of voices from the stairs and Jane came in, followed by Alfred and Rosemary.

'You win by your graceful neck, Janie,' Adrian said. 'Are you all coming to hunt the wily fox? Where's Cynthia?'

'She cried off,' Michael said. 'She's staying behind with Mummy. They've both had trays sent up.'

Alfred moved over towards the fire, shivering. His face was pinched, and his nose red against the pallidness of his cheeks.

'It's cold,' he murmured. He shivered. 'Bitter!'

Adrian saw Jane watching him and tried to guess her feelings. Was she interested in this rather negligible young man? She was so difficult to understand; there was that determination of hers to stand on her own feet as though the family, and even Tallwood, were in some way a halter on her spirit. Difficult. Michael made room for Rosemary beside him, and helped her to kidneys and bacon. He contradicted Alfred cheerfully.

'Cold? Lord, no. It's only brisk. The temperature's well above freezing point; the ground will be as soft as cake. Perfect weather, if the wind would only come round a bit.'

Alfred came over from the fire and sat down. His hands were white and looked numb. He said peevishly:

'This time last year I was in Castellammare, with Vesuvius behind me, and the bay like a fantastic shimmer of sapphires in front.'

Michael looked at him hard.

'Don't come out this morning if you don't feel like it,' he said.

Alfred said quickly: 'I love hunting.' Adrian saw him dart a glance towards Jane, and he finished: 'I feel the cold keenly; that's all.'

Jane came over and sat beside him. She took his hands and chafed them between her own. Michael gave them a startled look and turned to Rosemary. A bad sign, Adrian reflected, if she habitually mothered him.

After breakfast Adrian went to his study, to glance through his mail and *The Times*. He looked down the Personal column:

'The Revd. T. Giren-Wilson, M.A., Vicar of Plaistow, urgently appeals for help for the *suffering poor*.'

Pity, he thought, how clear and lucid, how noble an emotion. Pity, by its nobility inspiring yet nobler charity. He had not yet made his donation to the Queen's Fund for the Unemployed; he would remedy it at once. He searched for his cheque-book. It was not under his papers, where he thought he had left it. He got up to look in his writing desk, but as he did his ears caught the faint clopping, and then a whinny, shattering the raw morning. He heard Michael's voice. Putting down *The Times,* he hurried out to join them.

By the time he had got his overcoat on and found his whip, the others were outside and mounted. Hawkes was holding Bucephalus for him, pulling hard on his neck to check his restiveness. Bucephalus always was restive on windy days. Adrian mounted lightly, proud of his agility for a man of nearly sixty. They set off down the drive behind Michael. As they looked back at Tallwood, sunlight splashed waterily against the front of the house, and Cynthia waved from it, her normally drab hair suddenly golden. Fine children, Adrian thought, watching Michael's conscious perfection and Jane's careless assurance. The girl, Rosemary, sat well, too, although she looked so painfully fragile. Even young Storn-Miller had a good, though rather flashy style. He rode as though the drive were the Row on a fashionable morning, too conscious of the faultless scarlet of his coat. Still, a handsome company altogether. Very pleasant, Adrian thought, after solitary hacking to the meets, to travel so gaily companied.

It was only ten to eleven when they dropped down the long slope of Otterbourne Hill towards the Galleon Inn. There was a good number there already; Lord Mornington maintained stern discipline and the field always moved off promptly. He saw Adrian and called out to him:

'Hulloa, Drake! Got the youngsters down?' He glanced critically at the little group. 'They're all with you? I'll warn McArdle not to cap' em.'

Spaniard reared as another horse came up behind, and Michael curbed him sharply. Mornington watched, approvingly.

'You haven't forgotten how to ride in the City, then,' he said. Michael flushed.

'What do you think of the scent, sir?' he asked. 'It looks rather bleak. A stiff nor'-wester and ...'

He pointed to where two of the hounds were rolling voluptuously in the grass. Mornington grinned.

'We'll see,' he said. 'Our foxes don't always bide by the rules.'

'Why,' Alfred put in, his voice drawling weakly, 'are they Leadenhallers?'

Mornington looked at him critically for a moment and rode off with a nod.

Jane said: 'Idiot! He would sooner hunt his own children than a bag-fox.' She looked amused but irritated.

Alfred said: 'I believe he would! He'd better give us a good day after that, though.'

Michael said shortly: 'It will be as good a day as you can handle.'

Promptly at eleven they moved off. It was only a little over two hundred yards to the first draw at Primrose Copse, a clump of small timber about a hundred yards across, with two good avenues of grass dividing it. The field bunched round the outside. Adrian saw Alfred edging away from the rest, presumably hoping to get a good start if a fox showed on the other side of the copse. He looked very handsome on a horse, but not entirely secure. Jane rode after him protectively. Spaniard was taxing Michael's efforts to control him.

Rosemary said: 'Do they generally find here?'

Adrian replied: 'This is our first draw this season, but it swarmed last winter. A new farmer's got the land, though, and he's not too keen on the hunt. Won't come out honestly against it for fear of offending Mornington. But he's put barbed wire down in places, and there's some talk that he's been poisoning foxes during the summer. They didn't find much in the cubbing.'

Michael had Spaniard quiet for once.

He said bluntly: 'I hate that kind of farmer. I can understand a man not liking the hunt and wanting his land clear, though any farmer with a grain of savvy can get whacking returns out of the Poultry and Damages for what trouble there is. But to put on that sickly grin of welcome and at the same time shoot foxes and wire his fences … a dirty game altogether.'

Rosemary said idly: 'I suppose fear has a lot to do with it.'

Michael laughed. 'Fear?'

Rosemary said: 'Well, I suppose the hunt could damage him in more ways than one if he were too awkward.'

Michael shook his head, bewildered. This young girl, Adrian reflected, seemed to have a far deeper, instinctive apprehension of human motives than Michael showed. And yet, as the casualness of her comments made clear, an even deeper-rooted lack of interest. It startled him a little. Detachment, indifference towards the human race, he had thought was an attribute to be gained only through the painful weathering of age. This thin dark girl seemed to enjoy it without effort.

A cold surge of air swept down the green aisle that ran through the copse and he settled, more deeply snug, into his heavy coat. But there were signs in the cloudy sky that a break might bring sunshine; away to the left a patch of blue seemed to be growing. Suddenly the blast of the horn floated back to them; the long drawn-out call that showed a blank covert. The field began to move off again, splashing through the churned-up mud of the lane that led to the next covert.

They drew two more blanks and Mornington gave the next three coverts a miss, making back towards Stoneham. As the field jogged along disconsolately, Alfred called to Michael:

'Not so brilliant so far, is it? I believe I'd rather chase Leadenhallers than stand around freezing.'

Michael said curiously: 'You look quite happy about it, though.'

He did, indeed, Adrian thought, and wondered if he were not, perhaps, glad of the blanks and the aimless jogging. At least, he flushed now, and started talking to Jane. He was still talking to her when they began drawing Saddle Gorse, and almost at once a wisp of reddish-brown darted out and clear across pasture down hill. Under the double-noted exultance of the horn half-a-dozen voices cried, raggedly:

'Tally aw-a-aey!'

Then the whole field was in rich, rewarding motion; under Mornington's cautious strategy letting the hounds make the running on their own. They were half a field ahead, and Adrian saw them tumble over the fence at the end like a black and white cataract. For a while he forgot all else in his concentration on the cantering horse beneath him, the wind strong in his face, and the tumultuous flood of hounds. He was among the leaders as they went over the first fence, and reined up at once under the admonition of Mornington's waving arm. The hounds had checked and were casting in wide, purposeful circles.

Michael reined up beside him.

'Scent must be practically non-existent,' he said. 'They're probably following her on sight.'

'A vixen?' Adrian asked. 'I barely saw it.'

One of the hounds caught the scent – Harkaway, Adrian recognised, vain of his knowledge – and they began to move with shrill yelps. But barely two fields away they checked again, and checked a third time before they ran her into a covert. Mornington called:

'Are the earths stopped in there?'

And a farmer, riding up, replied:

'All stopped, m'Lord. Saw to 'em meself.'

The wind carved the air with an iron coldness, and at its touch leaves see-sawed down in a yellow harvest. Birds rose in a startled shower, their tiny clamour striking against the chatter and the punctuating snorts of the horses. Breath soared in steaming plumes. Everything was alive and vivid and harsh with the vigour of November. Adrian leaned forward to pat Bucephalus's neck. He looked round. Michael, flushed and happy, was cursing the scent, with Rosemary, dark and smiling, very upright beside him. Further away Alfred seemed to have lost the brief excitement he had found in decrying the hunt, and was huddled against the thrusting knife of the wind, his face almost blue. Jane had reined in, commiseratingly, beside him.

Then the golden horn roared again down the frozen river of

the wind and they were off over rough country, high with wet bracken and well broken by fences. There was no checking by the hounds now; the cataract flowed without a break, with the field lengthening out behind it. Adrian saw Alfred on his right, thrusting ahead. He came to a tolerable fence and jerked his horse's head away. Adrian heard him cry: ''Ware wire!' as he hunted along for a gate. But Michael and Rosemary immediately behind him put their horses straight at the fence and cleared it well. Adrian followed them, glancing down as he felt Bucephalus lift from the ground. There was no wire in the fence.

He followed hard after his son; the field was in full gallop now and the horses had their heads. Rosemary was riding well, and he saw Michael glance at her in approval. Adrian knew he admired courage in a woman; and riding was a fair test of that as young Storn-Miller's ridiculous panic had shown. Certainly a woman who took a fence like that was a finer creature than those who spent their time gossiping and reading novels … and nursing bad heads. He recognised his own disloyalty and regretted it. But Rosemary would be a fine woman with a little more flesh on her.

A scarlet coat swept by him, followed by a black. He didn't realise who they were until he heard Michael call cheerfully:

'Make it up on the straight, Storn-Miller, by all means. Are you carrying your own wire with you?'

Jane looked back venomously at her brother and called something that was indistinguishable. Alfred himself paid no attention, though he must have heard what was said. He was urging his chestnut on as though by speed he might out-race some challenging demon. Fear, Adrian thought; or, more likely, wounded pride. A man who jibbed at a fence like that must be used to fear, but generally he might have better luck in concealing it. With charity he reflected on the disproportionate penalties of cowardice. Take a stiff fence and you might land a broken collar-bone; painful, damned painful, but then you could lie back for a while, a heroic invalid. But jib at a jumpable fence and you were utterly lost; any man's butt, safe only in hiding. How much easier the collar-bone.

The field began to bear to the left. There was a stone wall at the bottom of the hill – weathered, but still too high for jumping – and the leaders made for the gap in the left-hand corner. One rider, however, galloped straight on in the wake of the hounds who had sheered over the stones like leaping foam. Adrian barely had time to realise it was Alfred before he heard Jane's voice crying out and saw her swerve her horse to follow him. He reined in quickly, with quick apprehension cursing Michael's sarcasm.

Alfred must have heard Jane's voice just as he spurred his horse for the jump. Adrian saw him half look back before one hoof caught the top of the wall, pulling several stones down, and there was the sound of a fall from the other side. He himself was intent now on Jane as she set her horse to the wall well clear of the place where Alfred had come off. She rocked over triumphantly, a black-coated Diana. Trailing with the others through the gap, Adrian could not stem his pride in such children.

Jane was helping Alfred to his feet as they rode up. He seemed dazed and from the wide smear of mud down his clothes had obviously landed heavily on his left side. Jane wiped the dirt from his face with her handkerchief. She turned on Michael furiously as he dismounted.

She said: 'You damned, insensitive idiot! Why don't you keep your mouth shut?'

Michael looked guilty. Alfred shook himself like a terrier and grinned.

'My own stupid fault for showing off,' he said. 'And even then I didn't clear it. Let's have a look at this horse, anyway.'

The horse stood shivering a few yards away. Alfred went to it and ran his hands over it gently while they watched. He looked round at them, grinning.

'You know,' he said, 'I'm a fool to hunt. I never get any plea-sure out of it. Whenever I begin to get into a swing, something like this happens. Anyway, I think this gee's got a nasty sprain so I'm excused for the rest of the day. I'll find my way back with it. I'm more cut out for leading a wonky nag along coun-try lanes than riding a good 'un over stone walls.'

His confession seemed natural and right; it did not shock them as it should have done. Jane laughed.

'Poor old Alfred. I know how you feel. I was always the same about hockey. I'll come back with you. Don't argue. I've had enough for to-day myself, and in any case you would lose yourself in this country. We'll take it in turns to ride and lead.'

They saw Alfred and Jane on to the Chandlersford road, and then looked for the rest of the hunt. Michael stood in his stir-rups, peering into the rain-threatening distance.

He said: 'There they go – over Bishopstoke way! He's making for the rivers, I'll lay. Damnation! A check like this on what will very likely be the only good run of the day. Come on, let's find 'em.'

They came up with the field where they had checked by the ford over the first river. Mornington had the hounds casting along the banks on either side; they were a pleasure to watch, quiet and working low along the edges of the stream. A hound Adrian recognised as Iron Maiden seemed to have something for a moment, but if it were a scent she lost it almost immedi-ately. Mornington pulled out his huge hunter and consulted it. Reluctantly his huntsman called the hounds off.

With some annoyance Michael said: 'He could have given them another five minutes. It was a damned good fox.'

'Too good,' Rosemary said casually. 'If they found him now they would lose him again on the next river.'

Unpacking sandwiches, Adrian unreservedly admired her sagacity. Rare in a woman, phenomenal in a girl, and therefore the more striking. The majority of them hunted by habit and convention, chattering the whole time and almost completely ignorant of what was really happening. When she was out of earshot he said as much to Michael.

Michael munched stolidly.

'Too knowing really,' he said. 'Knowing women ... I do not approve of anything that tampers with natural ignorance.'

Adrian said with distaste: 'Oh, Wilde ... You're a worse reactionary than I am, Michael. Women are going to be clever in future; you can no more stop it than you could keep red flags in front of those confounded motor-cars. And it's not a bad thing either. The chattering of idiocies and banalities may seem attractive in girls, but as you get older you feel the need for more intelligent companionship.'

'You'll be preaching equality of the sexes next,' Michael said.

Rosemary came over as he spoke, but beyond an enigmatic smile made no comment. The strength of assurance, Adrian thought, the assurance of strength. Would she change in this so rapidly changing world? He thought: I would like to see what she's like at my age; and felt the brief sadness of knowledge that he could not. And yet, did anyone change in any real sense? Remembering his own youth, he could find no valid difference between the person he had been and the person he was. Only the outside altered, spinning across one's life like a fantastic whirligig, spoked with railways and hurtling motor-cars and airships. At the hub the man remained, puzzled or confident only in relation to his self-knowledge of his own eternal ignorance. That was the ultimate truth; the realisation that truth was unattainable. One might admire a clever, spirited girl (mentally, of course – she was thin and after all, there was loyalty...) but essentially her spiritedness could only be the measure of her superficiality. Intrinsically, she did not exist. That left one free to admire her disinterestedly, aware that one really admired a dance of coloured bubbles.

Deep waters! He was rather amused at his ageing self venturing so far out beyond the protecting arms of ordinary life. Though philosophy was commonly accepted as a province of age; and eventually he must concede the slothful years. Eventually, but not yet. Nevertheless at this time of day, with a bleak, unsuccessful morning behind and a less than promising afternoon before him, there was always a deeper pull in the thought of his quiet study and his undemanding books. I might, he thought, be eating a civilised lunch with a good wine, instead of sandwiches and a pull of brandy from a flask. And retiring afterwards to warm solitude, secure against the baffled onslaught of the weather, anchored with Livy or Tacitus. But these remained when one yielded place to others in the field and heard the hunt only in the distance on bright, wintery mornings, when the notes of the horn fell softly across the valleys, fell with the falling leaves.

In the afternoon they drew blanks again at first, but they flushed a dog-fox in the fourth covert and hunted him over three miles to a kill in the open. The sky had opened now, to a pastel, cloud-rifted sunshine, and the hounds were excited and keener after their blooding. They killed again within half an hour after a sharp, exhilarating run with some good fences for jumping, and ran another fox for a couple of miles until it went to earth in a drain. The day had changed for all of them. Adrian thought that this was the sort of afternoon he would like for his last, a finish on a high note. But not yet! He wiped the sweat from his face and listened to the furious, yelping clamour of the hounds. This too was a peak of living; more real than the aridness of philosophy and, in its impact on memory, more abiding.

They were back now on the Winchester side of Chandlersford. They drew just below Otterbourne and flushed a pair of foxes, a dog and a vixen. For a while they were in view running together, as though reluctant to be separated, but at last they saw the smaller vixen break off through sparsely-wooded ground, and the hounds followed her stronger scent. They checked once on the edge of the wood, but picked her up again when she cleared into the open. This was good country; cow-pastures with moderate thorn fences and very little wire. The unexpected efflorescence of sunshine was now discreetly fading in the west, and the air was touched with a dual crispness and dampness as it slid by their flushed faces. Adrian felt the keen benediction of the senses. Touch – the horse between his knees, the mastery as he lifted over fences. Sound – the shrill excitement of the hounds giving tongue. Smell – the late afternoon scent of wet fields and hedges. Sight – the red and black and brown and chestnut and grey and black and white, all dappled and vivid with motion against the unmoving softness of green. Here, momentarily, the years retreated, defeated by the transient moment. He set Bucephalus to a gate, and felt the response of the horse with a delight that no response of woman had ever given him.

Michael came up on his right, and with the excitement of a boy, he called:

'A good run!'

Michael shouted back: 'A good day!'

He smiled at the smiling face of his son, realising in the renewed companionship of shared exultation the artificiality of the guilt he had felt over the land sold, the birthright narrowed down. He understood at last how Michael accepted things; simply, with no need for explanations and recriminations. Life was there to be taken at its best; enjoyed like a woman, or a book, or a good wine. Argument only rendered it sterile.

He glanced round briefly. The field was strung out over more than half a mile. They were up with the leaders; Michael a couple of lengths away on his right and the withdrawn and imperturbable Rosemary just beyond. At a whim he thought: I'd like those two to marry. That calm, that assurance! Even if it's only coloured bubbles I'd like it in the family.

Up the spur of the hill, through a patch of timber, and the valley stretched before them, dim and darkening. Beyond the milling torrent of the hounds he saw a flash of brown, moving more slowly as her strange and unjust destiny yelped and barked and thudded and shouted at her heels. What have we to do with justice, he thought, answering her mute accusation with the humble pride of a god. We only live, we do not question or purpose.

Sympathetic as he was to each slight motion of the horse beneath him, he knew at once what had happened when Bucephalus began to crumple forward, dreadfully swift and yet perceptible, as though a ship were foundering. His right foreleg in a pot-hole – and a deep one, his mind added, as the collapse accelerated. He felt himself falling free and his head hit the ground and pain fastened on him out of the shadowy sky.

Someone was helping him up, out of the way of a horse that kicked in agony beside him. A man said:

'Are you all right, Father?'

He moved his head, but the pain lanced down into his neck.

He said: 'Yes. I think so. Thanks.'

It was like thinking in a fog. Something had happened. A fall. He looked at the horse, and looked away. He tried to remember the horse's name. If he could remember that, he felt, the fog would lift. But he could not remember, and the fog thickened.

It shivered as the sombre note of the *mort* floated over the hillside, but it did not lift.

CHAPTER TWELVE

1900

Jane

AFTER THREE DAYS in the house Jane felt completely at home. From the start she was predisposed towards being happy there; her escape from the schoolgirl confinement of Grail House was too recent and too complete for her to feel any other emotion. Now there was freedom. In the autumn there would be Paris. The world spun like a musical top at a flick of her fingers.

The door opened and a young man looked in. She looked up at him, half in real, half in pretty, pretended confusion. She knew them all now and knew all their names, but there was still occasional doubt in linking the two. Was it Alfred, or Robert? She smiled across the table at him. He came towards her. It was Alfred.

He said: 'Do I interrupt your writing, Janey? I'll retire at once if you want to be alone.'

'Lord, no!' she said. 'It was nothing important.'

'A *billet d'amour*?' he suggested.

She waved the paper briefly at him and he came beside her.

'Verses!' he said. 'Do let me see them, Janey. I had no idea you were a poet.'

Jane folded the paper resolutely, and put it in the front of her dress.

'I only showed you,' she declared, 'so that you would not tease me over imaginary love letters. I was merely amusing myself. They are very poor verses.'

'I am quite sure they are not,' Alfred said lazily. 'Do let me see them. You are being unfair, Janey. We always show our poems and songs and sketches to anyone.'

'Ah, but they are worth showing,' she said. 'And beside, these are only for my amusement. And it is not finished.'

'Then I shall see it when it is,' he said. He sat down on the sofa, yawning. 'How the afternoon drags. Find me something to do, Janey.'

'What are the others doing?' she asked.

Alfred stretched his arms behind his head. He recited:

'John is in the attic painting, setting on canvas the clear, serene, undisturbed grey of a May afternoon. Emily is with Mama embroidering, dutiful and diligent. Robert is playing tennis with Rosemary in the garden. Father is probably consuming coffee and cigars in a late lunch at the Carlton, furthering the cause of banking and this delightful, boring existence of ours. I, luckiest of all of them, am distracting a poetess as fair as she is gifted. And Pedro' – his gaze flicked to the large blue Persian cat on the window-ledge – 'is manifestly waiting for a bird to chip its way through the glass into his claws, being much too idle to chase one himself.'

'You should beware of chiding Pedro for idleness,' she rebuked. 'Some might find you guilty yourself. And you've forgotten someone.'

'Now who?' Alfred said thoughtfully. 'I feel much too weary to care. Ah, the gallant Hussar! Yes, Lionel is out with his soldiers. We see him so little these days that it is not surprising we should forget him so easily.'

'Will he be at dinner this evening?' Jane asked.

'I believe so,' Alfred said indifferently. 'And at the Levines' ball afterwards. If he can pull himself away from his warriors for so long.'

Jane felt a small flame of temper sear across the calm, grey afternoon.

She said: 'Really ... I don't wish to criticise, but you ...' She felt herself flushing. 'Lionel may be going out to fight. You should be less casual of him.'

Alfred looked at her, smiling.

'If it amuses him,' he said, 'to go off beyond the seas and paint the world a little redder, why should we dissuade him? Doubtless the Boers will attempt that. We are not casual of our soldier at all. We would much rather he stayed here with us, but he must please himself.'

The door opened and Rosemary came in, followed by a laughing, dishevelled Robert. Rosemary was smiling faintly and looked quite cool; all the folds of her dress in place, every ribbon neatly tied. Jane looked at her in admiration.

Robert said: 'I've beaten her! Or would have but she would not stay to finish. A mean trick. She was well beaten.'

Rosemary went over to the window and stroked Pedro with gentle hands. Robert followed her insistently.

'Do come and finish the game, Rosemary.'

Jane watched him curiously. How contradictory were his claims to have beaten Rosemary and this present pleading. Victory was strength, and strength did not plead. Strength commanded. Was Rosemary's superiority strength, then? Not truly, since she did not command. She made no claim on others.

Robert said: 'I'll give you a point in every set.'

Still stroking the cat, Rosemary smiled at him incredulously. He looked at her a moment as though testing something, and then turned away to Jane.

'You then, Jane. Do come for a game.'

Jane shook her head. 'I'm busy.'

Robert stared at the two girls, his long, mobile face now creased in petulance. From the sofa his brother drawled:

'You must play yourself, Robert. Leap from court to court, maintaining the ball in constant propulsion. Most diverting.'

Rosemary laughed softly, her head bent forward over the cat. Jane, watching, saw the petulance on Robert's face deepen into anger. He went over and caught Alfred by the sleeve, pulling his slighter body forward.

'Well, at least you shall play,' he said gaily, with a note of threat behind the gayness. He pushed him towards the door. On the threshold he looked back, calling to Rosemary:

'Watch the pussy-cat carefully. He has claws.'

Rosemary looked up briefly and smiled. Robert pulled the door loudly shut behind him.

Rosemary left the cat and came over.

'Are you busy?' she asked. 'Writing letters?'

Jane blushed. 'No, poetry. Do you – ?'

Rosemary waved her hand. 'No. Don't show me.'

She walked over to the bookcase and brought back a volume of Browning but did not open it. She sat in the place Alfred had left, the closed book on her lap.

'Are you liking it here?' she asked.

Jane nodded vigorously: 'Tremendously.'

Rosemary said: 'Don't you find the boys rather – trying, at times?'

Jane defended them. 'Oh, no. They are most pleasant. And Lionel is … charming.'

'Charming?' Rosemary asked.

Jane said: 'He's wonderfully handsome, isn't he? And a soldier. It must be so exciting to be going out to Africa.'

Rosemary said: 'Could that be the subject of the verses you have been writing? – the handsome soldier going out to the wars?'

Jane looked at her in dismay. Rosemary laughed.

'He will be in for dinner to-night,' she said, 'and will be coming round with us to the Levines' for the ball afterwards. Wearing his Hussar's uniform. You must wear your new green dress.'

'What will you wear?' Jane asked.

Rosemary shrugged. 'Oh, something, anything.'

Jane sat dreamily in an enfolding contentment. Beyond the windows the grey, immense afternoon folded like a cloth across the quiet square, the railed-in trees and the glimpse of meticulous grass. A carriage clipped along the road, its miniature thunder trailed flamboyantly before and after it. When it had gone the clock in the corner of the room ticked more distinctly, marking off seconds, scratching in the odd corners of infinity. She wondered at her own complacence, half afraid of it but indolent and relaxed despite her fear. Perhaps my age, she thought, and I will soon be like Cynthia, accepting, too stupid to challenge. But Cynthia was always like that.

Rosemary said: 'Dreaming? Of tossing plumes and an arch of swords?'

Jane said: 'No. Idiot! I was thinking …'

'You were blushing,' Rosemary pointed out.

Jane said: 'I know. I do for no reason. It's unfair. But I really was thinking. Rosemary, are we getting old yet?'

Rosemary nodded. 'Shockingly so.'

Jane said: 'It's so strange. Living in such stirring times, I mean. One ought to be more alive, more vivid. You understand?'

Glancing through the book, Rosemary said: 'I like Browning. Poetry is ridiculous if you can see what it means straight away.'

Jane stood up, sighing. She walked over to the window and laid her hand on the sleepy cat. It lowered an ear, and began purring. Across the road larch leaves flickered like a cloud of green spears against the great grey shield of the sky.

She said: 'Wouldn't it be wonderful to be a man? To go out to the Transvaal … How exciting it must be.'

She turned round, looking inwards, away from the leafy spears and the embracing sky, towards the piled domestic intricacies of the room and Rosemary, lying with half-shut eyes against the sofa. From the garden a cry drifted back. Robert or Alfred, protesting or exulting.

She continued, half-earnestly: 'I thought – didn't you? – that when we left Grail we really would be free. No more Latin, no more French. That we could do what we wanted.'

Rosemary said sleepily: 'What do you want to do?'

Jane said: 'Oh, I don't know ...'

Rosemary sat up. 'Go out to the Transvaal? How fantastic! Surely we can leave that to the men.'

Jane said pointedly: 'To those like Lionel. But anyway it's unfair.'

Above the chimney-piece hung a vast gilt frame, enclosing a picture of a broad-shouldered, moustached officer. Jane went over and looked up at it.

'That is – your guardian, isn't it?' she asked Rosemary.

Rosemary nodded. 'That's Roderick.'

Jane giggled with some embarrassment and Rosemary looked at her inquiringly.

'Your calling him Roderick,' Jane explained. 'It seems so strange. As though he were a boy, or you a staid old woman.'

'It used to be Uncle Roderick,' Rosemary said, 'but the last few times I've been back I haven't bothered with the Uncle. He doesn't seem to mind.'

Jane glanced at her, appraisingly, worshipfully. She was still the same Rosemary she had so admired at school; still calm and unruffled. That unconscious grace and mastery was more effective than mere physical charm ever could be in its effect on men. She shivered. Men. Everything related to them, as though woman were an appendage. Dared one resent it? She thought of asking Rosemary if she too were aware of this crippling comparison, but realised the futility of it. How could Rosemary be aware of anything but her own superior aloofness?

Looking up at the gold-rimmed warrior, she said:

'I could never marry a man unless I knew he were brave.'

Jane received a cup of tea from Mrs Storn-Miller's vaguely hovering hands. Her daughter, Emily, sat as usual on a cushion at her feet. Rosemary, in real as well as spiritual remoteness, sat under the window, cup and plate expertly poised. Beyond her, Jane observed, it was beginning to rain, the wide greyness dissolving into feathery, drifting spray. Rosemary looked out through it, though with no real sign of attention.

Mrs Storn-Miller said restlessly: 'The boys should be here.'

Emily made a motion to entrap Pedro, who stalked haughtily away.

She said helplessly: 'I don't know, Mama. John is painting, of course.'

Jane looked at her curiously. She was so strangely subordinated to her mother, accepting in herself blame for any of the small obstacles and hindrances that Mrs Storn-Miller found in her path. It was a futile form of atonement. She would not go and seek her brothers to allay her mother's anxiety, but would sit in an atmosphere of guilt, no less wretched for being undefined, until they came.

From the window Rosemary said: 'They are coming in now from tennis.'

Mrs Storn-Miller said: 'Oh dear, playing in the rain ...'

The door opened and John came in. He smiled at them briefly. He stood, silent and immobile, by his mother's side as she poured tea for him. He was the youngest of the brothers but, Jane thought, the eldest in his appearance. Alfred and Robert, bursting in together, were like two tousled boys.

Robert said: 'Yes, please, Mama – hot tea, and lots of sugar and milk!'

His mother said anxiously: 'You have been playing tennis in the rain. You should go upstairs first and change. And you, Alfred.'

Robert seemed disposed to obey but Alfred, to whom he looked as though for a cue, simply bent down and poured tea himself from the silver pot. Then, holding the cup, he went over to his mother and rested a hand on her shoulder.

'It barely started,' he said. 'Just a drop or two. Feel how dry my sleeve is.'

Robert watched them, his mouth slightly open. Emily, from the humility of the cushion, reached across to pour for him.

Mrs Storn-Miller rolled her head sensually backwards against her son's arm. Her plump, white face relaxed. Alfred rested his cup on the table and with his other hand stroked her forehead. He said softly as he stroked:

'It's going to rain all evening, and all night, and all to-morrow and all our to-morrow's and all our nights, until the waters rise over Kensington and the Cairngorms and up, up over the Pyrenees and the Apennines and the Alps, and at last over the Himalayas until Everest stands like a tiny, futile pinnacle above the watery waste.'

Mrs Storn-Miller closed her eyes.

'You can be so restful, Alfred,' she said.

John relaxed his immobility to carry cakes round. Jane looked up at him as he reached her and saw that he was looking directly at her; a calm, unembarrassed inquiry from steady, dark eyes. She took a cake, locking her gaze with his, but had to look away again in humiliated defeat. He went over to Rosemary, and Jane saw that his eyes were making the same unselfconscious inquiry; but Rosemary did not seem to notice anything.

'Think of it,' Alfred said, dreamily. 'Eternal starlight on unending sea.'

John rang for fresh tea and stayed by the chimney-piece as though carved, his fingers still lightly holding the tassel of the bell-rope. In that position, Jane thought, with his face tilted away towards the Dresden clock, he seemed quite handsome. But didn't he usually? She considered, remembering, picturing. The eyes, she decided at last, that dark gaze. Seeing them one knew somehow that standards of comeliness were unreliable. But now the eyes were turned away and John was an ordinary, handsome boy.

Robert closed his mouth and came over to sit beside her. She drew her skirt away from the chair and smiled to welcome him. He looked at her with admiration.

With an attempt at bravado he said: 'You must save all your dances for me to-night, Janey. I most absolutely demand it.'

She said: 'I can't promise that. But how nice of you to want them.'

Alfred still drew his hand rhythmically across his mother's forehead. He spoke in a low, crooning tone, so that Jane could barely hear him.

'Only fish ... The wink of scales in the starlight, the phosphorescent flash of fin. No animals, no birds' – he glanced indifferently towards Jane – 'no soldiers ...'

Robert looked at her, his mouth beginning to hang open again, marring those regular Storn-Miller features.

'But I shall insist,' he said, 'I shall insist.'

Mrs Storn-Miller said, from under the gentle, stirring fingers of her son:

'Do you think, Emily ... another cake? You have had three. Your figure ...'

Emily's selecting hand dropped from the cake dish, and she subsided into a small huddled paralysis of remorse. She looked towards Jane and Jane smiled sympathetically but evoked no response. Instead Emily turned away, as though embarrassed by her own temerity in seeking any human contact.

Jane saw Rosemary watching something and followed the direction of her gaze to the door, which was slowly opening. The large bearded figure of Colonel Storn-Miller appeared, enjoining silence with fingered lip. But Rosemary's clear voice said:

'Why, Roderick! You are back very early.'

How the coming changed them all. Alfred's fantastic drawling changed in an instant into servile silence. Mrs Storn-Miller turned towards her husband like a plump and startled sacrificial heifer, and Emily beneath her grovelled in new, dispirited abasement. Robert's mouth sagged further in his reddening face. Even John, shaken from his statuary by the chimney-piece, seemed humble and propitiating. Jane herself was unnerved by the unexpected majesty.

The majesty moved in front of the hearth, twisting his beard, and looked round with satisfaction. Emily sat, between his feet and her mother's, as though petrified.

Colonel Storn-Miller said: 'We had a good morning and things were quiet this afternoon, so' – he raised a gesturing, benevolent hand – 'I thought I might be in time for tea. Am I?'

Emily slid forward to her knees and poured hurriedly.

Mrs Storn-Miller said reproachfully: 'Roderick, you surprised me.'

Lifting the tea to her father's hand, Emily quivered guiltily. She said in a small voice:

'It's quite fresh. Cake, Papa?'

The Colonel accepted her ministrations. He said blandly:

'Surprise is an excellent thing, my dear, especially for the digestion. But unfortunately I was surprised myself before I could achieve my aim.'

He turned to look at his assembled children.

'How are you all?' he asked pleasantly. 'All strenuously idle, I hope?'

With some recovery of self-possession, Alfred said:

'Of course, Father. You know how you can rely on us for that.'

The Colonel walked over towards Rosemary's seat by the window. He said, over his shoulder:

'All but Lionel. Lionel takes after me in his distressing propensity for doing things. How the pair of us must disgust you.'

He looked round quickly as though watching for a sign of that disgust, but they all attended respectfully. Mrs Storn-Miller, still plump but now more composed, less sacrificial, protested:

'John has been painting all afternoon.'

Her husband said: 'Ah. Painting …'

He stood in front of Rosemary, his profile vivified by the square luxuriance of his beard. Jane watched it with interest. To feel it, rough, against the softness of her face … She refused the thought, fearing the betraying blush.

The Colonel said: 'I haven't had a chance to look at you properly since you came back. Let's see you.'

He stepped back a pace and examined her critically. Jane looked round at the boys. They maintained their respectful demeanour, like young bulls in the presence of their leader. Mrs Storn-Miller lay back, her eyes half-closed, expressionless; but beside her Emily's sympathetic unease was glaringly evident.

Rosemary said: 'I haven't changed much, have I?'

The window panes were clouding over with the fine spray of the rain that further out blunted the green spears of larch in swift, shifting gusts. How dreary this weather would be at Tallwood, Jane thought, but here in London how unimportant it was. From somewhere out of sight smoke drifted with the veils of rain across the window.

Colonel Storn-Miller said: 'No, you haven't changed. You're still pretty enough.'

He turned back towards his wife.

'What are you all doing this evening? Theatre?'

Mrs Storn-Miller said: 'A ball – at the Levines'.'

Her husband considered briefly. He put his cup down carefully on the tray.

'I may come with you,' he said. 'Change is as good as surprise. Will you excuse me now?' He looked at his sons. 'Despise work,' he said. 'Always despise it.'

As the door closed, Alfred said dreamily:

'For forty days and forty months and forty years and forty centuries, gurgling and sucking and dissolving, but always rising, always always rising, for ever and ever. And no Ark. Not even a raft, not even a board.'

It was exciting, of course – her first London ball – but Jane was surprised at her own easy acceptance of it, her confidence. The dress, perhaps. She knew how well it suited her, in contrast with Emily's pathetic cigar-brown. Rosemary, too, was suited in white, but there was no desire to emulate her. Accentuating her thinness, her dress had practically no bustle.

Lionel was tremendously handsome. In his face there was the nobility which, with the other Storn-Miller boys, was achieved only in parts. Nobility and courage and a kind of quiet tenderness, most fitting for a soldier. He stood beside her in his uniform, as a symbol of the obverse of the coin of man's dominion over woman. If all were Lionels, all brave, all gentle, then there was no bitterness. To this one could dedicate – what? Life, love, all the better things in one's nature? Yes, all that!

The room, the lights, the noise, one's very blood dissolved into the leaping sweetness of a Strauss waltz. She saw Rosemary gliding away with Alfred and looked up into the face of martial nobility. That silky, brown moustache …

Lionel whispered: 'Our dance?'

Dancing, any lingering trace of timidity was gone. She was here by right; of youth, of beauty, of this admirable silk dress. She felt the pressure of Lionel's enchantingly large hand, the mastery of his leading. She hummed the music, feeling the throb of it flicker in her mouth like a tiny flame.

Lionel said: 'You dance delightfully well.'

She smiled at him, the radiance, the compliment, the waltz, all dissolving together, coalescing into a revolving glitter in her mind, a witch-ball pleasantly distorting the world.

She said: 'Thank you. But you lead so well.'

He said: 'I think dancing's a serious pursuit, don't you? It should be done well. Good exercise, too.' He smiled faintly. 'One needs to be fit.'

She hazarded: 'When …?'

He looked at her inquiringly.

'When are you – going abroad?'

'Very soon,' he said. 'A week perhaps.'

She said impulsively: 'Oh, you must impress all this on your memory, soak it all up, so that under the stars on the veldt you can fling yourself back here with us by the glance of a thought. Remember it all!'

He looked down at her, the fine lines of his face creasing in less fine bewilderment.

'How could one?' he asked. 'Remember, I mean. Things grow hazy – there's only a vagueness, and the present stands out like a fire against the mist of the past. It all goes. Even faces. That's the terrible part of it, I should think, not being able to see faces clearly.'

She said: 'No, no, they don't! It's always there, everything, faces and music and all the colour and brightness.'

He smiled again. 'For you, perhaps.'

When the dance ended he released her to Robert and she saw him turn away to Rosemary. She felt the loneliness of watching them dance away together. One danced, one talked, and something was created – a duet, a little life. And then so swiftly it slipped away in the bubbling uprush of all the other duets and trios and quartets, all the other little lives, lasting so briefly.

Robert said: 'And I shall have every dance after this with you too.'

She looked at him curiously. The slack mouth was tightened into a quite unreal thinness, flesh wrinkled above the deep, close eyes.

She murmured: 'You are so determined ...'

The hand on her back gripped more rigidly. Robert smiled.

'... that I feel bound to wonder why you consider it so important to be determined.'

He looked at her, puzzled, the mouth falling open. She felt the hand behind her slacken and his forceful leading faltered. She pressed her point relentlessly, half-ashamed of her own cruelty, half-contemptuous of the grotesque weakness under the surface vigour.

'You keep recounting the things you are going to do ... with admirable severity. But you know none of them will be done. Don't you?'

He gave a little, embarrassed laugh.

'How could I press a lady against her will?' he said. 'I don't like asking for things … Do you resent my demanding?'

'I ignore it,' she said.

She felt the bright strength of her own cruelty; her small voice so quickly lost in the sweep of the waltz, the chatter, and the colours that seemed to sing like angels, and yet so deep-barbed to the man before her. The rest of the dance they were silent. She glanced at the crumpled face and looked away again. She could so easily have bolstered its attempted strength, merely by accepting, by not challenging it. But why blame herself? It fed like a fire on the dry sticks of acquiescence, until at last it had to be extinguished; the sooner it happened the better for Robert. Later it would put out tentative tongues of flame again, tongues that would leap where none resisted them until the fire burned again beneath the slack ruin, and swept higher and higher to another fall. Must he always fall and rise and fall again, always arrogant and humiliated? The music swung to its close. It didn't really matter.

Alfred, suddenly at her side, said:

'Lord, Lord! Did you see my late partner? The very compietest of the New Women, the prizest specimen to date. I expected any moment she would tear off her skirt and stand arrayed in bloomers.' He pointed to a figure disappearing towards the ladies' room. 'There she goes! Off for a spin on her safety bicycle. Rescue me, dear Janey. Hide me behind your bustle if she comes back.'

She tapped him with her fan. 'Alfred. At times you are shocking.'

'Not at times,' he corrected, 'always. People only notice at times. I say, you must let me have the supper dance. I feel so much less guilty about pushing my way in for food when I'm foraging for a lady. And what about a few more before you are all booked up? The last one, for instance. Yes, the last one certainly.'

She wrote him down for three dances, gratefully invading the unblemished whiteness although it was early yet and she had no thought of being neglected. She hesitated a moment over the last dance. She smiled at him apologetically.

'I'm sorry, the last one's booked.'

Lionel would ask her surely ... At least it was worth delaying for. The orchestra struck up again.

Alfred said: 'Hurrah, a polka! I may have this one instead, mayn't I?'

He jerked her out into the whirlpool of bright duets.

As the next waltz was starting Lionel started coming towards her, but Colonel Storn-Miller reached her first and he smiled and turned away. The Colonel danced with a ponderous, stiff grace and a strained look on his face. He relaxed to look down to her, the curly beard slanting above her like a dark cloud of wire.

'Haven't been to a dance for years,' he said. 'You must excuse my clumsiness.'

'But no, Colonel,' she declared, 'you aren't in the least clumsy.'

He smiled largely.

'That's what one likes,' he said. 'Flattery from a woman – better, from a girl. We older men ...'

She said: 'But you aren't old, Colonel.'

'Power ...' he said vaguely. 'We can break young men as we like; cut off their money, ruin their careers. It's so easy for us. We can even buy their women from them. But they thrive on defeat, and we rot in success. What's our power worth?' He looked at her hungrily. 'And you are going to Paris with Rosemary in the autumn?'

She nodded, half scared, half exultant in her power over this large, virile man. He bent down towards her until his beard brushed her forehead.

'I get over to France a lot,' he said. 'If I come to visit you, will you be kind and entertain an old man? You and Rosemary?'

She looked up demurely, proud of her ability to make his earnest male gaze turn away in confusion. She felt her own virginity like a veil round her, dazzling his eyes.

'Of course, Colonel,' she said. 'It would be most kind of you. Will you take us to tea somewhere; and show us the sights of Paris?'

'I shall be honoured to do so,' he said. After a pause he went on: 'How do you get on with my sons? Have you a favourite amongst them?'

Her eyes sought automatically for Lionel's bright uniform among the circling dancers.

She said: 'They are all very charming.'

Colonel Storn-Miller nodded. 'Yes, very charming … They are all under twenty-one. If one could buy years … I would be a poor man to-morrow.' He was beginning to breathe heavily with the physical exertion of dancing. 'Are you going to marry a poor man for love or a rich man for money?' he demanded.

Jane turned her armour of chastity on him again and he flushed.

'I conceive it as not impossible that I might combine the two,' she said.

He released her with a little, choked bow to Alfred, who had clearly been drinking. His eyes were round and rather bright.

'Janey!' he exclaimed. 'What an age since I saw you. Is this the supper dance?'

Looking in the mêleé for Lionel, she said with some crossness:

'Don't be ridiculous, Alfred. You danced with me less than ten minutes ago. And if you continue drinking at this rate you shall have no more dances to-night.'

He went at last. Another waltz began and Rosemary smiled remotely at her, dancing past with a Robert vivacious again, the little flame leaping to a new conflagration. Behind her a voice said:

'Ah, there you are. I've been looking for you everywhere.'

She turned to him and knew she was not concealing her gladness. He swept her in among the dancers. She thought how strange it was that dancing with Colonel Storn-Miller, or Robert, or Alfred, there was the physical movement, deliberately made, with one's mind directing limbs and the music as a pattern to which to hold. And yet dancing with Lionel there was no such direction – hardly even volition – and their two bodies and the music and colour and warmth were all together on a plane beyond thought and prudence.

Lionel said: 'I've been thinking of what you said …'

It was an excuse to look up at him brightly, to rest her eyes on the deep lines of strength and the curves of gentleness.

'… about remembering,' he went on. 'It's still hard. Some must be good at visualising. John, for instance. He can probably call back a thousand scenes at will, with his artist's eye. And you, too, have it perhaps. I haven't though.'

Looking up, knowing she would never forget those lines, those curves, the fine gleam of light on that moustache, she said:

'You have to love what you see to remember it. Then it doesn't matter what – who – it is. You can never forget. Never.'

The waltz was round her, like the branches of a broad tree lifting to the sun.

Lionel said: 'You're young, Jane, but you seem very wise. It's so pleasant talking to you. And dancing, too, of course. Is your next free?'

She nodded, feeling a richness in her throat, like a swelling song.

He said: 'Would you mind if we sat it out in the garden, where we can talk?'

As he led her out through the great windows she saw John standing back in an alcove, expressionlessly watching all, like a statue whose eyes had been given life by the turning years. She pressed in to Lionel, clutching his arm. They came out into the shadowy darkness of the terrace. The air was warm and damp, but the rain had stopped and the grey-black mesh of cloud was starred by a patch of silver, where the moonlight thrust at it and filtered through. They found a seat overlooking the blurred wetness of the garden. Jane shivered a little, feeling the chill from cold wood and the damp air.

'You are cold,' Lionel said. 'How thoughtless of me. Shall we go back and get your cloak?'

From the spreading lights of the ballroom the notes of the Lancers drifted out, curling like frost-twisted leaves in the outer air. Jane shook her head determinedly.

'I'm really quite warm,' she said. 'That was just an odd shiver.'

Lionel said: 'If you are sure … Do you mind if I smoke a cigarette?'

She watched the small flare of light spread to a pool in the darkness, and die away again to the tiny red glow of the cigarette. The smoke from it drifted warmly up to her nostrils.

'You're comforting,' he said.

'Comforting?' she echoed.

'Yes. Some women – some girls – have it. Men run to them for it; especially men on the verge of being afraid …'

She listened attentively, conscious of a destiny, an inescapable future. Intentions, dreams, desires were nothing; faculties were all. It was too late now to draw back from the edge of loving Lionel. It must come and drench her with bitterness and perhaps never wholly go away, but to see the futility of it so soon – that was an advantage. At least, one would not be made a fool. And always be like this? The longing to love balanced for ever against the ability to comfort. She protested against the stupidity of it, the waste of longing and gladness. But after the protest there could only come the acquiescence. The gift of comfort was something, anyway.

Lionel said: 'I hope that didn't shock you – about being afraid?'

She could feel him looking to her in the wet dimness, searching her face for that sustenance that was there, against her will, for the weak and hungry. She wanted to say something bright and flippant but her voice, when she spoke, was tender:

'Only the utterly stupid could ignore fear,' she said.

He said: 'Yes.' His voice was rather uncertain, as though anxious to be persuaded. He reached down and caught her hand in his.

'You know, I've always been fond of Rosemary,' he went on, 'ever since she first came to live with us. And now, with things sharpened as it were … she seems utterly wonderful. And not quite real. Like a dream. Do you know what I mean?'

Jane nodded, and the red speck of the cigarette glow bobbed up and down.

'I know exactly what you mean,' she replied.

Lionel laughed nervously. 'Of course, everything seems like a dream just now, all swollen up and seen through the wrong end of a telescope. But it's not that that makes her so …'

'Splendidly virginal?' Jane suggested wearily.

'Yes,' he said eagerly.

Of course, she thought greyly, it doesn't occur to him that I might be laughing at him. How could I? I am the comforter, irrevocably serious and maternal. For me the male barriers of pride and arrogance come down; they stand before me, unclothed and ludicrous, entreating pity. As fast as I puncture the pretentious Roberts and confuse the Colonel Storn-Millers, they will return for more, until in despair I accept myself. I am even forbidden the mystery and seeming virility that might be fuel for my longings. I shall know the truth, and the truth shall bind me in chains.

Lionel said: 'I had hopes … you know … that the uniform, the glamour, might lift me a little towards her height. But it's not a height, is it – in the sense we know. It's something different. Jane, you know her well. Do you think I have … well, not a chance, but … Has she said anything? Just a clue …'

Jane remembered Rosemary in the afternoon, shrugging Lionel off in a few words. 'The handsome soldier going to the wars.' She felt a movement of warmth towards his hopeless-ness, the more hopeless for still hoping. My talent, she thought with a flicker of humour, and I'm developing it naturally. All these poor, futile, ridiculous men seeking shelter. Marvelling at her own age, she said:

'She's young yet, isn't she? She likes you, I know. Why not let things wait … ? Soon you will be back …'

The words did not matter; all that mattered was the inflexion of sympathy, the comforting voice, the warm hand in the dark. She felt his fingers tighten on her palm and all her body above her waist constricted with a pain that burst up into her throat. Just a foretaste, a glimpse of how bad it could be. Even without the mystery, without the virility, there was something that could tear her like an animal. She half-turned to Lionel, but withdrew again. Who comforts the comforter?

Lionel said: 'If I come back.'

There was the edge of drama in his voice, so that she guessed he was enjoying the thought of lying cold under foreign stars while his splendid virgin danced heedlessly in the warm lights of London. Forsaken men must be magnificently forsaken.

'You will come back,' she said, pressing his wrist despite the tightening, bursting pain. 'A hero, with medals and a bronze face. Quite, quite all-conquering.'

'You're good, Jane,' he said. 'I wonder if you realise how good.'

The music had stopped in the ballroom. A couple came out on to the terrace, opening the high windows and spilling the chatter from inside out into the wet, low-hanging night. Jane stood up. She had done her duty – no, that was dramatic, silly. Fulfilled her function, rather. Now that she recognised it, it would be easier in future. If only the pain, the stupid, unnec-essary pain, would hold off.

'Let's go in,' she said. 'The lights will cheer you up.'

He took her arm with tender competence and led her in.

'We are proud of you, Lionel,' she said. 'All of us. There's

Rosemary on the other side, quite unattached.'

He smiled delightfully and went. She turned to go out again to the cool darkness of the terrace, but a figure stopped her. It was Alfred, flushed and rather unsteady. He put his hand, restraining, on her arm.

'Janey!' he exclaimed. 'Let me go and find you some food.'

'So early?' she said.

'I'm hungry,' he said. 'I have a ravening tiger to feed. Be my excuse.'

She went with him, docile. How weak they were, she thought. Would Alfred, too, want comfort and confessional absolution? Watching the cynical curve of his mouth she doubted it. This one was too weak even to surrender.

CHAPTER THIRTEEN

1896

Alfred

ALFRED WOKE UP FIRST, feeling a tingling excitement and re-membering almost at once. Christmas Eve. There were movements about the house, but it was still very dark. He dressed quickly, calling to the others to wake up, and ran across to the window to look out. Fog pressed against the panes like soft yellow fur. He opened the window and put his head out, feeling the damp tang and the exciting smell and the bite of frost beneath the yellow cloak. Behind him he heard Lionel cough-ing as he sat up in his bed, and an indistinct noise of movement from Robert and John next door. He opened the window wide, letting the fog roll in.

'A frost, Lie!' he called. 'As sharp as a needle. It will be thick enough on the Big Pond this morning. I'm sure of it. Do get up. We'll sneak out before breakfast and test it.'

Lionel stretched his arms, shivering, and threw the blankets back. As he pulled off his night shirt and stood exposed, Al-fred felt the cold although he himself was now warmly dressed, and shivered in sympathy. Strange that he hadn't noticed it so clearly when he first got out of bed. Did Lionel now? Leaning backwards out of the window into the mist, he asked:

'Do you feel the cold, Lie? I mean … I didn't notice it when I got out of bed.'

Lionel said: 'Well, I do, young 'un. Close that window.' He coughed and deepened his voice which had only recently bro-ken. 'And tell Bob we're going out to Big Pond.'

Alfred banged the window shut and ran through the connecting doorway into the other room. John was standing in his night shirt by the far window, gazing blankly into the fog. Robert was still hidden under the mounded bedclothes. Alfred ran across and shook him by the shoulder.

He said: 'Bob. Come on! We're going out to test the pond. There's a good, thick frost – it should be all right this morning.'

Robert stirred, only to burrow still deeper beneath the blankets. His voice came up muffled and drowsy with sleep.

'All right … Gosh, it's cold. I'm getting up.'

Alfred said: 'John, you ass. Get dressed. You'll freeze standing there. I'll throw your clothes over. Catch!'

John half turned towards him but failed to catch the bundle of clothes which dropped at his feet. He stooped to pick them up and, holding them in his arms, turned once more to gaze out into the blind morning. Alfred went over to him, curious for the moment of his preoccupation. But it was only one of John's false alarms; there was nothing to be seen but the gleam of frost on the ivy and the red bricks between, all disappearing after a few feet into the pervasive yellow. Alfred tugged at his arm.

'Come on, then. You can't stand day-dreaming in this weather. Come on. It will be prayers before you are dressed and we shan't be able to get out till after breakfast.'

John said: 'I like those curves the fog makes … Changing all the time into new ones. Look at that. A line, and yet your eye can't follow it.'

Alfred paused, wondering. What could John see? How could he see anything except that which he saw himself; the ivy, the fading wall, the yellow fog? And to stand there looking at nothing on a morning like this. He looked round. Robert was still hunched under the bedclothes. He wondered whether to call him again, and decided he would not. If Robert stayed in bed and John gawped out of the window instead of dressing there would be only he and Lionel to go down to the pond before breakfast. And this time he really would establish an alliance with Lionel, against the bullying stupidity of Robert and the moony stupidity of John. He would get in early this time and cut Robert out. He looked at his brother's huddled figure with calm distaste.

When he went back Lionel was washing. He stood by the washstand, his feet wide apart and his face immersed in the water, snorting into it the way Papa did when he washed. Alfred watched admiringly. Lionel raised his head at last, reaching blindly for the towel.

He said: 'Well, did you get them out of bed?'

Alfred began eagerly and felt the words spluttering incoherently out. He restrained himself, and spoke in the slow drawl he was cultivating to avoid his stammer.

'Bob's too lazy, and John's mooning out of the window. Let's go along to the pond together, Lie. They'll probably be late for prayers.'

Lionel pulled his jersey on without answering. He walked to the connecting door and looked through. John was still holding the clothes in his arms.

Lionel said quietly: 'Better get dressed, Johnny, or get back into bed. It's the wrong weather for standing like that.'

John looked round towards him, as though suddenly waking up.

'Going out?' he asked. 'Can I come?'

Alfred said jealously: 'You're too late. Isn't he, Lie? You should have got dressed before, when I told you.'

Lionel said: 'Get 'em on quick and we'll wait for you.'

He walked across to the bed and shook Robert, firmly but not roughly.

He said: 'Come on, Bob. There'll be a row if you're late for prayers again. We don't want to spoil Christmas. You know what Papa said last time.'

Robert stretched up, yawning, and Alfred watched, hating him. All his advantage was on the point of slipping away again, leaving him defenceless, younger and physically weaker, against his brother. It was so unfair that he could never escape him.

He said vindictively: 'Oh, leave him, Lie. Serves him right if he is late for prayers.'

Robert stared at him, treasuring up the remark for later repayment. Alfred felt panic at the thought of it. Why must he always antagonise Robert, knowing how Robert resented and would punish his bitterness? He shifted uneasily and looked away.

'Going out before breakfast?' Robert asked, turning his attention to Lionel. 'Oh, the pond ... It should be thick enough for skating if there's been another frost. Hang on, I'm coming.'

Alfred said: 'I told you about it,' half-propitiatingly, half-petulantly.

Lionel said: 'Can't wait for you any longer, Bobby. We'll see you down there if you hurry. It's past a quarter to eight. Come on, youngsters.'

Alfred and John followed him eagerly, Alfred edging himself to Lionel's side as they clattered downstairs so that John had to trot behind them. Things were not so bad after all, since Robert had been abandoned. John did not matter much. It was only Robert that must be scored off. They ran down the back stairs, bursting into the kitchen and out again with only a brief glimpse of Cook's astonished protestations. Then they were lost in the silent, unfamiliar world of the fog.

It was like a dream; like the bright, ballooning spaces of a fever where touch and sight and smell were all lost in a new, vivid, indefinable apprehension. Trees, bushes, statues, sprang in their path like a defending army, so that they had to watch for them and dodge them with a queer exhilaration. Underfoot the grass crackled with frost, but the known contours of the ground had changed into fantastic dips and rises growing out of the fog. At one point – surely the pear-tree wall must be over there on the left? – Alfred slipped, and felt the chill of the frozen earth strike through his clothes while the other two faded away in front. He sprang up, his hands tingling with frost, and ran after them, calling. His own voice seemed to echo round his ears, as though the fog were a wall throwing it back. The ground sloped more steeply downwards now, through close-pressing, shadowy trees, and he heard Lionel's voice just ahead, calling out in warning:

'Watch out behind! We're almost on top of the pond. Tread gently.'

Alfred ran towards the sound of the voice and slipped again – this time heavily – on the frosty slope. He cried out, feeling himself rolling down, and suddenly the hard, level surface of the ice came up beneath him. Bewildered, he lay there. There were voices and muffled steps and, looking up, he saw Lionel's figure – strangely long and distorted – melting towards him out of the concealing fog. Lionel bent over and gave him his arm to get up. He struggled to his feet, pleasantly numb from the fall and the chill of the ice.

Lionel laughed. 'Hardly needs any testing now. Hang on, though. I'll come down and stamp around a bit. Come on, John.'

The three of them stamped around on the ice, walking, sliding, and now beating their arms for warmth. The ice was quite firm. Alfred screwed his heel in, and bent down to look at the crushed star he had made. Then up, and stamping round again, further out towards the middle.

John laughed, and they looked towards him, startled.

'Like elephants dancing,' he explained. 'Round and round … A dance. A procession.'

They laughed with him, though unsure of the reason for mirth. It was just something communicated – an infection from John's strange thoughts. Perhaps it was because in this new fluid world his strange visions and apprehensions were more reliable. Known, clear-cut standards were in abeyance. Still laughing Lionel drew out his watch, the sign of his responsible seniority. Alfred watched him click the silver cover open with pride and satisfaction. He might envy Robert, but Lionel was beyond envy.

'Jiminy!' Lionel exclaimed. 'Time for prayers. Come on back. Follow me and keep together. Let's run. Come on now.'

'Shall we come down with our skates after breakfast, Lie?' Alfred asked.

Lionel said: 'Yes. Run now. Mind that log!'

There was the barest of frowns from Papa as they scuffled into their places in the chapel. Robert and Emily were there already, but Cook and one of the housemaids scrambled in after them, and the frown turned on them and smouldered. During the hymn Robert turned to Alfred, whispering:

'What's the ice like? Will it bear?'

The hymn crowned the cold, lifeless air of the chapel. Alfred considered Robert's approach. Despite himself he was flattered by the friendliness of it. It had happened before – this approach of friendliness from Robert, but the betrayal had always followed. Perhaps his fault? Perhaps if he accepted the offering and looked for friendship, friendship would, miraculously, be sustained? Or was it best to refute him now; to score by rejecting his approach? He tried to stiffen his hostility. Remembering … On the way back from school, in the train, Robert had set the others on him, laughing, utterly cruel … Only yesterday, climbing down the old fir, Robert had stood below the lowest branch and called to him to drop and he would catch him. And then stood aside, to watch him drop and fall … He would hate him. He would.

More urgently, Robert whispered: 'The pond? Will it bear?'

His hatred relaxed before the paralysing certainty of Robert's sure retribution against rebellion. He turned round, smiling, pretending only to have heard the second whisper.

'Yes,' he replied. 'Firm as anything. We stamped on it.'

In front of them John heard and turned round quickly. He smiled and whispered:

'Like elephants. Dancing …'

Alfred ignored him. John's foolishness again; one might laugh at it out there in the fog, but not now. He gestured, shushing him and bidding him turn back before Papa saw.

Robert said: 'Oh, good. We'll get some skating in after all.'

They smiled at each other, warily.

Prayers came to an end; the servants filed out. Papa closed the heavy prayer-book and came across. He inclined his beard towards them, the late-coming forgotten.

They said, 'Good morning, Papa.'

He said, addressing himself chiefly to Lionel, but including the others:

'There is a little girl coming to-day. She is to be my ward, and therefore you must accept her as a sister. Welcome her. Play with her. Treat her with Christian gentleness and with propriety. She has no father nor mother.'

Lionel answered: 'Yes, Papa. How old is she?'

'Thirteen. A girl of tender years.' He looked round the chapel. 'Tender years ...' he repeated softly. 'Terrible as an army with banners.'

Alfred listened, trying to pity her. No father, he insisted mournfully to himself, no mother, no brothers nor sisters. Quite alone, while Christmas showered about her, like the picture of the orphan girl lying in snow in the grim white chasm of the alley. And yet, like a fugitive rising of excitement, he found envy creeping in with the pity. She had the escape he sought for. No Robert could bully her. In his mind the confusion of snow and pity, envy and escape, formlessly drifted.

Papa said: 'Breakfast parade now then. Plenty of hot porridge in weather like this.' He addressed himself to Lionel, almost confidentially. 'And what d'you plan for this morning?'

Alfred watched with admiration Lionel's response, the un-flustered assumption of near-equality to Papa's majesty.

Lionel said: 'Skating, Papa. The Big Pond is bearing now.'

Papa said: 'Have you tested it properly? Give it a good stamping over. And be careful of the fog. It's thickening if anything.'

Lionel smiled, accepting the inevitable commission of leadership.

'I'll be careful with them all, Papa,' he said.

'Good, good!'

Papa put an arm on his shoulders and led the way to breakfast. Alfred trotted behind them, worshipful and for the moment happy.

During the morning the fog clung thickly, showing not even the palest yellow ghost of the sun. The boys skated tirelessly over the dim surface of the frozen lake. They enjoyed the liberty of ghosts appearing to each other in the narrow scope of visibility and disappearing again with a shout or a laugh almost as suddenly. Alfred felt secure and happy. Robert had been unaffectedly amiable, laughing with him at the strange lunacies of John and reserving all his heavy barbs and resentments for the unconcerned Lionel. About eleven Cook came out – they heard her stumbling and calling to them almost all the way from the house – with a jug of cocoa and hot, new scones. They clustered about her, eating and drinking greedily. Robert, flushed and excited, teased her continually.

'Do come skating, Cookie,' he said. 'It's capital exercise. Let me put the skates on for you. Come on now. Sit down and I'll fix you up.'

'None of your silliness, Master Robert,' she threatened. 'I have my work to get back to. Not all of us can spend the day idling about on skates. I have to-morrow's cake still to ice, and all the little cakes and jellies, and to-day's lunch to prepare. You wouldn't be so keen to have me skating if there was no food for you afterwards.'

Robert said: 'Just for ten minutes, Cookie. Alfred and I will hold you up and skate you round. You don't need skates even. Come on.'

He caught her arm and began to drag her, protesting, towards the ice. Lionel came across between them and released her.

'That's enough of that joke, Bob,' he said. He turned to Cook casually. 'Has the little girl arrived yet?'

Cook collected up the jug and dishes.

'Not yet, Mr Lionel,' she answered. 'This dreadful fog will be holding her up, poor little dear.' She turned away, fading towards the house. Her voice faded with her: 'Don't be too long out here. This fog's terrible for the chest …'

Alfred said: 'What's the time, Lie?'

'Yes,' Robert put in, 'let's see your watch again, *Mr* Lionel. Be careful you don't wear the face away with looking at it, though. And don't forget to take us in before this terrible fog gets at our chests.'

Lionel kneeled down to adjust a strap on his boot. He said, over his shoulder:

'You should be careful, young Bob. If you give me any more cheek I'll punch your head for you. It will be no good howling then. I'm warning you now. I mean it.'

Hugging his satisfaction, Alfred gravely watched Robert. He could see his cowardice tearing him down from that recent peak of excitement, delivering him, bound and a slave, into Lionel's contemptuous power. Alfred, forgetting the pact, the temporary friendship of the morning, rejoiced in the revenge for all his own past humiliations. But he was careful, this time, to hide it. Lionel, he recognised, required no sympathy. Tacit sympathy with Robert was only ordinary prudence. And meanwhile, to himself, he could hug his savage joy.

John was watching all their faces with that detached, curious look that puzzled and disconcerted Alfred. But now it did not dismay him; he delighted in the part he was playing, and John's interest was only a compliment to his acting. Robert stood for a moment facing Lionel, and then skated swiftly away out of sight. Alfred, with a secret smile at Lionel, skated after him. Soon he caught up with him and they skated silently side by side. He did not want to miss a moment of Robert's discomfiture.

The affair had smoothed over by lunch time. They went back to the house playing an improvised hide-and-seek among bushes and trees, clutching at their fellow phantoms before melting themselves into the dark, drifting air. They were almost up to the house when they heard the deep groaning of the gong, and ran the rest of the way to the dining-room. Alfred and John, left behind by the longer legs of the other two, arrived panting together at the door. Alfred gazed in wonder.

The scene was transformed. The servants must have been busy during the morning for the room was bright with holly and fir and gaudy paper streamers. To Alfred the revelation that had come with the morning's waking was repeated again, now more insistently. This was Christmas Eve. The toneless fog, pressing at the window panes, enhanced the splendours of the decorations, the roaring, wood-crackling warmth of the fire on the hearth. He looked round, his eyes dazzled by the colours and the glossy, shimmering evergreens. Fir-cones, too, tied with cotton among the holly-leaves! He turned to John to say: 'There's something to look at!' but did not say it. John was gazing, too, with mild disinterest.

Papa appeared in the doorway, accompanying a strange girl dressed in white. The orphan, Alfred realised, summoning up his pity. No mama, no papa … He sympathised, indignantly. And yet she seemed in need of little sympathy; she looked round the four brothers with cool, appraising eyes, her severe, thin face tilted upwards as though by the weight of the bun of hair resting on the back of her neck. On the other side of Papa, Emily peeped into view, blinking uneasily at the room's unwonted splendour.

Papa said: 'This is Miss Rosemary Sedgwick who is coming to live with us. Rosemary, these are the boys. The tall one, Lionel; and in descending order, Robert, Alfred and John. You will soon get to know them.'

They all shook hands with her. Grasping her small cold hand, Alfred said:

'Hello. Do you like skating? The ice is awfully thick on Big Pond.'

She smiled at him remotely. 'Yes. Sometimes. You're Alfred, aren't you?'

He watched her carefully during lunch to see if, by chance, she would betray something of this mysterious, frightening, exciting world of being an orphan. Tears and timidity, he felt, were the least that could be expected in this world that, familiar and family-laden to him, must yet be strange and barren to her. But there were no tears, and no indications of timidity. She had a second helping of spotted dog. He sat on the other side of the table, disappointed but still watchful.

For half an hour after lunch they had to sit down, to digest the meal under Mama's careful vigilance. Alfred arranged it so that he sat beside Rosemary on the sofa under the window. It meant leaving Lionel with Robert in the big chairs on the other side of the room, but his curiosity about the girl outweighed even that. He looked down into her thin, calm face. By the vast rejoicing fire, Mama sat, rocking and embroidering, with Emily at her knees. He pitched his voice low, vaguely guilty about his questioning.

'You're an orphan, aren't you?' he asked. 'Papa told us.'

She nodded.

'How did they die?' he asked interestedly.

She looked full in his face and smiled.

'They were lost at sea. In a storm.'

'In a storm,' he repeated with awe. A real magnificence. How dreadful – how exciting – to imagine that Mama and Papa and all the others might be swept away in just such a storm at sea, leaving him like this girl, alone, friendless, undisturbed. He stared at her, trying again to drag out the secret of her participation in these fascinating events. Surely it must mark her – with triumph or grief? But she sat beside him, unconcerned.

He said, whispering more softly: 'Are you sorry?'

She said, serenely indignant: 'Of *course*.'

He was relieved and disappointed. Pressing further, he said: 'Did you cry a lot?'

She looked at him blankly. 'I never cry. Crying's silly.'

Alfred said: 'If Mama and Papa were to be drowned I should cry.'

She said: 'Would you?'

She glanced at him maliciously, and he shifted uncomfortably. Was she laughing at him because he had said he would cry for Mama and Papa, or did she somehow see down beyond what he had said to that shameful, rebellious core that exclaimed: 'But how exciting it would be!'? She could not. It was private. Only God – the all-seeing Eye, the awful pointing Finger – could see and punish that. He shivered, thinking again: 'I will repent before I grow up; truly I will. I'll repent to-morrow, in chapel.' But fear of divine wrath spurred in him the insistence that to all others his thoughts were private and concealed.

He said stubbornly: 'Yes, I should be enormously sad. I should be unable to eat. I should probably starve, and so soon follow them to heaven.'

She looked at him without interest, not seeming to notice, even less resent, his barbed allusion to her own appetite at lunch. The fire cracked like a whip, and Alfred looked across to see a burning ember fly out on to the carpet. Lionel took the tongs and replaced it in the fire. When he had put the tongs back he took out his watch, and compared it with the bronze chariot-clock on the chimney-piece.

'May we go now, Mama?' he asked.

She rocked forward on the chair. Emily, below, craned her head back to look into her face, dumbly attentive.

'Is it time, then, Lionel?' Mama said.

'It wants less than a minute,' he replied gravely.

She sighed. 'I suppose you must. Are you not tired with skating yet, having been all morning at it? And in this dreadful mist. You will be careful with them, won't you, Lionel?'

Alfred rose eagerly. He was surprised when beside him the girl Rosemary got to her feet also. She walked across to where his mother sat, and stood before her.

'I should like to go skating with the boys, Mrs Storn-Miller,' she said.

Mama stirred uneasily. 'I hardly think it would be entirely suitable. These harsh vapours ... You would be better to stay within doors to-day.'

Rosemary said with finality: 'Nevertheless, I should like to go skating.'

Alfred watched the conflict of strengths, fascinated. Mama had her strength in the family, which gave her position and authority; Rosemary in her detachment from it. He was pleased and startled when Mama finally dropped her gaze to her embroidery.

'If you really want to skate, my dear,' she said, 'then you can go. Lionel. You must take especial care of Rosemary. Do not stay out too long.'

Emily said, with an access of eagerness and vitality: 'May I go, too, Mama?'

Mama said immediately: 'No. Of course not. You are much too young to go out in such weather. When the fog lifts you may go skating with the rest. Now you must work on your sampler. Where is it?'

Alfred watched, feeling old and cynically wise. Poor Emily was tied completely; tied by her youth, by her docility, by being the only girl of the family. So there were worse states than his own. There were lower degrees of subjection. And of fear? The thought dismayed him. Fear more tense, more painfully real, than his own against Robert's torments? Fear of God, he thought driftingly. The Ancient of Days and Tortures ... to burn everlastingly for one's sins, with not just a finger, but every inch of flesh frizzling in the hottest of fires. God the Father. I will repent! God the Father.

They went out again into the fog and this time, coming from

the fire-warmed room, he felt the bleakness of the frost and the damp air striking through, as it seemed, to his very thoughts. He pressed his hands into his trouser pockets, against the burning warmth of his thighs. Lionel and Robert were in front; half real, half shadows, walking along together and talking of the figure 8 they had been practising all morning. On either side of him, close and substantial, were John and the girl, Rosemary. He looked at her cautiously. He saw the white clouds of her breath torn away from the corner of her mouth as she walked, and blew his own breath out between pursed lips like a steam-jet. He hadn't noticed it during the morning. Perhaps it had got colder. He felt the beginning of numbness in his finger ends.

They reached the lake, and sat against the frozen slope of the bank adjusting their skates. Bending down, Alfred saw the dull, powdery surface of the ice, flawed with scratches and scars by the morning's skating. The fog, licking all round them with wet tongues, seemed less yellow; more coldly white and bleak, but no less thick. Over on the left Lionel stood up with a shout and glided away. Alfred's own left boot was still untied and his fingers fumbled with it awkwardly. Robert balanced upwards, too, and struck off. He skated round in a curve, coming back to where the other three sat. He stopped, rockily, in front of Alfred.

'Too cold for little Alf?' he said. 'Can't he tie his boots up then? Better go back to the house and sit in front of the fire.'

Alfred looked up at him, despairingly. How did Robert manage to read his vague doubts and apprehensions, to twist and magnify them to torment him? And why, after the unquarrelsome morning? He had not exulted when Lionel humiliated Robert; not openly anyway. He tied the knot in his bootlaces clumsily, and stood up. Robert, in a quick turn, swooped down and hit him behind the knees with his arm. He fell, sprawling, on the cold, gritty ice. Lionel dissolved towards him out of the empty mists, and helped him to his feet. He was all strength. He said:

'Still falling over, young 'un? You should have your skating legs by now.'

'It was Bob!' Alfred protested. 'Bob knocked me over as I was getting up.'

Lionel looked down, god-like and careless.

'Don't tell tales, Alf. It does no good. Never tell tales.'

He turned, and was gone after Robert through the soft, shifting barrier of air.

Alfred looked back. John had not even begun to put his skating boots on. He lay back against the frosty grass, gazing tranquilly up into the blind, white sky. Rosemary beside him was almost ready. Alfred slid across and grabbed John roughly:

'Come on,' he said, 'you'll get frozen lying there. Come on, you idiot. What on earth are you mooning about now?'

John said: 'Nothing', but he smiled as though he were hiding a secret. The smile and the secrecy annoyed Alfred; he pulled him towards him with a shake.

'Hurry up,' he said angrily. 'You've got to hurry up.'

Rosemary stood watching, balanced on her skates. She said casually:

'Watch out; your brother's coming back.'

Alfred looked round quickly. Robert was darting towards him. He cowered backwards, almost off balance, and Robert's swoop towards him missed. He heard Robert shouting something and saw him turn, on the shadowy borders of visibility, to dart round again. He skated off awkwardly in the opposite direction. Somewhere behind him in the anonymous white mist he heard Robert's voice, calling excitedly:

'Tally ho! After him. I can see you, young Alfred. Watch out behind!'

He skated away desperately, twisting and turning away from voices and the melting wraiths of the others. He was on his own, but in the loneliness of flight, not the secure alone-ness he wanted. His breath came in gasps of ragged white steam, merging into the cold, concealing curtain about him. Even worse than the thought of his tormentor hunting him was the thought of the others, who did not care what might happen to him. But Lionel would. With Lionel he would be safe from Robert. He called: 'Lie, Lie!' but the fog threw his voice back with distorted, mocking echoes.

A figure darted up through the clinging folds of the curtain. It was Rosemary. She was skating well. Her pale cheeks were faintly touched with blue by the cold, but somehow it seemed natural for her.

She said: 'Hello. You're in a hurry, aren't you?'

He did not answer. None of them cared, he thought bitterly. The tormentor was not at their heels, so none of them cared. It was like a revelation of something he had secretly known and understood for years. None of them cared. They did not see, and they could not understand, and so they would not help. No one but God, and God, he reflected bitterly, was concerned only with watching for errors, for blasphemies and impieties, excuses for his own tortures and torments. Courage flared into him for a moment in his bitterness against all torturers and persecutors of the weak and helpless, but it ebbed again at the sound of Robert's voice, shouting, nearer.

He thought desperately – I must reach Lionel. With Lionel he would be safe. He needed only to anchor himself to that divine seniority and Robert would not dare to approach him. Vision curtailed, he listened intently for sounds that could lead him to his refuge. He moved with cunning, his senses alert. He could almost feel the crisp, biting edge of the noise of his skates against the ice, but all the other sounds were muffled in the stifling fog, just as his sight was muffled. There were phantoms and the sounds of phantoms. But at last the curtain, opening for a moment, revealed a tall figure foreshortened in kneeling. Alfred shot across towards him, calling. The figure straightened up, and turned. It was Robert.

Robert said: 'The fly walks into the parlour. Welcome, fly.'

Alfred moved in flight, but without real hope of getting away.

Robert, skating hard behind him, leaned forward to catch him round the waist. He kicked back, half-heartedly, and drowned in a new wave of panic as Robert muttered:

'Vicious, eh? We shall have to curb your viciousness, little fly, shan't we?'

He wanted to beg for mercy, but knew the futility of it. Robert's weight leaned against him, pushing him forward and off balance. They crashed down together on the ice, so that beneath him there was freezing hardness and above the pressing, vindictive warmth of Robert. He tried to wriggle up but Robert, kneeling across him, was too strong for his efforts. Robert pushed his face down against the ice. The cold fastened on his jaw, striking a great root of pain that burrowed up into his head. He launched his strength against the suppressing hand, but barely lifted his head half an inch from the ice before he had to fall back again, weak and defeated. Now Robert, kneeling more firmly astride his body, began pulling his hair with the other hand, and smaller gouts of pain tore raggedly across the larger one.

Robert said seriously: 'You must be properly punished, you know, little fly.'

He said, in agony: 'Why? I haven't done anything. Why do you always pick on me?'

Robert sounded almost surprised.

'You have to be tamed,' he said. 'You are much too fond of trying to be clever. I have to tame you. I have to keep you respectful of your elders.' He pulled hard, and Alfred cried out. 'Little flies must have their wings clipped.'

Robert shifted his position and Alfred twisted suddenly and jerked away. He crouched, breathing heavily, a few feet from Robert. His shame and rage made him want to fly at his tormentor, but against their impelling force stood the cold, ticking monster in his brain, warning of failure, vividly picturing defeat. He was glad he was dry-eyed. Deliberately he shut out the monster with his anger, and prepared to fling himself forward.

He tensed his body. There was a rush of skates, and Lionel glided up out of the concealing blankness. He surveyed them both with a serious, prefectorial air.

'Bob,' he said, 'have you been bullying Alf again?'

It was suddenly too much.

Bob said: 'We were only having some fun, Lie.'

Alfred felt the whole edifice – shame, anger, courage, even the watching monster – dissolve into self-sorrow and wretchedness. He wept, without reason and without restraint. Through his tears he accused Robert; wildly, bitterly, incoherently. He saw Robert move towards him, and cowered in towards Lionel's protection.

Lionel said: 'All right. Scoot off, Bob. Leave him to me.'

Robert turned and skated away, out through the clinging folds of the curtained air, the noise of his skates ringing after him. Alfred felt Lionel's hand on his snivelling head. He turned to him trustingly, but Lionel held him away.

Lionel said: 'You don't make things easy for me, Alf.'

He said fretfully: 'He's always bullying me, Lie. He never leaves me alone.'

Lionel said patiently: 'Things don't happen without cause. You must provoke him. I've heard you cheeking him myself. And when he does lace you ... You've got to learn to take that sort of thing. Everyone gets bullied occasionally; everyone gets kicked about. You've got to stand up to it, to face it. You should be ashamed of yourself; crying like a baby. You must develop enough backbone to stand on your own – not come running to me when anything goes wrong. I won't always be here.'

Alfred thought: he isn't here now. No one is. There's nothing here but the fog and the cold. He could think clearly again now, with an almost bland despair. There was nothing. Nothing in nothing, beginning and ending with nothing. It wasn't even a starting place.

Lionel went on: 'Don't let the young 'uns see you crying. Here's my handkerchief. Wipe your face. And then for the

Lord's sake buck up. Show some spirit.'

Alfred watched him skate away. He wiped his face carefully. Through its chill numbness he could feel a swelling tenderness that might be a bruise. He patted it carefully. The numbness was all round him and inside him, as though it were part of the fog, but a fog that sank deeply through clothes and skin and bone into his stomach and heart and head. He was alone in it. He thought suddenly of the island, and made towards it on uncertain legs.

The island, on the north side of Big Pond, was a tiny wilderness, barely thirty feet across, of grass and thicket. In the summer it was fun to storm it in the boats, and to leap ashore waving pretended swords. Now it was only a blot growing out of the enveloping fog, turning into bare, frozen bushes and patchy, frost-stiffened grass. He walked on his skates from ice to land and stood shivering. The thought of the island had been linked with summer and security. Now as he surveyed it there was only winter and death. He kneeled down and scrabbled at the cold, dry earth with his hands. It would not yield, and the cold bit through his skin with renewed and deeper agony. But his mind welcomed it. He fell forward, and pressed his bruised face against the burning brightness of the frost.

He heard the crackle of frozen wood trampled underfoot, and looked up. Rosemary stood before him. She had come through the brush from the other side of the island. She stared at him gravely. He scrambled to his feet.

She said: 'You've been crying, haven't you?'

He looked away.

'What have you been crying about?' she asked. 'Have your brothers been bullying you?' She smiled. 'I'm sure that's it.'

She walked across and dug the toe of her skates into the brittle, splintering ice.

'No one can bully me,' she said. 'No one. I shall do as I please. Always.' She glanced at him sideways. 'Don't you wish you could? Don't you wish you were free too?'

It was as though the fog flowered suddenly into white, close-pressing blossoms, protecting, not confining. His brief envy for her detachment was gone. Life was agony and joy, and without the fullness of agony there could be no joy. And without joy life was meaningless – a mere existence. Understanding this, he accepted all. Robert's bullying, Lionel's casual direction, John's involved vision, Emily's timidity – even Rosemary's sightless security. He had an insight that reached beyond the smallness of persons, out to the floating grandeur that pervaded them, as the fog pervaded the winter air. There was no escape. All must be felt, all known. All the moments of agony were realised and counted.

He looked up. The blossoms of the fog were becoming real; fragile, feathery blossoms that fell, drifting, around them. One rested on Rosemary's head like a star. He smiled.

'Snow!' he said. 'Snow in the fog. Come on, I'll race you back.'

She shook her head, and the star fell with the others to the ground.

'But don't you wish you were an orphan, too,' she persisted. 'Don't you really?'

He laughed for joy of the snow, and the knowledge he had found. The apprehension might fade, but the knowledge was real.

He said: 'I am sorry. That you're an orphan, I mean.' He took her arm lightly. 'Come on. Let's find the others.'

He skated away into the deepening flurry of snow. Ahead he could hear Robert's voice excitedly calling. He looked back. Rosemary was skating after him, looking for the first time puzzled and uncertain. The blossoms of snow brushed with cool petals against his cheeks. He soared in an ecstasy.

He called out gladly: 'Christmas Eve! Oh, let it snow, let it snow!'

She was still Alfred, her mind ringing with the agony and the exultance. His thoughts were mingled with her own, transforming the ordered, close-clipped garden of her mind into a fantastic jungle.

Life … agony and joy … without agony no joy …

She struggled to free herself. She had not asked for joy, she protested. She had asked for nothing – the calm, illimitable peace of nothing.

A whisper in the void. Was it her own thought, or a fragment from the retreating confusion that was Alfred, or even something else? Anyway, a whisper, a hint. That asking was not the same as getting. Ask, but it may not be given you. Accept. Accept. You may only accept.

Accept the agony and the joy?

Accept.

All that fear and pain, she thought greyly. A monstrous nightmare of it, spreading through men like a leaping cancer, tearing away dignity and respect and assurance. Accept that? Lance's twisted cowardice and deceit, and his furtive, joyless lust. The horror lurking behind Gordon's cheerfulness. Stephen's gnawing, all-obsessing guilt. Adrian's crawling doom. Jane's twisted love. Alfred's weakness and terror.

Accept?

There was Michael, she thought. An interlude. But joy?

Her thoughts flickered, kaleidoscopic …

… Lance stood outside the pub, his arm lightly holding Elise. He looked up briefly at the polished stars, the balloons fading into eventful night. A wind touched his face, blown down, far down, past the monstrously wallowing aerial slugs, through oceans of air and space, from the cold lamps of the stars. His mind leaped …

… The tiny, joyful finger! It flickered on in its glass and metal prison, beckoning, promising, exulting. The car throbbed beneath them with the urgency of their passage, a tumultuous, brazen chariot. Above the hill, like the foamy birth of a goddess, the full silver of the moon leaped from the black sea of clouds.

Eve whispered: 'Gordon, you're so good to me. I feel just like a bride.'

He was laughing, deeply beneath the fabric of tensed muscles and tender flesh; laughing at the moon, the hurtling road, the merry, flickering finger. Beside him Eve began to sing.

… Beyond the anger and disgust and guilty fear there was only peace left; a triumphant, ecstatic peace such as he had not known since childhood. Stephen looked upwards, up past the metal cliff that leaned over him to the dim, untidy sky. It did not open nor change; there was no revelation, no fiery angels swift to save. But he needed none. This sudden flowering transcended all the years of despair and mistrust, his past slavery and his present death. The cliff leaned, more and more swiftly. His small meticulous hands pressed uselessly against it. But in the smallness there was grandeur, and in the uselessness there was ultimate, unbelievable strength.

The words of the advertisement on the side of the bus hurtled towards him. He read them with vivid, sudden delight. BOVRIL, he read, PREVENTS THAT SINK …

… Adrian rose in his stirrups as he reached the crest of the hill. He had stayed up with the leaders; Mornington himself was only a few lengths ahead. And beyond the Master the pack, yelping downhill in a river of black-and-white fury. The air was a damp, cool brush drawn against the heat of his face and strong with the scent of November. Half turning in his saddle he saw Michael's serious, intent face on his right, and the girl, Rosemary, beside him.

The best of all, he thought. The last run of the day, on a good horse, behind a good fox. Touch and sound and sight and acrid November scent fixed in one divinity of apprehension. What have we to do with justice? We only live, we do not question or purpose.

… The waltz, lifting and enclosing … Jane looked up at the lines and curves of strength and gentleness and felt the exquisite, bright pain riding in on the wings of the music to transfix her. The polished floor glided under her tapping feet.

'You have to love what you see,' she said, 'to remember it.'

… Snow everywhere, blossoming out of the fog in flake and flower. He put out his hand and one came gently to rest on it. He remembered all the pain and torture and his own weakness, but with a tranquillity that purged all bitterness. Bitterness there might be again, but now there was the snow, falling from the dark, curtained sky like any Christmas miracle.

'Snow!' he said. 'Snow in the fog. Come on, I'll race you back.'

The orphan shook her head, shaking a star of snow from her dark hair, to float to the ground.

'But don't you wish you were an orphan, too? Don't you really?'

He laughed, knowing the moment of apprehension, the peak, the flowering of knowledge like the flowering snow. All counted; all must be endured, all must be enjoyed. And strangely his laughter gleamed into pity for this isolated one.

... He said: 'I am sorry. That you're an orphan, I mean. Come on. Let's find the others.'

They skated through the snow towards the voices of torment and deliverance, through the wide, dancing delight of white petals. He saw it all with the vision of John, and with something even deeper and more abidingly exquisite. His mind praised: glory, glory, glory!

He called: 'Christmas Eve! Oh, let it snow, let it snow!'

... She rested. The whisper that was less than a whisper, stirring somehow in the depths of nothingness, clamant, insistent:

Accept.

Agony. Brisk, incisive; a stirring of the spirit such as she had never imagined she would find in herself. Resentment and hate and rejection but somehow beneath it – as though life thrust brutally through old dead wood – a quickening and an excitement.

She concentrated her will. It was a cold world, she thought, cold and ugly. A world of fear and hate and pain. I did right – I do right – to reject it.

But there had been quickening; the agony of life in old wood. Almost without regret she realised that the longed-for calm of oblivion would not now be achieved. This thrust of life … What if I accept, she wondered, what then? The pain, the fear, the misery, the shame … all that and more. A cold, an ugly world.

Conflict; and again agony. She would not accept it. She would not accept. The struggle was within her and about her, a vast opposition of intangibles, but she would not accept.

The conflict ceased, and with it the agony.

She rested, not in peace but apprehension. This was not the end. When she felt the faint movement of the fall beginning she was strangely relieved. Faster, deeper, down into warmth, and then the slow swimming upwards through distortion into the world of sense again.

… She was Cedric Garland, a mourner.

South Kensington   *March-November, 1947*

by Sam Youd as John Christopher

with an Introduction by Robert Macfarlane

THE DEATH OF GRASS

The Chung-Li virus has devastated Asia, wiping out the rice crop and leaving riots and mass starvation in its wake. The rest of the world looks on with concern, though safe in the expectation that a counter-virus will be developed any day. Then Chung-Li mutates and spreads. Wheat, barley, oats, rye: no grass crop is safe, and global famine threatens.

In Britain, where green fields are fast turning brown, the Government lies to its citizens, devising secret plans to preserve the lives of a few at the expense of the many.

Getting wind of what's in store, John Custance and his family decide they must abandon their London home to head for the sanctuary of his brother's farm in a remote northern valley.

And so they begin the long trek across a country fast descending into barbarism, where the law of the gun prevails, and the civilized values they once took for granted become the price they must pay if they are to survive.

This edition available in the US only

ISBN: 978-1-911410-00-3

www.deathofgrass.com

by Sam Youd as John Christopher

The Caves of Night

Five people enter the Frohnberg caves, three men and two women. In the glare of the Austrian sunshine, the cool underground depths seem an attractive proposition – until the collapse of a cave wall blocks their return to the outside world. Faced with an unexplored warren of tunnels and caves, rivers and lakes, twisting and ramifying under the mountain range, they can only hope that there is an exit to be found on the other side.

For Cynthia, the journey through the dark labyrinths mirrors her own sense of guilt and confusion about the secret affair she has recently embarked upon. And whilst it is in some ways a comfort to share this possibly lethal ordeal with her lover Albrecht, only her husband Henry has the knowledge and experience that may lead them all back to safety.

But can even Henry's sang froid and expertise be enough, with the moment fast approaching when their food supplies will run out, and the batteries of their torches fail, leaving them to stumble blindly through the dark?

ISBN: 978-0-9927686-8-3

www.thesylepress.com/the-caves-of-night

by Sam Youd as John Christopher

THE WHITE VOYAGE

Dublin to Dieppe to Amsterdam. A routine trip for the cargo ship *Kreya*, her Danish crew and handful of passengers. Brief enough for undercurrents to remain below the surface and secrets to stay buried.

The portents, though, are ominous. 'There are three signs,' the spiritualist warned. 'The first is when the beast walks free. The second is when water breaks iron … The third is when horses swim like fishes.'

Captain Olsen, a self-confessed connoisseur of human stupidity, has no patience with the irrational, and little interest in the messiness of relationships.

'I condemn no man or woman,' he declares, 'however savage and enormous their sins, as long as they do not touch the *Kreya*. But anything that touches the ship is different. In this small world, I am God. I judge, I punish, and I need not give my reasons.'

Olsen's philosophy is challenged in the extreme when, in mountainous seas, disaster strikes: the rudder smashed beyond repair, a mutiny, and the battered vessel adrift in the vast ocean, driven irrevocably northwards by wind and tide – until she comes to rest, at last, lodged in the great Arctic ice-pack.

ISBN: 978-0-9927686-4-5

www.thesylepress.com/the-white-voyage

by Sam Youd as John Christopher

CLOUD ON SILVER

A disparate group of Londoners are brought together by
Sweeney, a mysteriously charismatic man of wealth, for a
luxury cruise in the South Pacific – they know not why.
Sailing far from the normal shipping routes, the ship drops
anchor just off an uninhabited tropical island. Whilst its
passengers are ashore exploring, the ship catches fire and sinks
beneath the waves.

With no means of communication with the outside world
and no hope of rescue, passengers and crew must find a way
to survive. In the scramble for power that ensues, the
distinction between master and servant becomes meaningless
as the more ruthless among them clamber to the top.

The inscrutable Sweeney, meanwhile, sits alone on a hillside.
Coolly aloof, he watches the veneer of civilization disintegrate
as his fellows fall prey to fear, desperation, barbarity …

As for Silver Island itself, with its lush vegetation and exotic
fruits, it had seemed like paradise. But as the days pass, a
subtle sense of unease gains momentum, and the realisation
gradually dawns that all is far from well in this tropical Eden.

ISBN: 978-0-9927686-6-9

www.thesylepress.com/cloud-on-silver

by Sam Youd as John Christopher

THE POSSESSORS

When the storm rages and the avalanche cuts off power and phone lines, no one in the chalet is particularly bothered. There are kerosene lamps, a well-stocked bar and food supplies more than adequate to last them till the road to Nidenhaut can be opened up. They're on holiday after all, and once the weather clears they can carry on skiing.

They do not know, then, that deep within the Swiss Alps, something alien has stirred: an invasion so sly it can only be detected by principled reasoning.

The Possessors had a long memory … For aeons which were now uncountable their life had been bound up with the evanescent lives of the Possessed. Without them, they could not act or think, but through them they were the masters of this cold world.

ISBN: 978-1-911410-02-7

www.thesylepress.com/the-possessors

by Sam Youd as John Christopher

PENDULUM

The sixties … a foreign country: they did things differently then. Or did they?

An Englishman's home, supposedly, is his castle, and property developer Rod Gawfrey was incensed when a gang of hooligans gatecrashed his son's party, infiltrating the luxury residence that was also home to his wife's parents and her sister Jane.

He had no inkling then of the mayhem that was on its way, as the nation's youth rose up in revolt, social order gave way to anarchy, and he and his family were reduced to penury.

Jane hadn't seen it coming either, despite her professional and more personal connection to Professor Walter Staunton, the opportunist and lascivious academic bent on fomenting the revolution.

A pendulum, though, once set in motion, must inevitably swing back. And who would have guessed that Martin, Jane's timid, God-fearing brother, would have a key role to play in the vicious wave of righteous retribution that would next sweep the land?

ISBN: 978-1-911410-04-1

www.thesylepress.com/pendulum

by Sam Youd as Hilary Ford

SARNIA

Life holds no prospect of luxury or excitement after Sarnia's beloved mother dies: potential suitors vanish once they realise that marriage to the orphan will never bring a dowry. Yet her post as a lady clerk in a London banking house keeps the wolf from the door, and the admiration of her colleague, the worthy Michael, assures her if not of passion, then at least of affection.

Then the Jelains erupt into her humdrum routine, relatives she did not know she had, and whisk her away to the isle of Guernsey. At first she is enchanted by the exotic beauty of the island, by a life of balls and lavish entertainments where the officers of visiting regiments vie for her attention.

But Sarnia cannot quite feel at ease within this moneyed social hierarchy – especially in the unsettling presence of her cousin Edmund. And before long it becomes apparent that, beneath the glittering surface, lurk dark and menacing forces ...

Her mother had scorned those of her sex who tamely submitted to male domination but, as the mystery of her heritage unfolds, Sarnia becomes all too painfully aware that the freedom she took for granted is slipping from her grasp.

ISBN: 978-0-9927686-0-7

www.thesylepress.com/sarnia

by Sam Youd as Hilary Ford

A Bride for Bedivere

'I cried the day my father died; but from joy.'

Jane's father had been nothing but a bully. His accidental death at the dockyard where he worked might have left the family in penury but it had also freed them from his drunken rages. He was scarcely cold in his grave, though, when another tyrant entered Jane's life.

Sir Donald Bedivere's offer to ease her mother's financial burden had but one condition: that Jane should leave her beloved home in Portsmouth and move to Cornwall as his adopted daughter.

To Sir Donald, Cornwall was King Arthur's country, and his magnificent home, Carmaliot, the place where Camelot once had stood. To Jane, for all its luxury it was a purgatory where her only friend was the lumbering Beast, with whom she roamed the moors.

Sir Donald had three sons, and Jane was quick to sum them up: John was pleasant enough, but indifferent to her. The burly, grinning Edgar she found loathsome. And Michael, on whom Sir Donald had pinned all his hopes, she disdained.

Sir Donald had plans for the Bedivere line – Jane wanted no part in them.

ISBN: 978-0-9927686-2-1

www.thesylepress.com/a-bride-for-bedivere

39090945R00171

Printed in Poland
by Amazon Fulfillment
Poland Sp. z o.o., Wrocław